SWIFT CURRENTS

—— A NOVEL ——

To Zach and Cole

Feel the freedom!

David Bruce Grim

David Bruce Grim

iUniverse LLC
Bloomington

SWIFT CURRENTS

In Swift Currents, fictional characters participate in historical events as the Civil War unfolds. These characters interact with actual individuals who played significant roles at this time and place in history. The slaves/freedmen communicate in a Gullah language made as authentic as possible. However, this is a work of fiction. Except as cited in the text, the characters' dialogue is a product of the author's imagination, and the incidents and locations described in Swift Currents are used fictitiously by the author.

iUniverse books may be ordered through booksellers or by contacting:

iUniverse
1663 Liberty Drive
Bloomington, IN 47403
www.iuniverse.com
1-800-Authors (1-800-288-4677)

ISBN: 978-1-4917-3394-3 (sc)
ISBN: 978-1-4917-3395-0 (hc)
ISBN: 978-1-4917-3396-7 (e)

Library of Congress Control Number: 2014908119

Printed in the United States of America.

iUniverse rev. date: 06/05/2014

In memory of the first freedmen of the Civil War

I hope I have done justice to
the strength of their character,
the power of their persistence,
and the depth of their faith.

Acknowledgments

This story could not have been told with authenticity without Osalami Lamoke, Gullah translator and St. Helena island teacher, composer, and performer. She plumbed the well of her experience, through six months of shared frustration and inspiration, to breathe Gullah life into the dialogue of the people on the fictional Oakheart Plantation. In "Notes from the Gullah Translator," she explains how she reached back to her ancestors for their words and wisdom. I am forever grateful for her thoughtfulness and our partnership in this endeavor.

Although I have benefitted from the perspectives of many readers, there has been only one editor for *Swift Currents* from beginning to end. Barbara Banus spent countless hours reading each draft, always making purposeful suggestions for necessary changes, mostly without bruising the ego of the author. Her thorough reviews and productive critiques kept improving the work. Through many years of production, her kind assistance, attention to detail, and guidance have been invaluable to me.

Both of my siblings, Carolyn Hill and Gary Grim, supported me through multiple drafts. Carolyn's edits and precision and Gary's solid comments and questions strengthened the storytelling. My son, Matt, shed light in thoughtful places and steeled my will to the finish. My effort to create *Swift Currents* was bolstered by the perspective and friendship of my former spouse Jacqueline Bolware and the wisdom and admiration of our daughter, Kelli.

Warren Slesinger reviewed an early draft and provided insightful guidance and common-sense notions about writing. When I thought I had finished this manuscript, Dr. Eleanor Barnwell and Rosalyn

Brown were kind to share their encouragement for the work and their thoughtful suggestions for improvements. Ideas from good friends Kate Joy and Rodney Cash also helped steer the project.

On my first day researching this project at the Beaufort County Library, Grace Cordial, Historical Resources Coordinator and Manager, advised me that I must read Willie Lee Rose's *Rehearsal for Reconstruction: The Port Royal Experiment*. She supplemented that sound advice by providing the wonderful map of the sea islands in the Beaufort area as of November 7, 1861, originally depicted in *Frank Leslie's Illustrated Newspaper*, November 21, 1861, pp. 8–9.

The cover is an original painting that beautifully depicts the day of the Union attack at Port Royal Sound. The artist, Jennifer, wishes to credit her young models who helped her portray the action—Tamashia, Leonard, and Tyrone. Jennifer can be contacted at artseaspirit.com.

With gratitude to all.

Notes from the Gullah Translator

Somewhere deep in my aged memory, a language that I heard as a child growing up on St. Helena Island was buried. Translating portions of *Swift Currents* gave me the pleasure of transporting myself back in time to find expressions that I had heard but never actually used myself, because as the child of a loving, educated schoolteacher, I was quickly corrected if any trace of Gullah slipped out. This language was nevertheless within me, or as I would jokingly say to David, "I have to listen to my ancestral spirits to hear how something would have been said by Callie, Lucas, or one of your other characters."

The reader may find it difficult to understand the Gullah expressions unless one tries to truly immerse oneself in the characters themselves and the time and milieu in which they lived. Trying to understand the expressions may slow down the read, but it's like learning a foreign language: saying the foreign words while keeping one's own accent, gestures, or intonations is not as enjoyable and effective as learning the ways of the native speaker from connecting with the culture of which that language is a part.

A glossary of Gullah expressions is provided to facilitate understanding, but to really understand, the reader must be willing to get outside of himself and be Gullah for a few chapters.

Osalami Lamoke

Author Notes on the Gullah Dialogue

It is important that *Swift Currents* presents as accurate a depiction of the Gullah dialogue as possible. I recognize that the Gullah spoken by a few characters may slow the read slightly, especially early in the story. Following difficult Gullah words or phrases, I have provided a standard English translation in parentheses and italics. I have also provided a Gullah glossary at the end. To the extent the reader is able to sound out the phrases phonetically, the richness of the Gullah language of African Americans on the southeast United States coast can be more fully appreciated.

Contents

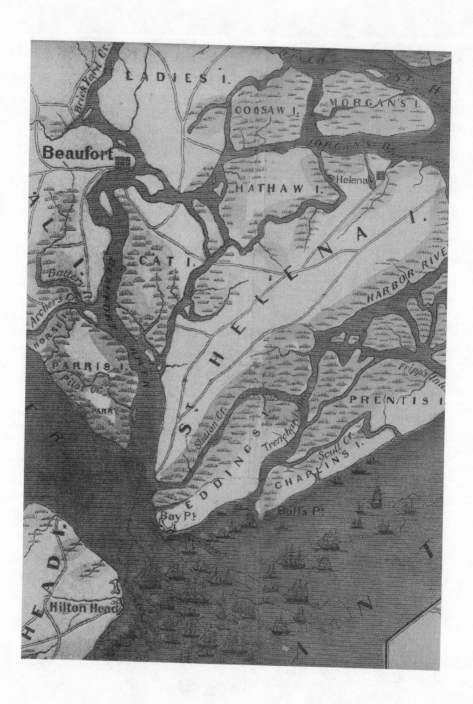

PART I

Late October 1861

Chapter 1

Though it was barely light, Callie was up early, her skin bathed in sweat before she even left her pallet. On this unusually warm and humid morning in late October, the tepid water in her washbowl added moisture to thick air but did not cool her. As she pondered the tasks ahead of her, Callie gently cleansed her sleeping daughter's peaceful brow.

Much was expected of Callie that day. After breakfast, she had to begin preparations for a feast on the plantation grounds before going to Beaufort to pick up the captain's favorite seasonings. After that, she would spend the rest of the day and much of the next in the cookhouse. Her thoughts wandered toward her younger brother, Lucas, the best slave boatman on the plantation, who would row her to town on the incoming tide. Missus Bowen had insisted gently that Lucas be on the Beaufort wharf to pick up her son as soon as the steamer brought him home from the Naval Academy.

Callie stepped from her one-room cabin to find the air so still that she felt a stir as mourning doves rose in a flutter just outside her door. With water on two sides of the point of land where the big house stood, the sea breeze would be up by late morning on most days. She looked forward to the relief it would bring, as soft light began to add depth to the dark shadows that moved with her up the familiar footpath.

Passing down the row of quarters reserved for the skilled slaves who worked directly with the planter and his family, she was grateful for the cabin she shared with her daughter. Their one-room home had a wooden floor and was sparsely furnished with a table, two chairs, and a bed just big enough for Sunny. Callie's pallet, near the small stone fireplace, had a blanket given to her by Captain Bowen that provided just enough cushion for Callie's long, slender frame. The captain had ordered his slaves to build the cabin especially for her about five years earlier. It was set slightly apart from the other shanties, affording some privacy for her. That the location also gave the captain cover for his dark purposes tempered her gratitude.

Typically, summer warmth remained on the sea islands through October, but the recent run of relentless sun, heat, and humidity challenged anyone attempting to work outdoors past noon. Callie watched the field hands in the dull haze as they moved slowly beyond the ocean of cotton plants to the sweet potato field. Digging out those wonderful roots from soil parched by the late-summer sun had been particularly exhausting since Captain Bowen was determined to get the sweet potatoes out of the ground and the cotton picked as quickly as possible. In that effort, one of the oldest hands on the plantation had died in the field on the previous day. From Callie's twenty-three years of life experience with Captain Bowen as master, she knew that his decision to cut work hours short by an hour for the rest of the week was an act of property protection more than one of human kindness.

With heart as heavy as the moist morning air, Callie knew she had to forge ahead. The words of her "mama" echoed in her ears as each new day began: "Dayclean, sunshine, wid Gawd, feel fine." She adhered to Mama Ruth's morning admonition, hoping for truth in its simplicity. Her spirit joined her faith to greet each new day with optimism, but her experience taught her to be wary.

Callie walked out from under the last live oak tree on her path to the big house, thinking that Missus Bowen must have been happy that morning as she awaited her son's return home. Then she saw Jacob, the plantation carpenter for the past ten years, standing motionless down near the tide line, facing sunrise over the salt marsh. His thin, wiry arms hung limply by his sides. Callie stumbled down the bank of sand and grass, startling him as he spun to meet her, so that he nearly fell into the shallows.

"You awright, Jacob?" Callie asked.

"Ain me you need fuh aks. You bes check wid yo fren, damn Massa!"

"Jacob!" Callie anxiously looked up the bank toward the mansion looming above the marsh, its windows and encircling verandas providing ample opportunity for Captain Bowen to view his property.

Jacob was not to be stopped: "Wuh wrong wid da man? He wuk dis cotton so haad (*hard*), he kill we."

Though sympathetic, Callie only said, "I jes know Massa worry bout time fuh git cotton pick."

"Don mek no sense. Wuh Massa know? Him see Franklin en Cato fall out … Massa lay em down en po water on dey head, den mek em wuk mo. No, Massa ain slow down til Hezikiah draw e las bret (*breath*)."

His eyes welled with tears and his chest heaved. "Yessuh. Wuk haad fuh Massa. Fuh wha? Fuh nuttin!" Jacob spat over his shoulder toward the big house, more gesture than substance.

"Jacob! You look fuh git whip yosef. I know you too smaat fuh act like fool in de sight uh Massa." His look to her, though respectful, came through watery eyes, a tear tracking down his clenched jaw.

"You know I right, Jacob. Ain gon leh Massa lash on yo ole skin. My haat kyah too much fuh oona. (*My heart cares too much for you.*)" She grabbed his arm, pulled him, and walked him up the shifting sandbank. "Gi Hezzie respeck dis day fuh way he treat we."

"Look wey him be now, Callie. Look wey him done git!" Jacob stopped walking with Callie as they reached the footpath, pulling back from her urging grasp of his arm. "Res of we ain sho like you, Callie, da nex day gon be awright."

She released his arm and stepped back, her eyes searing through his. "Wha I done been fuh Sunny, BB, Lucas, en you, Jacob! I tek kyah dem Bowen like I been do since I been small chile. I mek sho we git wha we need—wha you say don matta none fuh me." The fire in her eyes masked and stopped the tears that had begun to form, belying her words.

She calmed herself, watching a pelican family of five fly a perfect V formation at treetop level. "Jacob, you know yo fight ain wid me."

She paused. "You know wha I laan (*learn*) in da big house hep all we people roun yuh (*here*)."

Jacob hugged Callie; he knew he had crossed a few lines, but he never meant to offend. They moved off: Jacob to his carpentry and Callie to her list of tasks.

*   *   *

Callie was invaluable to Daniel Bowen for many reasons. She had gained the confidence of the Bowen household over a period of years. She provided all cooking services, and despite being just nineteen years old when Mama Ruth passed on four years earlier, Callie took on Mama Ruth's role of managing all domestic slaves working in and around the big house. Ruth, the only mother Callie had ever known, had shared her broad expertise gained through fifty years of enslaved service on Oakheart Plantation. From Ruth, Callie learned that each daily task taught lessons in life, so she was prepared to assume responsibility for "Mama's" duties and did so with grace unexpected from one so young.

Callie's knowledge of cooking extended well beyond recipes and seasonings. She had a knack for growing vegetables, herbs, and roots—talents that came to full realization when the captain allowed her to tend a small garden patch behind the big house. She learned the first signs of dry leaves and thirsty plants, when to pinch back, and how to prune. No book-learning made her an expert—just days of seeing and doing and thriving and suffering with her plants. Her calloused hands and muscled arms more resembled those of field workers than house slaves.

Yet, most times Callie knew that her work conditions were far better than others enslaved on Oakheart Plantation. She worried that some envied her position and believed that she was favored because her skin was of a lighter hue than most. Callie worked hard to get along well with her fellow bondsmen and to get necessary tasks done. She had a cajoling way about her that allowed others to feel good about themselves while doing as she wished.

"At Oakheart," the captain would tell his fellow planters, "less slave workdays are lost than on any other sea island plantation." This was a significant boast as there were more than one hundred plantations in the region. The reason for this acknowledged success was not the captain's stern management, as he led peers to believe, but rather Callie's knowledge of natural remedies. She was always willing to visit with slaves too ill or too injured to work, lifting their spirits while providing herbs and potions to heal their bodies. Her ability to help her fellow bondsmen gave her status on the plantation among both the free and the enslaved.

Callie consulted with Nickles, the plantation overseer, about field workers who were not able to do their tasks. Though his job was to get the most work out of the hands available, he was often persuaded by Callie to allow sufficient time for healing. They both understood that some hurts were not visible. Callie's approach gained the reluctant support of Captain Bowen also, as he saw his boast come true when he considered the quality of slaves' work when nursed back to full health. He reaped the profit from the harvest and boosted his reputation as a planter on the healthy backs of his Oakheart slaves.

Callie had made herself secure in a very insecure position, for she always remembered Mama Ruth's vivid description of Massa. "Gal, don neba fuhgit, Massa be a capn, and dis capn be a mean man. Das all oona need fuh know." Then she went on. "Him tell white man wha fuh do, en speck em fuh jump. Ain nuttin fuh him speck slave jump fas en high en say, 'Yassuh,' fo git back down."

While Callie had no doubt who was in charge, she was more than sure that without her, matters around Oakheart Plantation would not go so well. Callie understood the captain and usually deferred to his demands, but she was puzzled by Julia Bowen, his wife of ten years.

The captain's wife, or Sista Bowen, as Callie and the other African women of the yard called her, was a good enough soul, but had no natural gift for managing slaves. Her innate human kindness did not allow her to give orders without first holding an open discussion on the merits of a given matter. The slaves of the plantation, with the exception of Callie, did not respond well to her questions, as their slave training had not prepared them for such interaction. In ten years as the captain's dutiful wife, she never really settled into her role as "Missus" because she would never give the slaves a direct order.

It was not just her talkative self that puzzled the African women in the big house yard. "God ain gi Sista Bowen no smaats (*smarts*) bout how fuh fix food!" Mama Ruth used to say. "Nah, she ain know how fuh do nuttin in de cookhouse. We be de one tell she wha fuh do."

Other slaves in the yard would warn Ruth, "Jes wait, you see, someday Sista Bowen gon laan (*learn*) good how fuh move slave roun." Ruth always resisted the thought, saying, "We bless yuh, cause Sista Bowen ain ebil like some." Ruth said she had come to know the heart of the new mistress of the plantation, and she found it simple and kind.

But, whatever Julia Bowen's plantation status, she was the captain's wife. While she was not threatening in demeanor, inflicting none of the pain of servitude directly, she also seemed oblivious to all the cruelty that surrounded her.

⋆　⋆　⋆

Each day, Callie parlayed her knowledge into good eating for the Bowens, but the joy she took in being provider was tempered somewhat by her proximity to the life of her master. Though her tasks were on a higher plane than other Oakheart slaves, they still were within the tight confines of slavery. The cookhouse walls made of oyster shells did not limit the scent of shrimp, grits, and bacon cooked in an iron skillet over an open fire. One morning, Captain Bowen followed his nose directly into the peaceful space of Callie's cookhouse.

Some days the master was more oppressive than others with his questions and nags. Had Callie made certain that all tomatoes and sweet potatoes had been cleaned and only the largest retained for the feast? Were the shrimp and crab being pulled from the river in abundance this week? Where was Lucas? Did he know what he had to do before dawn tomorrow? Had the best corn from the summer harvest been saved for the shrimp boil? Was there any bug infestation in the storage shed?

"Callie, you must go check the storage shed. I'm heading that way—I'll go with you."

Callie watched the captain move a few steps down the path, noting, when he turned back to her, that his thin frame slouched to reveal a growing paunch. "Massa Cap'n, you know ain no time dis day for none uh da. Afta my regla tass (*tasks*), den I go wid Lucas tuh Beaufut fuh spice you like in de swimp boil." Callie, being keenly aware not only of her responsibilities, but also his intentions, managed the moment. She was the only Oakheart slave to call him "Massa Cap'n."

In the corner of her eye, she saw Lucas rounding the big house and heading for the dock. She shouted, "Brudda, we ready fuh row on de risin tide tawd Beaufut?" She hoped in vain that her question would insulate her younger brother from unnecessary, belittling morning instructions by Bowen.

"Come here, boy!" Captain Bowen barked. Lucas continued his pace but turned a right angle to move in the direction of his master. "You know how important it is that my wife's boy gets delivered in one piece today, Lucas?"

"Yassuh, sho do. Big boat ready fuh maaket, Massa."

Lucas, having registered the appropriate level of obsequiousness, was dismissed. "Well, then be off by God."

"Yassuh, Massa. I gwine (*going*) now, Massa."

Bowen further commanded: "Boy, when you return, you'd best be ready to get right back out on the next ebb tide tomorrow morning, and get back heah by noon with bushels of fresh shrimp. This batch has to be big and good, you know, boy?" His simple domineering ways would have been laughable, were they not intended to be threatening.

Lucas smiled as he turned halfway back, continuing in slower obedience than Captain Bowen wished. "Yassuh. Soon's I git back, mek ready fuh go on mornin tide, Massa. Massa be please wid wha Lucas pull from de crik." And he turned to head back to the dock.

Satisfied, the captain grunted, "Get on with it then. Callie, be sure you get your marketing done on time to catch the outbound tide down the river. I'll see you later about tomorrow night's dinner plans. Y'all be quick and you'll get a generous reward later."

"Yassuh." She threw the answer back over her shoulder, unwilling to further acknowledge his existence. To maintain her composure, she suppressed feelings of disgust rising in her stomach at the thought of his "reward." Callie and Lucas moved quickly down to the dock.

Chapter 2

Will Hewitt stood in the bow of the southbound steamer, *Carolina*, seeking a breeze to combat the oppressive heat that had settled over the sea islands. He was returning to South Carolina, his mother's home for the last ten years following her marriage to successful planter and boat builder, Daniel Bowen.

More at peace on water than land, Will thrived at the Naval Academy on Maryland's Chesapeake Bay. Summers spent training on the bay provided ample opportunities for Will to hone and demonstrate his seamanship. So, upon receiving word of his mother's illness, he worried both about her and the future of his pending career in the US Navy.

Now that the Southern states had actually seceded from the United States and South Carolina had started the fighting with the bombardment of Fort Sumter in Charleston, all plans had changed. Will and the other upper class midshipmen had been assigned to the *USS Constitution*, where he had expected to serve alongside his peers. He felt better about making the trip south after academy officials approved and even encouraged him to go.

The salt-marsh air and tidal currents of these simmering flat islands filled his senses. An all-enveloping moist heat made Will's breathing labored even while he was at rest. Yet the beauty was unsurpassed, with myriad shorebirds in flight and dolphins sharing their kingdom with his vessel.

It was clear to Will from his perch on the steamer deck that it was hotter and brighter here than on the Chesapeake Bay five hundred miles north. Morning reflections on the water made looking eastward impossible, though Will persisted in his childhood practice of squinting through cupped hands.

When his mother brought young Willy to these sea islands as a ten-year-old, he quickly fell in rhythm with the rise and fall of the tides. He watched creeks and estuaries swell as they pushed up into forests of pine and live oak trees that bordered the marsh. Will smiled at memories of easy days on these waterways of his youth, on low tides just like the one forcing the steamer to navigate so carefully.

By age twelve, Willy had persuaded his mother to trust him alone on the water. The area's pristine splendor, coupled with his own independent nature, compeled him to take early morning outings in his small bateau. He could not rush down the sandy bluffs and through the feet-sucking pluff mud fast enough to push out onto the water. Though told to stay near the shore, he soon ignored the instruction and rowed into the swift currents of the tidal creeks. Willy revelled in the wondrous movement of his craft as it surged through channels on rising, wind-swept tides. He craved the breeze on his face and the autonomy inherent in steering his own boat.

He learned to go with the flow of such powerful tides and, by reading the water, to keep himself safe. He studied inbound surges that were always followed by the ebb, twice each day with nearly a ten-foot difference between high and low tides. All beings scheduled their activities accordingly. Such knowledge, innate or learned, was basic to sea island living, and dying.

Warm, stifling salt air and sunshine enfolded the young midshipman in his reflections. Reaching to his full height, Will was savoring a deep yawn and stretch of satisfaction when his uncle clapped him on the back.

"Great to be back in the land of hungry bugs, eh, Will?" Uncle Harris, always seeking the silver lining, made light of the heat. He seemed not to notice the swarm of tiny flies around and in his full head of graying hair, or to mind their intensified feeding around daybreak— he never missed seeing the sun rise over the water.

Will shared many of his uncle's traits. Both six-footers were fit and trim, with kind faces that showed smile lines and determined eyes set in high cheekbones. He did not share his uncle's tolerance for swarming bugs.

The bond Will had established with his uncle Harris grew even stronger after he returned north to attend the Naval Academy. His love for Uncle Harris came from the deep, untapped, fatherless well of his youth. Though Will, as he became known at the academy, thrived on the rigors of maritime education, he took great solace and learned much in the "home" moments his uncle provided during those years.

Uncle Harris grabbed Will firmly around the shoulder, pointing to the largest of the majestic, low-sweeping live oak limbs overhanging the nearest riverbank. "See the strength and curve of that lowest branch? The strongest ships can be fashioned from such timber. And your stepdaddy's place is where they've done it best on these islands."

"I didn't realize how highly you regard Captain Daniel Bowen."

"To be sure, my boy, it is not him but his boats I prize, and the chance to visit your mother—to keep watch over her like I promised your father. Sadly, she made the task difficult with her unfortunate choice of a second husband."

The twinkle soon returned to his eyes as he cuffed his nephew on the back of his head. "But though we both love your darling mother, it's the water that draws us back, eh? Some of the finest waterways on earth!"

"Sounds like you grew up here too, Uncle."

"I remember my first visit down here, long before your mother married the planter and changed her life entirely. I was down here in the late fall, and I'll tell you, I thought I had found heaven. I was then, and remain, dumbstruck and in awe of this great expanse of water and the fresh sea air, especially at this time of the year. There must be hundreds of little islands with soil fit to grow almost anything—nothing better. Hard to believe now, but I even liked doing business with old Bowen back then, before he married Julia." Uncle Harris stopped abruptly. He shifted his gaze from the reflections in the water to the land. Gesturing toward the shore, he continued: "But then, if you stay around here at all, you feel the weight of human bondage in the air—of people forcing other people to serve them, on pain of death. You know, your stepfather uses his slaves for crops and boats and pockets the profits." His voice trailed off again, perhaps knowing of the hypocrisy in his complaint as he prepared to move a boat north for sale.

Just as Will started to speak, his uncle boomed, "And now, this godforsaken war!" He turned to Will. "These firebrand secessionists are making it awfully hard for an honest man to make a dollar at sea."

"Who would you be referring to, Uncle?" They banged shoulders together, both enjoying his small joke. Frowning, Will blurted out, "Sounds like your Union heart is aching to fight."

"No, nephew, I am not a warrior. But the sea provides other ways to serve and prosper during this rush to destruction. Besides, I made this trip not so much for another Bowen boat but to accompany you back here to see about your mother and, if she is well, to talk sense into her." Will looked closely at his uncle. "My sister-in-law has learned to live beside slavery, a fact I have never understood. But, like it or not, she needs to know that this war is coming her way—by one means or another."

"It didn't have to happen, you know! At the academy, I learned that the United States outlawed the importation of slaves more than fifty years ago. Why couldn't adherence to law bring an end to it?"

"Well, that law just said you can't bring any more slaves into the country. It did not stop slavery. Besides, you won't see too many people enforcing that law around these islands, that's for certain. There is great wealth among just a couple dozen families, and the rest of these boys down here will fight for the right to own slaves even though most of them never will. Make sense to you?"

Will replied quickly, "No, no more than my mother being married to a slave-holding planter from the heartland of secession. Uncle, I remember every time you would visit here while I was growing up, you would not stay on the plantation. Why? Was it slavery?"

"Not entirely, lad. Your stepdaddy and I did well in business together before he moved down here, but we developed a personal disdain for each other shortly after I tried to talk my former sister-in-law out of marrying him. I've enjoyed the freedom and delights of town on every visit since, while waiting to sail one more of his beautiful sloops to a customer up north."

"So Daniel Bowen profits from you taking his boats north to sell, but you're not welcome in his house?" Will found yet another reason to justify the contempt in which he held his stepfather, benefactor of his higher learning. When Captain Bowen had decided that Will should leave home at the earliest opportunity, he made "investments" with influential locals that ensured Will's appointment to the Naval Academy. Fortunately, his lessons at home filled gaps left by irregular schooling, so that he was prepared well enough academically for the challenge.

"Personally, we hold each other in low regard. But as much as I loathe his politics, I am respectful to him because he has married my sister-in-law, your dear mother. And he pays me good fees because he knows I can get his boats to top-dollar buyers."

"Through your Union contacts?" William probed.

"I would prefer to think he admires my seamanship." Harris Hewitt grinned at his obvious truth. "But as long as the boat gets delivered, your stepdaddy wants his profit more than he worries about the boat going north through a Yankee blockade. Besides, as a man very much seeking legitimacy in the elite planter class, he will pour his profit into the Southern cause."

Will erupted. "His profit be damned! I'm here to care for my mother and maybe visit with a few childhood friends. Then I want to return to my duties and find ways to pay off my debt to the captain. But I fear he will hold my education debt due and payable, starting right here and now, in service to the South."

Uncle and nephew searched the shoreline for answers among the changing shadows cast by live oak branches overhung with long beards of Spanish moss. Will spoke deliberately. "I remember how my mother felt seeing slaves treated poorly; I never understood how she went along with it. At the academy, I never could argue in its defense."

Uncle Harris broke the painful silence. "No, it's not my idea of a good day to see human beings in bondage—one of many wrongs done by one to another, in the name of profit." He continued. "Among my many vices, according to the planter and his friends, is that I see Africans in this country as people. He, of course, sees his slaves as property. But he would never abuse his desk or chair or horse. He treats his slaves worse than his dogs."

"I understand, Uncle, I've seen it. But what can I do?" Will moaned, frustrated with the ambiguities of his homecoming. "I cannot imagine my service to him or, indirectly, to the Confederacy. There must be another way to repay him for my education."

"Well, as you describe it, when you chose the Naval Academy, you committed to repay your debt to your stepfather on his terms. And for your mother's sake, you must honor that, I suppose. But remember, my help awaits your decision to use it."

As the steamer glided to a stop in the mile-wide semicircle of Beaufort Bay ahead of schedule, its anchor splashed into swirling waters that glistened with the brilliance of sunrise. The great white fronts of mansions on the bluffs fifteen feet above the normal high-tide mark took on a soft pink glow.

Uncle Harris drew the lesson to be learned. "That's the price of efficiency these busy days on the water. There's no berth at the wharf. This fine captain navigates his shallow draft sidewheeler through winding rivers and creeks so well he arrives early, only to wait at anchor."

"I guess there are worse outcomes, Uncle."

With transport "home" scheduled to greet him on the Beaufort wharf, Will settled on the railing to watch the colors of the morning sky mirrored on the incoming tide. He knew the river would carry him to reunions with his mother and his memories, and to an uncertain future in his stepfather's debt.

Chapter 3

It was not long before the steamer moved from its temporary anchorage in the bay to the town wharf. As soon as the ramp was in place, Uncle Harris urged his nephew to face the day. "Time for us to get on to our separate destinations, young Will. A beautiful mother is awaiting her only son. Old Bowen probably had his slaves row over in darkness to be sure to be timely. I bet they're here already, down the wharf somewhere."

Will turned to survey the other docks but saw no familiar faces. "Shall we see you soon, Uncle?"

"When your mother comes to town tomorrow or the next day, she knows where to find me. I will try to convince her that coming north with me is better than staying down here with the unknown. And that goes for you too."

"I don't know, Uncle. The planter has tried to give her everything she wanted, even making 'an arrangement' for my schooling. I don't think he'll let go easily." There was resignation in Will's tone.

"Lad, I'll be here in the tavern with all the boat people, picking a few lucky mates to sail north with me. Tell your mother her brother-in-law awaits her for a day of visitation."

After a handshake and manly embrace, Will walked down the wooden ramp from the steamer, alighting on the Beaufort wharf for the first time in three years. The once familiar now seemed strange to him. He viewed the scene on the Beaufort River as a young man whose world view had grown even more than his toned, twenty-year-old physique.

The docks in the summer of 1861 served a mixture of public, private, and military interests. The landing at the end of Carteret Street was used mostly by white folks who tied up there after crossing the Beaufort River from the neighboring sea islands, especially from Whitehall Landing on nearby Ladies Island. The big steamers from north and south secured their lines on the old slave-built wharf, the only structure solid enough to hold them through the ebb and flow of strong, swollen tides.

While Beaufort was a small port compared to the commercial port of nearby Savannah, the mouth of Port Royal Harbor invited vessels from the Atlantic over a thirty-foot bar into the deepest harbor on the eastern seaboard south of New York. Only two miles from the Atlantic Ocean over the Port Royal bar, a stretch of sheltered waterways known as the Beaufort River provided safer passage than the shallow water along the barrier islands.

When commercial vessels stopped in Beaufort, they off-loaded treasures for the planter class—pianos, heavy furniture, boxes of books, luxurious items of home décor, crates of rum, and the finest wines money could buy. Before the prohibition of the slave trade in 1808, the docks saw many a chained African arrive in Beaufort, destined to work the rice, cotton, or indigo crops that made the region one of the wealthiest in the country. After 1808, Africans were still brought to sea island plantations as slaves, but more surreptitiously, via its myriad island channels. The region's population consisted of approximately one thousand whites and ten thousand slaves who served them in their homes and worked their land.

Just downriver from the big wharf and the row of businesses on Bay Street, Beaufort's three-block waterfront, was a dock for local fishing boats of all sizes and descriptions. The waters of the low country had long provided an ample bounty of crab, oyster, shrimp, and fish, sufficient to sustain human life on the islands. As he walked to the end of the dock, Will wondered how many slaves it took, laboring intensely in the mud and heat, to sink just one piling that would last decades.

At this time in the morning, activity flowed around Will. Containers of all shapes and sizes were off-loaded down ramps onto docks where vendors offered fresh gifts from the sea. On the wharf, salt and sea smells competed with the pungent scent from the sweat-soaked clothes of slave workers.

Riding the incoming tide from the islands south of Beaufort, Lucas and Callie poled their large bateau into one of the last slips. It was formerly used by local fishermen but was rotting to such a degree that now it was used only by slaves. Lucas had crabs to sell from his early morning catch. Callie was looking for provisions she needed to cook for the Captain's big gathering of planters the next day.

Lucas held his sister's arm firmly as the bateau rose and fell with waves pushed up by a passing southbound steamer, not letting go until she had climbed onto the rickety dock. He could have used one of the better spots on the dock as he was there on a higher mission for Massa Bowen, but he had steered to his usual spot to off-load his crabs quickly, avoiding the certain questions the dock boss would ask.

After Lucas sold his crabs, he expected to wait for the steamer to give him the precious cargo of William Hewitt to take back to the boy's mother. Missus Bowen had come to his shack that morning before sunrise to ensure his promptness in meeting her son's boat. She did not know that he had gone out hours before to lay his crab baskets for the day and emptied other crab-filled baskets that had been soaking in the shallows all night. Lucas understood the importance of his mission.

For weeks before this day, Missus Bowen could speak of nothing other than William's return from the Naval Academy. She had visited him once in his first year as she had missed him more than she realized possible. The ache his departure caused her lasted longer and was more deeply felt than when she gave birth to him nearly seventeen years before he left home. So his return to her now, three years later, stirred her spirit and reawakened her appreciation of life.

She had been thrilled with island living during her first years on Oakheart Plantation with young Willy. The warm climate was much healthier for her than the chilled Chesapeake air of her youth. There had been nothing in her life to compare to the natural beauty of flowing waterways, constantly reflecting light back into the clouds above. She and her son would lie down anywhere to watch clouds sail by, their colors and definition changed by sunlight from above and mirrored reflections from the waters below.

On his kindest days, Willy's stepfather would take the family on boat trips around Constant Island. Even when the tides weren't favorable, he would pole up creeks and back out just before the pluff mud grabbed hold of the hull. He allowed Willy to learn the intricacies of the waterways just miles from the great Atlantic Ocean.

But when young William left for naval training, by his stepfather's arrangement, it was too soon for his mother, who knew she had seen the last of her boy. She struggled to accept that her wish to hold him close must yield to his reality. The hole in her heart left by William's departure would not be filled by her life with the master of Oakheart.

With Callie off to the lively market, Lucas quickly sold his crabs to the grocer on Bay Street and went searching the Beaufort wharf. While he was anxious to do his job to meet the missus's returning son, he knew that he was also meeting Willy, the boy who shared his growing-up years. He poled his boat to the more substantial dock fit for such a greeting.

Will wandered the commercial blocks of Bay Street before moving behind the buildings to the wharf where he could survey the waterfront. On looking east into the sun-glinting waters, then south down the bluff to the small docks, he saw a young black man staring back at him. He returned the gaze wondering if there was a problem, unable to recognize the face of the young man standing only fifty feet away.

"Da you, Willy?" Lucas asked quietly. "Memba me?"

As Will moved closer, he was dumbstruck at how familiar the face became with each word and step. "Lukey, I can't believe it." Eyeing the young slave's slender, muscular build, he said, "How did you get so big?"

"No bigg'n you I reckon …"

Will leaped onto the dock, hand extended. Lucas looked around quickly while stepping back. "Massa Willy, you ain been yuh fuh las shree yeah (*three years*), maybe fuhgit."

"What do you mean, Lukey?"

"Ain goot fuh shek (*good to shake*) me han. Don know wuh da do fuh yo han, but e sho gon git me han en trouble."

An awkward silence lasted seconds when the booming voice of Uncle Harris shouted over the docks. "You still here, Will? I know old Bowen has his people show on time."

Lucas spoke promptly. "Him people, suh, we right yuh. We been yuh wait fuh tek you en Massa Willy back, suh."

Will offered an explanation. "Remember those friends I talked about? Here's one of them. One of the best friends a boy could have growing up down here—Lukey knows everything about these waters."

Uncle Harris slapped him on the back. "Pleased to meet you, young man. I'm Will's uncle." And he grabbed his hand.

Lucas quickly touched and then withdrew his hand. Looking around furtively, he said. "Yassuh, please fuh meet you too, suh."

Will explained to his uncle, "I hardly recognized Lukey at first— sportin' all those muscles."

"You ain look same needuh (*neither*), Massa Willy."

Uncle Harris observed, "Well, you're not boys anymore."

Lucas nodded through a painful look. "Yassuh."

Callie arrived on the dock just then. "And a great good-homecomin day, Massa Willy." Perhaps it was his changed physical appearance from the young Willy she knew that caused Callie to cock her head at an angle and ask, "Da you inside yo grown-up-lookin self?" She smiled warmly, while appearing to look into his eyeballs to see whether he was indeed big enough to occupy that body.

Will remembered Callie. Although he assumed her to be only a few years older than himself, he always thought her to be quite mature because she conducted herself with great care and pride. His respect, or admiration, allowed him only to say, "Good day."

Callie laughed gently: "Good you home now. Yo Mama be too happy."

"Uncle, this is Lucas's sister, Callie—Callie, my uncle, Harris Hewitt."

Callie was unsure how to respond to her first formal introduction to a white man. Barely glancing at him, she spoke through her smile. "Mos please fuh meet you, suh."

"My pleasure, I'm sure." Uncle Harris nodded to Callie and studied her face, noting wide, dark, almond eyes, slightly cast down to wider cheekbones. He had just focused on the full, curved shape of her mouth when she said, "We bes go now, Massa Willy," gesturing forward onto the bateau.

"All right. Tomorrow, Uncle, I'll try to bring Mother in for a visit. No later than the next day."

"Fine, Will." Uncle Harris's words were not connected to his steady gaze that followed Callie onto the bateau. Callie looked briefly, unsure why Massa Willy's uncle was not joining them.

As they stepped off the dock, Will quickly said to Callie and Lucas, "Please, I am not 'Willy' anymore, not even 'William,' and I most certainly am not 'Massa.' I am 'Will,' or if you must, 'Mister Will,' but I am nobody's master."

"If you say so, Mista Massawill." Lucas responded, blank-faced at first. Will turned to his childhood friend to register his frustration again, only to see a widening grin, as Lucas and Callie poled out into the tidal currents now receding down the Beaufort River toward the Atlantic Ocean.

Chapter 4

The passage from Beaufort to Constant Island, some four to five miles, could take the better part of a day, with wind and tide against you, or less than an hour with both favorable. Of course, the number of oars in the water was a major variable in the calculation. Will quickly took over the other set of oars from Callie.

On this day, with two just reunited friends pulling together on the southbound tidal flow of the Beaufort River, they may well have been flying. Rather than hug the shallows most of the way, the boys put their backs into the first strokes—the bateau jumped into the heart of the wide river in just seconds. They sailed, without cloth, downriver several miles until a wide opening in the acres of marsh grass began to appear. Just past Cat Island, they turned east sharply into the mouth of the Chowan Creek, a tributary about five hundred feet across, whose depth and direction were wholly dependent on tidal flow.

Straining into their oars more than before, the boys knew they had turned "upstream" into the Chowan Creek current, as it, too, emptied toward the Atlantic. Having left the outbound push in the Beaufort River, they began to realize how much energy they had expended shooting downstream. Neither Will nor Lucas would admit it, but together they broke the rule they made for themselves as young "boatmen."

"Ride the river tide, when rest is best,
so strength will abide to meet the current test."

Instead, their sprint downriver left them winded just when they turned against the current. Now they were sweating profusely in the late morning sun. Constant Island came into view to the east less than a mile into Chowan Creek. A few more minutes' hard work against the flow, and they arrived at Daniel Bowen's dock, expanded to twice the size Will remembered. Sheltered beneath a magnificent live oak on the bluff above, it now commanded a sweeping view down Chowan Creek and into the Beaufort River.

Both Will and Lucas were spent and their words were labored. "Not bad, huh, Lukey?" Will sputtered.

"Yessuh, awright, Massa Willy!"

"Oh, yeah, and if I am still 'Massa Willy,' then you must still be 'Lukeyboy.'" Will looked up with surprise at his own assertion.

Then Lucas extended his hand. "I 'Lucas' now, jes like you 'Will,'" said the young slave, whose point was as clear as his spoken words. Will stood to accept Lucas's gesture. Their full grasp of each other's wrists kept them both stable when Callie rocked the bateau as she stepped onto the Oakheart dock.

Looking back over her shoulder, Callie laughed. "I real happy you boys back togedda again, but I gah wuk fuh do (*got work to do*). You boys bes hope Massa ain watch dis dock wid dem long eyeglass." Ever practical when in range of the master, Callie used her warning to mask her pleasure in the strength of the relationship between the two young men. She especially enjoyed seeing her brother being treated with respect by this cultivated white man, even if he was his boyhood friend.

Turning off the long path to the house, Will saw his mother surge through the front door onto the porch and down the eight steps almost without touching them. He arrived at the base of the porch steps as she descended them, tears streaming down her cheeks as she reached for her son. Their silent, heartfelt embrace was admired by all the assembled house slaves, until disrupted by the captain's voice from the porch above.

"Welcome, son, most certainly is good to see you here." His slight smile vanished. "Got a nice boat for you, and some hard work to be done in it."

"Daniel, please. He has not yet even stepped into my home and you are already recruiting him for your military supply schemes."

"The forts out at Port Royal harbor need our support, my dear. It's a noble effort, if South Carolina's sons are brave enough to stand up for it."

A pained look hid Will's anger, but he stood straight, stepping away from his mother and looking up at the captain. "Your worries are unnecessary. I am grateful for my education and am fully aware of my obligations to you. However—"

"However nothing!" declared Captain Bowen. He slammed his cane nearly through the porch floor for emphasis, whirled, and went inside. The storm that always surrounded the captain vanished, allowing Will to appreciate his mother's loving gaze.

"It is so good to have you home again. I have missed you so. Let's go for a walk around the house." Though it was October, they sought the shade of mammoth live oak trees as they walked down near the water, arm in arm.

"Mother, are you well? Clearly your heart is strong judging by your quick remark to the captain. But you look thinner than two years ago." He remembered his uncle's cautions on questioning his mother too closely, as women's health matters were suggested to be beyond men's understanding.

"Of course I am well." Smile lines that had sagged from lack of laughter quickly appeared. "But I know you must be hungry. Maybe some food together will get us past Daniel's ornery greeting."

"I know you love him, Mother." She looked at him without conveying her doubts as he leaned in to say, "But these short moments remind me of how grateful I am for my freedom from his ways."

"Your freedom is that of a young man, free to learn and live and sail on the winds."

"Am I also free to not support the captain's treasonous war, Mother? To oppose the Confederacy as it makes war on our country for the right to hold slaves?"

She loved her son but could not find a response. Her choice was to openly express her agreement with him, thus denying her life with her husband, or to defend the indefensible slavery on which she had come to rely, however uncomfortably.

Will saw the depth of despair his questions caused his mother and immediately regretted imposing that worry on her in a weakened condition. Quickly, he caressed her shoulder and gushed: "Mother, that is not your worry, nor even mine. What is most important is your health. The captain urged me to come see you promptly."

His mother's face grew more troubled as she began to understand. She had not known why her son and brother-in-law scheduled their visit with so little notice. She had resolved to ask Harris what he knew of this, but before that was possible, her son inquired directly. She wondered whether to perpetuate the falsehood. "I am fine now, son," she deflected, hoping such simplicity would suffice. "I know the captain exaggerates and must have in this instance."

Will, not wanting to press his mother, tucked away his confusion. "Well, I must have misread the seriousness of the captain's words, but I worry about you down here in the heat. So many ills that could befall you, Mother."

Julia hugged her son for a long, tender moment before they ascended the front steps. "William, I cherish your love, even though it is from a long distance and will remain so. But you know, now that we are close again, I believe that we both will benefit if you take advantage of the wash tub in your room before we have dinner together." She smiled gently. "You look, and smell, as though you may be tired."

"Ah, Mother, ever subtle when it comes to matters of the nose. Even I can tell that five days aboard a steamer did not leave me so very fragrant."

"Refresh yourself, William, and take a short rest. I'll call you for an early dinner."

He ascended the pine staircase; it creaked in the same places he remembered, though there seemed to be more layers and dimensions to the protestations of old wooden steps. On arriving in the room that was "his," Will looked out the second-floor windows, as he had done so many times while just a boy. The scenes were perfectly familiar, though three years older. From the window looking south through interwoven live oak branches, he saw Chowan Creek stretch into Beaufort River. From the west window, there were farm operations as far as he could see. Bent figures picked cotton in most of the near fields. Smaller figures stirred dust in the farthest fields, digging out sweet potato roots from the dark, fertile island soil.

Without doubt, the land, though flat, was still stunning, surrounded as it was by pulsing tides. Seas were always full of edible morsels; temperatures were as moderate as could be desired, with the exception of the blistering summer heat. It was a veritable heaven on earth. Will still viewed it as such. But he was disturbed anew to see that beauty through one window of his corner room and slavery in operation through another.

While growing up in Baltimore, Maryland, during his first ten years, Willy knew little of the South. But after his mother married Daniel Bowen, and they moved to the captain's home on Constant Island, South Carolina, he learned of a whole new world. For some time after his arrival, young Willy believed that the good things about their new life far outweighed any worries about his stepfather's harsh treatment of slaves. At first, he did not question the Southern society belief that slaves were not people, but merely property. Even so, he sensed his mother's increasing discomfort with the realities of slavery, at least as administered at Oakheart.

Captain Bowen utilized and, young William slowly learned, brutalized his slaves. The more he realized that his stepfather succeeded on the work of others, the more resentful he became. The whipping the captain laid on one of his most trusted slaves, when that man returned a day late from delivering goods to Savannah, scared and repulsed William. He never knew blood could be so red, or pain so severe that the torment produced only silent screams.

Despite his stepson status, or maybe because of it, William felt the fury of this rawboned man more than once and knew early in his teen years that his time under the captain's roof would be short. Physical violence usually took the form of face slaps, all out of sight of his mother, of course. The one time she saw her son kicked in the behind by his stepfather, Bowen quickly recovered on seeing her, laughing it off. His mother did not see the meanness in his stepfather's eyes that was all too clear to the boy.

His own sense of independence had become something of an obsession by the time William turned sixteen. In the following year, when he had formed his own plan to steal away on a northbound steamer, his relief came grandly and unexpectedly. Through his mother's powers of persuasion, her husband was convinced he should lobby local politicians to gain William's appointment to the United States Naval Academy. His influence consisted of several well-placed donations to local leaders' church funds—soon after William was notified of his acceptance into the academy. The next three years rushed the new midshipman forward with little time for reflection on his mother and what he had left behind.

But now he was back, and the world in which his mother lived was still beautiful and troubling. Having just begun his fourth year at the Naval Academy, he was surprised that his request for leave to visit his ill mother had been granted. Will was glad that he was permitted to go south, especially since his uncle had business in Beaufort at the same time, so they both could support his mother as needed.

Of course, the administrators of the academy did not know that Captain Bowen intended to have his stepson pay his personal debt immediately—first through his labor and then through his service in the Confederate navy. With the war at sea quickly moving south, others within the Naval Academy were pleased that Harris Hewitt, no Southern sympathizer, would accompany midshipman Hewitt on his intended round-trip journey.

After shedding his travel clothes, splashing water all over, and toweling off, Will's newly cleansed body collapsed on the bed. It had been days since weariness and cleanliness combined, and he soon was drifting in and out of awareness. Images of the surrounding sea and surging waterways at high tide swirled in his mind. Even as a young boy, Will trusted his own observations and intuitions on the water, though mindful of his stepfather's cautions and admonitions. "The rules of the water are stringent. Ignore them at your peril," his stepfather would warn during safety lectures. He remembered them now as he anticipated fishing with Lucas on the morning tides.

He drifted further back to the time he was a twelve-year-old boy. Willy, for the first time, had just worked up the courage to venture into the near-shore waters in the smallest skiff at the dock. He had watched men do this for nearly two years. He knew what he was doing, or so he thought.

The incoming tide swelled the river. Calm air meant a smooth-water surface for his inaugural voyage. He had quickly untied the skiff from the dock and pushed into the shallows when the captain's voice boomed down from the balcony of the big house: "Boy, what in hell—when I get down there, by God!"

As Willy poled bravely away from the dock, moving up the tidal creek that fronted the plantation, he grabbed the oar, waving it at his mother as she replaced the captain on the balcony. He saw only her encouraging wave, not her worried look. By the time the captain emerged from the first floor, Willy was well away from the dock, and clearly on his way. Either in his mind, or in fact, the captain's voice quickly receded, ineffective.

Willy felt free! Willy was free!

He felt as though the bateau, in contact with his body, was an extension of himself as it glided through warm waters. He moved with purpose. His arms pulled at the water and pushed it behind, his pace increasing with each stroke, his power more certain. The slight breeze his motion created caressed the smile fixed on his face.

Willy had learned the water depth throughout the tidal creek, as low tides revealed secrets of pluff mud, marsh grass, and oyster beds. He planned his inaugural trip to be just far enough up the creek and around the bend to be out of sight from the plantation house. However, the power of pleasure that day was so extreme that he continued well past his mark—the overhanging live oak at the back of the big house lot.

Before he knew it, Willy had extended the journey well beyond the cotton fields by the creek. Two dolphins surfaced twenty feet ahead of his boat and then quickly came up on his side, the larger one jumping over his outstretched oar. The boy took the challenge and rowed even harder for a minute, in full chase, before he realized there was no contest with dolphins. They took some final celebratory jumps well in front of him and disappeared up a narrow estuary.

Willy's spirit that day was substantially stronger than his preteen arms, for once he made his turn—he had punished the captain enough for doubting him and impressed his mother with his "manhood"—the boat made little progress back toward the south end of Constant Island. Though he tried and his arms did work the oars, the boat drifted further up the creek. He could not be seen by anyone from the plantation grounds. With no one working the nearby fields, no one would hear a call for help. Besides, he could not make such a call.

As the waters of this extraordinary high tide pooled and swirled, pushing his small craft into tangles of dead marsh grass, he began to doubt the wisdom of his plan, or at least its execution. Thinking hard on how to explain his exploits, Willy barely noticed the water begin to recede toward the Beaufort River and the ocean. He came to understand that he was caught in the last tidal push upriver and that all he had to do was stay clear of the branches and reeds, relax, and let the river carry him back with minimal effort. His sense of calamity faded, somewhat prematurely, it turned out.

So proud of his journey, and his futile race with the dolphins, Willy did not contemplate any result upon his return other than pride and praise. Later that day, he learned the captain had an unpleasant array of responses when he was unhappy.

Just as Will began to frown through his dream, the bell to ring the slaves out of the fields clanged him back to the present. Looking around, orientation to his reality came slowly. From his window, an orange glow on the western horizon was chasing the sun. Splashes of water from the bedside bowl did not clear a mind beset with travel weariness, unsettling dreams, and unpaid debts. Soon his mother called him to dinner, like so many times in the past.

Will paused at the top of the staircase, listening to sounds from the dining room below. After Callie brought out platters of shrimp and okra to accompany the bowls of rice, candied yams, and collard greens already on the table, she hurried out the door. The captain commanded her: "Gal, come here!" and Callie scurried back. "Where's that brother of yours? Haven't seen him around—I guess I can't count on him tomorrow neither. By God, I'll get some satisfaction!" He slammed his fist to the table, rattling the fine china settings that Callie had meticulously placed as instructed by Missus Bowen.

"Capn, suh, you know Lucas be ready fuh go out when dayclean (*sunrise*). You tell him jes dis mornin. Das all, suh?"

The captain did not like to be reminded of things he had forgotten and did not respond.

Missus Bowen dismissed Callie with her hand and suggested to her husband that they go out for a short sail tomorrow. She hoped to improve the relationship between the two men in her life. But her solicitous notion was immediately dismissed by the captain, saying he had already given too much to this "ungrateful boy."

Julia nervously called out to Will, who began his descent with loud footsteps, giving the conversation a chance to go a different direction. "Oh honey, I was just urging the captain to take us sailing tomorrow morning, but apparently he has a conflict in schedule." His mother lied with a graceful ease he had not noticed before.

"No problem, Captain," Will spoke coolly. "I know there must be more pressing matters for one so engaged."

"I expect after our cotton is shipped, you will become engaged, as you say, with the Confederate navy. We need help bolstering those forts out there." He gestured down the Beaufort River toward Port Royal Sound. "You took so long to get here I thought you were going to stay up north with Julia's brother-in-law." Julia's eyes dropped to the table.

Will was not intimidated by Bowen's rudeness. "Both Uncle Harris and I came as soon as we heard that my mother was ill. I am greatly

31

relieved to see that she is better now," he said, grasping her hand, "so much so that I am considering returning to school promptly, as many of my classmates already serve on boats of the United States Navy, and—"

"And your obligation starting next month, after you enlist with the Confederate navy, is to stop those Yankee boats from carrying out Lincoln's blockade of our ports. Since he started it in April, it's barely working anyway, but your job will be to help make sure that our boats loaded with cotton get through that blockade."

"With all due respect, sir," he replied, his voice dripping with irony not lost on his mother, "realistically, the Union is amassing every floating scow it can find for its navy, and the South has little strength to oppose it. Late last month they easily overpowered shore batteries up at Hatteras Inlet in North Carolina with coordinated attacks from the water."

"Well, I am sure there is no pride in that assertion, is there, boy? I'm beginning to wonder what side you're on, but I know this—once my cotton work is done around here, you belong to the Southern navy. Maybe you can make the forts on Port Royal Sound stronger than they were at Hatteras."

Will, seeking not to extend the debate, stifled his doubts.

"Stated simply, young William, it is a time for South Carolina's sons to rise."

Will could not stop himself. "But sir, you are not even one of this state's sons! Twenty-five years living down here does not make you a Southern man."

"I draw my strength each day from what South Carolina provides. So does your Mother, and so do you, boy."

"No matter how well I know my obligation to you, stepfather, I am on the side of my country! I don't fancy my participation in anyone's military that plots against our country."

"Don't presume to tell me what is 'my country.'" In seeking to rise quickly, the captain stumbled back into the chair, catching himself by its arms. His wife stood up to help stabilize him at first, and then she leaned her hand with some force on his forearm, pinning it to the chair. He glowered at her, pulled away, and turned to Will.

"When Hatteras has already fallen to Yankee attack by sea, you can sit there—a young man supported in every way by the fruits of the South—and lecture me about what is your country in this war of Yankee aggression?" His voice elevated with each word.

Will's mother quickly spoke to both men but looked at the Captain and took his hand. "My son understands his obligations. I just hoped we could help reacquaint William with these islands tomorrow—just so that we could enjoy family time a bit, while you shared your local wisdom?" Ever hopeful, she did not wish to see the vast gap between her son and her husband.

"My dear, this is not a time for family matters!" the captain snapped, pulling his arm away and standing abruptly.

Julia's hurt surfaced as she rose with him. "I have always known what comes first, Daniel. Your boats, your cotton, your profits, your property!"

"You live well off them, my dear," he said dryly.

Resigned, she sagged into her chair. "My blessing, my curse."

It began to appear to Will that he had interrupted an ongoing, nearly unspoken conversation. Then he provided needed relief. "Mother, I will go with Lucas on the early morning tide. I am well rested with so much idle time on the steamer. I will help Lucas bring in his catch and feel these island breezes once more for a good purpose, to complete the captain's feast tomorrow night."

"That would be fine, son." The mother's composure returned with her gratitude for her son's effort toward compromise.

Will continued in a feint of subservience. "Perhaps in some small way I can begin to repay your husband his due." His expression, as he cast his eyes back upon the captain, changed from steely resolve to grim acceptance.

The captain stomped away from the table to the stairs, muttering, "'Bout time we get some use out of ya. But for tonight, your insolence has soured my stomach." As the master of the house hoisted his angular frame up the pine stairs to the second floor, his dour spirit lifted from the room as well.

Mother and son spent the evening remembering, reminding, sharing—allowing Julia Bowen to see how the years changed her boy into this fine young man, this soon-to-be naval officer. After the deeply satisfying reunion dinner with his mother, Will was relieved that his duty on the water with Lucas early the next morning would spare him further discussion with the captain, for most of the next day at least.

Chapter 5

Lucas and Will surely got the jump on the day's fishing, both up hours before sunrise. Just as dawn breaking over the water once afforded the boys their daily escapes from plantation life, it now provided relief for young men still confined by circumstances not of their making.

For Lucas, as slave, the tasks at hand were his unpaid job—catching enough food from the sea to feed many others. These requirements were imposed by his "master," but he loved the work so much, he did it without coercion.

Will, as stepson, simply wanted to pay back his creditor on the best terms possible, and with minimal consternation, interaction, or compromise of his own principles. He hoped this small morning mission would be a good first step.

Whatever the motivation, they were at the dock while all the others slept, even the field hands who were working earlier every day to meet Massa's demands for the cotton harvest. There had been a particularly successful crop in this year of secession. While Southern men flocked to the cause, the priority of each planter had to be the harvest, followed by war-making.

Happily for Will, returning to his childhood schoolyard sea, getting on the water this early was not new. The academy imposed midshipmen hours that were more rigorous than this. To rise in full dark on Constant Island and feel southern breezes gently ruffling the waters under your bateau was one of nature's gifts.

Out in the Beaufort River, Will and Lucas pulled on their oars, leaning into strong strokes that pushed them eastward toward a rising sun. Will noticed the rippling muscles of Lucas's shirtless back, each stroke showing shiny scar tissue where the lash had laid open Lucas's skin. Will chose to focus on the muscles and had to ask, "Man, how did you get to be so big?"

"I kin aks you da too, Will."

Will quickly looked to himself, finding no comparison. He was strong, but smaller than his friend. Will responded, "Oh, the Naval Academy worked me pretty hard."

Then Lucas, between strokes, replied, "I wuk de pluff mud. Massa wan crop grow goot, so him aks Lucas cah (*carry*) de mud from de crik tuh de fiel. I dig em up when tide low, put em in de bucket, cah em tuh de fiel. Da wuk wuk me haad too, jes like da navy cademy wuk you."

"You never had to do anything like that when I was around, did you?" Will asked earnestly.

"Massa done figyuh e time fuh me do mo dan play wid you. When you gone, him mek me git outta de boat en wuk de fiel mos day. Mud so hebby (*heavy*) I mos kyan (*can't*) git em out de crik. Las yeah I say, 'Massa, suh, if I dig out dishyuh mud when tide low en put my bucket uh mud on de bateau, den wait fuh high tide tek me up nex to de fiel, I git mo done fuh you, suh.'"

"Sounds very reasonable. What did he say?"

"I ain neba tink Massa lemme do da, but him say awright, en I do jes wha I say. Whiles I wait fuh de tide rise, I catch whole buncha mullet and whitin, swimp en crab. Haul so much mud out, keep Massa off my back. Nowdays da wuh him wan me fuh do." After a pause, he said, "En da how I git so big deese shree yeah pass (*last three years*)."

"I see." Will did see, given the two ways the young men grew into their bodies. While he considered the Naval Academy grueling, he now viewed his labors of the last three years as privileged in comparison to what his friend had endured.

The cadence of their strokes breaking the water's surface rewound Will's memory to days past when he and Lukey, first as boys, then as young teenagers, plied these waters. He remembered their proficiency in the months before he left for the academy. In dugout canoes, they glided across glistening rolls of waves so swiftly and smoothly as to mimic brown pelicans in power glide inches above the breakers.

Early on, Willy did not realize the release their watery exploits provided for his best friend. They were just boys on their own, so he thought. The planter's stepson, raised for his first decade in the free North, made the comfortable assumption that Lukey chose to play with him every day. Only now, on looking back, did Will understand more clearly.

Back then, for young Willy, every day on the water was one not spent in the presence of his authoritarian stepfather. For Lukey, each day out with Willy was one not spent in the field. For the benefit of both, they kept each other out of reach of Daniel Bowen.

More lately, but always regularly, Bowen as "Massa" was a strict disciplinarian. The whip slashed the back of many a slave on the plantation, and that was just for ordinary, run-of-the-mill offenses, like forgetting an item on a trip to town, or dropping a place setting when company was present.

Young Lukey only felt the lash on one day and for just three strokes before his sister came flying through the front door of the big house. Lukey had been carrying hot water upstairs to the new missus of the plantation, a task he had performed many times during her first year. When he tripped, water cascaded down the stairs and into the parlor.

Massa's reaction was immediate! He moved with surprising speed from his study on the first floor, grabbed the always-handy whip hanging by the front door with his left hand just before seizing the thin arm of the slave boy with his right.

Lucas wasn't aware his feet touched the porch steps as he hurtled down them, gripped firmly by Massa's fury. His filthy shirt was ripped from his trembling body just before the first lash tore his skin open. With the second, the scream left his mouth from a place deep within. After the third, Callie's shout of "Noooo!" from the porch, stopped Massa's hand in midair, as it peaked to strike again.

As if a slave's objection to a whipping could stop it.

And yet it did.

As eleven-year-old Willy watched the scene with wide-eyed horror from the dining room window, the lash came down again, this time gently, brushing against the young slave's teary cheek. No more blows were struck, though the blood was rushing from newly opened, glistening wounds, stretching from one shoulder blade to the other.

After her scream stopped the violent attack on her brother, Bowen's hand still clutched Lukey's quivering skin and bones. Callie composed herself, stepping quickly from the big house porch down to Lukey's side. The looks exchanged between Callie and Massa were telling. Her anger was contained, unspoken. Massa looked, for the first time, as if he had done wrong by whipping a slave. For her part, Callie viewed Massa's concession to not work her little brother in the field as just compensation for the whipping he gave the boy, and for other outrages he had committed against her, for which at least that much penance was due.

From that day forward, Lukey was assigned full-time as Willy's playmate. Two young boys who did not fully understand their different stations in life, both scarred. They found refuge in their friendship, a fact that pleased Captain Bowen's new wife.

As teenage boys, they were constant companions. Shuffling through the sandy soil with bare feet, they were lost little souls on land and soaring spirits on water. Their outings on shimmering sunrise tidal creeks gave them new freedom. Each new incoming tide was teeming with life, making the boys very proficient "fishermen" with nets, hands, and poles as they caught crabs, fish, and shrimp at will. They soon learned that the bounty of their outings earned them favor, goods in trade, and money.

Neither Lucas nor Will could have known how their love of the water would alter their lives. Too young to see around such distant swells, they looked to the next crest and the exhilaration of riding it, not the great beyond.

As Will reflected deeply through his strokes, Lucas steered skillfully and powerfully, his oars digging into saline river water as it, too, rushed out to sea. Lucas interrupted Will's contemplations. "I say, Will." Will's attention snapped back with Lucas's call.

"We gah fuh (*got to*) be quick en good dis monin. We go way down de riba mos to big sea fo we turn up Station Crik. Massa wan fresh swimp en crab fuh all him planta fren."

"Well, you know where you're going. I'm the grunt labor and you're running the show. Tell me when and what to do."

"Da too funny. Me tell a white man wha fuh do?"

"Well, you know best. Makes sense, don't you think?"

"Ain de fus time I know bes. Ain nobody care wha slave tink. Cep when Massa lemme haul mud my way."

"Today is a new day, leastways on this boat. You, Lucas, are a captain, not a slave. I am crew. Crew awaits orders."

"Man, you been in da school too long, or up nort, or both. But you right. I know wha I do, da fuh sho. Dis day we go wey you ain neba be at low tide. I know hole in dishyuh crik wid all de swimp. Dey so much you kyan pull up de cas net."

Will audibly scoffed at the idea of too many shrimp to haul on board. "Is that a challenge, Captain?"

Lucas slowed his rowing. "Jes tell wha true. Deese yuh crik roun de plantation done been swimp-out—tek all day fuh fill one bucket. So I find spot at low tide wey nobody know en nobody go." They had made the turn into Station Creek when Lucas began searching for something along the bank. Will looked at his serious face, filled with purpose. Lucas saw Will watching, and explained, "I git done wid my tas real fas—gah mo time fuh fish en hunt. Jes so I do wha Massa wan en come back wid full boatload."

"Makes good sense, Lucas. I admire how you do your business."

"Turn yuh!" Lucas gestured with his chin and glance. As Lucas and Will pulled on their left sides and pushed on their right, two long strokes each, they turned and power-rowed quickly between the banks of spartina grass, oysters, and pluff mud into a small channel. Shallow water was overhung with live oaks leaning from the banks, their long branches draped into the marsh water. Lucas grabbed a ten-foot pole from beneath their seats, stood, and pushed the craft forward with powerful stabs into layers of mud. They glided into a large pool perhaps fifty feet across. In the far end nearest the shore, Lucas pointed down beside Will. "Crew bes stan wid cas net in teet (*teeth*) bout now."

Will did what he was told. He hadn't lost the knack of placing two hands on the rim rope circling the cast net, with a third spot gripped firmly in his mouth. All at once, he made a quick half turn in the bow of the boat, releasing hands and mouth simultaneously. A perfectly spiraling cast net splashed down onto the water, encircling unsuspecting marine life as it sank.

Will hit the spot as directed and began to pull up on the circular cords that trapped the unlucky beings below. He found that on first pull, there was only a little give. With a different stance and two hands firmly overlapping, he raised the net to the surface, fully rounded with brownish-green shrimp, a writhing mass, scrambling for the nonexistent advantage. And that was as far as the net was going to go, even with Will putting his "academy" fitness and training to work. Lucas knew before Will did that he would be needed and worked his way toward Will as they both hauled the massive catch of shrimp into the bateau. After three more casts, they had filled the large buckets between them and could catch no more.

"You told the truth, Lucas. That's more shrimp than I've ever seen in one place sitting in the center of our boat."

"Yeah—we done yuh. We jes gah fuh pull crab trap out de Chowan Crik. Seem like we git us some time fuh res."

"Thought we were in a hurry, Captain."

"Crew done do so goot yuh, kin lay low fuh now."

As they sat in the slowly rising tide that soft October morning, the setting moon slipping from view in the still dark western sky, the smooth "pond" showed them a second moon, mirroring the first. It seemed as if fortune had dropped the young men back into their boyhoods, where time on the water was great and keeping track of it was immaterial.

They shared stories of what each had learned on the water during their three years apart. Lucas demonstrated his abundant knowledge of the salt marsh tributaries and tricky sea island currents, while Will described how his instruction at the academy combined classroom and time on the sea.

"One of the most amazing things I have come to appreciate is how the navy can win wars that the army cannot. Seriously. What water divides and obstructs for armies, it conveys and enables for navies."

"Don know much bout army or navy. Do know bout de wada. You gah fuh go wid de way de wada go. Don do da, you gah problem."

"Man, you sound like my stepfather." Will mocked him. "'Actions have consequences, you know, boy.'"

"Well, dey do, ain dat so?" Lucas asked for affirmation.

"Of course, but ..." Will realized the truth more easily coming from Lucas.

Lucas said, "But if you git in da current, you bes know way e go, en when e go back tuh big sea, en how skrong e be. I ride deese current, Will, en I know bout how fuh scape ef supm chase me—git back home safe."

"Guess you've had some experience with that?" Will asked.

"Not me, but I know people who been chase ..." He hesitated and then went on. "I hep Massa chase down slave en deese maash crik (*marsh creeks*)." His voice dropped too low to be heard, and Will asked no more.

The quiet allowed gentle waves slapping the bateau to be heard. Lucas let silence work for a minute and then spoke. "Well, I figyuh we gah nuf (*enough*) fuh Callie bes stew. Huh crew git all dis peel en cook up by time sun go down."

"She is quite a chef, I understand. I remember her a little, but she didn't cook so much when I was here. Now she does it all?"

"Oh yeah, since Mama Ruth pass. Callie took ovah en do it jes as good as Mama. Ol' Massa brag bout de food be bes roun deese islan. Ebbybody know Callie de one run de show, ummm-hmmm."

Will noted that, as Lucas relaxed, his mind kept returning to the master. "Wish you didn't have to think of Captain Bowen so much. Seeing you work out here, teaching me things, I see you as an able man, more worthy than the captain to ask for a man's respect."

"Dem good word, Will. Dey ain real fuh me. I know wey I stan, and who stan on me." Will had no response, and Lucas went on. "Scar on my back don lemme fuhgit. I know you seen em and you know wey dey come from. You memba Massa scrap (*strap*) me? I memba too—yeah, I memba—hurt my head tuh dis day. I been a string bean den—dey call me 'bean.' Try real haad keep from cry. Ain know wha I do so bad fuh git whip like da—been good house boy fo da wada pitcha break. Ef Callie ainbe holla, Massa ain been guh stop till ..."

Will could not comment, and Lucas continued. "Yeah, I memba awright—always wonda when Massa lookin maddes at me, and hittin hardes, why he shout, 'By Gawd, I teach you, boy!' I figyuh him Gawd don teach him like my Gawd teach me, ummm-hmmm."

Finally, Will said, "It can be hard to have faith—treated that way."

"Ain haad. I got fait (*faith*). Me fait get me you."

"What do you mean, Lucas?"

Lucas explained, "My Gawd bring you tuh Oakhaart. My fait teach me da my Gawd ain gonna lemme down. I tell Him da I gi my life fuh Him if he gi me wha I need—and roun den, you come to plantation wid yo Mama. Fo I know, my job be fuh play wid you."

"That's pretty amazing, Lucas." Will actually was amazed and moved to the point that his quick hand swipe past his face caught the tear starting to fall.

Lucas finished. "I don know why you come yuh den en now, but de Lawd move in musterious way. Da be in de Massa plan."

"Ah Lucas, I don't care much for your Massa's plans."

"Careful, fren." Lucas cautioned him. "I ain say Massa plan. I talk bout de Massa, Lawd Jedus."

Will conceded this. "I see the power of it in your life, Lucas; part of me envies your faith." And then, nodding to the layered hues beginning to fill the eastern horizon, he said, "Look at your God's morning gift."

"Sun come up dis day and nex, Will. We talk so long I mos fuhgit supm I wan you fuh see."

"I thought it was this miracle shrimp hole here."

"Naw, supm mo den da. Ain fah from yuh." And with a few more strokes, the bateau, heavy laden as it was, surged out into the Station Creek current again. Less than a minute later, the ten-foot banks of spartina grass opened to reveal a large, filling lagoon, and beyond the far end of it, a man-made structure came into view.

Lucas rose in the bateau, using both arms to frame the new Hunting Island lighthouse for his friend to see. Will's jaw dropped at sight of the new lighthouse. Just then a bright flash lit the gray morning. A crashing boom followed immediately, causing Lucas to fall down into the boat and Will to cover his head. They both looked up to see a huge cloud of fiery smoke rise from the lighthouse as the structure's debris crumbled out of sight behind the barrier island tree line. Will, recovering, spoke first. "Good God, Lucas, just when I thought you couldn't impress me any more. What else can you do?"

Lucas stuttered as he stood. "I … I … I hep buil da lighthouse." They watched the fiery light subside while deciding without speaking to begin rowing back toward the open waters of the Beaufort River.

Suddenly shots rang out from a small boat at the far end of the lagoon, more than five hundred feet away. They assumed that they were being shot at by the same Union forces that must have just destroyed the lighthouse, but there was no time to verify that assumption. Shots were coming faster as Lucas and Will moved quickly into the narrow openings through the marsh grass. Soon they were in the Beaufort River and pulling the shrimp-laden bateau with the inbound tide using the most powerful strokes they could muster. Their worries grew as the patrol boat followed them through the marsh and into the river less than a minute later. Their worst fears were quickly realized as bullets zipped into the water around them.

"Hey, Will, memba I tell you, when tide low, lee boat kin go wey big boat kyan?"

"Yeah, Lucas," Will shouted. "Got a plan?"

"Time fuh go tuh de maash." Lucas gestured to the right and immediately rowed in a way to accomplish the turn, which Will mimicked. The bateau swung toward the marsh grass lining the river just as a bullet splintered the end of Will's left oar. He felt its impact in his hand and wrist but gripped tighter and rowed harder.

"Problem, Lucas!" Will shouted, looking forward. "There is no opening through the marsh, that's a bank dead ahead."

"Seem so, Will." Sure enough, they slowed moving into the strong stand of marsh grass, and then the bow ran aground, straight into the bank.

Will looked with desperation from Lucas to the chase boat, closing fast. "Got some tricks here, Lucas? What are we doing?"

Lucas ordered Will to move to the back of the boat and to haul the shrimp buckets back there with him. Will acted quickly, though he was doubtful. Next, Lucas went overboard, wading to the stern. Bullets increased in intensity as Lucas lifted the bateau from the rear and pushed it forward over the low embankment. He gave the boat a last shove, and in spite of the combined weight of the shrimp and Will, it slid quietly into the pooled water beyond. Lucas pulled himself out of the grasping muck of pluff mud and over the bank, as peering riflemen in the chase boat lost sight of their targets.

"Stay low, Will," Lucas whispered, and he began pulling on the oars. Together, they quickly cornered around a tall stand of grass and glided beyond a small island of scrub pines and myrtle trees. They were safe because the scout boat could not clear the embankment, and the shooters could not hit what they could not see. Only then, as their fear subsided, did they realize how close those bullets had come. Will looked through the shattered end of his oar at Lucas, who began to grin.

Though safe, they realized they had pushed deep into mud and dead marsh grass as they sought refuge near the island. When they heard no shots or shouts for a few minutes, Lucas assessed the status of their boat. "We stuck in da mud agin, Will—kyan row to deep wada."

"Don't jump back into that stuff unless you have to, Lucas," Will said.

Lucas looked at him with a pained but playful look. "Wha you tink I jes do? En been do all dem yeah you ain been yuh?" Then Lucas smiled. "Wha you say true—ain *me* gah fa go tuh de maash mud dis time."

Will jumped overboard, tugging with all his might on the bateau. He pulled it free of the layers of dead marsh grass, falling only twice and straining to lift himself from the suctioning mud each time. Will clambered back into the bateau, as fully coated with pluff mud as Lucas, and nearly identical in appearance. As their mud-caked exteriors hardened, they rowed through a back channel parallel to the river until they found an opening to the Beaufort River. They both were relieved that the chase boat had vanished, allowing their return to the plantation just after noon.

Will knew that shrimp and crab delivery was first on the agenda, but he felt obligated to report immediately to the captain on the military engagement they had just survived. Surely their good work and the intelligence they would share would leave a favorable impression on the captain, earning Will some respect and leverage when he attempted to negotiate a new arrangement for debt repayment.

Chapter 6

Callie had been sitting on the dock, anxiously waiting for Lucas and Will to return with a boatload of fresh delicacies from the sea. She had planned precisely for the food preparation, and all her cookhouse helpers were there, ready to work. She trusted Lucas to be back early enough so that they could get the meat picked from the crabs and the shrimp heads popped before working them into the pot.

Callie had prepared such mass feedings many times, and for her purposes, these planter gatherings were just another set of mouths. She knew her work well enough to anticipate any of the Massa's questions, except, "When are you getting started fixing the fresh shrimp and crabs?"

Normally, Massa Bowen did not give such attention to cooking details. His desire to check the corn storage with her the day before told her there was more on his mind than corn. It had been more than two weeks since he last insisted on "helping" her with her work. At such times, her own animal instincts were on high alert. Any time Massa came into view, she knew how to read his intentions—whether as a planter, a disciplinarian, or a male—and she acted accordingly.

"Hey, Callie gal."

Callie hated her status in life beneath this pitiful, nasty man. Though she knew he lacked civility, and she resented deeply his clumsy tyrannies, she also knew that she could still "manage" the situation. Callie had hunted enough times with her brothers to know the movements of hunter and the evasions of prey. Of course, as the hunted, she could not run an unlimited range. In other circumstances, evading her hunter would be all too easy. But within the confines of the plantation and the daily routines, and especially on this day of food preparation, Callie's whereabouts were somewhat predictable. Despite Callie's best evasive maneuvers, most recently her wait for the boys on the dock, Massa Cap'n found his prey.

His voice again penetrated her awareness. "Callie gal, I know there's some things needing your attention more important than sittin out on this dock." Callie sensed the dominance in his approach.

"Yes, Massa, dem boys say dey be back long fo now." She hopped up from her spot on the dock. "I jes go back tuh de cookhouse—mek sho Mabelle cut en wash de collard awright."

"Now, Callie, you know you can count on her." Her hesitation allowed his thin lips to unravel into a smile. "Just like I can count on you."

"Massa, you know you kin count on me. But don count on me jes now since I gah fuh cook." She approached him on the narrow dock, and just as Bowen reached for her, she bent over and pulled the rope of a crab trap, elbows flying as she strained her muscles against the weight of the trapped crustaceans. The captain backed away from the action.

Once on the dock, two small blue crabs scrambled free through the wooden siding of the trap. Callie grabbed both from behind in a quick motion and twisted her wrists so as to pass them to the captain's outstretched hands. "I tink deese yuh crab ain big nuf. Wha Cap'n Massa tink?" Her playful tone was just barely tolerable to the captain, whose subordinates in all other realms of his life never would slip from responsibility without his rebuke.

Callie lifted the trap to her shoulder and walked up the dock, leaving Massa holding the crabs. "Look heah, Massa, wha I got—we tank you so much fuh help wid de crab. Dem folk wha come yuh git soup chock full o crab, tank be to you and de good Lawd."

While she continued to worry about the boys and their catch, Callie pretended not to hear him say, "I will see you later then, gal." His intentions were clear, as he flung the small crabs off the dock into the shallows.

*   *   *

Later than expected, Lucas and Will arrived knowing they had set Callie's work back. After eluding unknown assailants, they had pulled in more crabs from the nearby creek, so their mission had been fully accomplished. Waiting on the dock, Callie's helpers unloaded the catch and carried it to the kitchen.

When Will and Lucas came off the dock, they saw the captain looking at them as though putrid air had just filled his overly large nose. "Well, aren't you boys a pair of sad mud balls."

Will stood to attention. "Sir, we must report to you on the destruction of the lighthouse by Union forces. They are near." He held up his "holy" oar. "They shot up my oar and chased us part of the way back here!" Patting Lucas's shoulder, he said, "He got us safely into shallow marsh where they couldn't go." Will felt he had done justice to the facts in his brief report.

The captain was less than impressed. "The day I take battle reports from a nigger boy and his lookalike friend will be when I'm dead and buried." He turned abruptly to walk away but turned again. "We Confederates blew up our own lighthouse, so it would not be useful to the Yankees if they are dumb enough to come here. Most likely, you got shot up by some of my friends out there." Pausing for effect, he then continued. "What do they teach you at that academy, boy?"

Will did not move during the exchange, nor flinch. Lucas shifted slightly on his feet, two steps behind his friend.

"I believe the South may be in good shape after all," mused the captain. With detachment, he looked past Will toward the Beaufort River. "Now I'm going to prepare for my guests. If you believe in the importance of first impressions, you may wish to do the same."

★   ★   ★

Darkening October skies turned the river waters a cold metal gray. For months now, each fourth Thursday late afternoon brought wealthy, hungry, angry men to the Bowen plantation from all the nearby sea islands. As they came up from the dock, they assembled in the yard around long boards wide enough to serve as tabletops, awaiting Callie's substantial meal. Callie and her crew knew their roles—to keep the food fresh, hot, and on the table—and then stay out of the way.

The gatherings had grown in size and intensity as the summer heat swelled. Though masters of all they surveyed, their stories reflected the dim mood of the day as did the surrounding waters. As shadows grew to dusk, their passions for the Confederacy heightened. Abundant food and drink did not diminish political talk, with speakers displaying their ardor in support of the right to secede from the United States, and their drive to right perceived wrongs, both past and future.

While serving the men, Callie focused on her tasks and acted uninterested in their conversation. She was careful never to look like she was listening, so that those with white skin would continue to ignore her but for the service she provided. They obviously assumed that she would neither care nor understand their banter about world and local affairs. Callie absorbed news of the world and gossip about the island families, information that she shared judiciously. From what Callie overheard that night while she placed platters of crabs on the long tables, she sensed that another element had been added to the roiling debates—fear.

As she brought another tray of oysters to the center table, Edward DeWitt grabbed one off the top, prying it open with a knife while standing to make his point. "You don't understand the immediacy of our moment here, Daniel. I'm telling you that the minute the Union Navy took Hatteras Inlet, they began looking farther south for a better deepwater port. They been watchin' Port Royal for months now. I've seen boats taking soundings in the last couple weeks!"

Bowen countered. "I'd still bet on Savannah or St. Augustine."

"Hell, boy, they ain't lookin' to do business. They lookin' to shut down our ships from takin' our cotton out and bringin' us the necessities for fightin' this war. No better place for them to bring their coal-hungry steamers than the deep water of Port Royal Sound."

Bowen wasn't convinced or was busy denying. "Dammit, DeWitt, all's we got is a bunch of cotton, bugs, and niggers. I don't think the Yankee navy wants any of it."

"Just cause you 'don't think' so, don't make it so. Keepin' your head down in the ground like a flock o' ibis birds won't change the reality of what's about to happen heah. Believe it or don't. Tomorrow, I'm packin' out my possessions on a flat boat and puttin' my family and house niggers on a packet to Charleston."

"What, by God, good will that do? What do you think the rest of your slaves will do? You think your driver will keep them in line with you runnin' out scared?"

DeWitt looked at Bowen with disdain. "Daniel, when Yankees come onto these islands, they won't find me or my family or our precious belongings. You may do as you think best."

Bowen, exasperated with DeWitt and unable to turn the tide of the discussion, turned back to his food. Callie witnessed his fright and frustration and could not help feeling a tinge of excitement course through her. Could DeWitt's worries possibly come true? Her reverie at the thought was interrupted by DeWitt's shout. "I said, gal, get over here with that bread!"

Just when Bowen was catching his mental stride again, his knife blade prying open a new oyster, Judson Feller, a planter from the north end of St. Helena Island, cornered Bowen on his bench. "Daniel, how them slave boys been workin' out for you on your new dock?"

Daniel could not show how important they had been, digging pilings into the pluff mud and building new docks, or else the wily Feller would want more in trade. "They gave me some good days last week, like I planned," Captain Bowen responded. "Why, you need 'em back?"

Feller leaned in. "You know you are deep in my debt, even before those boys came over here. I need the help of your gal, Callie. My wife is all but down in the bed full-time now. She's too sick to take care of herself, much less me."

Bowen leaned back with hands raised and shook his head.

Feller continued. "I promised help for the boys at the forts, and I'm late already. So I need your gal to take care of my wife now. I been tryin' to get my daughter down from Charleston to take over, but she's not here yet. Besides, your Callie makes medicine from roots and herbs." After pausing, he insisted. "You owe me, Daniel!"

Bowen hated the bind Feller put him in. He needed Callie around the plantation now more than ever. Not only that, he had promised Callie never to separate her from her daughter or her brothers. Over the years, she had continued to serve him loyally in exchange for that kept promise. Yet Bowen could not ignore the money he owed Feller. Even worse, Feller had helped Bowen keep some secrets in the past, and he relied on Feller to continue to do so. Against his will, Bowen relented. "I will lend you Callie for a period of weeks, until you find someone permanent. That's the best I can do."

Callie came into earshot as he spoke. Her fury rose in an instant! She turned on her heel abruptly and walked straight from the table down the nearby creek bank. High tide whipped by early evening gusts brought sea spray swirling into Callie's face.

The Captain had not dismissed her from service at the table. Such was her relationship with her "master," she believed that she could walk away with impunity. Besides, it was necessary to clear her head from the shock of separation from her family. She resolved not to be sent away. Had she not complied with Cap'n Massa's every wish? Had she not maintained perfect silence? All she ever extracted from Bowen for her years of full servitude was a promise to keep her family together.

Callie hurried back to her job and coldly finished serving, taking plates, providing drink, all without making eye contact with Bowen. She would deal with him later. Callie led her workers in the immediate clean-up effort, as the planters concluded their business and headed toward their carriages and the dock.

Determined to get back to her daughter, Callie slid away from the house after dumping the last plates of oyster shells in a bucket, hoping Bowen's liquored gaze would not fall on her. She did not know that, like a snake watching its prey, he awaited her departure with surprising stealth despite his intoxication. She walked, looking over her shoulder as she moved past the last live oak, its trunk the widest of the row. She only had to go another hundred steps to the quarters to be on safer ground.

As she moved quickly but softly, she heard Bowen's footsteps just before his hand held her shoulder to make her turn. She brushed off his hand and rushed away. As she quickened pace, so did he, catching her by both shoulders this time. She wriggled free again, for a moment.

Bowen raised his voice slightly. "Callie. I know you heard me. Callie!" He grew insistent as her walk away slowed. "Callie!" Callie stopped. At this he moved in behind her, taking both her shoulders in his hands, tightening his grip. She kept her eyes shut to his reality.

"I thought you were trying to get away from me," he slurred. "You know you shouldn't do that." His sorry attempt to be playful failed utterly. She started to pull away again until his command. "Stop!"

Without turning, Callie argued meekly. "Massa, you say you ain neba tek me from my Sunny, or Lucas en BB. Massa Bowen, you say da, fuh *all* I do—"

"Come on now, Callie. Won't be long you be right back with yo baby girl."

Tears welled, she trembled and then steadied. "You say da, Massa."

"I know, but I will get you back just as quick as I can." He rubbed her exhausted shoulders. "Meantime, Bella knows how to care for your girl, and I'll watch out for her too." Bowen spoke in a slightly tender tone that only a boorish man could believe alluring.

There was no consolation in his words. She breathed deeply, to contain her anger and stop a sob. Her bitter gaze slowly fell as she closed her eyes tightly and sealed her lips against the night air. The corners of her mouth quivered and turned down, her utter disgust unmasked.

While he moved in front of her, he did not see her face, as his eyes, too, were cast downward with lust. Now he commanded her. "Come to me."

Callie moved forward in the shadows of live oaks by the creek. For now at least, resistance was futile.

PART II

November 1
to November 6, 1861

Chapter 7

The next day dawned, but Callie did not want to see the light. This dayclean did not feel cleansing to her.

She awoke suddenly, her first thought being the imminent separation from her "baby," Sunny, an intolerable change that she had fought to avoid. Callie had learned to absorb Massa's feeble indecencies, to take them in her stride, but she was not emotionally prepared to be without Sunny.

At this thought, Callie shuddered, and immediately felt the small hand of her daughter, who had been standing watch over her mother's fitful sleep. "Mama, you be awright." Though an imitated phrase, it was enough, and Callie gathered her darling six-year-old firmly in her arms. Sunny, beautiful and innocent Sunny, reached out to smooth her mother's hair with tender strokes. In such moments, Callie's determination to protect her sweet child intensified.

The morning after the feast afforded uncustomary free time because the captain required little service, still digesting ample food and processing excessive drink. Callie used this small cushion of time to share leftover nibbles with Sunny. Cornbread and sweet potato cakes pulled from Mother's pouch lit up Sunny's face. Soon, the mother was stroking the child's hair, as parent-child equilibrium returned.

Callie hated to tell Sunny of her impending trip, not knowing whether she would be gone for several days or weeks. "Baby, you know yo mama love you?"

"I know da, Mama." Sunny looked up from her food, seeing the concern in Callie's eyes.

"I neba leave you les I gah fuh go, you know da?"

"I know da, Mama. Don cry."

At this, Callie breathed deeply to say, "Massa say I gah fuh go tend some missus wha sick. Ain be too fa way. I tell Massa I gah fuh come home fo moon git roun again."

Without skipping a beat, little Sunny assured, "Mama, I be awright. Auntie Bella look afta me mos goot as you." She looked quickly to see that her Mama understood.

Her Mama treasured the wisdom in her daughter's response and then reassured her, saying, "You know Uncle Lucas and Uncle BB gon be roun fuh mek sho you be jes fine." Callie held her tightly for minutes more before she had to get on with the day. Bella would have to shelter her baby for now.

Sunny's tender love gave her mother deep comfort. But nothing could heal either the sore places where she was roughly handled the night before, or the bitterness she felt in her soul about Massa's decision to send her away. Massa had promised that he would never separate them. Callie had kept her part of the bargain, too often. The part of her heart that had hardened in mute acceptance of her enslaved condition was wounded anew, bleeding despair and disgust into every fiber of her being. She startled at the urgency of her need to escape Massa's control.

Despite their need to hold each other close, to stay in the warm sphere of their shared love, Callie and Sunny rose to face the day. As leisure turned to a sense of mission, they left their cabin, embracing one more time, before sweet Sunny skipped down the lane to Aunt Bella's small shack. Callie felt her eyes fill, but she wiped them clear as she turned away. There was too much to be done, and it began with seeking the advice and assistance of her brothers.

* * *

Lucas was up early, as usual, sitting comfortably on the dock repairing his crab traps. Despite the captain's ridicule the day before, Lucas felt pride in catching all the main ingredients for Callie's seafood stew and in protecting his friend, Will. His sense of ease altered when he saw his sister walking quickly along the bluff above him.

"Slow down, gal—you gon blow up jes like da lighthouse do night fo las."

At first light, when Lucas passed Callie's shanty, he saw her red bandanna, placed on her door the night before, blowing sideways in the morning breeze. Her signal meant she wanted a meeting with Lucas and BB as soon as possible. Without warmth and with maximum efficiency, Callie said, "We need fuh talk right now, Lucas. Git done en git down tuh de meetin oak now." Callie went on her way to the meeting tree.

She knew BB was in charge of the sweet potato harvest that day. Midmorning would be the earliest they could meet under the great, old live oak on the far side of the fields, the place for discussion of all their urgent concerns.

Just as Lucas saw a fired-up Callie when he first spotted her that morning, BB could see that there was an extra jump in her step as he watched her turn onto the field at the far southwest corner. Lucas trailed behind his sister by a minute, laboring to catch up.

Callie's rapid movement matched the intensity of the day with its unusually strong morning breeze. Spanish moss, lifted by unseen gusts, often swung to a forty-five degree angle from live oak branches. Sustained winds generated white caps atop the river. The low gray clouds overhead raced faster than Callie walked, though she contested well.

Upon arrival under the old meeting oak, BB quickly cautioned her. "Take some deep air fo you pass out. Wuh ail oona?"

"Wuh mek you tink I gah time fuh deep air?" She shot him a look that was more pained than angry. And he backed down a bit.

On the entire Bowen plantation, BB was known as the most jovial presence, even when there was no reason to be. He always had a ready smile, but not of a mindless, foolish nature; instead, it was kind, so as to lift up his fellow bondsmen. In such simple ways, BB had become one of the leaders among the Oakheart slaves. Although BB was a big man whose strong muscles were masked by an extra layer of flesh, those who presumed that his girth indicated softness regretted their snap judgment.

BB could get Massa's work done by reminding all that the sooner their required "tasks" were finished, the sooner they could be about their own business. Most days, each slave had certain tasks, like digging four rows of sweet potatoes or picking a half-acre of cotton. When done, they were able to turn to weeding their own small vegetable patches, or pulling shrimp, fish, and oysters from the bountiful creeks and marshes. At least, that was so before Massa began adding extra hours. Now, the push to get cotton picked made it hard for BB to be a leader in the field because the work was too much, the land too hot, and the days too harsh. Little time or energy was left for slaves to garden or fish.

One of BB's strengths was in modeling behavior that proved successful, adapting to the circumstances and the people he met each day. After he had won them over by joke, grit, or muscle, he tried to be the voice for common sense, saying, "Wha we do nex? Wha we do today mek les fuh nex day, oona gree?" Although BB denied his leadership, he knew that people in his community followed his suggestions and actions.

For the wisdom BB brought, and for her love of him as a brother, Callie often rerouted her thinking after talking to him. But this day she had not come to him to be rerouted. Beyond a dreaded detour to care for the woman at Tidal Flats plantation, Callie had determined that there must be a change in her life. She just did not know how it would come to pass.

Callie had taken enough breath to begin. "BB, oona know I been good fuh dishyuh Bowen famly all deese yeah. Do all I kin mek sho me and mine be safe. We mek bes we kin outta haad time—but I ain sho—jes don seem like I kin do da no mo. Kyan put up wid Massa no mo—him lie en hateful."

Lucas arrived just in time to hear the last line.

"Whoa, sista ooman (*woman*), wha oona tink?"

"I gah fuh go, Lucas!" Her pitch and projection carried out to the sweet potato diggers, though only her angst, not her words, was understood by the field hands looking up from their labor.

Lucas stared at her intently. Then, with a glance at BB, his eyes asked why he was smiling at Callie with a look combining admiration and bemusement. "Mek huh see some sense, BB—ain nuttin funny fuh laugh at."

As he watched his younger sister's beauty become contorted with her anguish, BB's brow furrowed. "Taak, sista, wha Massa done do now?"

"Gon sen me way, BB, tek me from my chile. Mek me go dis day!" At this she allowed her strong outer shell to crack and tears to roll down softened, angular cheeks. As she settled, nestling into BB's substantial embrace, she explained that Massa promised Massa Feller he would send Callie to help his sick wife, at least until his daughter returned from Charleston. She hated most of all not knowing how long she would be away from Sunny.

BB started to respond. "My haat fulla yo pain, Callie. You know we gib Sunny good kyah. Ain nuttin gon hahm da sweet chile."

But Callie cut him off. "BB, supm goin on roun yuh, rile up Massa en all dem buckra (*white people*)." BB had learned from Lucas of talk in town about Yankees being out at sea or some such nonsense. Easing Callie was his first concern, but he wanted to know what she had heard at the feast.

She described how she had never seen these men so worried, but more than that, they looked and acted scared. They talked of now being a special time. "Dey tell Massa bout whole buncha Yankee boat head dis way from Virginny—Massa DeWitt say fuh sho dey come yuh cause dis haaba (*harbor*) be so deep."

BB said, looking at Lucas, "Yankee come dis way—da why dem buckra blow up dey own lighthouse. Dey mus know dey kyan keep Yankee from deese yuh islan."

Lucas mused. "Ol Bowen sho nuf try. Him tek food en odda ting tuh de foat (*fort*) ebby day."

Callie said, "I sho ain wan leave my chile when Yankee man roun yuh fuh fight. Lawd know wha turble ting be bout."

"No need fuh worry bout da, Callie." BB reasoned. "You go cross de islan in de boat wid Lucas. Goot way fuh fine wha so tween buckra and Yankee."

Lucas was quick to agree, and Callie did too, reluctantly. With the benefit of one another's thinking, and support, they helped Callie accept the task at hand. She knew that her brothers would care for Sunny, hiding her from Massa if that should become necessary.

When she had finished her list of worries natural to motherhood, it was BB's turn to instruct. Both Lucas and Callie were to make the most of this opportunity off the plantation, to learn all they could, so that when Callie came back, they could make their own plans. BB said he would talk to Jacob and others about protecting their families. BB almost agreed that Callie was right, that it was time to take care of some things that needed changing. But first things first.

"If Yankee come, en some big fight break out, Lucas tek de nex high tide up Chowan Crik, tek all de way to odda side St. Helena fuh git Callie. Callie, you be ready fuh Lucas on de same day. Head out afta low tide—ride high wada back yuh."

Callie sighed, knowing what had to be done. Her brothers gathered around her, for their six arms to enclose each other. BB whispered, "Bless us, Lawd. Hep we po folk git tuh nex day on dishyah lan. Fuh dis new day, gib we skrent (*strength*). Amen."

Their meeting ended, the day's tasks awaited.

★   ★   ★

Callie returned to the cookhouse to make sure no requirements went unmet. No food would be needed by the Bowens later in the day as they were going into Beaufort to visit with Missus's brother-in-law. She began packing her own food supplies from storage and the kitchen, as well as some of the catch from the dock. If she had to go to another plantation as commanded by the captain, she was going to be properly prepared.

As she worked, Captain Bowen appeared in the yard between the house and kitchen, catching Callie's glance ever so briefly before she turned to her business. Bowen chose not to correct her disrespect at this time. He leaned in the kitchen door, aiming his words generally in her direction. "I intended to go out to fortify our boys at Bay Point, but I wanted to check on your plans to travel today, Callie. You and Lucas should be out on that midday slack tide—best to use the high water for getting from here to north side of these islands. That's where your work is today, Callie girl."

She seethed silently, without recourse.

Done lording it over Callie, Bowen turned his attention to Will, who had just entered the yard.

"Will, welcome to the rest of your life, boy. Did you get enough rest?"

Will almost responded before realizing the captain would not care.

"Son, I will be escorting you and your mother to Beaufort later this morning."

"What about the wind, Captain? Are you sure either of us should be on that river, first into town, and then back later today?"

"We got the tides in our favor both ways, boy—the wind just makes it interesting."

Feeling wise enough to argue from his experiences at sea, Will retorted: "Look around to the southeast. There's a big storm brewing over the ocean. It'll get worse before it gets better. Is my mother able to travel on such a day?"

Captain Bowen turned back toward the house.

Thinking himself empowered, Will continued. "Could your secret war with my uncle be so strong that he cannot visit at the home of his own sister-in-law? Instead, on such a day as this on the river, she must come to him?" His baritone, forceful tone was incredulous and surprised even him.

The captain turned and stepped back squarely into Will's face. "Navy midshipman, huh? What do you know?" Bowen looked at him and said slowly, "About the weather, this river, your uncle and me, or anything else?" The moment lasted until Bowen emerged from his shock at Will's challenge. "Listen boy, we going to town *and* back! Today!" Walking away again, he turned. "Tell you what, though, if you are worried about going with me, you can take a skiff by yourself, if you can handle it—or you can get a small crew of niggers and row up the river. You could take Lucas, but he's busy boating Callie over to Feller's place."

Will knew that delay would cause him to miss their planned meeting with Uncle Harris, with Captain Bowen attending in his stead. Besides, he could not ask such an endeavor of Lucas—back-to-back hard rows—though the captain did not hesitate to ask it of him.

"When you come back from town, there will be a boat filled with supplies for you to take out to Fort Beauregard. Visit with your ma a little bit more, but as soon as this weather clears, you report for duty, and when you get out there, stay until you are no longer needed."

Bowen punched Will's chest with knuckles out. "That may not be the Confederate navy telling you what to do, but it is me! And I matter more than anything to you right now. Don't be thinking about leaving with your uncle Harris! Hear me, boy?"

His exit from the courtyard left two miserable souls behind. Callie pretended to have overheard nothing as she came through the cookhouse door, "Monin. Wey you been las night?"

Remembering his training to be civil and clearheaded, Will chose to ignore the severe aggravation caused by his stepfather. Besides, he wanted to explain to Callie that he did not attend the feast last night because sleep captured him upon return from his outing with Lucas. Will had awakened during the big feeding when he heard loud talk coming through his window from the grounds below. "Callie, please forgive me. I was more exhausted than hungry last night. When I looked out, I could not believe how many you were serving at those tables. Then I fell back in bed."

She smiled, uncertain where to go with the conversation, a signal that Will took to go on. "You managed preparations and service so well, taking care of all the men's needs." At that phrase he hesitated. "I hope you will forgive me … for not getting to sample your stew while it was hot. I know how hard you worked on it."

Callie turned her head forty-five degrees, while still staring at Will, uncertain what she just heard. She responded, "Wha you say shock me mo den I ebba been shock."

Will looked confused, not knowing whether shocked was a good thing, and not knowing which thing he said did the shocking.

"You aks me fuh fuhgive you?" Callie hesitated. "You be de fus white man aks da, and you ain done nuttin to me. I ain gah no worry wid you, cept may be da yo mama leh Massa do wha he wan do roun yuh." Her face hardened.

Will wanted to know more. "It seems we both don't feel too good about Captain Daniel Bowen this morning." This shared territory left both of them speechless. Will finally broke the silence, barely audible to Callie though she was just a few feet away. "Do you think I am obligated to Bowen, to uphold my family honor? Should I have to pay back the captain by fighting his fight?"

Callie shook her head "no" but remained silent.

"Or does what I believe matter—my ethics, my own honor—that my father's and uncle's name can never defend slavery."

She did not know whether or how to advise this young white man, but she sensed his question to her was genuine. "Will, we know you jes do wha Massa tell you is all, and do da fuh yo mama. All Oakheart folk know who be fren en who ain."

Will was pondering the great statement of acceptance he just heard, when Callie went on.

"Ain bout yo promise tuh Massa Bowen." She shook her head resolutely. "You right fuh keep yo word tuh yo Mama—ain no need fuh do da fuh Massa. You don owe him nuttin. I ain owe him nuttin. I done pay him mo dan he deserve. I pay him fuh my chile, and fuh my two brudda. Da damn man done tek mo dan wha right. Forgive me, Lawd."

Will understood that more was being discussed than just his dilemma.

After her pronouncement, Callie looked at Will to see him staring at her intently. She felt a strange draw to his presence, like attraction, but she was quite sure that was not the case.

Will reached out and touched her arm gently, below the elbow. "Thank you, Callie, for speaking with me. You've helped me."

For Will, this moment of long gazes and lightness of touch started other thoroughly involuntary thoughts. It allowed Will to see Callie for the first time as a woman, or maybe it was the first time he, as a man, saw Callie as the whole person that she was, including her femininity.

For Callie, it was the first time she was truly alone with Will. She did not expect to receive a tender touch from him, and her reaction surprised her so that she quickly suppressed it. She smiled at him sincerely and, just as sincerely, moved away from him, turning to her preparations for travel.

Chapter 8

Callie and Lucas began their five-mile journey later that morning on windswept tidal creeks that made passage rough and wet. Though a challenge for Lucas, the rising tides were favorable and the winds from the southeast mostly pushed them along, as did swells in the creek as they rolled up from behind, lifting and dropping their boat. Lucas was confident he could deliver Callie safely to the north side of St. Helena Island, despite deteriorating conditions.

But travel up the Beaufort River that afternoon was not sheltered like the back creeks weaving through the islands. Waves were rolling and breaking, some two to three feet high. Will was just about to question his mother about the wisdom of their intended river trip to Beaufort, when she informed him that the captain decided the river was too dangerous, especially for a return trip in the late afternoon. It appeared the storm had persuaded the captain, when, earlier in the day, the midshipman could not. Will observed wryly to his mother that "despite what his crews always said about him, the captain could be reasonable." He was promptly hushed by his mother, too late though, as the stepson's remark had been heard.

Bowen ordered the slave crew of four to remain down at the boathouse for departure "as soon as the wind subsided." The oarsmen huddled together against the windblown spray in the structure that, open on two sides, clearly was not built for a storm shelter.

Will whispered loudly that their discomfort was a monument to the captain's inhumanity. When his mother spoke of her husband's pride as an attribute, Will said it blinded his stepfather to what was right and just, and then he quoted Harris Hewitt, hoping his uncle's views still held value for his mother. "The captain's belief in the rightness of his every position will make him a casualty of his own certitude." Julia Bowen nodded while telling Will not to say such things.

After nightfall several hours later, Bowen dismissed the men while intensifying winds blew hard rain at sharp angles. It was about then that Lucas returned to Oakheart, having fought strong gusts and wind-whipped tides for more than three hours. Even he struggled with the powerful surges against his boat. The smaller rivers and creeks roiled, resembling the raging Beaufort River. Lucas felt small in God's fury, and yet he rose to embrace it. His exhaustion was earned, as he collapsed on his pallet that night, more confident after being able to handle such conditions.

★ ★ ★

For more than a day, storm winds transformed land, sea, and sky, only subsiding late the next afternoon, when sunlight streamed through cloud breaks low on the western horizon. By evening, sea breezes were nearly normal. After "all hands" and the family spent the day locked down against the storm, the captain announced that the next morning, Sunday, would be safe for passage to and from Beaufort.

Daniel Bowen knew the effort to attend church would please his wife. It also would allow him to hear the latest news about the Yankees. Bowen intended to intrude uninvited into the meeting between his wife and her pro-Union brother-in-law. He had reason to believe that Harris Hewitt's visit to Beaufort involved more than his concern about Julia's health.

Julia regretted that the planned feast delayed her visit to town by one day and was even more vexed that stormy weather kept her from seeing Harris for another two days. With her husband in a dither over war preparations, and her son being pressed to become a Southern warrior, the fact that her former husband's brother was visiting in Beaufort was secondary at best. While she knew that Harris would understand, she loved him like a brother and wished that they had not lost valuable visitation time.

Will and his mother were rowed up to Beaufort by a crew that was assigned to load the big longboat with supplies for Fort Beauregard. The crew of four bondsmen worked as one in cadence with their rhythmic chant. When they broke into a familiar soul-stirring song Will had heard through the forest on many a night, he and his mother exchanged looks full of appreciation for their escorts. The captain followed behind in his small rowboat. Later, the slave crew would carry him and the supplies to the fort on the outbound tide.

Julia Hewitt Bowen had long accepted and regretted the animus between Harris and her husband, though she did not fully understand it. For many reasons, she arrived at the Beaufort Hotel early that Sunday morning feeling guilty. At least her son would be there to help alleviate the awkwardness she felt, which was complicated immeasurably at the last minute when her husband decided to join them for the hotel breakfast.

The fast passage to town heightened Will's anticipation of seeing Uncle Harris, though he knew that his uncle would return north without him. Harris Hewitt sat at the dining table next to tall windows looking east over the wharf and ferry operations on the Beaufort River. Seeing him, Will was reminded how much he identified with his uncle and the Chesapeake Bay area, and how much he missed the life with his classmates at the academy. Almost all, except the first-year midshipmen, now were serving aboard the *USS Constitution* as it prowled the Atlantic coast. And yet Will felt bound by his debt to Captain Bowen, who required his labor in service to the Confederacy as payment. Could his uncle understand? Did Will even understand?

After warm greetings were exchanged, Will excused himself to allow his mother and Uncle Harris a private reunion. He had his uncle all to himself on the trip to Beaufort, and he knew that his mother always benefited from their time together. Their greeting was genuinely, but quietly, euphoric, as Julia so appreciated the role Harris had taken after his brother's early death. He helped Willy grow up and was everything a loving uncle could be. As they ended a lingering embrace, Julia said, "I wish we could have gotten to town to see you sooner Harris, but you know how it stormed."

"Of course I knew, and I also knew you would be here to see me as soon as the weather permitted. Not to worry." As they embraced again, Julia began to cry. "What is it, dear? Are you feeling poorly?"

She described how she had been in relatively good health. Shaking her head, she whispered, "It's Daniel." She intended to explain her husband's determination to enlist Will in service to the Confederacy, if only for a short period. But before she could go on, Harris turned his ire on Daniel Bowen.

"What is it, then? Is Bowen harming you?" Harris continued forcefully, not waiting for an answer. "I am sorry I brought you down here so long ago. If you are happy, then I will refrain, but I'll admit, I've never understood your marriage."

Julia placed her hand gently but firmly on Harris's arm. "Were you always able to support yourself, Harris?"

"Yes, why?"

"You are so involved with your view and your dislike of Daniel, that you do not see the reality and insight of my question. You do not understand my life as a woman."

He reflected on this for a moment. "Ah Julia, I always underestimate the depth of your thinking."

And at this, Julia decided not to complain further about Daniel's pressure on Will to help fortify the two forts defending Port Royal Sound. Instead, she responded more to his inquiries about her health, though she did not understand why there was such confusion about it. Will had asked her such questions also.

Just then, Will seated himself at the table with a quick handshake for his uncle. Will informed Harris that Julia's husband was in conversation outside the hotel and would be joining them shortly. Harris immediately turned the conversation to matters at hand, urging Julia to return north with him.

"Why, Harris, whatever are you talking about? I may be deep, but I am not dense. I see no urgency to flee. This war will not come to our islands, and if it does, Daniel is confident that we will be safe."

Harris shook his head. "Stop! I hear the conviction of your beliefs, my dear. But you cannot put faith in that man's bluster. You must know, Julia, that your husband's confidence in all things is overblown by far. And in this instance, rest assured he does not know what is coming." Harris hesitated, but went on. "If I cannot convince you to leave with me, then let me implore you to just stay on the plantation. Do not venture out on any trips to nearby islands. You should both feign that you are ill, Julia, to keep Will around the plantation for another week or so to care for you. Besides, you both deserve that time together."

They were puzzled by his insistence but did not ask further, as Bowen appeared at the door to the dining room. Julia quickly closed the line of discussion with assurances that she would be fine on the plantation with her husband.

Harris rose to greet Captain Bowen with ritual cordiality. "Well, I must say this is an unexpected, uh, pleasure, Daniel. I was not aware that you wished to dine with me."

"Always good to keep the family together. Especially at these stressful times, Harris. I sure am happy to have my boy, Will, back heah, I'll tell you that. He is going to make us proud." At that the captain smiled, falsely sincere. "I do hope I am not interrupting. All three of you looked to be engaged in the most serious matter when I arrived."

Harris quickly said, "Oh, we were just talking about taking a little trip on the river."

"Which way would you be going, Harris?" The captain drawled out the sentence meaningfully, as if he was a long-term son of the Deep South.

Ignoring his innuendo, Harris responded only that he expected to be heading home soon.

Daniel bore in. "I hear from some of my townspeople that you been out on the river already, a couple times in fact. Once on the first day you got here and again, yesterday, as the storm clouds cleared."

Harris considered his next words carefully. "I got out for a little fishing, Daniel. Not too unusual around here, is it? Besides, I had to do something while waiting to see dear Julia and to see this new boat you want me to take north."

Bowen's surprised look was genuine. "Why ... I don't have a boat for you, Harris."

Harris continued the offensive, staring earnestly at Bowen. "Well, I distinctly recall you said last year in a note from Julia that I should come on down for that new sailboat by the fall."

"I said no such thing recently—may have put it in a note about three years ago." Bowen sat back in his chair, confident of his terrain and curious at the evident deception. "Things have changed a bit since then, Harris. Haven't you heard? Your president has declared war on the Confederate States of America. Why, he's even taken on the notion that he can blockade our coastline as he pleases." Such talk fueled Bowen's fire as he grew louder. "You must think you are a pretty special seaman to come down here thinking you could even get my boat through a blockade—either special or damn well connected. Which is it, Harris?"

"Not at all, Daniel," said Harris, trying not to get caught in his lie. "I'm just trying to keep our agreement going, since it has been so lucrative for us in the past. Besides, I also came down with Will to check on Julia, after he heard from you that his mother was sick." Harris, feeling on high ground, began fishing. "I know you intended to tell me of her illness as well, didn't you, Daniel?"

The captain stammered uncharacteristically. "Well, she's ... she's much better now. You ... you really didn't need to come down here at all."

Harris set the hook. "In fact, Daniel, you only wanted Will to come here, isn't that right?"

Julia looked to her husband for explanation. Only then did she fully understand his plan to lie to Will about her illness, drawing him home to impress him into Confederate service.

Bowen ignored his wife's inquiring gaze and focused on Harris. "This conversation is not about my intentions. I also hear that you sent a telegram—about fishing, it seems. Hmmm." Bowen pulled a paper from his coat pocket: "Be back soon, only caught three, not that big, not worthy." Bowen smirked. "I have to ask, who up north cares about your fishing?"

"Enough, Daniel!" Julia declared. "What is the point?"

"I think Harris may be visiting here for more than just your health concerns." The captain looked at Julia, while clearly aiming his response at Harris.

Harris laughed loudly. "Do you think I could possibly be so stupid as to send a message north that had any military value? And if so, what would fishing have to do with it? I believe you have slipped into some form of Confederate paranoia, Daniel. I am here for two very good reasons—to support my sister-in-law at a time of illness by accompanying my nephew to see her, and to market another of your fine watercraft. Is it really an issue that I fished in waters that I love, or that I shared my lack of success with one of my sportsman friends?" He stopped lest the explanation go on too long.

"Consider yourself fortunate to be related to my wife, else I would turn you over to the authorities."

"Yes, I have always considered myself fortunate to have her as a sister-in-law, Daniel. Now ever more so." He knew that his deceptions were thinly veiled at best.

The comfort level did not rise during their light fare consisting of country sausage, eggs, and benne seed bread. It was clear that there were many conflicting agendas not to be discussed, especially involving Will's participation in the encroaching war, and definitely not the war itself.

When conversation turned to family members and places known only to the Hewitts, and not to Bowen, his thoughts drifted from the table, but not very far. He recalled with displeasure his last conversation with Judson Feller, who now had Callie in his service. He remembered Feller's taunting tone as he whispered to him at the feast.

"I know who's in town right now. That's right. I saw Harris Hewitt downtown last night. Wonder if he knows the history on your plantation—things he might even want to tell your wife—now wouldn't that be a fine kettle of fish? So I know you want to help me with my wife's illness. Getting Callie to help me helps you, Bowen!"

Bowen's mind snapped back to the dining room conversation when Harris Hewitt's voice grew louder and he began to wax poetic, as Julia and Will had seen him do on many an occasion, but in less intense times. Describing the wonderful array of southern cooking to which he had been subjected during this stay in Beaufort, Harris sailed to new heights. "Of all its charms, with which this little town disarms—waterways and seas, rich soils and breezes—its food from the sea, a rich bounty indeed, is by far the most worthy to me."

This proved too much for the captain, who had things to do, and more to the point, had had his fill of Harris Hewitt. "I'm off to the churchyard, Julia. Come quickly. Will, you do the same." He stood with a nod to Harris. "Sir, I wish you well, as long as you intend no harm to me or mine."

Harris stood. "Same to you, Captain. I guess it is in the definition of who or what is being harmed, is it not?" They did not shake hands, and Bowen moved off sharply.

Harris knew he must be on his way. "I was fairly sure that you, dear Julia, would not come with me now, as you have enjoyed the life that you have made here in the South. And I am grateful that it has brought you improved health. And, Will, I know you feel you must stay now, for your mother, for reasons I cannot argue." Will nodded. "Since I cannot persuade you to go with me, I must go now."

Will urged him to reconsider and stay longer since he did not have the boat to take north.

"I have secured different passage north than planned and must be about it. Please don't think me abrupt, but I have been sojourning in the heart of the great South for three days now. It is time for me to go. Julia, my dear, please stay out of harm's way, from whatever its source."

"Whatever do you mean?" she asked, not sure she wanted an answer.

Harris Hewitt gave his brother's wife a long, enfolding embrace and then stood back from Will, hand extended. "I know your course will right itself. Your internal compass is too resolute for you to go awry." Their eyes held each other's full attention as they shook hands. As they left the hotel together, Harris turned off of Bay Street and quickly walked away from them, through town, and away from the Beaufort docks.

Julia grabbed her son's arm. "He always means the best, even when he disappears abruptly or for too long. I believe your uncle carries on enterprises of which we are not aware."

"Is that not true for us all, Mother?" Will asked with some innocence.

★　★　★

The scene outside St. Helena Episcopal Church was not typical for a Sunday. Usually there were many more slaves waiting about with carriages and many more whites streaming in just before service. Inside, attendance was strong downstairs, though not all parishioners were dressed in their Sunday finest. Instead, some wore travel clothes. There was quite a stir among the congregation. Upstairs, there was still a large contingent of slaves in their balcony pews, sitting quietly as required. Julia regretted that neither Callie nor Lucas could come with them this Sunday morning, as was their custom. She had always made it clear that her house servants were to attend the Christian service every week.

Julia had other causes of angst this morning. Unpleasant rumors of war continued, but even more vexing were her husband's deceptions about the reasons for Will's visit. Further, he treated Harris in the most uncivil manner—worse than ever before. Her anger with her husband was compounded by his arbitrary decision to ship Callie off without Julia's approval or even any discussion. She had many grievances with her husband this Sunday morning, and none would be addressed easily.

Julia hoped that the message and music of the day would soothe her spirit, but the church service did nothing of the kind. To the contrary, the reverend instead used his pulpit to terrorize the congregation with warnings of imminent invasion by forces of the US government. Whatever religious message he shared was secondary to telling his parishioners to go home and prepare for the worst. There was nothing comforting about the service, at least to the folks downstairs. In the church balcony, the news was received differently—it gave slaves reason to hope that their prayers might be answered.

There was greater urgency than usual in the Beaufort streets after church as carriages rushed away in a manner out of character for a Sunday. Daniel Bowen walked quickly ahead, leaving Julia on Will's arm several paces behind. On their way back to the dock, Julia suddenly stopped still, sighting a young woman coming their way. After greetings and introductions were exchanged, Julia explained to Will that Eva Feller had been a piano pupil of hers for several years, before Eva married and went off to Charleston.

Eva was courteous in the conversation that ensued, but she seemed consumed by her travails such that her otherwise attractive face was beset by a general scowl. Julia asked, "Whatever is wrong?"

"I have returned at a terrible time, Missus Bowen. My mother is ill, and after a miserable muddy carriage ride from Charleston, my father is not here to meet me. I have no way to get out to the plantation. I am so worried about her. And now there's all this talk of Yankee invasion."

At this explanation, Will recognized the situation and told Eva that the Bowens' very best house servant had gone to care for her mother. Julia then understood where Callie had gone and decided that Will must help Eva get home as quickly as possible. She hailed her husband, now well down the street.

"Daniel, this young lady is here at the urgent request of her father!" As Bowen walked back to the group, she went on. "She is heading home to care for her sick mother—and her mother really *is* sick. I insist that you let Will take her home, as I know how I would feel, *if* I were ill and needed the comfort of my child."

The captain recognized that her sharp words barely cloaked her displeasure at his deception. "Why yes, dear, whatever you wish." While compliance with his wife's direction would delay Will's service to the Confederacy, he reasoned that his wife should not be crossed on this matter. Plus, if Will could hasten Eva's arrival at Tidal Flats, it would allow Callie's prompt return to Oakheart, solving problems on a number of fronts. The captain's added relief that Callie would no longer be subjected to the whim and wickedness of Judson Feller did not occur to Julia Bowen.

He barked orders to Will: "You will take the skiff and deliver young Eva to her home and bring back Callie while you're at it. When you report back to Oakheart, be prepared to defend your home by running supplies out to the forts guarding Port Royal Sound and staying there as long as you are needed."

Chapter 9

Will received the Captain's new orders to row Eva to her home as a reprieve from a sentence of "war." And it relieved him, if only temporarily, from acting in defense of slavery.

At least Will had more time to order his thoughts away from the captain's bombast. Still, he worried about what was to become of his mother, whether she would or should remain with the captain, and what naval warfare along the coast of South Carolina would mean for the residents of Oakheart Plantation. Uncertainty hung in the air, with the possibility of dire events intimated by Uncle Harris.

For Eva, war's unknowns could wait while she tended to her mother's convalescence. She was grateful for the immediate transport back to Tidal Flats, since her father did not provide for it. Will assisted Eva and her one bag into the skiff, and his swift, confident strokes moved them to clear water away from Beaufort to the northwest.

When Will told her that he was very familiar with the south end of St. Helena Island, Eva assured him that she could navigate him to her home on the north side. As soon as they were away from town, Eva's smiling countenance grew serious. "Will, what do you think of all this talk of Yankee invasion around these parts?"

Will deflected the question. "What's 'all this talk'? Do you mean the preacher this morning? Seemed to me he was a bit of an alarmist."

"No, Will, I heard it in Charleston before coming here. It's even in the newspaper up there. All people can talk about is this large number of Yankee ships that left Virginia, and some were seen heading south off the North Carolina coast before that big storm the last few days. Where do you think they were headed?"

Through the first long stretches of the Beaufort River, Will's breathing began to deepen as they talked. But he knew if wind and currents stayed the same, that he was up to a five-mile row in this sleek skiff. This challenge he could master. He was not so sure he could or should master those that lay beyond, and he was equally uncertain that he should tell his story to Eva. But he needed to talk.

"Well, I should tell you, Eva, just three weeks ago I was assigned to duty aboard the USS *Constitution*. The older midshipmen at the Naval Academy had begun to serve on board. Please understand, that gives me no special knowledge about the fleet, since I was not informed of war plans."

"I see." She hesitated, puzzling. "Actually, I don't see. Does that mean you favor the North? What are you doin' down here?"

"It's complicated, Eva. I came down because my mother was ill, or so I believed. Now I am here and my stepfather is directing me to give support to the forts across Port Royal Sound. If the Yankees are coming here, that is likely where they will go."

"My God!" She drooped her shoulders in despair. This was almost too much for her to digest, and she turned back to her own family sadness. "What a terrible time for my mother's illness to worsen." She shook her head and placed it between her hands. Shortly, she whispered, "First things first must be the way, I suppose."

Will's rhythmic strokes had established a steady pace through relatively calm water on the narrow portions of the river. He listened as Eva sought balance in the events around her. The trip around the west side of Ladies Island took longer than expected, and Will was grateful for the chance to hear the concerns of someone else. It helped him gauge his own dilemma.

Eva looked up, laughing. Now Will was puzzled. She said, "Every other time in my life when I have been out on these rivers and creeks, I have been filled with joy. And today, I have not even looked beyond this boat." At this, Eva drew up straight, turned at the waist, propping her hand on the rail, and reviewed all the beauty to starboard. She then pivoted halfway around to discover what bounties of nature were passing by to port.

"So much beauty!" she drawled. "So much beauty!" As if spellbound, she sat for long minutes, turning from side to side, stretching and breathing deeply but slowly. Her silence allowed the muted slashing of Will's oars in the water to be the only sound, interrupted by the gulls and the occasional deep-throated squawk of a great blue heron surprised into flight. Will was grateful for the respite and the time to retreat into his own thoughts.

Inevitably though, conversation between these two strangers interrupted their private reflections. They discovered similarities in stories of domineering fathers, sick mothers, and their own escapes from home as they grew to be young adults. But then Eva stopped abruptly.

"But I almost forgot, Will. You aren't on the side of the South."

Will hesitated. "It is confusing, Eva. I have conflicting feelings. The key fact for me though is that I owe my stepfather and this is the way he has demanded payment. I can barely reconcile the fact that I may go to war to defend these islands from 'terrible Yankees,' many of whom are my friends." Will even laughed in time with his cadenced breathing. "Please, Eva, if there is a quick solution here, please suggest it."

At this, Eva shook her head. "I just want my family home and my parents to be safe. Is it too simple just to want things back the way they were?"

"Yes!" Will's clipped response sounded too harsh after it had been uttered. He explained, "Wish as we might, we can't stop what has been started." He stopped rowing to look at Eva. "The South decided to leave the United States, asserting a right to independence, to continue the practice of slavery."

He apologized in advance for his opinion, declaring, "I could never own slaves; I could not claim the right to dictate the work people must do and not pay them; I could not confine other humans to a patch of land in service to me and my family. And I certainly could not enact the level of violence that is necessary for a slaver to keep control of his slaves."

Eva sat without comment, listening but not looking at him as he rowed.

"I mean no offense in my vehemence. Those feelings are rather strong, and I must be true to them." Will sought a softened approach with Eva, seeking to reason with her by explaining Callie's worries. "Apart from the sheer physical brutality of slavery, I think about what happens to real people. An example is the need to find assistance for your mother during her illness. Your father all but forced Captain Bowen to send Callie to your home. While we are all glad that she has knowledge of medical herbs and gives good care to the infirm, to come to your plantation meant that she had to leave her little girl behind." He saw Eva's frown deepen, but continued. "What do we think of the human condition of these slaves, whose lives we treat as if they are nothing?" He decided to stop his morality lecture right there, probably too late.

Eva tried to present the best case for her father's work and life. "I know he was determined to sell cotton and sell boats. That's how he and your stepfather got into business together. They put money up for projects and then got some slaves long ago. Got more successful and bought more slaves. They have been partners off and on through the years, building boats and trading slaves back and forth. I never really questioned it, Will." She shot him a quick look—defensive, yet seeking his understanding. "That's just the way it's always been, at least when I was growing up."

Will felt remorse for having been so harsh in response to Eva's wish to return to easier days. But he noted that she avoided discussing the problem he presented, of mother and daughter trapped in slavery. They continued on in silence.

Will and Eva completed their semicircle to the north, pressing through the choppier waters of St. Helena Sound. When Will turned to check his direction, he thought he saw the glint of what appeared to be masts in the late afternoon sun, well out into the Atlantic Ocean. He was wiping his eyes to get a better glimpse when Eva shouted, "There, just beyond the pine forest, see that small building just above the waterline?"

Will turned his gaze from the east over the ocean to where Eva pointed at wooded land on the island to the south. A dwelling of considerably less grandeur than their house at Oakheart was in the clearing. It was built on low bluffs that could not be more than five feet above Will's and Eva's heads as they arrived at high tide. Will maneuvered the boat up to a very old pier, quickly looking back to confirm what he thought to be the masts of substantial ships, but ocean mist left them as phantoms of his imagination and weariness.

Will could study the Atlantic no longer. Having docked, Eva quickly disembarked to run to her father. While Judson Feller appeared pleased to see his daughter, he was busy and seemed aggravated. After embracing her and nodding briefly to Will, Feller moved out smartly to the barn. He returned with his whip in hand.

Seeing this, Eva said, "Father, what could you be doing? We must think about Mother now; she is our only concern."

Feller slowed his pace, seeming to acknowledge her point. "Leave this, please," Eva said pointing to the whip. As he set the whip on the front porch table, he explained that he would still have to use it later on one of "these uppity niggers."

As she headed into their home, Eva slowed to introduce Will. "Father, forgive me, I should have introduced you and Will Hewitt. He is Captain Bowen's stepson, who brought me here from town when you were nowhere to be seen."

"Well, daughter, your mother took a turn for the worse, and I was having problems with this nigger woman."

With a knowing stare at Will, Eva continued: "In fact, young Will here has a message for you from Captain Bowen, something about you and your sloop being needed over at Hilton Head real soon. Remember, Will, what your Daddy was saying just as we were leaving the Beaufort dock this afternoon?"

With that, Eva disappeared inside. She moved quickly to the bedroom where her mother lay comatose. Callie had heard the arrival and loud talk on the porch and wished she could stop it for Missus Feller's sake. Her patient was sinking away; she'd lost control of speech, consciousness, and bodily functions, with all the attendant consequences. Callie was cleansing her with tepid water from the wash bowl when Eva entered her mother's death chamber.

Eva stood at the door catching her breath. She was shocked at how wasted away her once vibrant mother appeared and how foul was the stench of illness. At the same time, she was in awe at the tender care being given to her mother, who was not aware her daughter had returned home.

Soon Callie finished. She straightened Missus Feller's gown and gently turned her head toward the door, fluffing the pillow to better support her. Callie cajoled her patient. "Look who come. Da yo chile, Missus? Open yo eye and praise de Lawd. Yo chile here tuh love yuh." She signaled to Eva. "Come hug yo mama."

Eva was grateful beyond measure to the young slave woman who dealt with all the consequences of her mother's illness, in ways that Eva knew she could not do. She drew deeply into her lungs a breath of fortitude, though the fetid air of the room struck her immediately, slowing her advance toward this form that did not resemble her mother.

A short while later, Eva asked Callie to come out to the parlor. "It means so much to have you here for her." She introduced herself to Callie, thanking her, awkwardly moving to embrace her and then halting.

"Yes, mahm," Callie said to the white woman who was only slightly older than herself. "I done do wha I kin fuh huh. We mos los huh las night. Yo pappy say I keep huh from dead." Callie looked into Eva's eyes. "I tink she wait fuh you." Touching Eva's arm gently, she said, "You know, she ready fuh go?"

"Will told me you had to leave your daughter to come here. I am sorry for that, and we will send for her to come to Tidal Flats, if necessary."

Callie decided not to correct Eva's misconception of how long her mother might yet live. They began a short conversation about what Missus Feller used to be like and how Callie should not worry about Eva's father because he was ornery to everybody. Callie tried not to let her face show her feelings about Eva's father.

"Well, you are truly special to this family, particularly my mother. I just want you to know that I will never forget your kindness. You will be rewarded, if not in this life, then the next." Of course, Eva, having used that social phrase many times with her friends, had not calibrated its effect on a slave.

"You go rest now, Callie. You've done so much. I'll take over tonight." And Callie, exhausted, gladly went to the back room where she had laid a pallet, very relieved that the conversation had ended.

★   ★   ★

At first when Will was left alone on the porch with Eva's father, a long silence prevailed. Feller finally said, not really to Will, "You know it's hard when your wife is dying and you can't stop it."

Will felt sympathy for the older man and his impending loss. He also wondered how Feller felt about being countermanded so directly by his daughter. Will realized that he was being used in Eva's lie, designed to redirect her father's attention from disciplining one of his slaves. For that, Will was gratefully supportive.

Will told Feller that Bowen had already gone out to Bay Point with more deliveries and that he urged Feller to get out there. "The captain was telling us all that 'now is the time.' I guess he thought you would know what he meant." Will's first lie in service to a higher cause felt reasonable to him, especially if the lie lessened the chance that there would be harsh discipline that night for one of Feller's slaves.

Feller studied Will, trying to size up his messenger. "Well, all right then. Never remembered you as such a grown fella. You used to be a gangly thing—long neck, skinny body."

"Yes, sir. I've done a lot of growing in the last several years. I left these islands three years ago to study at the Naval Academy before coming back here." Will decided to display his "Southern" credentials. "When I return to Oakheart I am expected to take a vessel filled with goods for the soldiers at the forts."

Feller concluded his inspection. "Well, you done good."

Will followed his training. "Yes, sir."

"All right then, young man. I appreciate you coming here with the word from Captain Bowen. And I especially thank you for getting my Eva here, in time ..."

No sooner had Will thought the earlier storm had calmed when Feller stood up abruptly, squinting into the sinking sun. "Well, if I'm goin' to head out there at first light tomorrow, there's one thing I got to do before I go. Got me a nigger woman here that thinks she can read."

This caught Will's attention directly. Could Feller possibly be referring to Callie? Will found out immediately.

"Damn woman in there," said Feller pointing into his house. "Caught her readin'. Imagine that, a slave woman readin'." He slapped his leather strap twice against the table top on the front porch so loudly that Eva stepped outside, leaving her mother's bedside.

"Father, what are you doing making such noise?"

"I'm leaving out tomorrow morning, Eva. Now that you are here, you can care for your mother and handle other things around here as well."

"I certainly will, Father."

"One thing needing attention now, before I go, is that nigger woman in there. I caught her readin' today. Nothin' more dangerous than a readin' nigger."

"No, Father. This woman has been giving Mama the most vital care. What wrong could she possibly have done?"

"She was readin' the Bible to her, Eva. Imagine, a slave wench readin'."

At this, Eva had just too much. "Father, I have missed you, and I do love you so, but ..." She hesitated only briefly. "Father, look at yourself. In your zeal to keep these darkies from reading, you would deny God's word as comfort to my mother, to your dying wife? Do you understand yourself at such times?"

Eva's intervention did not quell his urge to punish. "I understand everything I need to know. We can't have a nigger readin'. She knows what she did!" And with that he yelled, "Callie-gal, get out heah."

Will, growing angry, braced to stop Feller, but did not know how. Callie came through the front door within seconds.

"Tell these good people what I caught you doin'."

"Massa, I been tek care uh yo missus, Massa."

"What else were you doin'?"

"Too much ting fuh tek good care, Massa. I mek sassfrass tea en mo tea from de mullen plant down by de road wid de yellow flower. En I feed huh en empty huh bedpan, en—"

"You were readin'," Feller interrupted. Callie looked at him puzzled. "You were readin' the Bible, little gal."

"No suh, I memba Bible vus fuh time like dishyuh. So I tell yo missus wha I memba fuh hep huh."

And with that came the scriptures. "Yes, Massa Feller, you know Psalm 23:4 … 'Yea, doe I walk tru de valley uh de shadow uh death, I will feah no evil.'" Callie looked straight at Feller with profound coldness and, shaking her head, said, "Thy rod and thy staff dey comfuht me." She raised her gaze to the sky. "And I will dwell in de house uh de Lawd fuhebah."

Feller was unconvinced, but he felt his zest for punishment fade with Callie's recitation. Perhaps he realized that his wife's interests were not being well served by his inquiry. "I was certain I saw you readin', gal, but go ahead, get back to tendin' my wife then. Don't you be a smart gal around me."

"Yessuh, Massa. Don be smaat." Callie hurried back inside.

Her father's persistence was a revelation to Eva, and she had to speak. "Look, just once look, at what we have done to them!" She gathered herself. "But don't doubt it, Father, I will make sure that Callie is properly treated, including a fine reward for the loving care given to my mother."

"Daughter, just 'cause you are grown doesn't allow you to come back here with disrespect."

"My only concern is my mother. If it helps Mama's last days to have that young woman sing Bible verse like a songbird while reading the good book backward, then that is what I want to happen." Finally, she said, "Sounds like the fight you want is coming your way, Father."

"Well, you best know that I am fightin' for you."

"You and thousands of men like you. I hope you know when to stop fighting."

★ ★ ★

After dark, Will sat alone down near the water, congratulating himself for deciding to stay the night. Not only would the trip through the island creeks have been difficult in evening light, but he also believed he was serving a noble cause, helping to prevent hateful acts from occurring on this plantation, if only for one night.

As he sat, he saw a figure come from the house toward him. Callie said that she could not sleep, even though others in the home were quiet. "How are you holding up?" Will asked.

Neither felt at ease but both needed to talk.

Callie responded: "I miss my chile too much."

"I'm sorry, what's her name—Sunny?"

"Sunny be de right name fuh huh. She bohn (*born*) when day been bright hot en fiel slave wuk long til night. So, she my Sunny."

"Beautiful name, Sun–ny," said Will as if he was fitting it to the child for the first time.

"She sho Sunny awright." Callie said, her smile broadening. Then the corners of her mouth turned down, lips trembled slightly. With a deep sigh, tears tracked down her cheeks.

"E don matta wha Massa Bowen or Massa Feller do tuh me—tek da and mo (*take that and more*). Jes wan hol my chile en mek sho she awright." Callie could not go on, her hands covering her face.

He strained to see her in the darkness of dusk. He glimpsed her silhouette just before she sat down, but that was enough ... he noticed how completely, perfectly slim she looked in her loose-fitting clothing. Will hated himself for having such thoughts during this emotional time for Callie, but her discernible curves moved Will's active imagination. He stopped himself.

"Callie, you are amazing. The way you have helped that poor woman and then to quote from the Bible and to withstand that imbecile's verbal assaults with such grace. You astound me." Though true, Will knew he was going on a bit.

She laughed, for the first time in days. "Will, you kind, but you don know. Da damn man ..." She stopped. "He wuss (*worse*) dan two Daniel Bowen. I leave da be."

"Well, don't worry. He will be leaving at first light tomorrow. I'll stay until then and take you back to Oakheart."

"Don tink da gon wuk, Will. I stay fuh hep Miss Eva tend her mama til she pass. No mo hahm come tuh me yuh. You can tell dem I be back tarectly."

"Tarectly? Do you mean directly?"

"Da wha I say."

Will smiled and was greatly moved by her generous, giving spirit. And at the same time, he did not want her to sacrifice more time from her child. "You've done what you can do here, Callie. Let her daughter take care of her now."

Callie felt comfortable enough with Will to argue with him. "No, Will, I stay fuh now. I see in huh eye da Miss Eva need me. I know da Lucas come fuh me—di-rect-ly."

In his desire to comfort her, he wanted to do more, at once reaching out toward her and then pulling back. It was as if he reprimanded himself for violating his own sense of propriety.

Callie noticed the struggle he was having, and that his forehead wrinkles had deepened, when suddenly she reached out to brush his cheek gently with the back of her hand. She wished to show a gesture of understanding and support.

Will took it that way, and more. Passion in him rising and face flushed, Will wanted to reach out to her after he felt that light touch on his cheek. He wanted to believe it was more than just an act of kindness.

Callie, too, felt powerfully drawn to Will. Yet in spite of their closeness, she could not bring herself to place her arm around him, as he had just circled his arm around her shoulder and moved his hand to her upper arm.

Trembling, she broke free and stood apart, not appearing to hear his apology as she moved quickly down to the water. She was nearly enclosed on three sides by the evening's flood tide. She sought waterside relief for all the worries she carried: having to adjust to days without her daughter, caring for a dying woman, almost getting lashed for reading the Bible, and being raped by two massas in just a few short days. Into this mix, came this young man Will. "Jes kyan do nuttin bout dem ting now," she said to herself.

Her thoughts kept returning to the conversation she had with Missus Feller late the night before. The old woman had awakened and attempted to sit up in her bed, so Callie propped her up and began feeding her soup from a small spoon. Missus Feller turned her head slightly toward the third spoonful. Looking up into Callie's face, she said softly, "I know who you are, gal."

"Yeah, I tell you when I come yuh—tell you I run de Oakheart big house fuh Massa Bowen—tell you I do da now since Mama Ruth pass many yeah back."

"No, I been knowin' you since you was born." She leaned toward Callie. "You're Callie Bowen." Missus Feller's voice grew weak and dropped below whisper. "I knew your mother, too, till they sent her away." Her voice was barely discernible as she sunk into the bed. "Yes, gal, I did … know all that." She drifted off to sleep, though fitfully at first.

Though Callie's desire to talk to her grew, there was no more conversation. Missus Feller had lost consciousness. Callie picked up the Bible next to the bed and began reading, at first silently to herself, and then aloud, to the dying old woman.

Chapter 10

Eva and her father stayed up most of the night, sharing final family moments. Missus Feller had not awakened, and by morning her breathing had slowed. They emerged from the house red-eyed, arms around each other, not acknowledging Will as he waited on the porch swing. Feller hugged his daughter good-bye; she held him closely while they talked, their relationship strong despite their differences the night before.

Earlier that morning, Eva had brought a breakfast biscuit to Will in the barn, where he had made an adequate pallet. He slept deeply from the moment he lay down, until the old wooden door creaked open at first light.

Eva walked several steps and stood over him. "Thought you might be hungry."

"Thank you, ma'am," said Will, stirring awake with civility and lucidity learned at the academy. Not knowing quite what to say at such a tender time for Eva, he simply asked, "How's your mother?"

"Not good, Will. I don't think she will awake today." Eva changed the subject. "Before events of this day hurry on, I wanted to say thank you for bringing me home, and also for helping me ..." She hesitated, unable to put into words the realities that confronted her the day before. Finally, she said, "You helped me to see my home differently."

"It took courage to do what you did," Will responded, smiling.

"Maybe so." Eva quickly added, "It took courage for Callie to come here to tend my mother during her last days."

Will agreed. "I believe Callie has had to be courageous every day of her life. We just have not seen it." Eva smiled and exited the barn, leaving Will to finish awakening, biscuit in hand.

That morning, Callie stayed in the house, mostly in the small back storage room, when she was not needed for giving comfort to the missus. She had come to the front door after Eva and her father passed through it to the porch where Will was waiting. Though she and Will did not speak again the night before, she smiled with genuine warmth as he glanced at her on his way out to the dock.

Will was to follow Feller as he wound his way through the island channels, a much shorter trip than Will pulled the day before. He was grateful, since his fingers had developed new blisters near old calluses. Will theorized that the oar handles were irregular and rougher than he was used to, so he decided he must use a different grip on them during the trip home.

Will did not rush his departure, reluctant to leave these two women with whom he felt a certain connection. Eva he barely knew, but her sorrow was palpable. Yet, at such a time when she was losing her mother, she found strength within to challenge her father's brand of slavery. Will was deeply affected by her forcefulness. And, then of course, there was Callie, whose resilience amid adversity left Will in awe. He nodded politely to Eva and waved to Callie standing on the porch and then turned to the water. Will knew that he was no longer needed there, and that he was expected elsewhere.

Feller had cast off already in his launch and, with a crew of two slaves, was quickly down the island coast before Will pushed off from the dock. They apparently set a course hugging the shore line at near high tide and turned south into the first major tidal creek. So slight were the winds that morning that the lead boat left a clear trail on the waterway for Will to follow. He caught a brief glimpse of Feller and his crew two other times as they forged ahead through the creeks.

Mostly covered by the full tide, only the yellow-brown tips of marsh grass were visible; Will used the high water to cut a more direct path across the winding marsh channels. When he slowed his pace, he smelled and tasted the salty air, grateful for the serenity of calmer weather after the battering storm. Will began to notice that he was surrounded by wildlife that seemed to share his gratitude. Each with its own song to sing, the species that thrived in this lowland paradise were about the airy business of being—singing, flying, hunting, eating, and dying. Will slowed to watch these routine acts as beautiful expressions of nature, as if witnessing them for the first time. He tried to reconcile the discordant events of past days with the harmonies that surrounded him.

In a short week he had seen slavery up close again and felt the wrenching slog of horrible events that were its byproducts. Moreover, he had witnessed the lives of Callie and Lucas—his friends. He watched as they both deployed their coping devices. Their quick minds set stories afloat to misdirect Massa, with Massa unknowing. They also were able to redirect their focus away from their despair and oppression. Somehow, their fortitude strengthened each day that their bonds restrained them. Their faith in a better day thrived, in spite of many reasons for it to have been parched in the fields of fierce, hot captivity.

Will found himself captive to the currents that roiled his family and divided his nation. When he allowed himself to concentrate on the marvels of nature all around, despair receded like outbound currents to low tide. Yet with each peaceful stroke, Will drew nearer to his stepfather and the point where his "decision" would become a path of action. His easy rowing cadence reflected his certainty that what awaited at Oakheart would not be as pleasant as his morning journey.

Will was back to familiar landscapes in less than an hour. Upon his arrival in the creek leading to the old plantation, he saw that there was a sleek little sloop, white with a small mast, with beautiful lines and a clear inclination for speed. As Will drew closer, he saw it was stacked with cartons, undoubtedly supplies ready to go to the forts. Closer view revealed crates of oysters, freshly raked out of the marsh mud by Oakheart slaves, and boxes of sweet potatoes, kale, and corn. All were destined for the sustenance of the Confederate warriors at the forts.

Captain Bowen stepped quickly down to the dock. "Once again I find, to my distaste, I am waiting for you."

Will reported as if to a military superior. "The condition of Missus Feller and the family, and the weather in near darkness last evening, were such that I decided I must stay, in support of the mission."

"Please, spare me your excuses," Bowen snapped. "More important matters are afoot. I am on my way to the fort with more supplies, as will you be." Then he hesitated, looking around, and realized that Callie did not come back. At this time Will's mother descended the bank to the dock.

"Greetings, Mother, all is well." Will went directly to his mother, both as earnest display of affection and to act as Uncle Harris recommended—determined to tend to his mother's health.

Bowen shouted over them both. "Where in God's name is Callie? You had one thing to do, boy, and that was bring Callie back."

"To the contrary, sir, I was to deliver Eva to take care of her mother, and, to that end, Eva wanted Callie to remain with her, sir."

"Again, spare me that horsepucky." Remembering his pledge to act more kindly toward his family members, Bowen turned to his wife. "Please speak, Julia! Get on with this presentation of yours."

As if officiating at an awards banquet, Julia began. "For a welcoming present, Daniel had intended all along to give you this beautiful little sailboat—from him, and me."

Will's stepfather leaned in with a clap on the new boat owner's back. "I bet you can't wait to get out there, boy. I already named her for ya." Will looked down incredulously to where new paint read *Southern Will*. He stepped back, about to speak.

Bowen went on quickly. "You can take it with you out to Fort Beauregard, and then over to Hilton Head when you start your service with the local naval authorities. I took the liberty to have your boat loaded with supplies that must be delivered out there pretty damn quick. In fact, the Confederate navy might could use the boat more than you." His humor fell flat, except in his own dark soul.

Will's mother tried to lift spirits to a level fitting the joyous nature of the occasion. "I asked Daniel to build my boy a special boat for whenever he comes home again, and it is ready for you now, worthy of a Naval Academy graduate."

"Well then, Mother, it will take one more year for my readiness." Will could not deter her enthusiasm, and he gave her a long and loving hug. During their embrace, he whispered in her ear that she was supposed to be feeling ill.

"Why, of course you are more than ready," she said, clearing her throat. "After we arrived here, I knew"—she paused to cough—"that you were made to be on the water."

Will protested. "I was made for many things that now are postponed due to the failures of our modern politics."

Julia cautioned him. "Now, let's not turn this gifting moment into a debate." Her emphasis on the word *debate* was loud enough to be heard by the captain.

"Debate?" he roared. "Why, there is no debate. That sweet boat will cross these waters many times to help supply the defenders of these islands. Your butt will be in that boat when it makes those crossings. If the Union navy wants a fight, we will be ready." He nodded at Will as a comrade-in-arms.

And then, as if Will had won a major award, the captain clapped him harder on the back. "Congratulations! You better take care of her— she's one of the finest little sloops in the islands. Once it is discharged of its goods and you of your duties, may you enjoy it in good health."

Will stood still, caught without option in the flow of events.

The captain smiled more broadly than Will had ever seen before. "I'm going out to Bay Point now." He put an arm on Will's shoulder. "Julia, let me have a sailor's word with your young man here, please?" Will knew that the false kindness foretold the onset of the captain's dark side. While smiling all the while, he began: "You remember, don't ya, boy, when that slave man got whipped so bad after he violated my trust? 'Member what happened then and what I told ya?"

Will searched his memory; there were too many cruelties to sort.

"You know, boy, you were about twelve that time you first took a boat of mine without permission?" Suddenly Will did remember.

The captain pressed on. "You took that boat up the creek without my authorization, and I was determined to teach you respect. Well, to get my satisfaction, I couldn't take it out of your hide, couldn't even lash Lucas. But because of you, Thomas lost an eye, and he hasn't been able to run well after that day either, when he got his ankle twisted in my whip. Remember, Willyboy, I told you that day I did it just for you!" A sneering smile creased his face. "But Thomas never ran out in this salt marsh again. That whippin', boy, I did that for you."

Will worked to mask his revulsion.

After hesitating for effect, Bowen drew nearer to Will, his breath smelling of rum. "If you don't please me now, I wonder which one these slaves is gonna mean enough to you, to get you to do the right thing? I just wonder. What will it take to gain your loyalty to the Confederacy?" His stepfather released his firm grip on Will's shoulder, though its impact remained.

It was clear to Will that the joyful boat presentation segment of the day had ended. He felt trapped, with neither fight nor flight available. This loathsome human being feigned the illness of Will's mother to lure him, presented a boat as a gift to take to war, and would and did mercilessly beat other humans and blame it on children. Will simply wanted to end the tyranny over his life. And yet he knew he should say nothing sharp in retort.

Bowen turned to face him. "I don't know what measure of a man you'll turn out to be, boy. Sometimes I think you're getting there, but I'm always disappointed."

It was one goad too many for Will. "It disappoints me, Captain—Stepfather," Will said, nearly spitting the word from his mouth in a stern whisper, "that the measure of your manliness equates to a willingness to mercilessly beat women, children, and old men, in order to feel superior to something." His boldness shocked him, though he remained steady. "I know too well what you are capable of."

Before Bowen could speak, Will turned back to his mother, adding, "But I will take that boat out to the forts, making sure its contents, including myself, are delivered as assigned, and I will do what I can to support the defenders of these islands." Will stood to his full six-foot height. "A Hewitt man is good to his word. My debt to you will be paid."

Will's decision, only then finally made, relieved and sickened him. He spoke up for his mother and his family name, so he could not be accused of breaking a pledge to repay a debt.

Bowen turned away toward the dock with no sign of appreciation. "We'll see if you are up to it then." Looking back at his wife, he called out to her, "Julia, I'm leaving now, but you should begin packing some of your treasures, in case we decide to leave this area for a while when I come back from the forts."

Despite the warnings on Sunday morning, Julia had not wanted to believe such an evacuation would be necessary. Until this moment, her husband had not given a hint that they would not stay at Oakheart. Julia shouted to ensure that he heard. "But Will must stay with me at least one more day, Daniel." She coughed dramatically. "I insist, maybe two days, to help me pack. I am not feeling well, and now you will be gone. I need my young Will to steel my spine and help me prepare for what is to come."

The captain turned to protest but then thought better of it. "All right, Julia, as I said, you have not been well lately. Will, a day, no more than two." He ordered the "boys" to move the oyster crates and produce over to his boat.

Will smiled to himself. "Yes, sir. But first, my mother commands my attention, sir." Will knew it was no time for foolishness, and yet this moment was satisfying to him. By staying on with his mother, however briefly, Will felt he diminished the captain and his Confederacy.

Through a glowering gaze, the captain commanded. "Don't push it, boy. When you come out, bring another fresh load just like what I've got today—BB and Lucas know what to do." The captain turned to look out over the water, but his words were still distinct. "Don't make me come back for your boat."

★   ★   ★

The captain drifted down Chowan Creek, standing in the bow as rowing slaves worked through waves created by the southeasterly breeze colliding with an outbound tide. As he grew distant on the river, calm descended on Oakheart Plantation. For Will and Julia, respite from his persistent nastiness was like a cool morning fog lifting to reveal a gloriously warm day. They decided to spread their sense of ease to all residents of the plantation.

Suddenly the big house bell rang out, signaling the slaves to stop work earlier than normal. Backs straightened across rows of cotton, and workers stood up in the sweet potatoes, but there was no movement from the fields. Will rang the bell again, as his mother instructed.

Julia called down to Lucas, hoping he was still at the dock. Reliable as always, Lucas appeared in a minute and stood tall beneath her. "Lucas, I need your help. Spread the word to all hands to stop for the day, and that tomorrow will only be a half day of work. Since you have all been in the fields extra time, start work late in the morning and quit earlier than usual—as a thank-you from the Oakheart Plantation."

Lucas grinned widely, nearly singing, "I do da right now, Missus." He sprinted toward the first field.

Will and Julia decided that there would be time the next day for any needed packing. After seeking a quick dinner from the food prepared earlier, they settled on the front porch. The evening was so quiet they could hear a slight breeze rustling the tops of live oaks and pines. They agreed to make the next day more like a holiday, for themselves and others.

In the distance they heard many voices singing a buoyant melody with phrases that were repeated, each time with more passion. Though the words were inaudible to them, there was no doubt that joyful songs of praise were spreading over the plantation.

Chapter 11

Celebrations had ended late the night before, but several hours into the day, almost all hands were back in the fields, an energized pace in their song and work. Julia smiled and commented that she had never heard such zest and joy in their voices while they worked, and that perhaps they should try this half-day program more often. She resolved to tell Daniel of her discovery.

Will looked on the fields in wonder as she spoke. Turning to her, he said thoughtfully, "Mother, I believe their singing may be about more than starting a short day of work a little late."

"Whatever the cause, I rejoice in it. Their mood fits this perfect November morning. I am happy for their lifted spirits. My joy is to have my boy all to myself!" She broke eye contact with Will to pull him into a powerful embrace. "If I must let you take that laden boat to the fort tomorrow, then so be it. But today we will focus on the good things."

By that comment Will understood that he would not be leaving for the fort that day, if his mother had any say in the matter. Her ability to focus on the good things is what had allowed Julia Hewitt to live relatively at peace in a house with Daniel Bowen and on a plantation full of slavery. As long as she could play her piano and give lessons to young girls, Julia's days were full, even after her son left home. But she noticed a growing discontent with her husband that deepened each day. It was beyond her ability to remedy.

Will chose to let the day be as good as his mother would have it. They laughed and talked, walked and sang together, as if waves of war were not lapping at nearby shores. Will suppressed the urge to think of his impending involuntary service in the Confederate navy. Instead, he basked in the glow of the maturing relationship with his mother.

By evening, Will had convinced Julia that he needed to prepare for the morning trip, if there was to be one. He also wanted to visit with Lucas before it got too late. At that point, reality interrupted the easy pace of the day.

Lucas bounded up from the dock, clearly anxious to report some news. "I talk tuh Sam en Cuffie from Capers Plantation—dey been out tuh de big wada (*the Atlantic Ocean*). Dey see mo ship dan dey ebba see. Dey see small boat move tween Bay Point en Hilton Head. Dey drop line in wada, but ain be fuh git fish. Den dey go back out tuh de odda ship. Supm ain right—so I run back—mek sho oona know."

After thanking Lucas, Julia's first thought turned to her child. "It's settled then. You mustn't go out there tomorrow either, Will."

Laughing at her enveloping and yet confining love, Will wrapped his arms around her. "You know, Mother, I have been training to be at war on the sea."

"Not on this sea!" Julia gestured broadly, adamantly refusing to accept that her son could become a warrior.

"Mother, did you hear Lucas? They all went back out to sea, no shots were even fired." He hugged her closely. "They are probably heading down the coast now as we are worrying about them." Though he knew better, his reassurances seemed to work with Julia, who drew comfort from her son's simple banalities.

All day Will felt the need to spend more time with Lucas and to get his best advice, but he had been determined to humor his mother first. "Now, my dear, let me go about my business. I want Lucas to share more of his wisdom about these waters before I go out on them in that new vessel you and Daniel gave me. I did not properly thank you earlier, but I love what you persuaded him to do for me."

After convincing her that they just might need to move inland for a day or a week, should unpleasantness break out, Will left her alone to pack her essentials. With a kiss on his mother's forehead, he was out of the house.

*   *   *

Will found Lucas where expected, down on the dock. A more natural fit was hard to imagine. Lucas loved his work. That he performed it as a slave was another matter altogether. But he was a contented man when allowed to pursue his craft, hauling life from the water so that others might eat.

"Will, you jes in time. How you know I need yo hep fuh git knot out my crab line?" Lucas enjoyed his own joke and beckoned him over sincerely, handing him a line of thin rope with tangles such that there were not three feet without a knot. "Watch out fuh dem hook." Once the line was untangled, Lucas put rotting chunks of mullet on the hooks so that a blue crab would work hard to get the bait off. When Will's knot-puzzle was solved, Lucas handed him a knife, the clear point being that the fish chunks needed help getting onto the hooks.

With feet dangling in the wide creek as it curled west toward the river, the young men worked two crab lines and talked. Once again, they found themselves together on this sea island shore, the calm of their friendship holding steady before an unknown storm. As they watched sunset colors brighten, the sun dipped just below the last low-lying clouds. The daylong breeze relented, if only slightly, making it easier for the small, biting bugs to swarm the assembled fish and nearby humans.

"You ready fuh go cross wide wada?" Lucas was feeling his way, pointing to *Southern Will* tied up along the dock. "Wha mek you tink you kin wuk dishyuh boat en deese wada wid da big load up top?"

Will reassured him. "They made us do something like that this past year at the academy. I had to take a boat usually crewed by two, loaded with weights. They wanted to see how we could handle a rolling vessel in the open water of Chesapeake Bay on our own. I can do it, Lucas. Besides, the wind is dying down."

"I wan hep you. Wada flo tween deese yuh islan strong en change day by day. Lotta boatmen be surprise, eben me sometime. Too much folk go out when ain de right time—need fuh know right time. I kin hep you be safe, Willy, and I wan do da."

"Forget it, Lucas!" Will softened. "Lukey, not another word about you helping me help the Confederates. It's odd enough that I am doing it, but you most certainly will not help defend Captain Bowen's desire to keep you as a slave."

Lucas knew Will was right. He also knew he must agree with Will now and help him prepare. But he was sure that, the next morning, he would follow his friend to the fort.

They traded banter and shared long moments of silence. When Will pulled his legs onto the dock and stretched out, Lucas kept talking at first, aware that he was losing his audience. He stopped his stories when Will's snoring grew too loud, allowing Will to harmonize with the crickets uninterrupted. For nearly an hour, Lucas let Will's deep sleep proceed, making sure his friend didn't roll off the dock.

Will began moaning and mixing in some words, inaudibly at first, as Lucas leaned closer to hear. Soon Lucas realized that Will's sounds came from his dreams and were growing louder. At that, Lucas shook his friend. Will sat up, breathing hard and looking puzzled at his surroundings. Lucas explained, "You been sleep. Fall out on dock, ummm-hmmm. Sun go down—you go down." Lucas stood up and pulled Will to his feet and then directed him off the dock to the house. "See kin you fine yo bed. Come dayclean, ifn you gah fuh go, I be on dishyuh dock. We figyuh wha fuh do nex."

★ ★ ★

Early Wednesday, uncharacteristic morning winds blew Spanish moss nearly horizontal. Gusts picked up whitecaps on the river and sent them spewing ahead. Julia still believed that her son should not conduct warlike activities but had given reluctant approval of his call to duty. To her glee, the weather dictated that today was not the day for passage out to the edge of the Atlantic Ocean. Though Will felt compelled to make a good-faith effort to deliver to the forts and knew he could make the trip successfully even in these poor conditions, he was willing to wait another day.

He sought his mother's opinion over breakfast that morning, and she remained supportive of his intention to keep his commitment. She simply did not want her son exposed to hardship or harm. When Will questioned her closely, she began to waver, saying she would support whatever his judgment directed him to do.

To Will, that sounded very much like Uncle Harris's departing comment: "I know your course will right itself. Your internal compass is too resolute for you to go awry." Those words hung in Will's mind like a promise he did not know how to keep. Taken with Julia's "advice" to trust his judgment, Will began to doubt his decision to supply the forts at all.

He was grateful when Lucas came up to the front porch looking for him, offering respite from his ceaseless deliberations. Will explained his decision to wait one more day. Lucas smiled and immediately offered to train Will to crab with the lines they worked on the evening before. Will jumped at the chance for one more outing without the worry of war. He checked with his mother who was wise enough to know what Will needed, even though his needs no longer always coincided with hers.

Despite the wind churning on the river, Lucas found spots on the creeks sheltered from the gusts where he guaranteed the crabs would be hiding. They rowed slowly through the area Lucas identified and extended the crab lines behind, each with terrible-smelling chunks of dead fish firmly attached. Then Lucas said, "We kin wait a lee bit—ain gon tek long."

When Will complimented Lucas for all that he knew and could do, Lucas felt honored and was encouraged to share more of his wisdom. "Tide be up tonight, wind push em up mo. How high dey go? How fas? Kyan say. Today wind push up mo wada from da sea. Nex day be betta."

Though Will thought he understood the winds, he had not always given the sea island currents their due for mystery and uncertainty. The currents were the topic of Lucas's lesson yesterday; today, midshipman Hewitt was given the tides lecture.

Will found himself starting to worry again about the real world of military life that awaited him. Lucas noticed the furrowed brow and distant look of his pupil and popped Will on the head. "If you wan know bout wada flow, watch wha de fish en bird do on de wada."

Will began to laugh. "Are you saying that fish affect water currents? Birds, too?"

"No, man, but dey change wha dey do long wid de tide change, ummm-hmmm. Ebba see long-neck white bird stan on leg fuh stab little crab when tide high?"

"You talking about that egret over there?" Will shook his head no.

"You ain neba seen da when tide high. Da egret bird wait fuh hunt in de maash mud when tide low. Den he git him catch." Lucas had Will's full attention.

"De big fish wha jump out de wada—I laan from him."

"Dolphins?" Will asked.

"You say so. Dey catch mos dey food in low tide when dey don wuk so haad—chase fish up on pluff mud bank. I see two trap en eat mullet down on crik bank dis monin—see da wid my own eye, ummm-hmmm."

Lucas was satisfied that he had rich nature stories to share with Will, pleased that the things he knew to be so might help his friend. So he went on. "Look deh. See dem bird fly all togedda in line."

Will watched ten pelicans as they followed their leader in formation just above the water. "Yeah, Lucas, my mother and I used to love to watch pelicans glide, but we never understood how their big bodies could be so graceful in flight."

"Dey so smaat—dey mos always take off wid de face tuh de wind. Dey get up high real fas—see! De air lif em. Fus ting dey do, dey git up in de air. Mos time fly togedda. But ifn dey see wha dey wan fuh eat, dey go dey way—don wait fuh de res."

"So let's see, professor. Are you saying I should take off like a big pelican, into the wind, but act on my own needs when I have to do so?"

"I know fuh long time pas you be smaat too, Will."

"But I should be patient, like an egret waiting to feed?"

Lucas smiled broadly. "Now you see de way ting be."

And Will was learning. Species adapt and figure out how best to meet their needs. At least that was the message Will took from Lucas. Somehow, through the Lucas stories, he had begun to understand what his uncle said was true. "Your internal compass is too resolute for you to go awry." Was that a pronouncement, or a challenge? Did Uncle Harris believe that, or hope it was true? Will concluded that the combined message from Harris, his mother, and Lucas was to trust his instinct, his sense of direction, his sense of what was right. When he also tried to think of what would be best for the people that he loved, he found confusion and conflict, but he also found purpose. Being true to his own internal compass was best.

Will decided he must make Lucas aware of the threat Captain Bowen issued to him, possibly to harm either Lucas or Callie. "Lucas, I worry that Captain Bowen may hurt you or others if I decide to leave, especially if he thinks you may have helped."

Lucas was direct. "Ain bout me en Callie, Will. We look out fuh each odda, en we kin tek kyah uh ole Massa if need be. You gah fuh tink bout yosef, and wha right fuh you."

"Lucas, you know that you and Callie and the others are important to me."

"I know da, Will. I glad you feel da way. Da ain wha e bout. Wha you yuh fuh? (*What are you here for?*) You yuh fuh do wha Cap'n Bowen say, or you yuh fuh do wha in yo head—in yo haat (*heart*)?"

At that moment, they heard the firing of large shells from the forts. Will and Lucas listened keenly for more, but none came. Suddenly too real, the prospects for warfare might be only a sunrise away. Lucas and Will saw the seriousness in each other's eyes.

Finally then, Will knew what he had to do. He began to consider how he might slip from this onerous obligation, still hold his family honor high, and somehow keep his friends safe. He decided that he must deliver the goods, but that he then must extract himself from any obligation to the Confederacy, as soon as possible thereafter.

"Lucas, if I do get the supplies out to the fort at Bay Point, what do I do with this new boat? This gift is like an anchor. Where it is, I will be expected to be. If my stepfather stays at the fort tomorrow, I will be under his direct supervision."

"Wha if you don be wid de boat? Wha if you be someplace else?"

"Lucas, I'm taking it out there, how will I ... get back?" He realized he was looking at the answer to his question.

Lucas nodded and quickened his talk as his enthusiasm mounted to help Will find a way out. "Dis wha you fuh do. Drop de load, anchor de boat, den settle in de foat. When tide low in middle uh night, come out back tuh de maash crik behin de foat. Stay low in de maash grass. I leave dishyuh boat fuh you."

Will understood, but without precise plans, especially at night, he wondered how he would find Lucas. Lucas knew the terrain and quickly added, "When you leave de foat en git out on de Beaufort Riba, row tawd Oakhaat. I be up in de brush en pine at de fus big crik. When you git deh, I gon see you."

Will was reassured that the next day had a chance of working out. Through his worry, he was faintly amused that his Confederate service would end with the gift boat moored at the fort, in deception of the captain. His amusement ended, though, with the thought of the hasty good-bye to his mother that would be necessary, the danger to his friends, and how near he was to actual warfare. "What if there really is a Union fleet just miles away ready to attack?" Will mused aloud. "Might find out pretty soon."

Lucas smiled at the prospect. "If dem Union boat come yuh, ain gon be jus de tide run out. Massa en him people run out too."

As Will pulled the line slowly, Lucas scooped a big net attached to a long pole beneath the feeding crabs. Over and over again, to the end of the line, Lucas scooped crabs. After a while, Lucas said in his understated manner, "See, Will, some uh Gawd creachah pretty smaat. Den some don know when fuh jump off de line."

"I guess I'll find out tomorrow if I'll know when to jump off a line." They smiled reassurances and continued scooping crab until well past sunset.

PART III

November 7, 1861
to May 13, 1862

Chapter 12

Startled, Will awoke to the muffled sound of artillery shot, fired from quite a distance away. Then there was more rapid fire from smaller-caliber weapons coming nearer, followed by larger explosions, and then nothing. He opened his eyes to see only a faint glow coming from the east. Had he been dreaming? Rising quickly from his bed, Will called to his mother, and they found each other in the hallway. Her words of insistence that he stay away from whatever caused those explosions fell without impact on his all-too-attentive ears.

Will had convinced her previously, and yet again this morning, that the least he must do was to deliver the supplies to the forts. He reminded her that those same skirmishing volleys were heard last evening and came to nothing. Final reassurance to his mother that he would sail close to the shoreline all the way to Fort Beauregard, and thus out of any line of fire, allowed him to exit her loving, suffocating embrace. Wish as he might that he could be coddled away from hardship, this moment was his.

Down at the dock, Will prepared to shove off when Lucas appeared. Lucas made one brief effort to dissuade him, but Will remained focused on securing the load and completing its delivery. With a smile and a brief glance, Will acted as though it was just another launch. Lucas advanced for a handshake, and as they pulled each other closer, they felt the gravity of the day. Will quickly jumped on deck and caught the dock line tossed by Lucas.

The push provided by Lucas combined with Will's first pull on the oars caused the still waters of flood tide to swirl slowly around *Southern Will*. Stacked with fresh vegetables, crab, and oysters, *Southern Will* was carried toward the fort as the tide turned back to the sea. Will was relieved that this long-awaited, much-debated task was underway. He had the best of intentions—to be true to his promise to deliver the goods and then to find a way to remain true to himself.

Just another quick river run to the ocean, Will tried to tell himself. He set his sail to catch any slight morning breeze, something he had done on these waters many times as a teenage sailor. Then he began the arduous one-man task of rowing the loaded craft toward the Atlantic Ocean. He knew his stepfather wanted him to use a small slave crew, but Will did not consider it.

As he rowed out Chowan Creek and turned into the Beaufort River, Will peered into the sunlight to find his objective, the southernmost point of a chain of barrier islands, now home to sandy Fort Beauregard. Will understood there were more than five hundred troops assembled there, and even more across the channel at Fort Walker on the northern tip of Hilton Head Island.

Squinting from the morning light reflected on the water, Will looked past the farthest point of land, Bay Point, to see dozens of ships! Amazed, he stopped rowing to cup his hands over his eyes, simultaneously horrified and elated to see so many ships of the United States Navy all coming in his direction. Will realized that the Union command also was taking advantage of high slack tide to push into Port Royal Sound this fine November morning.

Will assessed the strength of the fleet, marveling that it survived the howling storm during the week before, and that it had assembled such an overpowering array of vessels. He recognized the *USS Wabash*, the fleet flagship, able to carry forty cannons, leading a line near the center of the channel between the forts. A succession of at least twenty warships with at least one hundred big guns followed. Looking farther out into the Atlantic, Will made out the shapes of many transport ships. By the fleet's alignment and approach, Will recognized the intent to attack the Confederate forts guarding the mile-wide entrance to the sound. He could not imagine the forts or the men withstanding what the Union Navy was capable of delivering.

Will searched for Confederate vessels standing in to resist. He saw just three armed tugs and a steamship, all withdrawing past Fort Walker and heading up Skull Creek behind Hilton Head Island—Union gunboats moving in their direction. He turned his attention back to the fleet as the familiar sounds of fife and drums rose unexpectedly from Union warships.

Will noticed the *Wabash*, just a few thousand feet off Bay Point, drawing near Fort Beauregard and angling more toward him. While surveying the awe-inspiring scene before him, Will realized, belatedly, that he had drifted farther from the riverbank than he intended. Will pulled hard on his oars to regain position nearer the coast where he hoped to remain unnoticed.

As the *Wabash* opened up a huge barrage on Fort Beauregard, other ships in the fleet followed suit. Then a tremendous shot lifted from Fort Walker, rushed over the *Wabash*, and fell harmlessly into the sea. A thundering roll of cannon fire reverberated across calm waters as both Confederate forts responded. In an instant, Will's mission ended. The Confederate fort on Bay Point began disintegrating under the brutal Union bombardment.

From the chaos of fire, smoke, and noise, Will glimpsed a gunboat moving out from the fleet toward him. He briefly wondered its purpose before realizing that, to the Union navy, he captained an unknown vessel in an enemy position during battle. He started rowing hard to port when small-caliber artillery shells splashed in the water about fifty feet short of his boat. Instinctively, he veered toward the imagined shelter of the riverbank and quickened his stroke. Will heard the next round of fire as he saw the splashes, this time only ten feet away.

Will knew he had only seconds before another, more accurate volley would scream at him. It must have blended with the thunderous shells beginning to break down the sand berm walls of the nearby fort. As he started to dive over the side of his boat away from the attack, Will saw the wooden bow crack apart. He plunged headfirst into the river, along with splintered crates full of sweet potatoes, greens, and fresh-caught crab, blown apart as Union shells wreaked havoc with items entrusted to him.

Will surfaced gasping for air and attempted to swim, but only his right arm responded. With it, Will wrapped himself around a floating wooden barrel, only to find half of it intact and barely buoyant enough to support him. In his last seconds of awareness, he struggled to pull himself onto it. Through the haze of semiconsciousness, he saw the *Southern Will* list to starboard and then sink.

Lucas was keenly aware of Will's predicament. He had been tracking Will since he pushed off the plantation dock that morning but stayed well behind him. Lucas had rowed slowly in one of the Captain's finely honed dugouts, moving tentatively toward a bigger fleet of ships than he ever could have imagined. All the while, he had kept a sharp eye on Will's movement up the shoreline.

The first blast of cannon fire startled Lucas so much that he dropped an oar. He had just retrieved it when the Union navy unleashed all its power on Fort Beauregard. Then, from nearly a half mile away, Lucas looked on in horror as his friend came under attack. Lucas immediately pulled into his oars as if Will's life depended on it.

In less than a minute, he glided into the still-floating debris near the sinking boat. Will was adrift, his feeble efforts to paddle having no effect. Dazed, he did not notice his lack of progress through the water, though miraculously he remained on the floating remnants of the barrel, recently full of oysters for hungry troops. He was not fazed by the nearby explosions. He did not seem to know where he was, nor could he function to protect or save himself.

The smoke of battle masked Lucas's arrival on the scene from any who cared. He immediately stroked to Will's side and carefully pulled his limp body across the bow.

Lucas braced his feet up on the gunnels and used his substantial strength to get Will into the boat. As gently as he could, he lowered Will between his legs, keeping his head upright, and tried to comfort him. As Lucas pulled on the oars, he spoke words of encouragement interspersed with pleadings to God on his friend's behalf.

Lucas veered into the first break in the river bank. The boat disappeared through stands of yellowing spartina grass as powerful strokes pulled it behind a small island sprouting scrub pine. Lucas made certain that they could no longer be targets for Union fire.

Immediately inspecting his unconscious patient, Lucas discovered that Will's left side was covered in blood. He searched and did not find a wound in Will's chest, finally seeing that the source of blood was on the back of his upper arm. Lucas tied one of his thin fishing lines around a rag on Will's arm to slow the bleeding.

But Will's breathing was labored, and just as Lucas pulled the dugout deeper into a protected cove shaded by a large wax myrtle tree, he saw Will's arms fall to his side. Reaching for him, Lucas could not stop Will from sliding down into the boat. Momentary panic gripped Lucas as he thought the worst. He propped Will's head up, holding him against his chest, rocking gently. So focused was he that he could hear Will's breathing, sounding cluttered as if through cotton fibers, and it seemed to be slowing. Lucas knew that Will needed more help than he could give. Until that moment, no sound could have distracted Lucas from his concern for Will. But a thunderous roar of cannon started up again, and Lucas had to look. Carefully, he propped Will up against his legs, straining to look over a sand ridge while holding him against gravity's pull.

What he saw defied his imagination—more than fifty ships in sight, some still steaming past Fort Beauregard; the lead ships passed in front of the north shore of Hilton Head Island where the larger Confederate fort stood. Even heavier bombardment had opened up on Fort Walker, and the Confederates were responding. The cacophony of hundreds of shells caused Lucas to cover his ears.

From about two miles away, Lucas watched transfixed as explosions in and above the fort made him wonder how life could survive beneath the fury. Lucas felt sorrow for those caught in that hell on earth, but then he questioned himself. His empathy diminished as he remembered that Captain Bowen was likely in one of the forts.

Having confirmed that no warring forces followed them up the river, Lucas felt momentary relief. Then Will shifted in his grip, at once coming to consciousness and clearly experiencing pain in his chest. When Will's breathing became more difficult, Lucas decided he must get Will back to the plantation. After steering the longboat into the river, Lucas hugged the shoreline for twenty minutes of hard rowing against a tide that was starting to turn out toward the battle. Soon, around the bend into Chowan Creek, Lucas came in view of Oakheart Plantation. The bluffs and dock were lined with his fellow bondsmen, straining to see around the bend and upriver where the roar of the big guns compelled their attention.

Lucas thought old Bella could fix almost anything, a lot like Callie could, and she had been using healing herbs longer than Callie. He stroked quickly toward shore, hoping Bella would know best what to do for Will. He decided to row up under the old live oak, its overhanging branches sheltering them from watchful eyes in the big house. Lucas was determined to protect Will from any further demands by Captain Bowen. He felt badly for Missus, but he could not take Will home for fear that Captain Bowen could be there too, wanting more from Will than he could give.

From the bluff, BB saw Lucas veer toward the shore of the creek about five hundred feet short of the dock, the spot overhung by an ancient, draping live oak tree. Not knowing why Lucas pulled up, BB sprinted there and found Will laid out in the boat. Lucas knew that BB would share his burden of worry and care. BB immediately reached down with one move and began hoisting Will up.

"Tek kyah, brudda, he hurt roun unda lef ahm."

And BB slowed down, cradling Will in his large arms. "Ga fuh git him tuh Bella—quick, fo anybody see him yuh." Lucas did not worry about that, since large explosions, sometimes visible over land and trees, continued to draw all eyes in their direction.

Bella had remained in her small shanty, too aged to rush down to the bluffs with the others. Besides, she was holding Sunny close in her weathered arms as she rocked in her only chair. She whispered stories to the little girl to distract from the powerful roar of cannon fire.

When BB entered carrying Will with Lucas close behind, the five of them filled Bella's home. Will was unconscious when laid upon the small pallet Bella used for sleeping. Despite her age, Bella stood right up, gently handing Sunny to Lucas, and in seconds knelt on the floor at Will's side.

"Lawd ha mercy! Wha ebil strike dishyuh youngun?" Bella's hands began rubbing Will's forehead, at once giving comfort and telling her of any fever. She tended Will with kind competence, finding his wound, removing the makeshift tourniquet, and cleaning shallow lacerations across his left shoulder and the puncture wound under his arm. "Dis po boy tek supm powerful on de side. Hurt outside and inside—him ain breed (*breathe*) so good. Him been sleep?"

"Mos de time," Lucas said, shielding Sunny from the view.

Bella's close examination yielded more. "Seem like him git bang up good wid dishyuh big lump back him head."

At that, Will awoke coughing. "What's happening … my boat … what … owww … what's going on?" Bella held him closer, BB knelt to better support Will's back, and Lucas reached down to touch his head, though Sunny's weight almost made him fall into Will instead.

"Bella say you hurt. Wha you say?" Lucas asked.

Will looked at him and, drifting to sleep again, managed to utter, "She's right." Will settled back in Bella's arms.

Lucas needed to tell BB what he had seen. With the description of many boats blasting both forts, Lucas said, "Look like dem planta and all dem boy in gray git beat real bad dis day."

BB began to contemplate the reality of the situation. "Don know wha dem planta gon do ifn dey kyan keep de Yankee out."

"You ain worry da Yankee gon tek we people from yuh, is you BB? Da wha Massa say happen ifn dey come yuh."

"Don know fuh sho, Lucas. Seem like Yankee bring buckra mo worry dan dey bring we." BB took charge. "Keep em yuh, Bella. I know you kin fix em. Keep Sunny too. Den we watch out fuh Massa. He come yuh from de foat, he gon be mo mean dan ebba."

"Wha we gon do, BB?"

"We gon be ready fuh do wha we gah fuh do. Him ain gon be massa no mo roun yuh. Lucas, you on de bluff—watch de dock. I look out fuh de res."

Assured by whatever plan BB had just asserted, Lucas left his friend with the healer and her assistant, little Sunny. He did as BB suggested, standing facing south, watching the explosions, some of which were visible, but most were only heard. From his position, he could see Bella's shanty on slave row and most of the creek coming from the Beaufort River. Booming warfare continued for another hour, stopped for an hour, and then resumed. Those slaves who came by wondered what Lucas had seen, so he told his story again and again, leaving out the part about rescuing Will.

He did not see how Massa could have survived the shelling he witnessed, if he tried to seek shelter in the sand embankments on Bay Point. But there was no reason to assume that he stayed through it. Lucas realized that Massa could have left out the back, hiking over sand dunes and through marsh mud to the creeks where flatboats were moored after the troops moved in.

Lucas waited, growing tired in the midafternoon after consuming the shrimp and biscuits Bella had provided. He sat with his back to the live oak overlooking the water and started drifting to sleep. The shelling had subsided, allowing his slumber.

Soon he stirred to the sound of distant cheers and then music. Bands on the Union ships were playing the tune he had heard in downtown Beaufort when all the buckra folks gathered on Flag Day. He thought they called it the National Anthem. He could have sworn that's what he heard, coming from Port Royal Sound. And then, no more music. Instead, more explosions ripped through air that had just been so pleasantly filled. He rose to catch a better view, rotating to once again look down the lane to Bella's and then back to the big house.

Bowen emerged from the tree-lined creek just behind him, as if he rose from the water, pluff mud caked on his boots and pants. Lucas abruptly stopped surveying the landscape when he pivoted and saw the barrel of Bowen's pistol pointed straight at him. "Hey there, Lucas. I know you are surprised to see me. Well, I'm here to take you and your sister with me. We gonna have to go away a while, so you'll be all right."

"Yassuh, Massa, I know I be fine—ain no need fuh hol da gun on me, suh. Lucas do wha you say him whole life, suh."

"Well now, Lucas, I been shot at a few too many times today not to know who might be my enemy." And indeed, though there was no apparent wound, the captain was scratched and cut and splashed with mud, indicative of a fast, low run through the creeks and forest as he escaped Fort Beauregard.

"Lucas neba been Massa enemy, suh. Neba."

"Well, shut up about it, boy, I mostly want to find your friend Will. Just before all the ruckus started, I saw him coming out to Bay Point, and then he got my boat shot up." He drew very close to Lucas, while keeping the pistol in full threat position aimed at Lucas's chest. "You wouldn't know about that though would you, Lucas?"

Lucas had seen Massa on many a day, and Lucas always saw the evil, even when Massa was trying to be benevolent. But today there was no veneer of benevolence. "You around here, Willy boy? I know you are—hidin out like the girl I always knew you to be. Saw blood in Lucas's boat here." He looked at Lucas with newly threatening intent. "So I figured that blood must be yours, since Lucas is not bleeding— yet. Anyway, I'll be leavin' the plantation for a little while, so you know, takin' your mama inland. 'Fore I go, I got some unfinished business with you, Willy boy."

Silence.

The captain cocked his head, turning slowly to listen. He leveled his gaze squarely at Lucas and continued shouting at Will. "I told you, boy, that if you defied me—worse, if you betrayed me—I would make you regret your ways." The captain proceeded talking to the surrounding trees while keeping his pistol pointed at Lucas. "Clearly either your judgment generally is poor, or you grossly underestimated me—and what I will do to prevail in adversity." He listened, scratching his head with the pistol butt, before aiming again at Lucas. The bombardment had stopped. "I say, Will!" He was shouting now. "Is there anything you think I should know before I decide where to put a bullet in Lucas?"

Of course, there was no response forthcoming from the unconscious Will, only two hundred feet away. Captain Bowen turned to Lucas. "Well, boy, since Will has decided not to respond to me, I'm thinking this isn't going to be a good day for you. If you have a God, you best be talking to him." And he aimed his weapon at Lucas again, his hand tightening.

When Lucas started to say, "Massa, I kin hep you up de riba," he detected movement behind Bowen. The captain appeared to be considering the offer when BB rose from the same creek bank that had cloaked Bowen's approach. BB moved fast for a big man, lunging at Bowen as he turned, plowing into his midsection, driving him down, and snapping his head to the ground. Stunned, Bowen offered no defense as BB's fist pounded the older man's face. For Bowen's sake, it was good he stopped at one blow. Though dazed, Bowen tried to get up, and BB shoved him back to earth.

Lucas quickly picked up the pistol that had threatened his life. "Wha you say, BB? We gon show Massa de same mussy (*mercy*) him show all we life?"

"We show da en mo. Fo sho he deserve wuss." BB paused for effect, looking directly in Bowen's bloodied face from one foot away. "But we ain ebil like Massa. We know de Lawd wan we fuh be bedda dan da (*wants us to be better than that*)."

Lucas sighed. "Yeah, BB, you right. Dis ol buckra gon burn in hell fuh sho!" Staring down at the powerless Bowen, he said, "Lawd tell me da wha he wan fuh you, Massa."

BB set the tone for how Daniel Bowen would be treated, slowly turning to him. "You bes git on yo way fo some odda people come yuh. Dey ain gon sho dis mussy." Smiling the most sinister grin a kind face could muster, BB whispered, "Betta hurry fo I change my mind, Bowen. Betta move yo damn ass."

Lucas was impressed and a little frightened by the menace in BB's demeanor.

They let Bowen up, with blood still streaming from his nose, BB escorted him into the house where his wife had been cowering in her room all afternoon, afraid even to go out on the balcony to look for her son. After only a few minutes, he emerged with a suitcase in each hand, racing down the stairs and across the yard toward the dock. He glanced at Lucas, then back to BB and Julia as she stumbled behind him.

Julia asked, "Where are we going?" and then, "Where is my son?" Bowen replied curtly to both questions and arrived at the dock ahead of her.

When Lucas approached Missus, she looked at him with fear. He stopped a few feet away from her, saying, "Missus, got supm fuh tell you, but you bes not tell Capn Bowen." Time did not allow him to wait for her agreement. "I fish yo boy safe out de riba. He hurt, but he gon be awright. He sleep jus now, kyan go no way. Das all I kin say."

Will's mother was fortified by these assurances and started to inquire further when Bowen rushed back, grabbed her arm, pulled her toward the dock, and loaded her onto the small sloop. She mildly protested her forced departure but, looking over her shoulder at Lucas, did not disclose to her husband what she had learned.

Bowen was quite aware that the Union forces were too preoccupied securing the forts to venture up the Beaufort River yet. He knew also that his refuge lay inland, up the Combahee River where he hoped to find temporary shelter at the plantation of a friend. Unlike many of his planter brethren, Daniel and Julia Bowen did not have other property where they could retreat.

Bowen had witnessed the destruction of forts expected to protect his property and way of life. Not only did he see his defenses of sand fall around him, he then suffered the indignity of being knocked down by a slave, followed by the humiliation of being allowed to stand. But now he had to flee his own home and do his own rowing on the arduous journey to the unknown. As he pulled out into the creek, he looked back to the dock where Lucas and BB remained, watching his departure. They barely heard Bowen as he yelled back, "You niggers will regret this day. I will be back, and you will regret this day, by God!"

He continued shouting at them beyond their range of hearing. Lucas and BB turned and left the dock, walking onto a plantation now without a planter.

Chapter 13

Of course, BB and Lucas had been on the plantation many a day without Captain Bowen. But there had never been a day when a planter was chased away by threat of a slave—as supplemented by the military might of the United States.

BB hugged Lucas to him with an embrace more fervent than he had ever given his brother before, and they walked up from the dock with arms around each other's shoulders. When they arrived on the bluff, BB held Lucas at arm's length. "Brudda, wha we jes do?"

"BB, you ain had no choice. He been guh kill me sho nuf."

"I know da. I stop da buckra fuh sho."

"Stop um." Lucas repeated.

"Jump um en crush um tuh de groun!"

"Jump um en crush um."

By now the cadence was set and with each phrase they got louder than before.

"Scaid um fuh sho, en sen um outyuh!"

"Scaid um en sen him outyuh!"

"Pack um en ship um up riba like cotton bale."

"Pack um en ship um like pick cotton."

The brothers hugged again and spun together as one.

By now a crowd of laughing, shouting, smiling, cheering fellow bondsmen had gathered around them, their bonds loosening. And when the shouting between the two brothers came to an end, so also did the celebration around them. All eyes were cast on BB and Lucas.

"Sista and brudda, dis day like no odda fuh we slabe (*slaves*). Sho nuf, we sen Massa way from yuh. Seem like from wha Lucas see dis monin and wha we yeddy (*hear*) dis noontime, dem Yankee come, en dey done beat buckra bad out at de foats."

"Wha da mean, BB?" asked one of the older women.

"Fuh now, less (*unless*) all dem massa come back, we free of em, sista ooman. Maybe de good Lawd keep dem from yuh fuh ebba."

They shouted praises to God, embraced each other joyfully, and some spontaneously began rhythmic stepping, clapping to the beat, and curling in line around BB and Lucas. After several minutes of hilarity, BB held up his hand, and the celebration calmed slightly, allowing him to speak again. "Fa true, les gib praise en tank tuh de Lawd—He done sen down deese yuh Yankee fuh chase Massa way." Heads nodded and then bowed in prayer.

"Praise Gawd! Tank you, Lawd!"

"Please Gawd, mek Yankee haat (*hearts*) good ifn dey come roun we people nex day."

"Amen! Amen!"

And someone shouted, "Don matta bout nex day—dishyuh day ain no mo Massa!"

It took no more than that to send half the crowd out and about, to tell the story, to jump for joy, to share this unknown feeling with those they loved. BB's cautions followed them as he shouted over their celebration. "Tek kyah (*care*) people! We ain know who chase who dishyuh night—could still be buckra on de run from Yankee. Tek kyah!"

Lucas immediately knew his next step. "Callie!" And he started moving. "Kyan wait fuh flood tide, brudda. Ain right she up wid Feller. En now dis big gun shoot?"

"Go Lucas—I stay wid Sunny en Will, case he wake up agin."

★ ★ ★

Lucas was more exhausted than he knew, after fishing Will from dangerous waters earlier that day. Yet he virtually raced toward Tidal Flats until he got to creeks where the waterline was so low that he had to get out and push his boat. Strong enough to make it through those

120

"dry" patches of marsh mud, he lifted and shoved the slender, long boat forward through shallows full of tall grass and oysters. While fiddler crabs stopped waving single large claws at him and scattered into their holes, Lucas realized anew why most island boatmen took boats in those creeks closer to flood tide than ebb.

Finally Lucas emerged from the shallows to deeper creeks as incoming tides filled in the north side of St. Helena Island. He rowed smoothly out into the Morgan River and then into St. Helena Sound where he spotted the dock at Tidal Flats. Upon arrival, Lucas gave in to his exhaustion, draped over his oars, and slowed his breathing before lifting himself onto the dock.

It was just past sunset when Callie sat down to rest on the porch. She had worked through the day to keep Eva moving after her mother had finally passed peacefully during the night before. Callie had convinced Eva that they should bury her mother promptly so that Callie could help before she went back to Oakheart. They had begun digging just as the cannons started booming on the south end of the island and then finished the hole that afternoon, just as it ended.

Eva was terrified that invading Yankees would be about and, due to her exhausting grief, had become hysterical when she thought about being alone on the plantation without her mother. Callie had just helped Eva drift off to a fitful sleep, when she walked to a rocking chair on the porch where she could keep watch over the water. She jumped up the second she saw Lucas standing on the dock in the dusky light. As quietly and quickly as possible, she ran off the porch, skipping the few steps, and raced down to him.

"Lucas!" Callie whispered loudly, and vaulted into his arms, hugging him with a desperation borne of death and a day full of cannon fire. "Oh Lucas, I jes been aks Gawd fuh sign so I kin know you awright—en deh you be, up from crik."

She hugged him again and felt the slack in his spent muscles.

Callie backed away and pulled him up, bracing him as they walked up the path to the porch where she could feed him leftovers. In no time at all, she came out of the house with a plate of still-warm sweet potato mashed with shrimp. Her tension eased as she watched her younger brother fill himself and lean back against the porch railing. She waited with her questions.

Lucas had never needed a meal more. Finally, after quickly cleaning the plate, he looked up to Callie. "Sista, don madda wey you be, you know how fuh fix food da hit de spot right."

And at that, her inquiry began and her eyes widened at the description of Lucas dragging Will from waters beneath hell's fury. Assured that Will had survived and was receiving Bella's loving care, she got similar assurances for Sunny's well-being.

Lucas told her that the slave-quarter celebrations were starting to get rowdy as he left, and Callie shook her head. Lucas quickly added that BB cautioned them to be careful until they knew more about what was happening.

Many of Callie's worries were eased by what Lucas reported, but she had to ask, "En Massa, wha bout him?" Lucas decided not to tell her about Bowen yet, not knowing if Eva might hear. His hand signals on the porch closed the matter.

They heard Eva stirring inside her home, drawers opening and closing. She came to the front door with suitcase in hand, saying she must go now to Beaufort and on to Charleston. When Callie asked who would take her, Eva said that Lucas would, of course.

Lucas lost no time in replying: "No, mahm." And without really considering it further, he said, "Mahm, some ting done change dishyuh day wha mek me say I kyan do da jes now. I gah fuh tek my sista home to huh chile en family. May be I kin tek you some odda time—bes I kin say now cause I ain know wey Union navy gon be dis night."

Eva was not thinking clearly enough to be shocked, but she was left without suggestion, a void Callie quickly filled. "You kin come back tuh Oakhaat wid Lucas en me dishyuh night." Eva was too frightened at the prospect to say yes, but more afraid to stay on at Tidal Flats, alone with the Africans who had been in service to her parents.

Callie was insistent, not just because she was anxious to get back home, but also because she hoped Eva might be able and willing to give her more information about Callie's own mother. "I know fuh sho you be safe wid me at de Bowen Plantation. Safe yuh? Deese good people know who been good to dem, and who ain." Callie let that thought simmer with Eva, aware that there were some factors that might push her decision to leave.

With only moments' more consideration, Eva consented, realizing there was nothing left for her at Tidal Flats, at least not then. Her mother was buried, and her father and husband were fighting for the Confederacy. She wanted to head home to Charleston, since she had little hope of finding her father. She was too scared at the day's events to stay alone on her parents' small plantation where she could not feel confident of the slaves' intentions. At least she felt secure in Callie's company, so much so that she asked Lucas to carry one more trunk from the house to the dock. He did so reluctantly, saying, "Dishyuh boat ain mek fuh hol shree people, en all dishyuh bag. Dis gon be hebby load—we gah fuh mek sho nuttin shif in de boat too much."

Callie recognized the tone and words that Lucas used when he was trying to make his point to a white person but not sound too smart in the process. His expertise extended beyond the local waterways to the workaday ways of having lived enslaved.

★　★　★

Callie, Eva, and Lucas caught the inbound swelling tidal creeks, floating several miles toward the heart of the sea island cluster. Though only an occasional directional paddle was needed, Lucas muscled the boat faster than the current. He had a finely honed sense of the day's urgency and was grateful for the push of the tide.

This early evening, a crescent moon shone down upon Lucas and the women as it set in the southwestern sky, its angled sliver smiling on their mission. As they floated on silken waterways, they came upon different voices around each bend, lifting up passionate thanks to their God for the freedom he had bestowed upon them. From the largest plantation, the energy from praise songs rushed toward them like a flock of ibis suddenly lifting their heads together in flight. As those melodies became faint behind them, another chorus of inspiration rose from the opposite river bank. Not much further downstream, they neared the plantation with the fine new praise house from which rhythmic thumping of shuffling feet kept cadence to a quickening "shout" of love for a God so merciful. For all their lives, the slaves had sung spirituals to ease the ache of the present, to lift hopes for the better day coming, and to affirm their belief in an all-powerful God who would right the wrongs of the world. Now, their aches had eased, their hopes had been realized, their God had moved, and they sang of their freedom.

Lucas and his passengers were content to ride the wave of river and song ... no conversation needed. Once, when they were passing through a quiet area in their journey, Eva whispered as she drifted off to sleep, "Those spirits liftin' my mama to heaven tonight." Callie responded that her people did not fear death but saw it as an open door through which to return home. Callie began to sing softly, lyrics known especially to boatmen around the sea islands.

> "Michael row de boat asho, hallelujah,
> Michael row de boat asho, hallelujah,
> Riba Jordan chilly en wide, hallelujah,
> Milk en honey on de odda side, hallelujah."

Just as Callie allowed Eva to believe that her song was only about Christian comfort in the afterlife, with no reference to the freedom yearned for by all slaves, she also let Eva rest in the belief that the spirituals from the forest that night were meant to lift her mother's spirit. Perhaps later there would be time to explain that the music expressed the feelings of a newly freed people.

Lucas took the opportunity of Eva's sleep to quietly tell Callie about Bowen—and his forced departure from Oakheart. Her eyes widened, first in fear and then hope, as she began to wonder about life without Bowen. Her shoulders slumped with relief, and tears came to her eyes. Then more spirituals came from the forests, washing over them as they flowed with the swift currents of freedom. With the smiling moon now below the watery horizon, the stars above shone more brightly than Callie had ever seen.

As they floated up the creek to Oakheart just after midnight, they heard their friends' familiar voices singing and shouting out to each other. By that hour, their zest was only slightly muted from the day's celebrations which had resounded throughout the islands.

Lucas was first to smell the smoke of cooking meat, purloined from the captain's smoke house, wafting through the trees. The feast for the stomach, though superb, was nothing like the sweet taste of having no master to fear.

Freedom!

They had only imagined. Now they witnessed their friends, slaves no more. Dancing and shouting continued through the night, with no seeming limit to the shared elation. In each step, there was a little more jump; on each brow, the furrow smoother. From each mouth a free voice sounded every phrase.

All tongues were busy giving praise to God. To the faithful Africans of the South Carolina sea islands, no one but God himself could have brought about such an event, though high regard was expressed for Abraham Lincoln, who had sent his soldiers to scare away the planters. They did not know the future, but they did know that this day, they were no longer slaves, and they did not choose to think about what the Yankees might do—not yet.

Callie and Lucas rushed up to the big house from the dock with Eva, who had just awakened to what was, for her, a discomforting return to Oakheart. It was a very different place from the time of her piano lessons with Julia Bowen. As she saw only black faces around her, celebrating, she stayed well within the protective sphere of Callie, who carried herself with authority the moment she stepped off her brother's boat.

BB saw Callie from the big house porch, which he had used as his base of "operations" during this tumultuous day. He had moved Sunny to one of the upstairs bedrooms that afternoon because she desperately needed rest after the daylong explosions. BB also wanted to give Will more space and peace to recline and recover in Bella's cabin.

Callie followed BB's pointed directions in response to her question, "Wey Sunny be?" She quickly climbed the porch steps and walked through the front doors of the big house, entering the living room where former cookhouse and field slaves now lounged comfortably on furniture arranged in a circular fashion for ease of conversation. Hearing her mother's voice, Sunny dashed down the narrow stairwell to hug her as tightly as her little arms could.

After Callie was reassured of her daughter's well-being, she went about organizing the situation before her. She assigned her best cooks to the morning meal. "Tek two mo fuh help en git busy. We got whole buncha folk fuh feed, en de wuk don stop roun yuh."

Turning to Lucas who had stretched out on the library room floor, she said, "Brudda, you res up, den you know wha fuh do in de crik. We gon fix meal fuh all us free people."

Though most of the former slaves respected Callie for all that she did and could do, a few looked at her skeptically. When she realized that Eva had been standing just behind her shoulder, Callie explained Eva's presence to the puzzled crowd. "Eva yuh fuh grieve. I jes hep huh bury huh mama—les hep huh out bes we kin. We gon all try fuh git tru deese days togedda now." She asked Eva to step out onto the veranda and turned to her people. "Sides, we kyan blame huh fuh wha her daddy done."

Callie thought she had said enough. But many among the former bondsmen of Oakheart, just now free of the tyranny of the planter class, did not welcome to their newly freed enclave an offspring of a buckra whose business had been to buy, sell, and catch slaves. Callie added: "So leave huh be so me en BB en Lucas kin figyuh wha fuh do wid huh." Callie gave lingering stares to several in the room.

Then Callie lifted her voice for the ears of those inside and out to hear clearly. "New day staat right now, right yuh. Massa gone. Yankee chase all dem off deese yuh islan. BB and Lucas move ol Bowen out, and he ain gon come back. Now, we tek kyah dishyah place. De good Lawd mek way fuh we. We gah fuh show how skrong (*strong*) we kin be."

As she directed Eva upstairs and to the Bowens' bedroom, Callie turned to go out the front door, leaving behind her grudging acceptance. Before she could settle in with her child, she had to check on Will. He slept soundly on Bella's pallet while Bella dozed beside him in her newly acquired rocking chair. Callie leaned over him, gently touching his forehead, brushing his hair aside, listening closely to his congested breathing. By a simple smile and nod of her head toward Will, Bella reassured Callie that he was better, needing sleep. Callie left them, rushing quickly back to Sunny, whose mother finally ended her first day as a free woman with her arms wrapped snuggly around her daughter.

★　★　★

Just four hours later, as sunlight filtered through lifting fog, Callie rose to find Lucas and BB talking down by the dock. The canopy above them, alive with chasing squirrels and singing birds, brightened as first light from the east showed an island at peace.

They greeted that day, unlike any other, together in a great embrace. They admitted to each other that they were glad they didn't have to work that day. But all three were anxious to see what the new day might bring. Though they weren't required to be productive, they knew there was work to be done.

"Bruddas, I jes ain know wha fuh tink bout dis feelin da run tru me. Wuk be wha I do bes, but ain nobody mek me wuk right now, nobody sides my own sef." Callie shook her head from side to side and uttered a loud and heartfelt, "Tank you, Jesus!" The discovery of freedom came to her in waves, with new revelations by the minute in the choices before her. "We gah fuh do right by people on dishyuh plantation. Wha come nex? How we gon shaya (*share*) wha we got wid ebbybody? Dey gah freedom same as we. Don madda who wuk in de

127

fiel and who wuk in de big house. Wha we mek we mek fuh all—but all gah fuh put supm in de pot—ebbybody kyan jes do wha dey feel like."

"Sista, some wan know why we save two buckra on dis fus day we free." BB looked at Callie for her explanation, though he knew her instinct was to help somebody in need.

"We done do wha right in we haat (*hearts*), brudda. You know why Lucas save Will."

"I kin see da. But wha bout Miss Eva?"

"Like I done say—Miss Eva jes los she mama." Both Lucas and BB nodded. She went on. "Sides, fo she mama pass, she say she know me en my mama. I wan fine out ifn da famly know supm bout my mama fuh sho." She looked around at them for understanding. "En jes now, Miss Eva ain gah no place fuh go."

BB warned her. "Da be awright fuh now, but she bes watch out roun dis place, cuz dem new boys come yuh shawt time back gon memba wha Massa Fella done tuh dem."

"Da may be so, BB, but right now we gah mo fuh tink bout den da." That was about as far as Callie's emphathy extended. "Eva gah fuh tek kyah huhsef roun yuh, or stay in de big house."

Callie and her brothers agreed to meet late that afternoon, adding Bella and Jacob to their group. Lucas headed straight out on the creek to check his traps and pull some shrimp. BB had asked some of his best workers to meet out at the sweet potato field, convincing them all that they were harvesting not for Massa, but for their families and friends at Oakheart.

Callie first assured herself that the cooking tasks were well underway. She knew that people who were well fed would be ready to listen and work together. Callie had put on so many feasts for the planters that she could not wait to prepare one for the eighty souls newly breathing free air at Oakheart.

Then she went back to the house to get Sunny so they could go see Bella together. Coming up the lane of shanties, Callie was shocked to see Bella walking in front of her home with Will propped up on her, taking small, uncertain steps.

Callie moved in to hug Bella and, at the same time, replace her as human crutch for Will's measured progress. Callie whispered in her ear: "Kyan tell you how much love in my haat fuh you, sweet Bella—I tank you so fuh de kyah you done gib my chile."

Bella just smiled and shook her head. "Dis chile no trouble, she jes so sweet. Now dis one yuh," she laughed while pinching Will's good arm, "he de one been worry me so."

Will received Bella's pinch as a sign of the tough love to which he had become accustomed. He pressed his cheek against Bella's in gratitude, as Callie took over his support.

"I gon tek em tuh de big house fuh res. You awready done do so much good fuh me I don wan aks mo, but I need you fuh look afta Sunny one mo day. So much gwine on."

Bella's simple smile signaled the favor was granted.

★ ★ ★

Will told Callie that he had slept so much, waking occasionally to sip more of Bella's special brew, that when he finally regained awareness, he was without headache and only sore in his ribs. He reported that the wound where Bella found wood splinters had been cleaned repeatedly and, though still raw, no longer caused pain. Nothing was broken. It was fortunate that Will dove from his boat just in time to be clear of the burning lead that shattered it and its cargo.

Just as Lucas had told Callie about BB's heroic handling of Captain Bowen, Will heard it directly from BB. But BB's version also included an apology to Will for having to be so "skrong" with the massa, and for sending his mother away. Will thanked him for his apology, and they laughed together that they were both made free by BB's willingness to stand up to Bowen. When Will told Callie that his laughter with BB had hurt his ribs anew, she smiled through her sympathy, saying, "We been wait all my life fuh git free uh Massa Bowen."

They rejoiced in the story as Callie supported Will all the way back to what had been his family home. Callie reflected on what she had been through over at Tidal Flats. "I tank you fuh bring Eva. I been aks de good Lawd fuh git me out da house en way from da man—en nex ting I see you en Eva. Da mean mo dan you kin know."

Will studied her eyes as she spoke, taking Callie's words at face value, feeling her genuine gratitude for helping her through some hard times. Callie went on. "I know you ain wan fight fuh Bowen. You try fuh do wha right fuh yo mama—I tink you good man fuh da, Will."

"Enough about me, Callie. These days are about you. I was a free person all my life and knew that I would be away from Bowen. But you, you are no longer a slave."

"I ain slave no mo, fuh sho. Haad fuh know wha da mean. I wan shout out loud wid joy en cry same time. Now I wuk fuh my people—don wuk fo no massa. So much bring cause fuh rejoice. Jes don know how fuh tink bout deese change."

"I could say—" Will started to speak as Callie guided him into his room, but she put her fingers to his mouth.

"Will, you still gah fuh res mo. I be back tarectly."

"Directly?" Will asked.

"Di-rectly, wid some good food." When she checked on him later that day, he was sleeping soundly.

Will was surprised to awake the next morning to find Callie sitting next to him. She then started to clean his wounded shoulder. He closed his eyes to remember how his mother used to comfort him with such light touches but then gained enough consciousness to know that this beautiful, caregiving woman was not his mother.

Callie told him BB and Lucas were both sure that the Confederates were indeed gone and the Union navy was in control of Port Royal Sound. At the news, Will tried to lift himself but still was not able to lean on his left arm. With limited movement and soreness in his ribs, he needed help changing shirts.

Callie supported his weight while holding the shirt open for him. "Seem right fuh tek kyah you. Da please me whole lot."

Will protested. "You're giving me too much of your time."

Callie argued with him. "I free now en kin do wha I please. Dis wha I choose fuh do." "Sides, you ain been well in yo head. I gah fuh mek sho you git bedda in head en body." Will's resistance to the soft, easing hands was minimal. Soon, after cleaning up a bit around the room, Callie gave Will a gentle but forceful tap on his good shoulder. "Git up now, time fuh tek walk."

Will considered protesting but knew that he needed to get moving again. After all, his legs were not injured.

They walked down the lane, past the fields, and across the spit of land that connected Constant Island to St. Helena Island. They basked in the sunshine of a crisp new day unlike either had ever experienced. Will found it hard to breathe several times when they walked a little too fast but he felt stronger with every step.

They did not talk much, so busy were they absorbing their surroundings. Mockingbirds sat on their perches, filling the air with varied songs. Cardinals and Carolina chickadees were intent on sorting through the seeds that Will's mother always threw around the side yard. A slight breeze allowed the pelicans gliding over the river to pause in midair as they took aim before plunging on the helpless fish below.

Yes, the wildlife was on the move. But it was not alone. The pulsing of a free people was evident everywhere. The main road was packed with folks walking, mostly to visit their kin and loved ones, moving without limitation or direction from others. Some had loads on their backs and heads, sacks full of food to share with friends and family on other plantations.

Will was stunned at the numbers of people out walking and looked to Callie in amazement. Sensing his wonder, Callie explained, "We walk tuh visit famly en such. Fus time folk be free fuh walk in light uh day. Slave time, we walk in de daak, so Massa don see we. You ain know da?" She enjoyed her own humor.

Callie and Will came upon one group of women, embracing and crying. There appeared to be no outward source of grief. No one in sight was injured or dead. Yet, this knot of women held onto each other in inconsolable sadness. Callie reached out to touch the shoulders of some, as if to ask the source of their pain. Hannah, a good friend of Callie from a nearby plantation, turned to her and saw her sad, inquisitive face.

"Callie, we full uh joy now, but we jes wish Emma been yuh fuh shaya dis joy. Ain been mo dan one yeah she pass—en she know de good Lawd gwine mek we free. We jes sad she gone tuh de Lawd fo she see dis day. Now she look down on we free folk en she crack e teet (*smile*) in heben wid de Lawd—en we cry, we be so happy." Callie understood and passed on with a hug for Hannah.

Will's face fell in the presence of such grief, though he tried not to be too intrusive with his curiosity. He asked why they would be so happy about her cracked teeth.

Callie laughed loudly and then placed a huge smile on her face, showing a mouthful of teeth. As she pointed to her smile, she said, "Will, dis wha mean 'crack e teet.'" And she laughed again louder this time.

In mock offense, through a partial smile, Will said, "I'm glad you are having so much fun at my expense." He shook his head as Callie pushed on his good shoulder.

They soon came upon an old woman sitting on the side of the road, facing the risen sun, singing in deep resonant tones with no particular pattern or progression. She was making beautiful random notes deep in her throat and only opened her mouth to let the sound out when she took a breath. Will and Callie were mesmerized, watching her sing, and sway, and smile. When she seemed to have finished, she saw them before her. Will asked about her health, and if she needed assistance. She smiled quietly bending forward and rocking side to side.

"Whiles I sit, I try fuh see wha gon happen down de road. Kyan bleib (*Can't believe*) da we people be widout buckra planta man tell we wha fuh do day en day out." After a pause and wide smile, she went on. "We talk en wait all yestuhday en when we see da de buckra run fuh true, we fall down on we knee. We sing praise to Jedus fuh dis blessin. We know de Lawd sen soljuhs uh Abrahm fuh free we people. De Lawd be good fuh sho, en we people be bless bless."

She finished and looked down several seconds before swinging her eyes back to Will, staring at his face. She did not speak until she was sure their eyes were engaged. "Guess you kyan know, kyan magine wha e be like fuh be slabe. Tink you kin?"

Will knew he could not and silently shook his head.

"Den you kyan know dis freedom wha I feel." At that she gripped her own midsection with cradling, weathered arms.

Will sat down beside the old woman and motioned Callie to join him as they listened to the occasional spirituals lifting above the trees. "People all over the islands are celebrating, up the creeks and on every plantation," Will said. Then he asked about the drumbeat he thought he heard clearly across the water, remembering that drums were not allowed at Oakheart since Bowen feared too much communication among slaves.

"Da ain no drum," said Callie, swaying gently with the dull pounding sound. "Da be dem folk free foot, wha dance skrong wid de shout en de song."

They continued to sit with the old woman, absorbing the quiet dignity of her celebration.

Chapter 14

While autumn winds chilled northern regions, warmth lingered in this semitropical climate where life continued to leap from the fertile island soils—sugar cane, sweet potatoes, winter cabbage, and greens. Cool nights followed bright, beautiful days well into December, accommodating all living, growing things. Rays of sun slanting in from southwestern skies gave a strong illusion of afternoon warmth, a deception that faded earlier each day with the setting sun.

Seasonal change was most evident in the expanse of salt marsh grass, the brilliant greens of summer turning in fall to golden wheat hues before dimming to winter's soft browns. The forests, too, announced that they held more than pines, live oaks, and southern magnolias, as families of maples blended seasonal splashes of red, gold, and orange. Spanish moss, draped beautifully on the limbs of imposing live oak trees, retained its grace and mystery. But its misty green faded to more somber gray as late fall wind chased humidity from the air and winter approached.

Such change was a constant, experienced yearly in the ebb and flow of life. In November of 1861, a change in humanity more monumental than the seasonal movements of earth, air, and water occurred on these small flat islands. Where once lived ten thousand bondsmen of African descent, there now lived that many free people.

The newly freed experienced a range of choices each day. They did not know what hardships might await under Union authority, and their future was uncertain, but they savored the right to decide what to do with their time. Their backs straightened without the weight of subservience. Their minds no longer raced to say words to avoid the lash. Their labors worked crops to sustain life of those they loved, not to make profits for those they feared. Children played as their parents watched in pleasure, no longer fearing unjust discipline.

Their joy grew in proportion to the numbers of loved ones who returned to the islands since the freedom came. Each day there were new stories of enslavement and escape, freely told. They began to have confidence that they would not lose another child, sister, husband—sent away to satisfy master's debt, or whim, or jealousy. For some, there was the realization that they, or their loved ones, would not again have to submit to the forced touching of their bodies or even worse cruelties.

Their smiles now came naturally, given freely, not for self-preservation or to placate the master's mind. Stated differently, the sea islanders had ample cause to "crack dey teet."

* * *

Unlike many plantations where planters had deserted and freed slaves stripped the big houses bare, at Oakheart there was no looting of the mansion, though several items had disappeared from the cookhouse behind the big house. Callie figured some people had earned the right to a new cook pot from the master who no longer controlled their lives or needed his pots. Callie also asked BB to take one of the porch rocking chairs to Bella's home.

In the first uncertain days, Callie and her brothers worked with others to lead the freedmen in a positive direction. The group at Oakheart seemed to take the admonitions of BB and Callie seriously, choosing to continue laboring. They agreed to work the land together and to share whatever benefits might come, and to leave time for their own pursuits like fishing, hunting, tending small gardens, or fixing family homes.

Of course, for Lucas, that was both the old and the "new" way to pass time—fishing for work, subsistence, and relaxation. He launched into every day as he had the days before "the big gunshoot." Lucas, like his sister and brother, did not rest on done deeds. Lucas was proud that he fished Will from the river and got his sister back home safely, but that was in the past. Each morning, he was out on the water early, tending his traps and lines, bringing in a bounty large enough for all the people of Oakheart to share one good meal a day. He did stay to the island creeks, not venturing into the river where Union navy patrols passed daily.

After Lucas finished two full days hauling in buckets of shrimp, he found Will returning from a long walk with Callie. Lucas had been very worried about Will, so he was greatly relieved to see him up and moving so well just days after being bloodied and unconscious. They embraced like the brothers they had become, but Will flinched when Lucas compressed his tender ribcage in enthusiasm. They smiled broadly as they stepped back.

"You kin stan? How you feel?" Lucas looked over his friend closely.

"Still sore around my ribs and having trouble breathing deep sometimes, but I'm gonna live, all thanks to you, and dear Bella, of course." Then Will got a mischievous look on his face. "And I understand you have lost your master?"

"Los em. Chase em way from yuh. You be proud uh me en BB. We stan up tuh him. When he raise gun tuh me, BB beat him down."

"Hard to believe." Will shook his head in wonder.

"Yeah. I tell yo mama I hep you git back safe en you be awright— den she go wid da damn massa."

"Thank you for telling her that, Lucas."

"Yeah, huh look pretty scaid but seem betta when I tell huh da we take kyah uh you. Don seem like she too keen on Cap'n Bowen no mo. She ain wan fuh leave de islan wid him."

Will took those words to heart. "When I get all healed up, can you show me what river they went up? Somebody around here has to know how far inland the rivers reach and the places where Captain Bowen might go."

"Sho nuff, brudda, ain know much bout da, but I aks some folk."

* * *

As they watched over the next days and weeks, they learned that the Union navy was present in great numbers at Hilton Head. The rivers were busy with patrolling gunboats, trying to head off Confederate raids that might come from the mainland or from other islands where Union troops were not in control. Only once in the first week did Union forces move up the river into Beaufort, putting landing parties ashore that did not stay the night.

On most islands, there were no soldiers, at least not yet. The people were left on their own to decide what they would or would not do. Some chose to live each day as it came. A few began planning for beyond tomorrow. Such options were not familiar to most slaves, especially the field hands who previously had little choice in the various tasks that would fill their days.

But even for those like Callie and Lucas, who had developed specialties that kept them from repetitive labor, it was difficult to know what the next day would bring. While they were without the oppressive rule of the planters, they, too, waited to see whether Yankee troops would arrive to become their new rulers.

Most adults turned to the immediate family needs, like improving shelters, starting a winter garden, and fishing. Others went on the road to locate and visit relatives. Some, like Callie, BB, and Lucas, took a broader view. They had no way to know what to expect from the opposing forces—Union and Confederate—that surrounded them. Though they sensed that change was on the way, they knew it was beyond their power to control, so they resolved to use their freedom to try to be ready for whatever would come.

Early on in the first days after the battle, Callie, Lucas, and BB met with Bella, Jacob, and a few others to discuss what they should do. Over the next weeks they had many such meetings. Everyone seemed to agree on the first priority—to defend themselves and not get captured back by Massa or any other planters. But they let BB know they feared the Yankees. "You tink wha Massa say true? Yankee gon mek us slave en sen us way tuh Cuba?"

BB reassured them. "Naah, dey busy fight dishyuh wah (*war*). Ain gon sen us off no way." But they agreed to be on alert for Union soldiers too. They decided who would be responsible, by day and night, to watch over the river and creeks, and who would cover the approach to the big house from the main road. BB said, "Anyways, we gah fuh keep we own lookout, en da true for all ting. Afta we watch wada en we watch road, we gah fuh watch de cotton—mek sho we wuk de res uh dishyuh cotton crop en finish off de pickin right. We gah fuh do all da."

Though the immediate days of freedom were relatively calm on Oakheart, there were undercurrents even in the early meetings. Who was in charge of things? The old driver who let BB run things before freedom came vanished the day of the battle. Who would work on the plantation, and what would they do? Who wanted to leave, and where would they go?

One of the first disagreements was about cotton. Jacob saw no reason for slaves to continue to work cotton and said so strongly. "Naah, Callie, ain be no need fuh wuk cotton. Fuh wha? Ain gon do da fuh Massa no mo, ain gon do da fuh Yankee ifn dey come roun yuh."

"Naah, Jacob, we do da fuh we sef (*for ourselves*). We speck (*respect*) we sef, dey gon speck we. We keep do good wuk, we gon git speck." Jacob's silence encouraged Callie to continue. "Ain gon be like ol time wid Massa. Don madda wha you do good, you still be slabe en you git treat like slabe. Naah, dis new day. We gon reap wha we sow in dishyuh new life."

She talked with confidence not supported by her knowledge of things to come, but by her hopes. "Look yuh now. We in chaage uh all dishyuh cotton we done grow. We bale em up, sto em so Massa en Yankee kyan (*can't*) see whey dey at. We sell de cotton, da how we gon git wha we need fuh live. Ifn we be smaat, we kin mek money yuh."

"How we gon sell dishyuh cotton?" one of the oldest field hands asked, trying to be respectful to Callie as the youngest in the meeting.

"Ain know da yet, Uncle. Gon fine a way, I know da."

The old man shook his head, but he smiled. Callie had convinced them that even though they no longer had a master telling them to work cotton, it was smart to finish the harvest and prepare bales for storage, because they were worth something. They even were willing to get it done fast, so that the cotton bales could be put out of sight quicker.

★ ★ ★

Later that night, Callie and Lucas were resting on the big house porch, sharing their relief at how things stood so far. Callie had been thinking about Lucas and how easily he got around to so many different places on the water. "Lucas, you know wha be good ting fuh do?"

Lucas said, "Anh-anh, but somebody fix fuh tell me."

"Da be right, lee brudda, you gah fuh lif yo head—see mo dan fish en bait. Be free ain jes bout wedda we pick cotton aw wedda we don pick cotton. Ain jes bout wedda you be boatman aw don be boatman. You gah fuh lif up yo head fuh see wha out deh you kyan see."

Lucas was quick to doubt. "Da don make no sense. See wha you kyan see."

Patiently, Callie urged him. "Try fuh look pass dis day en look pass Oakhaat plantation, mo faah. Wha kin oona do da gon madda fo oona en yo fambly de nex day, en de day afta de nex day?"

Lucas admitted, "Don much tink bout de nex day."

Callie gave the look usually reserved for urgent disciplinary action by Mama Ruth when Lucas was acting out in church.

"Wha da look bout, sista? Why I gah fuh tink bout nex day when ebby day be so haad?

"If oona be smaat like oona tink, you laan fuh read—hep git ready fuh de nex day. Da how you kin git mo smaat en kin show how smaat you be. Den folk listen en heed wha you gah fuh say, specially when you use dey wud—you, not oona."

"Don need fuh read. Wha bout BB? He ain gah no book smaat. Da don mean he ain smaat. He life smaat. He kin lead we people."

"We know BB tek real good kyah right now, but ifn he laan fuh read, he do mo bedda."

"BB do wha he do. Me? I ain one fuh talk out tuh odda folk like BB. I ain one fuh read like oona, Callie. I fish. Da wha I do."

Callie gave Lucas credit for his accomplishments. "Oona good like oona be. Folk know wey dey stan wid oona—dey gon git real good fish, crab en swimp fuh good price, en oona gon be fayah (*fair*) en tell trut."

"So?" Lucas loved his sister but felt she was pushing too much.

His look of boredom did not stop Callie, though. "Whole lotta way fuh use freedom. In de boat, you free fuh go new place. You kin tek deese yuh crik en riba en leh em (*let them*) tek you faah in yo life."

"Yeah, Callie, I kin do da—when I go on de wada, I look fuh wey my life kin go nex." But his tone was not as serious as Callie hoped.

"Da wha I talk bout. See wha you kyan see. Mek nex day be wha you wan fuh be."

"Dey you go wid mo taak bout 'see wha oona kyan see.' Why oona don tek de riba en see wha oona kyan see?" Lucas was pleased with his challenge to Callie.

"Me? Da life ain fuh me. Me en Sunny gon stay roun yuh. But you kin fill yo life wid new ting."

Lucas grew tired of hearing from his big sister, and she saw that, so she slowed down. "I jes say you kin tek wha you know bout dishyuh wada, en mek da wuk fuh you. Folk pay you fuh hep em git round deese islan."

Lucas asked her straight out, "How you know da?"

"I got fait (*faith*) big change staat rounyuh en we kin hep mek de change. We ain gon jes sit en watch."

"You gah da fait, huh?"

"Yeah I do, brudda. Wha bout you?"

Lucas had to be honest with her. "My fait in de good Lawd be skrong, Callie. Da don mean we kin mek de change come. Da be in de han uh de Lawd."

Callie didn't let his doubtful stare stop her. "You use yo fait day by day—e fill yo spirit wid ting you don see. Use yo fait en mek yo nex day betta. Das all I say—see roun da nex turn in de riba, fo you git deh. Same ting in life, ummm-hmmm."

She was done.

And Lucas agreed that she was.

Chapter 15

Sure enough, though, as days passed into weeks and December arrived, Lucas did branch out to distant waterways in his boats, the ones left behind by Daniel Bowen. But he did not have Will as a healthy companion in adventure. Will rebounded from his immediate wounds but contracted an infection while still in a weakened condition. Despite the layers of loving care administered first by Bella, and then by Callie, Eva, and Sunny, Will's illness kept him in various stages of sleep over the next several weeks while his body fought through it.

During this time, Lucas covered long distances around the islands and into the blackwater rivers that flowed down from the mainland. He particularly liked the long dugout canoe with a paddle fashioned on both ends of the oar, allowing rapid strokes from both sides. With it, Lucas moved quickly in his probe of the many creeks and tributaries between Port Royal Sound and St. Helena Sound, discovering the new realities of sea island life under Union occupation.

Twice Lucas was stopped by Union patrol boats, telling officers where he lived and that he was a fisherman. Behaving with the utmost respect, he was allowed to go on each time. His travels showed him where the local ferry points were for islanders crossing the river to Beaufort or connecting with other islands. He discovered that he could, in fact, offer ferry rides to folks and be paid with various foods and goods, sometimes even in money.

He began talking with several members of Union gunboat crews as they met on the river. His answers to their questions about quirks in river currents and best places to catch their food gained their admiration. To his astonishment, he was building relationships with the Yankees—unimaginable just days before.

Lucas did not tell Callie immediately of his pleasure in exploring new creeks, ferrying islanders, and talking with Yankees. He was beginning to see around the bends in the river, and he was enjoying it. By looking hard around a corner, he had discovered unexpected opportunities.

Some people were not as interested in any interactions with Yankees. Through her first weeks at Oakheart, Eva kept herself hidden away in the big house. She was not comfortable in the presence of former slaves, though she preferred them to the Yankees. Callie had asked Eva to limit her time out among the Oakheart people, so she spent many hours singing with Sunny and reading books from Bowen's modest library, away from the new days dawning outside.

Sunny's bright and quick running commentary on the world around her surprised Eva, and she enjoyed answering the little girl's endless questions. Indeed, Eva's presence in Sunny's life was a gift to Callie, and Sunny's giving and inquisitive persona were what Eva needed then to pass through her grief. Eva saw clearly that Sunny's mother had spent many hours with her in thoughtful conversation. The benefits of Callie's love were evident.

But times had surely changed for Callie. Although still Sunny's loving, doting mother, Callie had assigned herself certain tasks in the new days of freedom that took her away from mothering. Eva's arrival at Oakheart enabled Callie's activity. Ever since the big gunshoot, Callie made it her business to visit each family and "household" on the plantation to determine their health and other needs, especially those of the elderly. She finished each day making food or "medicines" for her next day's visits.

For some of the women on the plantation, Callie provided a garment from Missus Bowen's collection. These women had received only one simple dress a year from their master, so they were grateful at the distribution of Missus Bowen's wardrobe. Callie had heard that freed slaves on other plantations were not as fortunate as those at Oakheart, where, with the master's rapid departure, most of the family's clothing and possessions were left behind. On some plantations, the absence of food and clothing made conditions desperate for the newly freed as chill December air enveloped the sea islands.

Callie considered it her main job to make certain that Oakheart people got the help they needed. When not working on those tasks, she cleaned the big house and checked the women she left in charge of the cookhouse and the daily food preparation for plantation residents.

On many occasions over the first month, Callie told Eva how very much she appreciated Eva's affection and patience with Sunny. Eva was complimentary to Callie as well, as Eva scarcely believed how well Oakheart continued to run. They had warm discussions over tea in the big house, as Sunny drifted off to sleep on the daybed beside them.

Once, Callie told Eva that she enjoyed getting to know her mother, even if only for a few days. "Yo mama had skrong spirit whiles huh body been git weak. I kin see you skrong like huh." Callie told Eva about losing Mama Ruth, and even though she was not her real mother, she thought she could not go on without her, and yet she did.

Callie became more direct. "You know my real mama?"

"No, Callie, why would you think so?"

"Yo mama tell me fo she pass she been know my mama. I ain know if da be true or if she jes been talk out huh haid wid feebah (*fever*)."

Eva considered her answer carefully before she began. "I know my father had a lot of slaves come through our dock. He had a long hut down by the marsh creek where people stayed as they were passing through. I always thought he was giving them a place to stay when I was young." Looking at Callie finally, she said, "Then I realized that all the people there were dark-skinned, and some had chains." She stopped, turning away and raising her hand as buffer between them. "I never knew your mother, Callie, and I'm most sure my mother didn't either. She probably was too sick to make sense."

Two days later, Eva asked Callie, "When should I leave Oakheart?"

Callie wondered whether anyone told her she should go. "Anybody say supm bout you—I mean—say you betta leave dishyuh place?"

"Well, no, but I just thought—"

"You know, you be welcome yuh. Ain no need fuh go less da wha you wan fuh do."

"Callie, I'm not sure where I should be. No husband in Charleston. No father here. No mother on this earth."

Callie reached out and took her hand. "Yo place be yuh as long as you wan stay. When you feel yo time come fuh go, go wid wha you feel. You ready fuh go?"

"Don't want to be around those Yankees if they come heah. I know that."

"I gon talk wid Lucas en Will—fine out how dey kin git you back tawd Charleston."

★   ★   ★

Unfortunately, Will was not in a position to afford anyone assistance during most of November 1861. Before the early December nights when his fever peaked, he barely remembered the feel of damp cloth in Callie's cool hands. He had lost weight and looked pale, appearing weak enough to require great attention from his caregivers. The long period of convalescence had allowed Callie and Will to grow closer through their conversation. And just as she did in the days after the Yankee invasion, Callie had begun insisting that Will get out to exercise. Though they both delighted in the walks together, she soon realized that Will had regained the strength he needed to function independently.

Callie began to tell him that he was too well to continue taking hours from her afternoons. But as she spoke, she stumbled over mole mounds in the yard, leaning heavily into Will to prevent a fall. Will caught her, his arms beneath hers for support, but his aim was off. He realized he had a different grip than intended, and he now held the fabric-enclosed flesh he had longed to touch. And just as quickly, he stood her up and backed away. Immediate thoughts filled his head, and his red face told it. Sure that he had done something to offend, he considered confessing to his boorish behavior, at least in his mind. He had only uttered, "I'm sorry," when Callie stopped him.

"I jes glad you been deh fuh cotch me. I been gon say tank you, but now I see how red yo face done turn, maybe bes you pologize." She looked at him again and said, "Ain nuttin bout e be nice, so you bes be sorry." She turned to hide her uncertainty.

Will read her actions as rebuff, and he walked away shaking his head.

Callie stepped quickly to his side to reassure them both that their mutual support remained. "I tank you fuh keep me up same way I do fuh you when you been down. I know you jes cotch me fuh stop me from fall."

Will's relief was immediate and heartfelt. There were many reasons he held Callie in such high esteem. Her kindness and beauty were regular features of his day, and they were having a cumulative effect. He thought her face was the strongest, softest he had ever seen, and when Callie was amused by something, her spirit and smile lifted all those around her. Beyond his personal admiration, though, he respected her journey, most of which he could only surmise. He was in awe of the fully accomplished person Callie had become, overcoming unimaginable outrages her entire life. His considerable regard for her, he reasoned, viewing matters objectively, was rational and high-minded. That respect was complicated by the irrational mental meanderings of a postpubescent, infatuated male.

He realized he had been given a reprieve. While holding Callie may not have been his intention, he was nonetheless thrilled for the occurrence. He now labored to put it from his mind. He stuttered out a few words that sounded like, "You're welcome," and felt slightly faint.

Callie was quick to observe and ask, "How you be now?"

"Feeling dizzy, Callie."

"Might be bes stay in bed one day mo. You don look steady on dem two foot."

After a pause, Will muttered, "No, I feel better—on two feet. In fact, I just learned today how well I am feeling." Callie did not catch his self-absorbed humor as they moved up to chairs on the front porch.

"I been watch sick folk fuh long time now, en I know when I see somebody who don be awright."

Changing the subject from his infirmities, Will said, "My dear nurse, I'll tell you the truth, now that I am healing, uh, healed. I need to get on with it. I've got to get back to the academy. This war is happening now whether I like it or not, and I know which side I'm on."

Callie's look told of her disappointment. "Nobody say you gah fuh rush way from yuh—di-rectly. You ain gah fuh be in dis waw. You done been injuh."

"I owe it to my mates at the academy, and to my training, and to my country. And I owe it to you and Lucas and BB and Bella. I do have to go."

Lucas heard the last words while mounting the steps to the porch, and he did not hesitate to join the conversation. "I know you ain plan fuh go back to da waw. Ain been too many day pass I find you, piece uh Will stew, mix up wid collard en crab in de wada. I ain fish you out jes fuh leh you jump back in." Lucas went on to explain that Will's lingering illness was a classic case of the unseen moving hand of God. "De Lawd wan you fuh stay yuh, res en git well. Lawd say, 'Son, lay down yuh while mo.' Jes like when Him sen me fuh pick you from de riba—da be jes wha de Lawd wan fuh be."

At which point Will, after considering the matter, decided to question the major premise of Lucas's assertion. Will proceeded carefully. "Lucas, do you really think that your God directed you to be there for me? You know I give you all the credit, my man."

"I gib Gawd all de credi, Will. Him de one put me in de wada fuh hep you."

"But your skills and your foolish willingness to risk your life for me is what saved me."

"Dem be gif from Gawd. He protek me en you. You kyan see da?"

"I don't mean to argue with you on such things, Lucas. And I hope you know how much I do respect you and your God." Then Will's thinking meandered on, aloud. "But I just don't see a god being that active, that widespread, like a giant live oak over the world, sheltering all believers. I wish I could act as you do and talk as if that God of yours is real for me—like a lantern to light my path."

Will saw the hurt on his friend's face and went silent, contemplating their situation. Lucas had all the faith in the world and hope for the future, and no apparent basis for either. Will had the blessings of wealth and education, but no faith in God. One man was steeped in the Christian word, the other unable to embrace its peace.

Will felt the need to say more in explanation of his beliefs. "I never could understand my mother's brand of Christianity. I respected her faith and how she practiced it, and yet she was able to condone slavery, to live with Daniel Bowen as he behaved in a most un-Christian fashion. So, since I saw their religion manifest itself in the worst kind of treatment of human beings, I grew to distrust my mother's religious beliefs."

Lucas earnestly sought to understand. "Dey jes ain follah de way de Lawd set down, das all. Jes cause dey ain do right, da don mek de wod uh de Lawd wrong."

"Well, the combination of Christianity and slavery created such a feeling in my gut that I just could not accept either. And when I went to the academy, I studied philosophers and the men who founded our country. The best way I can explain my beliefs right now is by what Thomas Paine said—something like, 'My mind is my religion, and I just seek to do good.'"

Lucas absorbed this and then responded, "You ain de onliest one wha use e mind. I use my mind too, brudda. I jes know in my haat wha my Gawd tell my mind fuh do."

Will quickly jumped in. "And I know the same in my head. If we both do the same good deed, does it make a difference why?"

Lucas thought and started to agree but then said, "Da be why I like you. You don taak tuh my Gawd, but da don stop me from know whey you stand." They shook hands, holding at the wrists, cementing mutual lifelong understandings.

"Speaking of getting things done together, I was just telling your sister that I owe you both, and that I am going to do something to repay you."

"Owe me?" Lucas asked.

Callie chimed in. "Wha you owe we?"

Will was emphatic. "You mean besides my health, my life? I've been thinking. I want to help you both, and BB, and everybody here. I think I can sell your cotton up north. I want to take it before anybody else gets to it. They'll find wherever you hide it, eventually. Either that or Bowen will come back and burn it—that's been happening around these islands, you know. Be best if I take it up north and get a better price up there. I will bring the money back to you."

Callie shared her news about Eva. "Now you be the second person talk bout leave. Eva wan go back tawd Charleston."

"Well, I can't help her with that. I am quite sure I won't be going to Charleston."

Lucas quickly said, "Ain nobody gon leave yuh lessn (*unless*) Yankee leh you leave. Mo en mo uh dem Yankee out on de wada."

"Well, I'm not ready to go just yet. I still need to find where my mother went with Captain Bowen. Any news, Lucas?"

"Ain been look fuh needuh one uh dem. You kin go wid me fuh git Eva wey she wan go, en den we kin figyuh bout yo mama." A look of amused brilliance came across Lucas's face. "We kin look roun da ben in de riba en see wha we kyan see."

He turned to see his sister, who broke out laughing despite her attempts to stifle it. "Da right, brudda, tek yosef roun de ben en see wha you kyan see."

Lucas's laughter continued as he clearly was enjoying the moment more than Callie.

She protested. "You mek fun uh me, brudda, when all I try fuh do be talk sense en yo haid, en laan fuh taak betta wid (*and learn to talk better with*) de white folk. Da way, dey know betta wha we tink. Like right now, we taak wid Will bout how fuh git Eva back home, en how fuh mek Will stay yuh."

Lucas relented. "Awright, we gon tek her, den we gon fine Missus Bowen—we gon see wha we kyan see, right, Callie?" Lucas couldn't stop himself from making one more joke.

*   *   *

Lucas and Will launched the dual-purpose river trip around midnight a few days later, with Eva and a few of her possessions perched between them in the long dugout canoe. They were optimistic, despite the uncertainty about their mission. They accomplished little other than to deliver Eva to an accessible shore, suggesting to her that the Confederates were reported to be just up the road a bit through the pines. From the rickety dock where they left her and with the assistance of others, Eva expected to make her way back to Charleston.

From there, they moved forward on sparse information. Lucas had received a vague description from one oarsman at Oakheart who had taken Massa to hunt foxes on a mainland plantation several years ago. Lucas had already steered past expected large bends in the river and literally did not know what lay beyond. It was cold, and there was no sign of a major plantation along the flat, wide river.

Will and Lucas came to realize that there was little prospect of finding Will's mother, and that they were moving into very risky territory. Lucas's capture would return him to slavery; Will could be treated as spy or deserter, or both. With no Yankee gunboats in sight, there was little assurance that Confederates were not waiting to rush from a tree-shrouded cove. As each new bend in the river felt more threatening, Will conceded that the possible consequences of their venture were not worth the chance of their success. Lucas concurred, assuring Will that he would remember the river bends they navigated that night. As they turned toward the southeastern horizon, Will looked back to the dark, flat riverbed they left behind, resigned not to know of his mother's safety or location.

In the first glimmer of morning light, they slowed their rowing to a fisherman's pace as they came back down the river, quietly passing Beaufort. Through the low haze hanging on the water, they saw Union troop transports tied at the wharf. Floating farther downriver, they could see lines of troops on Bay Street, moving south. Clearly, overnight the Yankees had made a move into Beaufort.

Will pulled his hat low over his eyes as he quickly cast a fishing line. While Lucas steered their dugout canoe to the far side of the river away from the docks, he provided reassuring waves to any Yankee sailors looking their way. Lucas did not hide his pleasure at the moment. "Ain neba tink dis ting kin come about. Plantaman out. Yankee in. Ain neba tink da. But da wha I see yuh."

Will said, "I have never doubted they could take this area or, for that matter, win the war eventually." His assertion of Union victory was based more on enthusiasm than information. In fact, from what had been reported during the first six months of fighting, it was clear that the war was not going well for the Union. But Will's perspective was that of the US Navy, which expected to establish a clear dominance in force along most of the Atlantic Coast.

They rowed back to Oakheart in silence, the sliver of new moon grinning at them. Upon their exhausted return, they confirmed to Callie that Eva had been delivered safely up the Combahee River. Then they spread the word that Union forces had entered Beaufort in strength.

Chapter 16

Will smiled to himself as he drifted off to sleep after Lucas and he returned that night. His philosophy of just wanting and trying to do right was now being played out before him by the might of his country. Slavery here had ended. It took the will and force of the Union, raised against the Confederacy, to make it so. The freedoms he was privileged to witness compelled him to rejoin his "classmates" and take his place in the war.

Then, through a thickening haze, Will's mind began assessing the alignment of forces as if in an academy exam. He reasoned that though the war might not be going so well for the North at that time, the Union had captured the region's best deep-water port and, with it, the ability to throttle Confederate trade. Through fully closed eyelids, he saw again the flickering lights of Union campfires dotting the Beaufort bluffs early that morning as he and Lucas floated by quietly on the far side of the bay.

The next morning, Lucas went fishing near the mouth of Port Royal Sound, away from Beaufort. He observed intense activity by Union forces at the docks on the north end of Hilton Head Island. Large transport ships lined up out into the ocean to offload troops, supplies, and construction materials. While scanning the area near the remains of Fort Walker, Lucas watched several small boats growing larger as they crossed the sound in his direction. As he hastily rowed back up the river toward Beaufort and then up Chowan Creek, the Union boats docked at Lands End, the southwest corner of St. Helena Island.

Over the next several weeks, Union soldiers spread throughout the islands, as ubiquitous as grackles in a spring migration, with their shoulders glistening iridescent blue. Troops visited each plantation, requisitioned "supplies" as needed, and asked about owners and other island residents. Though Union soldiers brought the message of freedom, former slaves usually stayed out of sight while they were nearby.

All contact was not avoidable, however, and on Oakheart, Callie and BB were heartened by the kind demeanor of the army captain who conducted an orderly entry onto the plantation. However, after the troops had camped there for several days, there were allegations that the acquisition of supplies was not always carried out in the good manner exemplified by the captain.

Old Bella surprised Union troops leaving her shanty, taking spices from the only shelf where she could store such things. She surprised them a second time when she said: "You boys ain gah fuh tief (*steal*) from me. If oona need dis, I gib oona. If oona belly ain full, we gib oona food fuh eat."

The soldiers received her forgiveness without celebration but thanked her for her kindness and started to leave.

Bella then asked, "If oona tek dem dry leaf wha season de pot, pot ain gon tase so good. Leave me da en I kin cook up supm gon mek finga git lick en mout say tank you."

Confronted as they were with a tiny, dark woman acting feisty and benevolent, they acceded to her request, muttering to themselves as they walked away. Bella called out to them, "Oona wan eat dishyuh day, I cook fish fuh oona. Nex day, come yuh dayclean en you laan how fuh git dem fish out de wada. Den I show oona how fuh cook em up jes right."

★　★　★

On river trips throughout December, Lucas saw more blue-clad soldiers filling camps around the outskirts of town, so that Beaufort was securely surrounded either by Union troops or salt water. Officers moved their commands into the substantial dwellings along Bay Street, constructing perches atop the highest with the best sightline down the Beaufort River.

The spread of Union forces brought many "visitors" to the sea islands of Hilton Head, St. Helena, and Port Royal. Hundreds of slaves took small boats, waded through marshes, swam, and hiked through pluff mud at low tide—seeking the freedom conveyed by the Yankee presence. The pace of these arrivals accelerated after mid-December, 1861, when Confederate General Robert E. Lee, assigned to bolster the defense of the Savannah–Charleston railway, authorized confiscation of property, including slaves, to support the work. When mainland plantation slaves learned that the Confederates would use their labor to help defend the rail line, many more still enslaved near the coast sought the safe haven of the Union-occupied islands.

Just after General Lee issued his order to "requisition" slave labor in defense of the Confederacy, the US government sent representatives south to visit the region and learn how best to take advantage of the opportunities presented. Colonel William Reynolds arrived in Beaufort on December 20, directed by Secretary of the Treasury Salmon Chase to collect "contraband" cotton from the Confederacy and ship it north for sale.

Weeks before, the free Africans of Oakheart decided to complete the cotton harvest, ginning, baling, and storing. Callie had convinced them that it would be worth something to somebody, and they intended that "somebody" to be themselves. They used the cotton barn, but they stacked the bales high on the front rows, blocking the view of empty storage space behind. Remaining bales, nearly half the harvest, were hidden in new storage space on the far side of the fields, dug into a bluff over the river.

When Colonel Reynolds passed through the plantation just before Christmas, he made clear that the US government intended to "complete" the cotton harvest, with the cooperation and labor of the plantation's field workers. He directed Callie to gather the slaves on the front yard of the big house, where he spoke from the porch stairs about his expectation of full cooperation on the cotton harvest for the good of the war effort.

Standing next to the colonel one stair down, Callie collected her thoughts and made her best effort yet at speaking in the words and cadences of the white people she was getting to know. "I promise you, Colonel, that Oakhaat folk wuk cotton bes we kin, suh." And when Colonel Reynolds said that they might be paid for their assistance with spring planting as well, at first Callie hesitated. But before anyone else could speak, she said, "We do same wuk ebby spring when we slave wid no pay. Yankee can be sho we people wuk for you now. You give us pay for wuk, we too thankful, suh." Satisfied and smiling, Colonel Reynolds descended the stairs briskly to his horse. As he spurred his mount to a trot, the freed people of Oakheart smiled, nodded, and waved, as urged by Callie and BB, knowing their cotton deception was underway.

★　★　★

But confusion lingered for two of the oldest field workers who argued with Callie following the meeting with Colonel Reynolds. They questioned why Callie and BB had just promised to deliver their cotton harvest to the Yankees after Christmas.

One man asked: "Jes like befo wid Massa, all de Yankee kyah bout be cotton. Wha bout we people da been pick de cotton?"

The other chimed in. "Wha we gon pick cotton fuh? Massa gone. Yankee ain no massa. We gah fuh tek kyah uh we famly. (*We've got to take care of our family.*) We gah fuh grow crop fuh eat."

BB said halfheartedly, "Now, we gon git pay fuh wuk cotton."

Callie quickly added: "We still gah time fuh famly en wuk cotton fuh hep Yankee. I don be happy wid all wha go on roun yuh, but I tank Gawd de Yankee set we free."

The old man reasoned: "If e be fuh dem da set we free—if da mek ole Abe Linkum happy, e be awright. Sides, don want no mo worriation."

Those persuasive words were enough for his friend. "Ga fuh gib Gawd de glory! Dis be time uh yeah fuh celebrate Jedus's birt, and say tank ya Jedus—now no mo be slave."

Indeed it was a special Christmastime in 1861. With wariness matched by gratitude, they began to follow Bella's example to interact with the Yankees, these blue angels who carried out the work of a most merciful God by setting the slaves free.

Perhaps it was the spirit of the season, but the presence of Union troops at Oakheart had become more comfortable, to the point that former slaves began to share a few of their secrets. For the freedom and protection they provided, Yankee troops were taught the intricacies of slinging castnets over the water to gather unsuspecting fish below, baiting areas to draw shrimp close for the castnets to work, and raking up oysters from just below the high-tide line along the marsh banks.

After one particularly succulent noontime meal, including oysters freshly raked from the pluff mud by the freedmen, the troops were lounging on the riverbank interspersed with freedmen who had shared both their food and some tips on catching it. A sergeant rubbed his stomach as he leaned back into the bank, face to the sun. "So you folks don't go hungry down here, do you?"

"Naw suh, we be mighty fine. Long as eyeschuh don run, en crab en swimp do (*as long as oysters don't run, and crab and shrimp do*). Mix da up wid hominy, en yas suh, we people be mighty fine." Then the fisherman added: "Eben en slabe time, afta we git we tas (*tasks*) done, deh be time fuh we sef. We feed all de buckra en still git plenty fuh we sef, ummm-hmmm."

* * *

Despite the pleasantries, it was clear who was in charge. Callie and BB understood that it was necessary to appear to be in complete compliance with the troops occupying the land. The Union forces intended to control the plantations and their production. Callie and BB also realized that, with more Union troops and vessels about, it was more likely that their cotton stores would be found, and it would be less likely that they could get the bales of cotton out on the river undetected.

Will had recovered but remained out of sight during the holidays when Union troops were around the plantation. He became less cautious after they left, and one day in mid-January, while crossing the courtyard to the kitchen, he did not hide at the sound of horses pounding up the lane. Two Union soldiers, part of a larger detail, dismounted and approached Will directly. They grabbed his arms behind him and briskly questioned who he was and what he was doing at Oakheart.

Callie appeared on the back porch of the big house, shouting, "Gentleman, please do not touch this patient." She hesitated slightly, remembering Julia Bowen's reference to one of Daniel Bowen's brothers who had died of tuberculosis. "He has contagious … consumption, and cain't be touched at all." Callie's demeanor was a fairly solid impersonation of a Southern matron serving as head nurse of a hospital ward.

The Union soldiers withdrew abruptly from the front yard with apologies to Will, and a tip of their caps to the "medical officer" on the porch. As they left the front yard, a bemused man in long civilian overcoat tied his horse to the fence and walked slowly toward Will, so as not to disturb the scene. Extending his hand, he offered, "Greetings from the United States government. I am Edward Pierce, representing Treasury Secretary Salmon Chase."

Will was stunned and moved quickly to shake his hand. "Good day to you, sir. It is a pleasure to meet you. I highly regard Secretary Chase, sir. I had the pleasure to hear him speak at the Naval Academy earlier this year."

"Is that right? Very good." Gesturing to the front porch where Callie had stood her ground against the Union soldiers, he said, "That was a very impressive display. Where is she from?"

"Well, sir. You are standing on her home soil. She is one of several who have been in charge of this place ever since the planters ran off."

"Well, isn't that something?" Pierce was genuinely impressed. "And you are?"

"Pardon me, sir, how could I be so impolite to not introduce myself? I am Will Hewitt, fourth-year midshipman."

"Will, I am anxious to hear any stories you may tell of this beautiful land and its people," he said, again gesturing to the porch, "but first I just have to ask, what are you doing here, if not attached to any Union military outfit?"

After Will explained briefly how he came to be "stranded" on this plantation and his intention to return to duty, Pierce described the task assigned to him by the treasury secretary. He was to study the situation on the islands and recommend what to do with thousands of newly freed slaves whom the government considered contraband of war and neither slave nor free.

Will quickly realized he could help steer Pierce's inquiry, to last only several weeks, and perhaps improve the response of the US government to the conditions of the people of St. Helena Island. Will spoke strongly on their behalf. "These people are courageous, smart, strong willed. They are so able—clever at tackling problems, finding a way to do things. They believe in themselves and in their God. I hear from them every day that their faith made them certain that they would be free one day."

Pierce listened intently, nodding frequently.

"They now need help in becoming citizens of our country, and because of what we allowed to be done to them, we owe them at least that much. Mr. Pierce, please make sure there are no obstacles, legal or educational, in the way of their march out of bondage to freedom."

"Well, young Will, I must say, that sounds much like some politicians I have heard, more eloquent than most. What is your family name, again?"

"Hewitt, sir, Will Hewitt."

"I know a Harris Hewitt—fine sailor in Annapolis—are you related?"

Will grinned and nodded.

Pierce smiled, "Father or uncle?"

"Ah, my uncle, sir, and an inspiration to me."

Pierce offered to take Will back to Washington with him and promised that he would assist in Will's career in any way he could. It was then that Will saw the cotton solution. He asked if Pierce would write a pass that would allow him to take a boat through the Union blockade for his Uncle Harris. Will decided to be more honest, informing Pierce that he also intended to transport cotton and to return any profit to the people of Oakheart Plantation.

Pierce disapproved governmentally but realized Will's intentions were just. After meeting Callie and her brothers, not only did Edward Pierce write Will's pass, he offered to assist the family if any of them should ever come to Washington.

With the arrival at Oakheart of this fine civilian agent of the government, Oakheart's "cotton problem" was solved. Soon questions about next steps were flying between Will, Callie, BB, and Lucas as they set their cotton plan in motion.

It was just a week after Edward Pierce returned to Washington that Will made final preparations to leave for the North. The sloop chosen for the journey was made to the specifictions of a Northern buyer who would never see it. It was small enough to be managed by one man, sleek enough to make the run north some five hundred miles, sturdy enough for hard sailing, and large enough in its hold to carry six bales of the finest sea island, long-fiber cotton, with four more balanced fore and aft on deck.

Will argued repetitively with Lucas trying to make him understand that he did not need help sailing north, and that the pass Pierce wrote was only for him as a solo sailor. Will tried to convince Lucas that he had important work to do at the plantation with Callie and BB and on the water where his talent fed so many.

In the course of several days' debate, Lucas revealed that he had begun assisting Union captains. For weeks, their patrol boats had run aground on low-tide shoals that the captains had not anticipated. When Lucas said he was out fishing, instead, many times he was piloting

Union captains around dangerous spots on the waterways around the islands. Lucas said he also showed the Yankees places on mainland shores where hidden Confederate docks might exist.

Lucas gained the confidence of Union officers who asked him to help assemble available flatboats for cotton transport from nearby plantations. He even helped pole one of those flatboats up the Broad River toward Gardens Corner, carrying army troops for a raid against the Confederates on New Year's Eve. Lucas was proud as he told Will his story, but his eyes widened and saddened as he described the wounded men he saw, one of whom died next to him as he helped row the raiders back to the less dangerous waters of Port Royal Sound.

On hearing his experiences, Will said, "Then you understand better than anybody why I have to go. This fight is worth having, for our country and for men like that willing to die. And for you and BB and Callie and thousands more."

Lucas nodded, giving his friend permission to return to war.

Callie did not want Will to go and made her feelings clear, though they were not exactly clear to her. She felt protective toward him and appreciated his commitment to do the right thing, even though she questioned his decision.

Will was completely certain now, and he used Callie as an example of why he had to go. "You've shown me that one person can make it better for others. I've thought that but done nothing. And now it's time. Right now, for me, that means trying to get Oakheart cotton up to Northern markets and bringing the profit back to you all down here."

When Callie was still not in favor of his plans, Will said, "You and BB trust me? You know I will come back with your money, don't you?"

At that, Callie shook her head and drew Will to her. "Fo sho, we trus you. It just, you been such hep to us and, you know, we ... we kyah bout you."

Will kissed Callie on her forehead. "I care too, Callie. More than you know. That's why I must take your cotton now and do my duty in this war." With that, he was off to make a special round of good-bye visits, lingering with Bella and Sunny.

Callie and Lucas each had time with Will before he left, helping move ten cotton bales onto the sloop and leaving just enough room for Will to stretch out for all-too-brief moments of rest on his journey. The moment of departure had been preceded by many prolonged discussions and attenuated good-bye hugs. They were both at the riverbank on the far side of the cotton fields, just down from the secret storage shed, to help Will push off into a flood tide on Chowan Creek.

As the nearly full moon set hours before dayclean, they watched Will go around the creek bank toward the river, and craned their necks to see what they could no longer see. Callie wiped tears from both eyes as she stood with Lucas, brother and sister, arm-in-arm in the parting.

Chapter 17

Just as the island people adapted to the prolonged northwest winds in the winter of 1862, they made their adjustments to the needs and intrusions of the Yankee presence. They were free, but they were subject to the order and direction of the Union military. The soldiers had made themselves both a blessing and a problem with persistent demands for food and labor. Though they learned the ways of harvesting from the surrounding sea, they also depleted plantations of corn, sweet potatoes, rice, and winter kale. As cold days dragged on, and barren fields turned to brown mud from strong coastal storms, supplies dwindled and life grew more harsh and uncertain.

Large numbers of freedmen began working with the army engineers on Hilton Head Island, and at Lands End on St. Helena Island, building docks and a network of roadways. An endless stream of navy and merchant ships, anchored side-by-side in Port Royal Sound, waited to unload cargoes of coal, weapons, supplies, and more troops. More transport vessels lined up in the Atlantic Ocean waiting to enter the harbor.

Pierce was true to his word, reporting the needs of the South Carolina freedmen to Secretary Chase in early February 1862. His recommendations included paying wages for cotton production work and educating those who had been kept illiterate. Pierce's report coincided with the request of the Union military command at Port Royal for managers and teachers on the plantations.

Soon, more than fifty "missionaries" descended on the islands, most of them previously affiliated with efforts to abolish slavery. Coming from Boston, New York, and Philadelphia, they were intent on providing support and help to former slaves. By the end of March, most missionaries were assigned as plantation superintendents. Freedmen were suspicious of this new group of Northern white people now given the authority to manage their plantations. The US military had concerns as well.

*   *   *

For those who worked the land and lived from its production, spring was always a time of hope for new growth and bountiful crops. Cleansing winds and rains accompanied strong storms out of the northwest. When the last of the live oak leaves fell to earth, spring buds immediately filled the branches of these twisting behemoths. A sheltering cover of mint-green leaves formed just prior to the onset of summer heat.

On Constant Island, BB always welcomed the challenging newness of spring. The Oakheart slaves had a reputation of being willing to work long hours to get crops in on time. This year, they knew that if the farming work was well done, all would share the benefits. BB, Callie, and Lucas would have welcomed the arrival of a Northern superintendent to demonstrate their abilities and accomplishments. They had kept the plantation operating quite well, and they would have been proud to show anyone how they managed their own work with no external direction. They would point to the cooperation of most hands, from farming and fishing to food preparation, working to meet the needs of all in the community.

They achieved this during those first months of freedom, despite the fact that army troops confiscated much of the harvest during the winter of 1862. In this regard, Oakheart's experience with the Union army was common across the islands. Former slaves had endured the tyranny of their masters all their lives, and now they learned the cold reality of "freedom" under military control in a few short months.

By mid-April, when most of the superintendents were in place on other plantations, Oakheart still did not have one, for unknown reasons. A kind army captain informed Callie that Oakheart would be supervised by the new missus on Oaks Plantation, just up the creek from Constant Island. Callie was pleased. By then, she had heard that lessons for children from several plantations had already begun at Oaks. Though she was proud of what she had taught Sunny, she was determined to get her daughter the best schooling available near Constant Island.

Callie rowed herself up Chowan Creek a short distance to the Oaks Plantation. Walking onto the grounds from the dock, she was surprised to see a young missus in the yard feverishly scrubbing several dresses, muttering that they were not fit to give away. Callie approached with great caution.

"Pardon, missus. I been hopin my daughta could git some schoolin and dey say you might be teachin heah."

"Indeed we are, young lady. And who might you be?"

"Callie, missus—heah for my baby girl, Sunny."

"And I am Laura Towne, and I hope your Sunny will be with us on the porch most mornings to learn her letters."

"Mean no disrespek, but my baby awready know de letters."

Miss Towne lifted her kind but serious face to study her visitor more closely. She ushered Callie into the garden area and offered her a seat before entering into a long conversation. Miss Towne explained that because two missionaries had returned north, there simply were not enough to assign one to each plantation. Her supervisor believed that since Oakheart was being well managed by the freed people living there, it could go on without a superintendent. Miss Towne was stunned as she realized that it was this wonderful young woman and her two brothers who had accomplished so much. The more Laura Towne and Callie Bowen talked, the more impressed they became with each other.

Miss Towne told Callie that the Oaks Plantation was to be the center of relief operations for the islands and that the Union military would also use it to host visitors. Miss Towne spoke of her determination to provide education, clothing, and medical care to those who had been denied basic humane treatment during their lives. She ended her small speech with the statement: "We have come to do antislavery work, and we think it is noble work and we mean to do it earnestly." **

Callie was completely in awe of Miss Towne, and that made it harder for her to say, "Well, missus—you might be a lee too late. Slavery done awready end heah now."

Towne laughed heartily and took Callie's hand. "Of course you are right. All my adult life I have worked to abolish slavery. Now we must decide together what the next steps are, now that, here at least, slavery is no more."

"Honest, missus. I neba know somebody white believe in freedom for us all huh life. Neba know dere been people like you."

★ ★ ★

Within weeks of Miss Towne's arrival, it became clear to all in the sea islands that she was full of energy and resolve. She got things done! Clothing from the North was distributed, classes for children were started, and most important, medical care was provided.

Callie was amazed. Just as she knew the local healing roots and special concoctions to cure the ills of the islanders, Miss Towne knew natural remedies from all over the world. At the end of their first visit, Callie invited Miss Towne to Constant Island to treat some people whose maladies were beyond her own knowledge.

Miss Towne agreed and asked Callie for a favor. "I really want to go to all your neighbors on nearby plantations, you know, to see what they might need. Would you help me do that? It would mean so much to see you coming with me ... put people at ease. You do that rather well for such a young lady."

Callie felt honored and immediately agreed. Miss Towne asked her to row over the following Monday morning so they could ride together in a carriage. Callie knew that Miss Towne was part of the answer to her prayers—to find ways to help more people in these troubled times. She had started with those on her own plantation and was thrilled to be asked to cover a little more ground.

That Monday, before they even left Oaks Plantation, Callie told her new friend that she had heard some stories about things that happened to slaves at the Oaks. Troubled, Miss Towne asked her cook, Susannah, to join them in the garden.

Though Miss Towne had been working with Susannah for several weeks, she had not yet heard many details about the treatment of slaves there. The direct question from Miss Towne, coupled with Callie's presence, encouraged Susannah to start her story. Soon, Susannah removed her flour-caked apron and settled her ample frame on the garden bench. They did not leave Oaks that day.

Susannah said, "Massa been mean en haad to him slave—ain gib no shoe, salt, mlasses, or clothes fuh Sundy. Ain gib no meat, ain leh we raise pig—he whip we plenty. Massa be scaid Yankee come, so he keep all we in fiel from sunup till sun go down, en ain day go by we don git lash." ★★

Her voice trailed off. "Da wha you wan fuh yeddy (*hear*), missus?"

Miss Towne explained that she hoped to never hear the awful realities of slavery, but the truth should be known to all.

"If anyone wanted to tell it," Callie reckoned aloud, "someone should be ready to listen."

Encouraged, Susannah carried on, describing how she avoided being whipped as an adult. "I tell Massa e don do no good fuh lash me. I splain nex time I do bedda. Jes leh me know wha you wan me fuh do en I do da. I tek pride in wuh I do, and da be wha mek me do right—lash don mek me wuk." ★★

She told us once when her master finally let her raise pigs, he threatened to shoot them to discipline her. "I holla, 'No, Massa, you kyan do da. How we gon git salt ifn oona shoot pig? How we gon git shoe fuh we chirrun when e col?' Ain shoot pig da day." ★★

And then she left even Callie speechless with the next disclosure. Susannah birthed twenty-two children but was only allowed to raise three boys, until they, too, were sent away from her. Master let one come back from his son's plantation when Susannah was very sick, but he told her that as soon as she was well again, the boy would have to go. Susannah looked up from relating her story, and saw both Callie and Miss Towne weeping. Quickly, as had been her fashion, she rose up and enveloped them both in her large arms, so that the three could cry together.

As Callie prepared to leave later in the afternoon, she promised Miss Towne that after she had a couple of days at Oakheart with her daughter, they could schedule another time to go out visiting. They committed to meeting again the next Monday.

On the carriage ride over to the north side of St. Helena that Monday morning, they came across an old man slowly walking the road. His shoes were more worn than the tattered hat he lifted to the ladies. Miss Towne stopped to ask, "Good sir, how are you getting along? I work with the government's relief effort," she said. "What can I do for you?"

To which he promptly replied, "Dey say govment fight fuh we so we wuk fuh govment. We ain aks fuh money. We jes wan clothes en salt en sweetins. I been born slabe, mahm, and now sence govment fight fuh me, I wuk fuh govment. I do da, en welcome." **

Miss Towne exclaimed on driving away from this humble, gentle man, that the trust and kindness he and others had displayed, after having been through so much, utterly overwhelmed her. Laura Towne explained that she had great respect for the island people. She said, "These poor, anxious people have lived on promises and are starving for clothes and food while patiently working for the government." ** It made her know that this was the job she was meant to do and that she must work harder at it.

They ventured nearly all the way out to the Jenkins and Edding places, passing some of the most awful conditions. As Laura Towne rode, she spoke, "These wretched hovels with their wooden chimneys and the general squalor show the former misery." **

Just as they were looking at one place, with its gaps in the walls that let winter winds go straight through, a woman emerged, giving praise to God, her arms stretched up to the sky. She shouted: "De change wha come wid Yankee be like Gawd done sen anodda Moses down yuh fuh lead us oudda bondage. E be like heaben on eart en eart in heaben now." ** She continued shouting her praise as the carriage rolled on, nearing the end of the road at St. Helena Sound.

There they saw a woman who told them her two children had been whipped to death, and as they looked at the group of former slaves, surely it was true. There was none without welts. The woman went on. "One baby, two, shree, fo baby don been kill in me from whip. When I been mos hebby wid chile, massa mek me wuk jes like fiel han." **

Laura Towne asked Callie why the woman cried so hard now. Callie and the woman talked awhile before Callie explained, "She cry cause she tink maybe you tink she a bad mama, on account uh she let so many baby go."

The woman pleaded. "I try haad fuh keep dem two lee boy in line, tell all de time fuh ack (*act*) right. Bu dey be up tuh mischief—da mek Massa trade em way."

Laura Towne shook her head, sad that this woman could be left feeling guilty for the awful things that had been done to her. As Miss Towne completed her physical examination of the woman with an embrace, she walked away, speaking to no one in particular. "How could any man, any one, be so cruel?"

Most of the way back to the main road, Callie and Miss Towne rode in silence. Finally, Callie could hold it no longer. "Missus, da back dere be worse than I ebba hear, and I done see and heah some bad ting." She reached over to touch Miss Towne's arm. "I too sorry you had to heah all da sadness."

Miss Towne drew the carriage to a stop. She turned to Callie, reaching both arms around her. "I am so sorry that you and your neighbors had to live through all that."

As they reached the main road, they met Mr. Boutwell, whose work surveying the coastline made him a frequent visitor at Oaks, even before the war. "Mr. Boutwell," Miss Towne started, "we just heard some of the worst imaginable things today. I never knew how badly slaves were treated."

Mr. Boutwell described what he had seen on his trips up and down the coast, visiting with many a planter and fisherman. He told Miss

Towne that "the St. Helena people were hard, and not considered well educated or good specimens of planters" and "that they were hard to their Negroes," especially at Oaks where Miss Towne lived now. **

Mr. Boutwell had come to be known as a reliable source of information around the islands. That day, he told of a current problem out on the old Coffin Point Plantation, where two men refused to work the required four hours a day on cotton. Instead they wanted to work their own crops all the time.

Callie had heard the story and told Miss Towne that the same thing happened at Oakheart, only BB had handled it in a good way. BB listened to the complaints of some of his most reliable workers, wanting to work their own fields, go fishing, take care of their families, and not tend anybody's cotton. Callie told about BB's solution, as she heard it just the night before.

"Shree young men come to him firs. BB meet wit em to work it out. Then he watch em fa shree days. Two uh them work haad on cotton and do many different job. The other one didn't do so much—work, anyway. He lay up with some ooman down by the riba bank one day, sleep through mos of the nex. When they come back for the ansa, BB stan up for the two men, defen dey right fa full pay en rations. They work half time in their own fiel or boat en half time in the cotton fiel to earn money. We work togedda so there be more for ebbybody at Oakhaat to shaya."

"So what did BB say to the third man?"

"BB jes look at this man same way Mama Ruth look at him in chuuch on many a day. When the meetin ova, BB call him en splain wha he see—tell the man not to be so triflin and to stand up for hissef wit de trut. Nex day, man left plantation like his freedom say he can." To conclude her story, Callie said, "Seem to me BB got ebbybody in those fiel behind him since he stan up for dem wha do de wuk. They even wuk cotton part time when he aks—no problem. I got even more respek for BB than been have befo."

*   *   *

Miss Towne and Callie arrived back at Oaks to find BB waiting to take Callie home. The wind had come up so strong that he decided to row a bigger boat up the creek, pick up Callie, and tow her dingy back to Oakheart. Callie introduced BB to Miss Towne, who was quick to refer to the story Callie just shared. "Excellent work, young man. Sounds like you can lead the people of your plantation to do good things. Good luck to you."

"I wuk dis lan all my life. So good fuh git my finga in dishyuh dut, toe too—lov fuh mek crop jump out de groun."

Callie said, "Watch out, Miss Towne. Betta tek yo seat. I kin tell BB got supm to say."

BB barely slowed down. "Ain madda how much I love de lan. I jine up wid de Yankee right quick ifn I kin fight gainst de buckra planta. Ain right dey hole we people, whip we, en sell off famly. Jes wan chance fuh fight em—fight fuh my ownt freedom."

Laura Towne listened in awe to the passion and marveled at the character on display before her.

"Like I tell Oakhaat people, ifn I kyan fight fuh my freedom right now, I sho kin hep dem wha mek we free. I kin wuk fuh Yankee en be proud—don mine pick cotton sence now we git pay."

"If it is a matter of more pay, well, the government has limitations, I'm afraid," Miss Towne said.

"No, mahm. Ain bout de pay. We sho be proud fuh git pay fuh we wuk. We ain de kine fuh jes play en do nuttin, when we kin wuk fuh tek kyah uh we sef en we famly. Been da way befo, en be da way now."

Then BB paused and decided to return to the subject first raised by Miss Towne. "Deh be some young buck say dey ain gon wuk no mo cotton. Dey say we free now sence big gun shoot. Da mean we ain gah fuh wuk cotton. I stan up fuh wuk wid Yankee, but dem young folk mek some sense. We wan grow crop fuh eat, ketch fish, mek net—da way we kin mek ting bedda. Missus, kin see da? Massa gone—we don wuk fuh no massa—govmint ain no massa—Abe Linkum ain no massa needuh, right, missus?"

Miss Towne answered: "You're right, Abraham Lincoln is no master for sure, for he wants to pay you for your work. You work some on your own vegetables, fish, home, whatever to make your life better. But you work tasks in cotton and get money from President Lincoln, the US government. You don't have to work for a master ever again, and you work for yourselves some too. Is that better?"

BB nodded, though only partly satisfied.

Miss Towne added, "On some plantations, they were saying to people, unless you work some cotton, there won't be any more education. And you know what happened? That made some people come to the cotton fields so that they could get their schooling."

"No need fuh say da yuh, missus. We been know education be wha madda. Folk know ifn dey git some education, da wha gon hep dem down de road. We wuk cotton now fuh Yankee cause dey been good tuh we people."

"Sounds like you earned your respect, BB," said Miss Towne.

"Yes, missus, he did," said Callie as BB kept his head down.

Because of their apparent full cooperation with the US government, neither BB nor Callie were comfortable with their deception about shipping some Oakheart cotton north with Will. But everything else BB said about willingness to work for and fight for the Yankees was true. That would have to be enough truth for the moment. Besides, they reasoned, the cotton secret allowed the money for the cotton work done at Oakheart to go to the people who did that work, and was therefore, a righteous secret worth keeping.

** Denotes quotes and Gullah adaptations of actual quotes or phrases from *Letters and Diary of Laura M. Towne*, ed. Rupert Sargent Holland (1912; repr., Salem, MA: Higginson Book Company, 2007). The passages are from Laura Towne's diary. Some are adapted into spoken Gullah by the Gullah translator for this book. While Callie's presence is fictional, these descriptions of slavery are taken directly from slave stories Laura Towne was told 150 years ago.

Chapter 18

Days later, Callie, BB, and Lucas reaped the harvest of their deception. Will returned, looking resplendent in his navy blue fine-flannel jacket, the small gold cord on the collar signifying his ascension from midshipman to ensign. The captain allowed him two days' leave from the ship while it was anchored at Hilton Head Island to take on coal and supplies—Will had promised to return with a large haul of shrimp and crab.

Will left out the details of his trip north and how he came to be in the good graces of the US Navy in such short order. Instead, he waited not even a minute more after greetings were exchanged to pull an envelope from his pocket. Callie and BB grabbed each other's arms, and Lucas looked up from the fish head he had just severed. Will had their full attention. "I sold your cotton. Got me a good price for it, too. I figure after I took out my expenses, this belongs to you and yours."

BB stepped forward to claim the prize, opened it, and pulled out a stack of hundred-dollar bills. "Count dis fuh me, Callie, I don bleib wha I see."

Lucas jumped up from the dock. "Da fuh real, brudda. Don gah fuh look roun de ben en de riba fuh see dishyuh, huh, Callie?" He punched Callie's shoulders, almost making her lose count.

"How we gon use dis money?" Lucas showed his impatience.

BB responded, "Time gon show da."

And as Lucas looked pained, Callie finished her counting. "We don know wha time gon show. We neba had such money befo. BB right—bes we keep money til time show we wha fuh do."

"Naw, Callie, wha you don unnerstan—I kin make mo money ifn I git supply fuh my boat. I kin buy anodda boat I know fuh sale right cheap now. We kin tek mo people cross de wada en mek mo money."

Callie gave Lucas an icy look. It was the look he had learned to dread when it came from Mama Ruth. Callie looked right through his eyes to the back of his head, and he could feel it. Then she cocked her head slightly and was doing it with only one eye directly on him. "Look yuh, Lucas, you my brudda en I loves you, but don tell me fus ting wha I don unnerstan. When you say da, I unnerstan I don wan yeddy wha you gon say nex."

Again the look, right through his eyeballs. Lucas grabbed the back of his head in protest but said no more.

At that, BB spoke up in a commanding voice. "Stop da!" BB's shoulders drooped in frustration. "Callie, Lucas, look each odda in de eye—be kine." They did so, reluctantly, finally holding each other's gaze, gently. "May be plenny uh fight roun yuh, but ain gon be mongst we. We kin fix dishyuh problem bout money. We gib Oakhaat folk dey shaya (*shares*). We keep ownt shaya, en we don leh money come tween we. Ain nuttin wort da. We save dis fuh now, talk mo layda (*later*)." And thus ended the dispute.

Then BB told a story he just heard, but from a lifetime ago. Six boatmen on a plantation on the islands were tied together by their massa and made to whip each other till they all had drawn bad blood from each other's backs. BB stood up. "We ain gon lash each odda no mo!" When his anger subsided, he went on. "You know why dey mek em whip each odda? When dey mek trip cross riba tawd Beaufut, one dem white missus git clothes jes a lee wet."

They sat in silence for a while before Callie told of the terrible slavery stories she heard from the people on the north side of the island. But she ended the short summary with typical Callie optimism. "We on a new time now." They rose to make it so.

Will sat by silently, not wanting to intrude on their deliberations, but took advantage of the break in their conversation to ask, "So are you ready to do some fast fishing, Lucas?"

Lucas didn't skip a beat. "Now, you know a man don know much bout wha him talk bout when him say fas fishin." After shaking his head long enough to make Will wonder whether he would get some help, Lucas looked up. "Got supm fuh mek sweet dis deal?"

"My friend, when we live through this," Will said, pausing for effect, "you will be the first person I tell of the secrets to my success."

"Da spose tuh mek me wan go kyetch fish fuh you? Don know if I kin wait fuh all da success."

Will played along. "No, we won't have to wait. We're living it!" Will shouted. "Your success is my success." The self-proclaimed "brothers" went out to check nearby crab traps and shrimp holes in the low tide water. Will's crew would not be disappointed.

★ ★ ★

The next day, the freedmen's tentative, fearful hold on freedom was tested anew when word spread that the Union army intended to take all island men ages eighteen to forty-five to Hilton Head for military training. Under orders of General Hunter in early May, former slaves in the occupied sea islands were free, and they would form the First South Carolina Volunteers.

Through months of interaction, the Union soldiers had made the former slaves feel confident that they were free, and that neither old nor new masters would ever be allowed to own them again. Then, suddenly, the Union raised an old fear: their masters had told the slaves that Yankees would capture them and sell them in Cuba.

Throughout the island plantations there was great sadness and audible angst from the women. Some men had been taken to Hilton Head Island in boats. Others hid themselves in the salt marsh on small islands, out of reach of the Union soldiers. Though not known to the Union officers at the time, most freedmen were like BB, willing to be trained and to fight. What they feared most was leaving their loved ones without protection when their masters still could return. They also feared the unknown, including the Union soldiers' treatment of their families and meager possessions.

Civilian authorities, like Miss Towne, and her supervisor, Edward Pierce, were required to cooperate with this military venture but were none too pleased. They saw it as a breach of trust with the former slaves. They also thought taking workers from the fields undermined their objectives as plantation superintendents—to create a successful cotton harvest and prove the advantages of wage labor.

Nonetheless, BB and many more freed Africans from Oakheart willingly joined hundreds from around the islands for military training on Hilton Head. Though BB stepped forward as he said he would, Lucas did not share his brother's zeal for military life, unless it involved being on the water. Lucas did not see himself as a navy man like Will, either, though they were working smoothly on the dock as a two-man team when Union soldiers raided Oakheart looking for recruits.

When Lucas was ordered off the dock to join the young men being marched off the plantation, Will intervened and told the corporal that he had been instructed to keep Lucas for a special naval assignment. Will shouted up to Callie on the big house porch to find his jacket with the orders involving Lucas. She hesitated at first and then dashed inside. Callie quickly wrote on a notepaper and placed it in the coat's breast pocket. Tired of waiting, an army sergeant moved toward the steps just as Callie came flying down to Will with jacket extended.

"Sorry to keep you gentlemen waitin."

Will reached in the pockets, started to speak, and then stopped as he pulled a note from one of them.

> *Ensign Hewitt -*
> *Boatman from Oakheart needed.*
> *-Captain McGuffrey-*

The signature on the last line was barely legible.

Never guessing Callie had written the note Will pulled from his jacket, the Union corporal glanced at it and accepted its legitimacy.

Pointing to Lucas, he declared, "He stays with you!" They turned and moved quickly down the lane of cabins, invading each dwelling, as though the people had not suffered enough indignities.

Will looked inquisitively at Callie. "You are quick, aren't you? I was going to pretend to lose my orders. Then you ..."

Callie smiled. "I been listenin tuh white folk talk my whole life. I watch ole Bowen do his business fuh long time. Now I free, I learn mo bout the world ebbyday. I see how deese officers do things, all orders and propa. I say I kin do da, too."

Callie savored her competence another few seconds, appreciation still evident from Lucas's prolonged hug and Will's smile of amazement. Then she turned to what had to be done next, as always. "Lucas and Will, you boys bes be off tonight on your secret job—stay clear all dis mess for a day or two. Will, you bes git yo navy clothes off while you first mate on Lucas boat." Once again, they knew that Callie was correct. Not only that, over the next night and morning, they had to bring in a haul of seafood fit for a ship's crew.

Lucas and Will cast off the dock lines to the rowboat, headed down Chowan Creek, and turned north toward Beaufort, where Lucas knew of more prime shrimp holes. Away from the intense search for army "volunteers" on the islands, they planned to dock in town for a late dinner before they worked. They felt like celebrating Will's return and the money he brought back to Oakheart's cotton workers who still waited for government pay.

Crossing the river toward the Beaufort wharf, they saw a sidewheeler rounding the bend and moving in the same direction. They prudently decided to wait for it. Will and Lucas peered at it through the low fog on the river. Lucas thought he recognized the lines of the steamship *Planter*, a boat that had been in service to the Confederate navy before the Union invasion at Port Royal. He had seen it navigating the tricky shallows of the tidal creeks as it ran supplies for the Confederacy. "We in bad place, Will." Lucas muttered as he began rowing hard to move away from the approaching vessel. "Da be buckra navy boat."

"What's it doing here?" Will asked, telling Lucas all he knew about it.

Their rowboat passed in front of the steamer as it slowed to a crawl. Lucas was first to notice the captain emerging from the wheelhouse. Through the evening mist, the captain's coat and hat became visible at the railing. Lucas recognized the garb from past sightings of the *Planter.*

Fearing the captain would blame their boat for crossing closely, Lucas immediately shouted plaintively, "We sorry, Massa Capn, suh. We jus tek injud man cross tuh town, suh. We gwine tuh hospital on de point, suh." Lucas hoped their stated mission to one of the hospitals would mitigate the captain's anger.

"Thank you for the explanation, sir." A voice boomed through the fog. Then his face came clearly into view as he stepped forward from the shadows—an African face, strong but—in this instance, at least—kind. "Be about your business, young man. You did nothing wrong. You have no apology to make."

His words echoed across waters still as glass but for the movement of the two boats. Lucas's eyes were riveted on the captain, not registering the forgiveness he received so much as the reality that a black man captained a Confederate steamer.

Will could not stay quiet. "Sir, we are not combatants, but we would ask who are you, sir, and for whom do you fight?"

"I am Robert Smalls. I now fight for my freedom, and for yours, young captain." Turning his gaze from Lucas and back to Will, he said, "Earlier today, this boat lay in Charleston Harbor. My family and friends liberated it, and ourselves."

Neither Will nor Lucas could quite imagine it. Yet here he was, and his boat. Soon two gunboats emerged from the fog, close behind the *Planter,* prompting Will to shout, "Are they chasing you, sir?"

Smalls responded, "The Union navy is my escort. I am leading them from the north down to Hilton Head. They struggle to keep up through these channels." A broad smile appeared on the dark captain's face. "Go safely, gentlemen!" And with that, Smalls moved back into the wheelhouse, and the *Planter* proceeded to dock at the Beaufort wharf. As Will and Lucas watched in wonder, standing off along with the gunboat escorts, the *Planter* discharged black women and children, with the captain, Robert Smalls, seeing off the last passenger.

"What do you think those six men lashing each other for wetting white folks' clothes would say about a black African man stealing a boat and guns from the Charleston Harbor?" inquired Will, a wry, irrepressible smile breaking across his mouth.

Lucas quickly responded: "Dey say, 'I ain fraid uh no buckra navy needuh.' Jes gib me a chance en leh me at em, like Mista Smalls." Lucas looked off into the water. "Kyan stop from wonda ifn I be brave nuff fuh do supm fuh my freedom. I tink about de story Callie jes tell, en wha BB tell bout dem boatman wa whip each odda. I know da be supm I kyan tek no mo."

"*Can't* take?" Will asked.

"*Ain!* Ain gon tek!" Lucas declared.

Will nodded.

Lucas looked on admiringly at Robert Smalls. "I feel like da man deh, jes don know ifn I kin ack like him."

PART IV

**May 1862 to
January 1, 1863**

Chapter 19

Now that most of the men had been swept up by the army and taken to Hilton Head Island, Callie began to worry about the farm management, BB's job. Most women continued to perform as they did during slavery, willing to work as hard as required by their circumstances. With strong backs and hearts to match, they filed into the fields for longer hours, determined to keep up with the work. Still, there was too much to do.

Bella looked after Sunny, which allowed Callie to follow her conscience and help others, assured that her daughter was in good hands. When Callie was not working crops, tending the sick and infirm, or checking on the children of the plantation, she turned her remaining energy to Sunny. Then her bone-tired body could relax and just be a mother.

Without the restraints of enslavement, their time together almost always resulted in Callie teaching something, not just letters, but life. With Callie's stories of crabs and birds and foxes and frogs, Sunny easily absorbed the lessons. On their trips in a rowboat up Chowan Creek to the Oaks Plantation, where Miss Towne held classes on weekdays, Callie called out words, and Sunny guessed the first letter of the word. Callie's pride in her daughter grew as Sunny began calling out, often correctly, the second letter in each word. Before they knew it, the stories Sunny loved had taught her to spell the words in them. Amid all the surrounding turmoil, Callie saw the light in her daughter's eyes and became proud of her own motherhood.

Most days, Callie rowed back to join the work at Oakheart late in the morning. After lunch, she worked the fields through the afternoons until she returned to the Oaks for Sunny and to attend some of the evening adult lessons on the porch of the plantation house.

But on this morning she delayed her row back to Oakheart. Callie had heard wailing throughout the night the men were taken to Hilton Head, as hysterical women feared they would never see their sons, husbands, and brothers again. On behalf of these fearful families, Callie felt she had to speak to the power of the United States, which would have to be Miss Towne.

Callie came up from the dock with Sunny to see a different, though familiar, face. Edward Pierce waited, the man she and Will had attempted to fool months ago.

"Good morning," Pierce called out.

"Good morning, suh. It's you, who—"

And he waved her off, saying, "Who was impressed by you and your brothers and your friend, young Will. I was so impressed, in fact, that I approved your Oakheart Plantation continuing without a superintendent on site."

Callie nodded her head as if understanding, though she didn't. She hugged Sunny and sent her on to her lessons in the big house. "You approved, suh?" She realized as she asked that Mister Pierce must be the "boss" to whom Laura Towne had referred. Callie now questioned the wisdom of complaining to the US government about the men leaving the island for military training. Instead, she expressed her sadness that BB had gone, and how hard it was to work the land without him and the others.

Pierce immediately agreed with her, explaining that he implored the army generals to stop this action. Pierce appeared crestfallen that he had promised a freedom to the people that they still did not have. Further, he told Callie that more than four hundred men were taken, interrupting farm operations across the islands.

Callie began to realize the scope of the problem and the different forces at work within the Yankee establishment. At least she and BB were free to manage each day as they saw fit. She told Pierce how very much she appreciated all he had done to help the people after slavery, and wished him well.

Callie rowed back home, very gratified that Pierce and Miss Towne thought Oakheart could function well without a superintendent. To know Pierce was there to guarantee the promise made her feel better about each day's business. Pierce, and the government he represented, provided security for the hopes of freedmen across the islands.

Callie believed that she and her brothers had moved nimbly on the ebb and flow of circumstances surrounding them. But suddenly BB's leadership and labor were missing, leaving her with a challenge unlike those that BB had already met—how to get good work done through other people. Having no choice in matters unfolding around her, she continued to manage the plantation with steadfast devotion. Callie trusted her keen instincts to steer her through the currents of change.

Although she attended religious services regularly while in bondage and drew great strength from her faith, Callie often found comfort from her worries in a quiet cove, nestled between the eroded roots of two giant live oaks that bent toward the shallow water. On this very early morning, still lit by the moon, while all souls slept, she visited her "flectin" spot.

Callie walked down the bank to the water's edge. Holding on to a live oak branch above with one hand, she leaned low over the water. With no wind ruffling the surface, Callie looked down to see her reflection in the moonlight. She muttered: "Da wha I look like to you fishes? Guess da why oona don come up en speak. When I look down I see me—en I see wey I been, wha I be, wha I done do. Mos time I likes wha I see, cause I know I done my bes. Fuh Sunny, I done git huh in class so she kin laan new ting ebby day. Fuh my people yuh on Oakhaat, done my bes, too. I kin say awright, Callie, umm-hmm."

But then Callie hesitated. "Deh be time when I don like my flectin spot da much—wada still nuf like glass—e tell me wha be in my face—see mo worriation dan I know I got." She looked up to see no one and returned to her reflections, uneasy. "Lucas en BB, I tink too much bout dem. Lucas talk bout he gon git train wid army on Hilton Head, but I know he ain gon gib up de wada. Maybe he gon fine waay fuh hep odda people on de wada. Supm light up in him afta him see how Robert Smalls free hissef on da *Planta* boat."

Callie laughed, remembering how Lucas told of seeing Robert Smalls on the river—how a slave man, raised up right in Beaufort, had stolen a boat from Charleston Harbor. When he spoke of Robert Smalls, his eyes sparkled in wonder and pride at the courage and the accomplishment. Lucas shared his stories with all those on the plantation who would listen, gleefully embellishing to enhance the entertainment value.

"Man steal boat from Charleson Harba. De name uh de boat be de *Planta*. Man tek de *Planta* right out de harba, right pas big ol Foat Sumta. Kin you top da? Tek de boat way from buckra navy. If I ain see da wid my own eye, ain no way I tink da fuh real. De *Planta* come out uh de fawg—move smood right tawd me and Will whiles de captain fight de current fuh come tuh de whaaf. Fus I tink he swing way too faah. Da when me en Will cut in front, him gwine so slow. Bad move turn out so good. Out de wheelhouse come Robert Smalls, call me 'suh,' tell me I done nuttin fuh haffa pologize, tell me I kin be bout my bidness. Him whole sef be so skrong, like de win be at him back, cep he de pilot uh dis big steamboat."

Callie clapped, acting as though she was in the crowd when Lucas first shared the story. Then she spoke aloud to herself:

"He been so bol (*bold*), tek him famly en odda people to freedom. Ready fuh gib him ownt life if ting go wrong. Da haad fuh magine— but I do same fuh Sunny." Callie paused in thought. "Praise Gawd. Him sho tek kyah uh de people."

Callie peered at the water, moonlight so bright that she thought she saw worry lines on her forehead. "BB off on him own jes like Lucas. Kyan reach em. Kyan much hep em yuh on dis lan. BB do sech good wuk, maybe I speck (*expect*) too much from BB on dis faam. Sides, maybe him wan be army man—wan be right in front ifn we git fuh fight in dis waw."

Finding solace but no answers, Callie left her spot before the sun came up and was back at Sunny's bedside when she awakened. Although she loved her brothers enough to worry about them endlessly, she knew that they could care for themselves, and no matter what, they were going to make their own decisions.

Most freedmen at Oakheart and throughout the islands had acted on a natural desire to take care of their loved ones first. During slavery, they had very meager provisions to do so and less time. Now, they built better shelters and worked on their own subsistence crops like corn, greens, and sweet potatoes. Recently freed to search for and reunite with family members, they were not at all interested in leaving each other again.

So when General Hunter ordered able-bodied men to be taken to Hilton Head for training, uncertainty among family members caused panic. The fact that Union soldiers who had brought the freedom originally and then been protectors, now took black men away—most often against their will—added to the fear.

Fortunately, the men returned after only a week on Hilton Head with their heads held high, purpose in their steps, and strength in their unity. Some came back from training with a new awareness of what might be possible in their lives. Some intended to make their future in the military. Others were sure they did not want to work in the fields but were doubtful that the army was their route out. BB was happy to get back to his work at Oakheart, though he was grateful for the new skills he learned and the trust shown in him by white officers. He was ready for the next call to army training.

Callie told him how much work she did and did not get done in his absence.

Within a week, BB confirmed to her that they were short some hands, and tasks were still going undone. "Day by day, less en less han in de fiel. Some folk don wan wuk cotton. Dey wan wuk fuh dey ownt famly, don wan wuk fuh no massa. Don madda dey say we git pay."

"I know, brudda. I struggle fuh crack my teet ebbyday you be gone."

BB took that as cue to continue. "All dis talk from two side de mout by US govment bout we git pay o don git pay. Ain do no good fuh wuk haad in da cotton fiel ifn de sutla (*sutler*) tek wha lee money you git. Folk jes go chase dey freedom ebby way but yuh."

BB, never shy before his training and further emboldened by it, wanted to take his irritation directly to one of the main sources of angst for the freedmen. Union authorities had allowed sutlers to sell goods, both to soldiers and freedmen. Some operated in Beaufort, and others took their wares out to the islands. There had been ongoing complaints about the prices and credit practices employed by these salesmen, who were taking full advantage of their position.

BB entered the Oaks Plantation sutler's store seeking molasses, a favorite of his and an ingredient in a cake Bella wanted to bake that afternoon. The prices on several items were higher than the last time, so BB asked the man, with no expectation of a satisfactory answer, "Why malasse (*molasses*) fiteen cent a quaat now, suh?"

Mister Whiting, round and soft, immediately took offense while his face reddened. "Boy, I think you better check your tone right now. I work hard to bring you people things you need, and I don't expect to get a lot of questions from a—"

"You were going to say something, sir?" Will strode into the space Whiting used for customers, surprising everyone. He was back in the area for the afternoon and evening if necessary, once again assigned by his captain to "requisition" supplies from local waters. Will had heard about Callie's frustrations with Whiting's unfair practices when he visited several weeks before. "I believe you were explaining why you overcharged these good people?"

Whiting mounted his defense. "Young man, I am sure your intentions are good. As a young naval officer, you should understand that I must make a living, too. Besides, this matter does not concern you."

"Oh, but it does. It concerns me greatly. Since I know you are here under the authority of the US government to support that effort and to lift these people ..." Will let his words hang.

"These people," Whiting said, gesturing toward BB, "are very fortunate we are here. Their lives have vastly improved due to Union military and merchants," he said. "I would expect a little more gratitude."

"Before you give yourself too much credit—" Will began, but BB interrupted, speaking firmly.

"Yo name Whitin, suh? Mista Whitin, we don need no new massa wha tek from we en say him gib we supm (*who takes from us and says he gives us something*). Da soun jes like wha we been yeddy (*hearing*) fo de Big Gun Shoot." BB slammed the molasses jar down on the wooden plank Whiting used as a countertop. "Day uh massa damn ovah roun yuh!" BB turned to Will, saying, "Pahdon me fuh de way I put da." Then he walked out the open side of the tent.

Will raised his arms as if to say, "To whom are you apologizing?" Then he turned his ire on Whiting. "See here, Mr. Whiting, I've heard some sad stories about you. Not just in your little store, but in your cotton dealings—seems you always want more money than you deserve. Then you pay a mere pittance to the laborers who worked that cotton from seed to perfection and have the nerve to pay only one-quarter of the amount due, telling them that the other three-quarters they can collect in goods from your store. You know, Whiting, that is just not right, and it isn't a service to the very cause the government sent you here to support. They wish to show the benefits of wage labor over slave labor, and you, by your practices, are undermining the best efforts of these hard-working people."

"You do not know the sacrifices my family and I have made to come down here, young man."

"And I see you living rather well in the overseer's house here at Oaks Plantation. I dare say that's the finest house you have occupied in your lifetime, sir. You have the nerve to live in that house, paid for by the government, and then overcharge for basics like molasses at fifteen cents a quart and act like you deserve it! That is shameful! You must be one of those scoundrels the commander of the fleet, Admiral Dupont, referred to as 'Ali Baba and the forty thieves.'"

Attempting to negate the problem Will was creating for him—a crowd of freedmen and soldiers were gathering outside his tent—Whiting curtly retorted, "Troublemakers are not needed here, young man. I respect your uniform, but you are not qualified to judge how I do business."

"No?" Will was fully engaged, as if the fight was his own. "Having watched my stepfather conduct his slavery-backed business for years, I can surely recognize the smell of greed and the stench of a man willing to live off the sweat of others. Not only that, I am a supply officer with United States Navy, and I will be filing a report with Mr. Pierce this afternoon. I guarantee there will be a change in your business practices—or your location."

Lucas, who had arrived on the scene after Will began his speech, said, "Seem Will like fuh stir ting up."

"Especially when I know I'm right." And Will turned back to Whiting. "You, sir, are plainly wrong and will be found to be so." Will picked up the jar of molasses and tossed a coin onto the plank with sufficient force that it skipped to the dirt floor of Whiting's tent. Will gave Whiting a brief, disdainful look without apology.

As they walked away from a shaken Whiting, Will was proud that he confronted someone who would profit from the plight of his friends. BB loved the support but was quick to ask Will, "Don git nuff fight out on de big wada wid de navy? Ga fuh come back yuh en pick fight wid a po ol buckra who try fuh steal from we Negro?"

"Well, Whiting just got my dander up." Will still fumed. "People like him need to be fought! But I don't need the action." Will settled down enough to report on his adventures. "I've been getting all I ever want out on the beautiful blue ocean."

"Da right?" Lucas asked doubtfully.

"Yep. I work below deck mostly managing supplies on a Union frigate, but I watched us chase Confederate steamers leaving Charleston. We are out there just waiting for them."

"Kyetch any?" Lucas leaned in.

"Been real busy lately. The fleet captured one last week and shot another up pretty bad. We got almost every sailboat that came out. It's been a little tough trying to catch all the steamers. They are fast and hard to see because now they are built so low. Hard to follow sometimes at night when there is no moonlight, or in the fog. And *phhhhhttt!* Gone. The ship you were chasing just disappeared."

Lucas started smiling to himself and then broke out in a sliding chuckle. Will shot him an inquiring look.

"Da be funny. You en de Yankee boat kyetch people when dey do de same ting you did—tek boat tru de blockade fuh sell cotton."

"It is pretty funny, isn't it? Glad I didn't get caught. Worked out pretty well. And now, coming back to Hilton Head so often, I can keep trying to find my mother when I get any free time. No more word about where she and the captain went, I suppose, now that you are all over these waterways?"

"Naw, Will, sorry bout da, we ain been look too haad fuh Massa. Fact be, we jes hope he stay wey he at. I see rebel light in de night when dey don know I on de wada. Dey keep busy like buncha bee."

Lucas swept his arm inland and then, smiling broadly at a passing Yankee patrol boat, waved his hat. "Mighty nice you boys in blue free we people. Keep Massa fah way from dishyuh place."

"So are you getting paid to carry people across the water?" Will wanted to know whether Lucas thought of himself as a money-making businessman.

"I done haul people up tuh Beaufut en back en tuh Hilton Head en back so mucha time. Dey got army boat en navy boat. Sometime dey need one mo boat, en da be me. I stay out de trouble, en guess you kin see, I stay out de army too."

"Happy for you, Lucas. You get to work hard at what you love, floating up and down on our favorite water. Now, so many people need you to ferry them places, do you still have time to fish?"

"People still like fuh eat?" Lucas dryly responded.

"They're lucky they got you to grab the best shrimp and crab right outa these creeks. As am I, I might add, since I promised my shipmates on board I'd come back with another bounty of Lucas's best catch. Yes?"

"I might kin hep you out wid da."

"You better. If you don't produce, Lucas, then I can't come back to visit."

Lucas did not skip a beat. "Guess da mean I gah fuh figyuh out wha I gon do, huh?"

* * *

True enough, Lucas's teasing notwithstanding, Will was always well received at Oakheart. Callie, Lucas, and BB were first among those who thought well of Will, but Sunny and Bella were similarly enthused. After Will returned with the cotton money, and Callie and BB made sure it was fairly distributed among the workers of Oakheart, the people came to realize that Will played a significant role in how that money came to them. They were most grateful to him and respected the effort expended and the honesty inherent in the deed.

Just before Will returned to his ship with bushels of shrimp, he stopped by the house to see Callie, finding her on the porch talking to Sunny about letters and words. He hated to interrupt such good work, but his crew was waiting at the Oakheart dock after loading the day's catch. Sunny raced down the steps to jump into Will's arms; her mother was more restrained. Will apologized for not visiting before it was time to leave, and Callie pointed out that they had spent little time together since his recovery. Callie smiled down from the porch, saying, "It such good luck for us that you can keep on comin by. Knowin you are doin awright make us people of Oakhaat too happy!"

Though always appreciative of the warm reception, he knew he didn't have much time to talk. "Say, not to be too serious, but I was thinking about you a lot lately."

"Fuh real?" And by her inflection, he knew Callie took his comment in a different way than he intended.

"Some of my crewmates have gotten sick on board, different maladies going around, I guess. But I was just remembering how much

190

you helped me get well. Not just the treatments, and the herbs, and the hot liquids, but your cool and gentle hands, and the wonderful way you cared for me. Everything that you did made me well, Callie. And I was just wishing for that kind of treatment for all the men getting sick and hurt by this war."

"Dere be hurt and sick people heah, too. Got all the work I kin handle at Oakhaat, tween these fields, and our own people. And now I tek Sunny to lessons at Oaks, and I tek lessons too." She realized as she spoke that it sounded like a list of excuses for not doing something—a lot like the responses Lucas gave after Callie urged him to look around the next corner at what he could not see.

"I understand, Callie. I just had to mention it. You were so good for me, I wanted to share you ..." He smiled, bent low at the waist, and, with a sweeping arm beneath him, said, "I must bid the gentle lady adieu." He smiled a silly smile and turned with a bow to Sunny. "And adieu to you, sweetheart." Sunny glowed openly, her mother slightly less so.

The notion that Callie could be a great asset in providing medical care had occurred to others as well. Laura Towne had been quite impressed with Callie's way with the sick and told her so. Callie took the compliment well but did not take it as guidance for her future. Typically, she stayed at Oakheart, only rowing up the creek for Sunny's lessons or to go with the good Miss Towne on one of her missions.

Important missions they were. Callie worked with Miss Towne when the best things began happening for the island peoples. Of course, when Miss Towne began her lessons for island children, Callie and Sunny were drawn to them, along with more than fifty students on most days. When boxes of clothing arrived by steamer, Miss Towne asked Callie and a few others to inspect them carefully and make certain all the garments were fit for distribution.

Callie looked at Miss Towne in amazement after she declared several pieces lacked sufficient quality or cleanliness and therefore were not fit to be worn by residents of the sea islands. That Miss Towne would judge a freedman as being too good for clothing from Philadelphia meant something special to Callie.

In fact, Callie was already an expert on clothing distribution before any of the Yankees came around, and was quick to tell Miss Towne about it. "I look in Missus's closet. Mek me tink how nice all de dresses be if dey get out on folk to walk roun Oakhaart. Now, at Oakhaart, de ladies look like well-dressed people. Sides, Bowens ain yuh no more."

It greatly amused Laura Towne that the work she arrived to do on behalf of the newly freed slaves was being done by one of those very people, at least on Oakheart Plantation. On their own, Callie and BB had organized the work of the plantation, provided for health care visits, assured everyone that they would get food from the general storage areas, and equally shared some of the clothing and other "luxuries" not previously available to most slaves.

Because the slave cabins were very basic, BB had told Captain Bowen's former slaves that they could take wood from several of the rundown, unused buildings on the grounds to improve their homes. Within weeks, the dwellings of Oakheart freedmen had new wood floors and built-in lofts to increase living and storage space. Since the plantations had been abandoned, busy carpenters were creative in their liberation of wood for other purposes all over the islands.

Despite their pride and progress, after the forced departure of the men for military training, island people were suspicious of Yankee intentions. Their doubts were greatly alleviated when Edward Pierce used available funds to provide payment for their past work, insisting that each get between seventy-five cents and three dollars, depending on tasks completed. For freedmen, promises made were kept, at least for the moment, making it easier for Callie and BB to ask workers to give some time to the cotton fields. Several weekends later, distribution of excellent bacon from the North caused further celebration and strengthened relationships. It was not clear whether the pay or the pork caused the greatest rejoicing.

Miss Towne and Callie went visiting on the Monday after the May weekend when all hands feasted. As they returned in the early evening, Miss Towne remarked, "My, there are so many people out walking tonight, and almost every night. Why is that?"

Callie explained to her new friend, "Nightime cooler, missus. Day heat up fas roun heah." Miss Towne readily agreed. Callie went on. "And thas the only time Massa not check on wey slave be, so we get a lot of visitin done at nighttime."

"Oh, masters didn't care where you were at nighttime?"

"Well, not exactly, mahm. More like he not know wey we be when nighttime come. Sometime people want to visit family so bad we travel without Massa permission. So nighttime bes time. You know, e daak, we daak." Though Callie amused herself, Miss Towne was uncertain how to respond, so Callie continued. "Mahm, I joke a lee bit, but, see, famly is too important to us. It not jus bout family by blood—sometime e bout dem who treat us like we famly, de first person who kyah (*cares*) for us, or who love us. Dey always be famly. Famly mean a lot fuh people and dey go long way to git togedda. Now freedom come, we can git out right regula to see famly."

"That's wonderful, Callie. Thank you for sharing. What were your best times when family gathered together?"

"You know, when folk get togedda—shaya dey love, dey favorite food, dey crabbin or shrimpin or fishin. Dey teach younguns what dey need to know bout how de world wuk. Where de younguns laan manners and respeck, en where de eldas show why dey git respeck. Yessum, seein how hard plantamen tried to tear up we famlies, I tank Gawd we heah stronga den ebba befo."

As Laura Towne went from plantation to plantation, she saw one example after another of what Callie had described—deep-rooted strengths that were, somehow, nourished in this impoverished community of former slaves. She saw how elders were so well respected, and that children were taught to be obedient and well mannered. She certainly noticed those attributes in Callie's little daughter, Sunny. Recognizing how well Sunny was doing, Miss Towne made a spontaneous offer. "Until my friend Ellen arrives to help manage our school, may I call on you to help with the younger children? You know—teach them letters through your stories the same way you did with Sunny?"

Reluctantly, Callie said, "Yes, missus, but I still want schoolin fuh my own self. Don know if I good fuh be teacha."

"Dear woman. You are a self-taught reader who has taught her very young daughter to read, and you say you aren't a teacher? But don't worry, as soon as my friend Ellen arrives, you can continue to be just a student." When their journey ended, Miss Towne asked Callie to stay in the carriage to hear one more suggestion. "There is a new arrival in town from the North who can tell you all about taking opportunities that life presents. Ever heard of the Underground Railroad?"

"No, mahm. But I most sho e ain gon wuk too good roun yuh. The one tween Chaaston and Svannah built up—ovah de maash wada, ummm-hmmm."

Laura Towne appreciated Callie's willingness to share the facts as she knew them. She stifled her amusement as she asked Callie more directly, "Do you know of a woman named Harriet Tubman? I think she also has been called 'Moses' because she took slaves to their freedom up north?"

"Oh yeah, missus. I heard of tha woman—heard tell stories of her good deed. Yes'm, I heard plantamen talkin about her, too. They tank Gawd she not roun heah, I memba em sayin."

Towne quickly added, "Well, she's here now, up in Beaufort."

"Guess Gawd not listenin de plantamen no mo then. What's she doin here I wonder, sence we not slave wantin fuh run no mo?"

"Helping the troops, doctoring their injuries, teaching, baking pies. You know, she's got talents in areas you favor—taking care of others, cooking, healing using herbs."

"She done so much, missus, I jes cain't be like huh."

"I thought you might like to know she's here, and that she knows some things about life and helping people, just like you. And, just like you, she doesn't let things get in the way when she decides to do something. Thought you would like to see her. It might help you know which direction you are going with your life."

"Direction, missus? I'm jes livin as ooman bes I can, raisin my daughta and carin for my people, wid no massa tellin me do dis, do da."

Chapter 20

Unfortunately, the world around Callie continued to disrupt her comfortable routine. Edward Pierce, their good friend in the US government, announced his intention to leave South Carolina for other responsibilities in the North. As shepherd of the government's freedom experiment, his impending departure not only created great sadness for Callie and many others on nearby plantations, it also increased anxiety about the level of Union commitment. Making it more worrisome, Pierce's planned departure in early June coincided with stepped-up raids on the waterways by Southerners who were determined to harass the Yankees and reclaim their property, including their slaves.

On Sunday, June 1, 1862, there was a farewell ceremony for Edward Pierce at the Oaks Plantation. As always, the freedmen were attentive as he spoke with optimism about their future. Their gratitude for Pierce's efforts overwhelmed him as he received their love and thanks long after the ceremony had ended. Callie was one of those who lingered. After saying a heartfelt thank-you in a formal fashion, Callie wanted to ask some questions.

"So, Mista Pierce, afta you leave heah, wha you tink gah happen to we, fa true?"

"You'll be all right, Callie. You know what you are doing and how to take care of your business. You will be fine."

"I ain aks jes for me. I aks da fuh we people heah. Dey don know if Yankees gah stay with we people, help we keep free from Massa. If you haffa leave us, please say we gon be free."

Pierce said when South Carolina and other states seceded, Lincoln decided to fight to keep the Union together, and that where the Union military defeated the Confederates, slaves were freed. Pierce was honest with Callie, saying that, first and foremost, the Union needed the deep-water port and that bringing freedom to the slaves, though important, was secondary.

"So, now you jes say Mista Lincoln don kyah much whedda we free?"

"No, Callie. What I said is that President Lincoln and his war department wanted Port Royal Sound as a harbor the Union navy could use to blockade the southeast coast. You became free as a result. But the president wants slavery to end as much as I do. He is just trying to save the Union so that it can be a place for all to be free together."

"Sound good, Mista Pierce. But I jes sad freedom not the reason for this war."

Pierce responded: "Well, I don't mean to sound too smart, but I do read a lot, and I write. I heard just last year that secession speeches given right here in South Carolina were all about slavery and keeping the economic system that was built on slavery. So, since the secessionists down here said they were doing it for slavery, I guess we ought to take them at their word. I know Lincoln stands against slavery, so if you want to think this war is about freedom for you and yours, since you've been freed by it, you just go ahead."

"Thank you again for takin the time to taak to me, suh. You always been a most kind and patient man. You look me in my face and explain tings. You goin, but you stay in we haat." Callie hesitated as Pierce reached out to embrace her, before turning to others who waited for him.

The Union navy's increased control of the Atlantic coast allowed Northern travelers like Edward Pierce to come and go at will on steamers from ports like Boston, New York, Philadelphia, Baltimore, and Washington. There were many people wanting to help advance the North's experiment with newly freed slaves in the southern tip of South Carolina. Callie stopped being surprised at the new faces she saw at Oaks Plantation when taking Sunny for lessons, since Miss Towne always was receiving visiting officials, both civilian and military.

Although the ocean was secure for travel, and the sea islands and surrounding waterways were controlled by Union forces, danger was nearby. As the summer of 1862 began, there were more sightings of Confederates on the creeks connecting the islands, and landing parties had come ashore in remote locations.

On the day before Miss Towne's schoolteacher friend arrived, four freedmen pickets standing guard at a plantation near Oakheart were killed. Word first came to Oakheart from Lucas, who saw three Union patrol boats anchored where Chowan Creek flowed into the Beaufort River. He approached the boats cautiously, of course, recognized one of the naval officers he had talked to before, and rowed in his direction. The young captain told Lucas that the four Negro guards were shot as a result of Confederate trickery of the cruelest kind. It seems a long boat passed the pickets on the river bank. When it came by again, black men on the boat jumped up, hollering, "Don't shoot!" When the pickets relaxed and lowered their rifles, a boatload of rebels stood up and fired.

Lucas knew two of the young men killed and was distressed by their deaths, but the deception the Confederates used offended his own sense of honor. "Dey hide behind we—to shoot at we. Wha kine uh man ...?" and his sentence trailed off as he let his rowboat turn in the tide. "Tank you, Capn."

"Tell them up Chowan Creek that our boats are standing in the mouth of the river here tonight," the captain shouted after him. "May have to come up to evacuate the Northern women if these secesh keep acting up."

"Yessuh, Capn. I pass de wud."

Lucas arrived with the news from the Union captain around the same time someone returned from Beaufort to report that Union commissaries there were evacuated the day before. The more widespread the talk of attacks and evacuations, the more Callie and other freedmen living near the Oaks Plantation feared that Miss Towne and other plantation superintendents would leave the islands. Though their strong independent streak gave them confidence, the freedmen were sailing in uncharted waters. It was not possible to know what might happen next, especially, they felt, since Mister Pierce had left them.

When Callie and Sunny came back to Oakheart the evening after the four pickets were killed, Callie was greeted at the dock with questions. "Mista Peeus gone now, we on we own, fa true?" "Wha bout dem mission folk?" "Miss Towne en dem gon stay on?" "Kin we trus de res dem Yankee gon stay?"

One of the young men who had most distrusted the Yankees answered. "Damn, if military tell em fuh go, dey gone. We be lef behin jes like da ifn da wha de boys in blue wan fuh do."

Callie responded. "Yankee ain gon lef (*leave*) we yuh, en we ain gon go no wey (*where*). Look a dem dock en ship way yonda cross da wada on Hilton Head—mo freed folk spread out on de islan. Yankee en free slave tek ovah da islan, fuh true."

BB saw the uncertainty in the eyes of his fellow freedmen. "We gon be awright, people. Wha oona tink? Buckra gon jes roll ovah en don fight back? Oona know dey ain gon quit. Dey be stubbin like mule. No need fuh be scaid uh dem. Jes git ready fuh em. Nex time dey show dey face roun yuh, we show how skrong en stubbin we is too." Hearing a chorus of affirmation, BB considered the matter closed.

The young doubter looked out over the darkened waters. "Dey out deh—dey watch we—jes be sho uh da." And then he shouted out over the creek, "Hey, all you nocount buckra, wha you gon do bout dem bad boy in blue? En ifn you git by dem, you gah fuh git by we nex!"

"Yeah, I know you wan be in de fight," said BB, who had reasons in the past to doubt the young man's word when it came to work to be done.

"Yeah, BB, fuh true!" He looked at BB, showing heartfelt hurt. "BB, I been da watch oona (*I've been watching you*). I know dis fight be bout freedom fuh we people. I ain gon be one fuh leh you down, da fuh sho."

* * *

Such bravado, always valued in young men during wartime, was much in evidence in the early summer of 1862. The Confederacy could not resist the power of the Union navy or reclaim any land masses near saltwater. But rebel raiding parties landed on occupied islands seeking to retrieve property, including their slaves, or damage that which they could not carry away. There were more deaths of freedmen around the islands, but most raids succeeded only in terrorizing their former slaves or burning stored cotton so that the profit could not go to the Yankees.

From Hilton Head Island north to Edisto Island, and past Beaufort toward the mainland, a zone of freedom had been established, with both sides in the war appearing to accept that Union naval strength would continue to control these South Carolina sea islands. Union attacks along the Georgia and Florida coasts harassed the Confederacy but did not make a material difference in the progress of the war. Northern forces were prevented from advancing any farther inland, as the defenses designed by Confederate General Lee to protect the Savannah–Charleston railroad held.

Despite the seeming equilibrium, Union forces pressed north toward Charleston in mid-June, suffering a brutal defeat on James Island at Secessionville. Casualties streamed into Beaufort, where the converted homes and churches along the river became Union hospitals. Miss Towne asked Callie to help the wounded, a request that was at once frightening and compelling to her.

The injuries some men sustained left them just waiting to die. As Callie gently cleansed their horrible wounds, she sought to soothe the young men's minds. Along with her smile, Callie brought continuous encouragement, stories, and questions about their homes. She recognized one soldier from months earlier when his brigade of New York Scottish volunteers lined up patiently at Oakheart to be served the seafood stew she once prepared exclusively for planters. The bullet that shattered his arm would not kill him, and he was well enough to be bolstered by Callie's manner and demeanor.

All through the day while her busy hands worked tirelessly to heal, she never noticed her exhaustion. Not until she rested, leaning back against the old boards in the longboat ferry to St. Helena, did she realize how spent she was, and finally she allowed herself to cry. Her tears fell with the vivid memory of men dying all around her, and in fear that BB's commitment to army training could get him injured or killed. While he might have looked quite dashing in his blue coat and red pants, and he did indeed seem to carry himself a little taller in the uniform of the First South Carolina Volunteers, Callie never feared that actual harm could come to him until she nursed injured soldiers.

Callie and other former sea island slaves had little interest in past observances of the nation's freedom from English rule, but the sacrifices she saw during her hospital work had stirred her. She had a clearer understanding of the cost of this war that brought freedom to her and her people. Callie was now determined to go to town for the Fourth of July, where there would be a great celebration of independence.

Moved by her experiences, she wanted to share the festivities with Sunny, Lucas, and BB. Bless his soul, BB chose to work the corn fields that day, as army training had put him behind on the Oakheart schedule. Lucas tried to refuse, but Callie reminded him that some of the injured soldiers she tended in the hospital were younger than him. He relented, noting that there would be a great breeze on the river that day to give some relief from the intense summer heat.

Sunny and her mother both wore flowered cotton dresses that Callie had made from one of Missus Bowen's summer frocks. Callie was thrilled that Sunny could see how the grand old Episcopal churchyard was decorated for the affair with a huge US flag dominating the scene. Under Spanish moss swaying in the breeze, the band played patriotic songs.

Sunny beamed, touching her braids tied in bright red and blue ribbons fit for the occasion, as she joined the children from Laura Towne's school to perform the "Song of the Negro Boatmen" composed by John Greenleaf Whittier. It included the words:

"Now praise and tank de Lord, he come.
To set de people free;
Ole massa tink it day ob doom,
But we ob jubilee."

As they finished their lunches of fish, melons, and hardtack with a sweet ginger-molasses drink, Callie asked Lucas to take Sunny back to the dock while she went to the general store. Callie walked on alone, laughing to herself about the conversation she had earlier in the event with a white woman whose northern accent and fast words clearly identified her as a visitor to the area. The woman was so very impressed with the children. "It's so precious the way these youngsters treat all the white visitors so well."

Callie responded: "Well, they treat everybody with respeck, mahm. We raise em to respeck dey elders no matter whedda dey be daak or dey be light."

"That's very good, of course."

"Of cos, dey also fear de light skin a little, you know—dey seen so much bad ting done by light folk when dey was little slaves."

Callie moved on briskly down Bay Steet, still smiling at the truths of her statements to the woman and the slow understanding she saw break across the woman's face, when she felt a hand on her shoulder from behind. She spun around to see a man in dapper civilian dress, and, as she looked up under the wide brim hat, she saw—Bowen's face! Callie started to back away, but he already had gripped her wrists between his hands in such a way that hid his forcefulness from others as he slowly walked her just off the main street.

Callie's mind raced. *How is he here? I thought Yankees were in charge? Will he try to take me away? Should I scream?* All this flashed through her mind, and more.

"Surprised to see me, Callie girl?"

She could not speak; she struggled for air.

Bowen leaned in, his thin face more gaunt than before. "Don't plan on being out there too much longer without me, darlin'. You lookin at the latest registered cotton agent let in by the Yankees." His breath reeked of bourbon. "Till I come back, there's some things I need from my small writin' desk up in the attic, so that I can do some business, you know. Julia loved that piece so much, she wanted me to get it, and

I expect you to get it for me." His voice strained with urgency. "Meet me at the Oakheart dock tonight." And then he cajoled. "You know how Julia loved that old furniture?"

Callie didn't know anything of the kind. In fact, Callie knew, from overhearing their conversations at the house, that Julia Bowen never went into the attic and still missed her old furniture from Maryland. *So what's old Bowen lying about this time?* Callie thought, even while in his grip.

Acting content with his hold on her, she smiled. "Sho, Massa, I gib you anyting you want." At that she delivered a fierce knee to Bowen's midsection, and as he bent over, an uppercut smashed into his chin from the depths of Callie's soul. As he writhed in the dirt, she looked back long enough to see blood streaming from his mouth. She hoped he bit his tongue off. Her hand began to ache as she raced back down Bay Street to the dock.

Lucas hurried Sunny into their boat the minute he saw Callie walking as fast as she could, just short of a run. As a good uncle, he placed her facing the river so that she could not observe her mother's approach. Callie signaled him to start rowing before she stepped into the boat, and she hurried his strokes with her hand as Lucas rowed out into the southbound current, away from town.

Callie helped row most of the way back home, masking her fear for Sunny's benefit while venting the burst of adrenaline still coursing through her veins. She recounted the story to Lucas when they arrived at Oakheart, and that afternoon, BB, Lucas, and Callie decided to tell no one about Bowen. Instead they warned all on the plantation that Union officers asked them to keep a close watch these nights.

The only two rifles the freedmen had found on the plantation were both loaded. One was held by young Charlie, Oakheart's best shot from army training, posted on Oakheart's dock. BB held the other, as he paced the bluff along the waterline. Lucas launched the captain's sleekest canoe onto the river, carrying the pistol Will had given him for emergencies.

That night Callie sheltered her daughter upstairs in the big house. When Sunny went to sleep, her mother sat on the floor at the window, head propped on the sill, eyes sharply watching the darkness.

* * *

The captain had scared Callie more than she thought possible. He had been a ghoulish presence throughout her life, and she had not missed him. She had started to forget the reality of her enslavement under Bowen until jolted by his rude intrusion into her otherwise glorious day of independence. That he could reach her now after he had been defeated, so Callie thought, was evidence of his persistence in pursuit of his property.

Callie was more determined than ever to act in her own defense. She smiled at the memory of her combination blows that took her tormentor to the ground, all the while soaking her swollen hand in cool water.

Now that Bowen had accosted her in Beaufort, she was determined to see what secrets he had stored away. She had explored the attic briefly once after the Bowens were chased away from the plantation but saw only old furniture and dusty boxes, most of which she had helped pack and put away.

After lunch the next day, Callie told Lucas that a terrible headache forced her from the field. In the first hour of digging in the attic, her search yielded clothing, old magazines, and Bowen family albums. But in the last box she opened that afternoon, Callie discovered the small wooden lap desk Bowen described, which contained several small books. The first one she opened showed records of his crops and profits. The next one intrigued Callie. It was a small black book, with the first page labeled "Acquisitions—Departures." The first column showed names of men, women, and children listed separately. Callie thought the second column showed ages, and then in a third there were four-number combinations that looked like years: 1856, 1845, 1828, and on. Callie puzzled over the fourth column with combinations of three or four numbers like 900, 1450, 600, 1175.

As Callie scanned the lists, she had recognized only a few names on the first pages, when Lucas called from below, "Callie, you up deh?"

"Yeah, I right yuh. Wha wrong?"

"Git down yuh quick. Whole lotta folk done git off boat down at de dock. Need you now!"

Hearing the worry in his voice, Callie closed the book, placing it in her deep apron pocket, and descended from the attic to see Lucas pointing from the hallway window of the second floor. She thought he was joking. "Wha gah oona so rile up?" Callie's jaw went slack as she saw nearly a hundred poorly clothed freedmen, under the direction of a Union naval officer, streaming up the bluff and sitting just below the big house.

The officer revealed to her only that they were refugees from Edisto Island, and they were brought here temporarily, he hoped. He reported that there were hundreds more in Beaufort and on the north side of St. Helena Island.

"But why are you heah at Oakheart?" Callie asked.

"We must stop at the Oaks Plantation to transport visitors from Washington. We offered to take these refugees from Beaufort as far as we could. Sorry, but we must drop them here before we pick up our passengers. Gives us time to tidy the ship a bit, you know."

Callie turned from the officer and his comment to see a woman, slightly better dressed than the other bedraggled refugees, approaching her from the group. Her odor was an overpowering combination of dried human and animal fluids soaked in salt. "Mahm, when we ain been on de wada, we been on de dock … day afta day. Dey mek we leab home on Edisto. We pray we kin res yuh jes a while. We so weary en hongry hongry (*very hungry*)."

Callie's focus on her own history and problems melted away as she recognized the desperation in the voice of this self-appointed leader of the Edisto refugees. "Fuh sho, sista. Oona kin stay in da baan, jes back deh. We gon bring supm fuh yo people."

"Gawd bless oona, mahm."

Callie quickly asserted, "Please, I ain no mahm. I try fuh fine my way jes like oona. We hep yo people now, no need fuh worry." Callie found the cookhouse ladies already firing up a pot full of corn, ready to add rice. Lucas offered to throw his catch of shrimp in the stew for these guests of Oakheart instead of taking it to Beaufort to sell.

Callie tucked her newfound book in the bedside table of the room she shared with Sunny, and with it, her immediate desire to probe further into Oakheart's acquisitions history. For now, there was a massive growth of freedmen at Oakheart that commanded her full attention.

The next morning Callie was greeted by about twenty Oakheart folk who were none too pleased with the new arrivals. Resources were already scarce, they argued, with the Yankee soldiers coming around taking whatever they wanted, whenever they wanted, so why did she think the plantation could feed more?

Some thought the Yankees were just dumping freedmen anywhere while they prepared to leave the area. One man said look what happened to the Edisto refugees, who were crowding before him emphasizing his point. "Dey tell me da de same ting wha happen on Edisto. Dey been grow cotton jes how Yankee wan, den Yankee say time fuh go en bring all de people tuh St. Helena."

Callie managed to reassure those assembled that she would get firm answers that day. The group disbanded, muttering among themselves.

The Edisto freedmen left that afternoon, just as quickly as they arrived, when the same Yankee boat came back to Oakheart. The young captain informed Callie and BB that they would be going to St. Helenaville and that they would no longer be her problem. Callie told him it wasn't easy, but it was no problem either. "Gib me joy when I help more folk lib free."

The captain thought for a moment and then smiled slowly, appreciating the caring woman before him. "Well, then you will surely enjoy the news I heard at the Oaks. It seems the United States Congress has passed some new laws that say African persons serving in the military are to be free, and that their mothers, wives, and children would become free also."

BB immediately shouted, "Huzzah!" as army recruits were trained to do. His zest for military service intensified, a feeling still not shared by all around the plantation.

One of their best workers who, like BB, also kept his own garden plot in perfect condition, said, "Da be mighty good—if I kin live yuh on dishyuh faam wid wife en chirrun, grow vegetable, ketch fish en swimp—I feel pretty free. Don rightly know how I kin git mo free, lessen da be when Massa stay gone en all deese Yankee go back wey dey come from."

BB couldn't argue with him openly, since all were experiencing new choices in their lives. But BB told all those listening that day, again, "We gah fuh be ready fuh fight to git free, and keep our famly free." Though Callie worried for him, she was glad he and others had army training, since the increasing frequency of rebel night raids around the islands had left all freedmen tense and fearful.

With so much open water and back channels, even more Union patrol boats could not prevent small raiding parties from crossing a river in the dark. Though Union soldiers occasionally camped on Constant Island, the men of Oakheart Plantation were determined to keep watch over their island. They had thrived during several stints of Army training, and BB wanted the men to feel in charge of their riverbank when they were on picket duty. It was a difficult assignment with only two rifles available to defend against a raid.

As if in answer to the prayers of dutiful but ill-equipped warriors, Miss Towne told Callie that a gift to the people of Oakheart had been placed in her boat. She told Callie that rifles had already been given to men at the Oaks, and that BB should decide who on Oakheart Plantation was worthy of them.

Following class, Callie rowed the heavy box of six Springfield rifles and ammunition back to Oakheart against an incoming tide. The longer-than-usual journey allowed her to realize that her gratitude for the weapons was tempered by her fright at the prospect of their use. Callie watched BB and the selected men receive their rifles, understanding their pride and pleasure in practicing the muzzle-loading steps they had learned in training. Yet she dreaded the feeling of encroaching violence. With the security of the weapons came the possible carnage they cause, and Callie feared for the Oakheart men as their chests swelled with newfound power and responsibility.

Ironically, and sadly for those like BB who wanted to fight, General Hunter disbanded the unit of freedmen in early August only weeks after the rifles arrived. Frustrated that he could not get authorization from his superiors to pay the black soldiers, General Hunter suggested that they return to their families and "gather crop." While such an order was not objectionable to BB, it led some of his men to complain, the oldest one saying, "Dey need fuh mek up dey mind! Wha dey wan we fuh be? We be soljuh? We be fiel han? We be free?"

General Hunter shared their frustration and wanted to help Washington's decision makers understand the value of deploying freedmen in the Union cause. He and his officers recognized the special qualities of determination, attentiveness, and respect that the freedmen brought to their military training. They also had developed great appreciation for the quality of information Robert Smalls shared about the water defenses of Charleston. General Hunter decided to send Smalls with a civilian delegation to visit President Lincoln, to help convince the president that Africans in America wanted to fight for their own liberation. They reasoned that the guile and courage Smalls demonstrated when he took the *Planter* would be persuasive in President Lincoln's decision-making process.

When Lucas heard that Robert Smalls went to Washington to meet the president, he again sang praises of him as a man who could make a plan and carry it through, because, Lucas said, he saw the miracle unfold before his eyes. Then he turned to his big brother and said, "A man jes like Mista Smalls be right heah fuh lead we people." The small crowd gathered round began to voice their agreement as Lucas turned his praise to his brother. "We gah leada tek chaage uh ting, whedda it be wid de crop or wid de army."

Indeed BB did take care of the plantation's business, whether it involved organizing crews to handle the field tasks or helping train new soldiers at Oakheart who had joined the First South Carolina. Just because the unit had been disbanded formally, there was no less ardor among the men for the fight at hand—BB saw to that.

Several times before sunrise, they had heard gunfire coming across the creeks from nearby plantations. With weapons in the hands of newly armed and anxious sentries, false alarms were not surprising, as there was ample reason for concern about Confederate mischief. The Union navy did not always keep its gunboats stationed at the mouth of Chowan Creek nor could patrols cover all the waterways.

One very early morning near the end of August, BB was finishing up a steamy night of picket duty and Lucas was just rowing out to drop his crabtraps when they heard the crack of rifle fire. Coming around the bend and just visible through the marsh grass was a rowboat with at least three men sitting as low as possible. There was no Union blue apparent in the dim light of early dawn. BB instinctively raised his rifle and aimed, just as another shot was fired by the rowboat crew. BB's first shot was precise—the head of the lead oarsman snapped back and his body slumped into the boat. The remaining two men quickly and powerfully rowed the boat into a small opening in the marsh across the creek, out of sight from the bluff.

BB and Lucas knew well that the tide was going out, and that the only way a boat could exit that particular stand of marsh grass was by using the tributary the Confederates had just entered. With the tide flowing strongly to the sea, the men would soon be stranded in the day's heat without a way to exit their pluff mud prison.

After BB's shot chased the "danger" into hiding, Lucas stationed himself in the boat just downstream from the rebels' entrance into the marsh grass. BB and his men remained across the creek with rifles trained on the far bank, ready for any movement.

In a few moments, the rebel rowboat poked out from the marsh just far enough so that Lucas could see it before those on the riverbank. He raised his pistol to fire but did not, allowing the boat to move farther out into the creek. Again a blast from the bluff took down the first visible target. Lucas saw the terror on the face of the lone surviving crewman as he frenetically pulled on the oars, backing the boat into the marsh.

That poor individual remained stranded through the heat of a sultry summer morning and into the afternoon. When the tide was at its lowest, the sun was straight above, baking the pluff mud. There was no wind for relief. Soon, a weak, young voice came up out of the marsh, crying for his mama.

BB said coldly, "I ain know deese yuh buckra soljuh be sech baby. Dey cry fuh dey mama when ting git tough."

Lucas did not join the ridicule, as moaning sounds rose for a while and then subsided, not to be heard again. Both men considered the suffering of the rebel to be awful, but BB had hardened to it, accepting it as what men have to do when at war. Lucas was uncomfortable with the brutality of death, even when the death was of an "enemy."

Above, at different levels, turkey buzzards had begun their languid circles as they honed in on the dead meat below.

BB caught Lucas looking at him with a sideways glance, and he took the questioning gaze head on. "I ain like you, Lucas—been raise up haad—gah fuh be haad fuh tek wha Massa do back den."

They both needed distraction from the carnage of their own making. BB redirected their attention. "When I tink bout dem haad time, en dem rebel in de maash right yuh, I ain happy. My haat need de sof time wid my ooman en all de chirrun roun yuh. Da wha mek me git up when dayclean—gah fuh see de chirrun be free right roun yuh."

Lucas shared his brother's pleasure in the pace of life and work of the plantation, before the war came too close. And yet Lucas added, "Deh be time I don feel sho bout all dis freedom—freedom good, fuh true—but haad fuh know wha nex day bring. Seem like I be on de wada, wid no ancha, jes drif."

"Wha oona mean, brudda?"

"Jes feel like supm ain right." Lucas tried to explain, but without details. "Some kine uh hole be in my life."

"Maybe ooman mek ting right." BB grinned, sounding like almost any other older brother.

"Maybe. Ain da simple. Sides, ain fine myself jes one ooman."

"Yeah, fuh true." BB thought it was time to tell his younger brother something he had only recently learned. "Time gon come fuh settle down wid one—wha mean mos fuh oona. Eben when you ain look, good ooman show up unda yo nose."

"Brudda—ain know oona been so smaat bout dis kine uh ting."

BB confessed. "I ain tell oona de whole trut bout wha keep me busy roun yuh. Dey be one or two gal I tek up wid."

"Da be good, brudda. Da way man gah fuh live, right?" said Lucas, bolstering the appearance of conquest beyond his reality.

To which BB responded, "Good Lawd know why He mek ooman en man de way dey be. Da be wha I gah fuh figyuh out. Why fuh de good Lawd mek we so? I been busy study bout de question." BB could not suppress a satisfied smile as he reflected on his research.

Lucas laughed at the humor in BB's revelation. "Oooooo, brudda, oona do ting ebby day wha mek eye open wide (*you do things everyday that surprise me*). Mek me happy jes see you be so skrong en smaat. I laan from you, BB."

"I figyuh I gah fuh do de bes I kin ebbyday. Wha be my bes? Da be when I bring joy in de life uh de people I kyah fuh, de people da kyah fuh me—en keep em safe."

"No need fuh worry bout da, big brudda, you done good fa true. Yo whole Oakhaat famly know da, jes like me."

*   *   *

Later that evening, just after sundown, the firelight burned down near the oyster pit where buckets of Lucas's crabs had been offered to everybody at Oakheart. The drama of the day, when Oakheart sharpshooters defended the land from rebel raiders, had peaked. The rising tide dislodged the boat, unseen, from pluff mud where turkey buzzards had feasted earlier. As the heat of the day subsided, the islanders were drifting back to their own dwellings, and the company of newly arrived Union soldiers, fully fed, had gone to their camp down past the fields.

BB, too, had disappeared before Callie took the last frying pan down to wash in the creek. She had just started up the embankment to the bluff when she was scooped up by both elbows so that her feet dangled in air. Though she had missed any signs of impending danger, her response to physical assault was quick and accurate. Callie wriggled free enough to get her feet back on the ground. She swung the frying pan in her right hand striking the figure on her left squarely in the forehead. As he tumbled backward into the water, she ran up the embankment and straight to the barn. The other man still standing pulled his pistol and aimed but then lowered it and ran after her. In full stride, Callie screamed when she looked back to see Feller chasing her, only ten feet behind.

Feller apparently intended to get Callie before he let Bowen know he had found her. He was so intent on his conquest as he entered the barn, he did not notice a large figure slide through the barn door just behind him.

Bowen had recovered just below the riverbank and had started to rise when he saw Union troops approaching on a full run. He backed down and watched as they headed directly toward the screams now emanating from the barn.

In the dim light, the soldiers saw two figures rise in hand-to-hand combat. The smaller man in a dark blue overcoat was lifted by his throat and held up struggling. His head was gripped in the massive, locking forearms of the dusty-clothed man in a light-colored hat with his back to the Yankee troops.

"Halt!" The soldiers' command voices had no effect on the struggle. When BB forcefully twisted his arms, he snapped Feller's neck and threw his limp body off to the side. Several Union troops fired at the same time. BB dropped to his knees before he could even turn. He looked down at Callie, where Feller had pinned her, a tight-lipped smile of recognition and pleasure in his accomplishment as he fell forward, a bullet through his heart.

Chapter 21

In honor of BB, all hands turned out to work the fields at dawn, but the cadence of their labor was halting and their tones subdued. Voices in mourning cried out to their God in uncertainty. Why was one so worthy taken down? Why did the Union troops do it? How did the planters come back? The scenario had changed for all: fear was in their eyes; sadness gripped their souls.

Perhaps their visions of freedom had been celebrated too soon.

Callie discovered in the hours and days following BB's death that there was no consolation. She could not accept the enormity of her loss. Nor could she fully absorb the reality that BB's love for her, combined with his freedman's heart and military zest, compelled him to act. In first light, Callie looked into Missus Bowen's mirror to see her eyes swollen from weeping through the night.

So many came to see BB "home" and to speak well of their experiences with him that Callie resolved on that day to keep the plantation running. She knew that her will to do so was ever stronger now in BB's absence and in his honor. Over the following weeks, as the workload increased without BB, Callie displayed a somber, duty-bound demeanor that did not allow her grief to surface.

Lucas, in contrast, could not hide his pain. His first reaction to strike back was futile, since a Union soldier fired the weapon that killed BB. Lucas was furious, having no place to vent his anger. As the younger brother, Lucas had never known a day without BB. He was not prepared to surrender BB to anything, and certainly not to circumstances that defied his understanding.

One night, Callie found Lucas standing on the end of the dock, his toes overhanging the wooden edge. She was almost sure he would not go into the dark, high-tide waters, but she watched in silence from just off the dock. He sobbed quietly for many minutes.

Then Lucas looked upward, arms outstretched, seeking to understand his God. "You tek my brudda? Why fuh you tek my brudda?" He lifted his open hands to the cloudy skies. "Why fuh I ain heah Callie holla fuh hep?"

Finally, Callie moved next to him, placing her palms on his back. "Lucas, come rest."

"Ain no ansa, Callie." He resisted her gentle pressure on his shoulders to step back, and he raised his voice. "Lawd, why fuh I ain been fus one tuh de baan fuh hep BB?"

Distraught, Callie scolded him softly. "Go ahead. Beat yosef up wid deese question. Ifn you git ansa, da ain gon change wha done happen. BB done gone en ain nuttin gon bring em back. Now we free to figyuh wha come nex."

Lucas said, "Free, huh? Free fuh wha? Fuh git shoot down by de people wha pose fuh mek we free? Fus time ting git tough—shoot no-count free Negro. Callie, dey shoot we brudda ..." And his anger melted into sobs, but now he turned to receive Callie's comforting embrace, as they shared the pain of BB's passing.

Over days of talking together, Callie managed to persuade Lucas that she felt every bit as miserable and angry as he did, but that there was no wisdom in reacting wildly. They agreed to go forward with BB's advice in mind. "Time fuh git ready be when you ain know wha you git ready fuh."

Both Callie and Lucas took solace in the fact that BB perished while avenging the cruel abuse Callie suffered at the hands of Feller. Callie also was pleased to have crashed her frying pan into Bowen's head. Though she was not positive it was Bowen whom she struck, she was almost sure his hand had stirred events that night, giving Lucas and Callie one more reason to loathe their former master, and to fear him.

Over the next several weeks, the Union army very lightly disciplined the two men who shot at BB, after a "fair" hearing in which one explained that he saw a man looking like a Confederate soldier breaking the neck of a man clothed in a long blue coat. He offered that, as a Union soldier, he instinctively fired his weapon when he saw the violence done by a supposed Confederate to a supposed Yankee. Under questioning by his captain as to whether the man he shot might have been defending his sister on the floor of the barn, the soldier answered that he did not notice the woman until after he fired. He could not have known that BB was defending his sister, he said, exclaiming, "Hell, I didn't even know they had sisters."

Orders were issued weeks later, requiring soldiers to be respectful of the life and property of "contrabands," the official army term for the freedmen. When BB's commanding army officer, Colonel Thomas Wentworth Higginson, visited Oakheart to convey his regard for BB and his heartfelt regret, Callie was able to emerge from her grief and accept this extension of respect that her brother had earned. Lucas was nowhere to be found.

⋆   ⋆   ⋆

For days, Callie's fitful efforts to sleep were interrupted by the scene she could not shake from her mind. Feller had tackled her into the hay as she shouted, "Massa Fella, you gon get huht roun yuh now!"

Feller pinned her arms and started to stuff his filthy bandana into her mouth. "Shut up, little gal—be too smart like your mama, we have to send you away, too!" And with those words he was swept up over her, suspended in air for seconds, before BB's powerful forearms snapped his neck.

Callie realized Feller's dying words took her one step closer to understanding her own story. Before then, she had only heard Missus Feller say she knew her mother. She had heard Massa Feller threaten to take care of her the way "they" took care of her mother. Callie surmised that "they" probably were Feller and Bowen, and that they decided to send her mother away because she was smart and hard to handle. Callie was proud to hear that her mother's toughness had caused Feller trouble.

Suddenly, Massa Bowen's record book, tucked away in the bedroom drawer, came back to Callie's mind. Nearly forgotten in the activity of recent days, she returned to it that evening. Plunging into the lines and pages, Callie deflected her thoughts from the scene in the barn.

While studying the page with columns of names and numbers, Callie thought about the ciphering classes she had taken at the Oaks in the last few months. She realized that the fourth column of numbers must represent dollars. Three numbers meant hundreds, and four meant ... more than hundreds. Now the columns made sense to her, and she studied the names of people on the pages, as well as the money Massa Bowen paid for his slaves. Her discovery was tinged with disgust as she understood what power Captain Bowen's money gave him and the suffering it had caused. She saw one of the first entries was crossed through. All she could make out was a name that began with "S," the year 1838, and four numbers in the dollar column, 1250.

Callie did not see her own name on any pages.

There were letters stuffed in the front pocket of the book, but she decided not to press the search at that time. She had more than enough to do every day without spending time or thoughts dwelling on the past. She opted to read Massa's secrets on another day when the present and future were not so pressing. Having made that decision, Callie was drawn back into the past when she saw Lucas return to the dock the next morning with new crab traps purchased in town, and a passenger. Eva!

Callie instantly lost control, marching straight toward the dock and opening her mouth to curse Eva's father when she remembered her advice to Lucas on the uselessness of reacting in rage. She stopped short, pointing the way for Eva to follow her to the porch. Callie left her sitting there briefly before returning with a tea service in her trembling hands.

Eva immediately sought to explain her presence at Oakheart, saying her Charleston home had been sold by her husband out of necessity while he was away fighting. "His business partner told me that there was a place in downtown Charleston for me. Went there. Too many people scurrying and worrying for me, so I decided to go where there were people I could care for, and who could care for me."

Callie could not bring herself to acknowledge Eva as the woman whose dying mother she had helped to nurse and to bury. Though Eva was noticeably forlorn and thinner, wearing a slightly soiled dress and scuffed shoes, Callie had little sympathy for her. She saw Eva ... and thought Feller.

Eva tried to break through. "I heard what happened here. Union army reports were sent to the Charleston papers to scare the Southern people. They said my pa died at your brother's hands." She shook with sorrow, undergirded by a submerged anger. "I know I can't be mad at you—or your brother. Report said my father died attacking a woman at Oakheart Plantation. I know it was you." She looked up at Callie, either to give an apology, or receive one.

Finally, after a long silence, Callie gave a measured amount of truth to a young woman who had denied it to herself too long. "Jes like he done befo, yo daddy been gon tek me (*was going to rape me*). BB stop him en git shot dead fuh da. Tek da story any way you like."

Callie started to step away when Eva grabbed her arm, turning Callie to her. "Papers didn't say a slave was killed."

Callie stared coldly at Eva. "No *slave* been kill, Eva!"

After a moment of hesitation, she said, "Of course, Callie, I am sorry, and I'm so very sorry at BB's passing. I know I'm not the right one to offer comfort right now. But my mother and father just died, and I can't stay up in Charleston any more. My husband is somewhere in Virginia." Eva asked meekly, "I want to help with the children. Besides, I can help you. Can you help me?"

Although Callie accepted Eva's explanation for being back at Oakheart, she did not completely trust her, a feeling that made Callie doubt whether Eva should stay. Why should the daughter of one of her tormentors, the cause of BB's death, be allowed to live on at Oakheart? What could she offer? Why should Callie accept whatever Eva offered?

Given the difficult hours they had spent together, Callie decided to let Eva stay, at least that night. She sensed Eva's path to be true, though confusing for both of them, so Callie embraced her as a friend. Over ensuing days, Callie and Eva spoke of the resilience required to get over life's losses. They helped each other by sharing a period of mourning, however different the causes.

Callie also knew that Eva's presence was good for her daughter. Eva could give Sunny special attention and lessons that she could not get in the Oaks schoolroom. As Eva's visit stretched through the first week, Callie gained needed free time to manage the plantation.

Nor was it lost on Callie that Eva might yet divulge more information about Callie's mother. Days after her arrival, Eva admitted that she had other memories to share. "I remember one time when my mother and I were walking and talking. We had more slaves than usual down in the water hut, Pa's covered cabin that let water in up to the waist at high tide. Some of the women were crying, and yet they stayed there, mostly quiet, taking it. I couldn't have taken it.

"Anyway, Mama said, 'There was one slave woman long ago who belonged to Bowen. She would not stay quiet in the water hut. She was very strong-willed and spoke up.' Mama even told me, 'Your pa beat her once with his whip, and she just stared right back at him, sayin' nothin'.' Another time, Mama told me, 'Daddy hit this woman on her head with a pistol, and she spun round on him so fast her elbow caught him upside his head. Made a big egg-shaped knot over his ear—he was so mad, he woulda killed her.' But Mama said he and Captain Bowen were determined to get some money back for her, and she wouldn't be worth nothin' to them dead." Eva looked up, hoping that the details she remembered were not hurtful.

Callie hated what she heard from Eva but had to ask, "You tink that ooman was kin to me? Jes cause Capn Bowen hep yo daddy deal with huh?"

"Don't know for sure Callie, but Mama said I was about five years old at the time, and she remembered this slave woman just had a baby."

"How old you be now?"

"Twenty-nine."

Callie tried to see the numbers in her mind, as her ciphering classwork had suggested. In her mind's eye she looked at twenty-nine cleaned-out oyster shells lined up and beautiful, and then she took away five. "That been twenty-four yeahs pass." Callie looked inward, considering her facts, and then said thoughtfully, "I be twenty-four." Her face expressed her growing recognition that there was a woman owned by Daniel Bowen twenty-four years ago who, having just given birth, was sold away by Feller and Bowen because she was too difficult to handle, and that all happened in the year Callie was born.

"Eva, I was hopin that you might rememba supm like that. Felt bad to aks right afta your mama pass."

"I understood why you had to ask. One of the reasons I came back was to tell you what I remembered—guess I owed you that, and more. I wished I told you before."

"Thank you. Don mean tuh push you, but that all you memba?"

"Yeah, I really didn't understand much of what I saw and heard, and I didn't see too much. When I was little I just thought my pa was helping people who didn't have a place to stay. I thought they were just on their way to someplace to work, just like we had them working for us. Pa tried to hide the worst of it from Mama and me. I think I started to realize that bad things were happening when my pa brought new people in to stay for a few weeks and they were always so poor and unhappy looking. Then I saw chains on their ankles … I didn't question much when I was growing up. Then I found my husband to carry me away from all of it."

Callie shot back. "Pretend e neba happen in yo life, in yo house, on yo land?"

"Maybe I tried to deny what I saw then. But now I see it for what it was. Partly, that's why I'm here. The other reason, I told you, is to teach the children."

Callie accepted Eva's stated desire to teach Sunny and the other children. She was too busy to worry much about Eva. She had put her search for family truth aside to deal with the current requirements of her long days.

Callie could not be sure that the Yankees would stay and that the planters would stay away. She started to wonder what she, Sunny, and Lucas would do if the Yankees left. But she hid her angst from the others and held her head high, remembering the admonition she heard all too often from her dear Mama Ruth: "Oona kyan see whey fuh go wid oona eye on de groun!" But Mama Ruth didn't have all these things to worry about. Without BB to help think it through, Callie felt fear rather than confidence. That was why, when Lucas came back to Oakheart with news that the Oaks school was closing, Callie panicked until he went on to say that Laura Towne and other teachers were going to open a bigger school at Brick Church.

Callie knew it was time for another visit to Miss Towne. She loaded the rowboat with watermelons as gifts for all those at the Oaks and used the strong inbound tidal surge to help float her heavy load up the creek. Callie remembered how kind Miss Towne had been after BB died, so comforting. She had insisted that Callie begin calling her "Miss Laura," as they had become friends.

When Callie arrived, she hugged her friend and wished her the best in a way that alarmed Miss Laura. "You are still planning to bring Sunny to our new Penn School, aren't you? Please let her be one of our youngest scholars."

Callie was relieved to learn of Miss Laura's ongoing commitment and responded, "Of course, missus. Thank you for callin—wha you call my baby girl—a ... a schol-ar? Tha mean you think she smaat?"

"Of course I do, just as her mother is very smart."

Callie was not searching for such a compliment, but it made her feel great. "Fuh true, I be so proud to bring my chile to Penn School."

Hoping for more good news from Callie, Miss Laura asked if freedmen at Oakheart were content with their work and the payments they received in September.

Callie bragged. "Yes, mahm, we wuk for pay and mos happy to do so. Some get two dollar, some up to five for how much extra they done." And then she said through a satisfied smile, "But we wuk for pride, too!" Realizing how boastful that made her sound on behalf of herself and her peers, Callie quickly added, "Sorry to say so, Miss Laura."

"Oh, no apology is necessary, Callie. Pride is very real and it's good to feel it, especially when it is pride in what you and the people at Oakheart have done."

"BB always say, 'We wuk fuh food en fuh money, but we wuk mos for our chirrun en ousef.' He been tell folk, 'Be proud of wha dey do fuh dem dey kyah fuh.'"

"What a wonderful young man was your BB. He would have been extra happy with the news I have to share."

Callie looked up expectantly. "Thas awright, Miss Laura! He still be happy cause I know he watch over me. Please, miss, what happen?"

"President Lincoln has issued a special order, actually a proclamation. To summarize, it states that on the first day of 1863, slaves in captured territories of the Confederacy are to be free. It means places like right here, Callie. I think the president wants to have freedmen all across the South do what young men across these islands have done—join the fight for freedom. He wants to abolish slavery once and for all."

"Sho is good news, Miss Laura, though I haffa say I been feelin a little bit free for a good while now. Glad Mista Lincoln know what we know all along—we be too please to fight to be free."

As she rowed back to Oakheart, Callie tried to find joy in the news about Mr. Lincoln's proclamation in Washington to free the slaves sometime in the future. She only knew that right there in her family, she and her people had tasted freedom, but her beautiful brother could no longer sip from that cup. Callie had struggled to come through the pain of BB's death. Usually only Sunny could pull her out of sadness, and sometimes even her child's joy was not enough. But, like any parent, Callie knew that she should be strong for Sunny, and that she would carry on as BB would have her do. It was just so very hard to be without him.

* * *

Lucas continued to carry out his responsibilities in a manner BB would praise. His solitary labors to feed people masked the depths of his grief. When he wasn't fishing, he provided transportation for US government agents at the Oaks plantation and shared his knowledge of local waterways with Union naval officers. This role suited his independent streak perfectly and allowed him to mourn his brother's death as he worked largely in isolation.

Free, no longer a slave, in the heart of family love, fishing for the good of all, Lucas believed his life had been a gift from God. Then suddenly his foundation had been destroyed by Yankee bullets. He could not reconcile the conflict between his belief in a loving God, and the reality that his God had allowed BB's life to be taken. Nor did Lucas want to face life without his brother, friend, leader, protector—a source of strength and character that had always bolstered him.

Lucas was sad and mad, confused and infused with an energy to do something—anything that would rise to the level of an adequate response to his brother's killing. He accepted Callie's admonition to avoid reactions that only satisfied the moment. But he justified the anger he carried for wrongs done and questions unanswered. As so often happens in conflict, violence begets a willingness to violate others, for real or perceived wrongs. That Lucas kept himself on the water fishing for hours at a time benefitted those not exposed to the barbed persona he had developed in the weeks without his brother. He even avoided spending much time with his sister, uncertain that his bitterness could be contained and unwilling to injure her further if it could not.

If Callie needed him to work in the fields, Lucas was willing, but he believed he served a higher calling on the water. For the first time, this calling was not firmly based on his faith in God. So Lucas rode the currents, ostensibly a fisherman with all the gear, but with BB's army rifle nestled at his side with extra ammunition. Lucas was more than certain that if he happened upon an enemy, he would not hesitate to fire. He intended to be ready for anything as he glided silently on the waterways, listening, watching, fishing, and waiting. Some nights he would patrol the shoreline around Constant Island, and on others he would venture up river with the incoming high tides, sliding into mainland waters controlled by the Confederacy. What was he looking for? What did he hope to find? Just like BB, Lucas was seeking the flashpoint of the conflict. But the enemy, real and imagined, was elusive.

Through September of 1862, bold Southern raiders continued to seek weak spots in island defenses. Their unwelcome visits were seldom so deadly as the night BB was killed. Increasingly, the raids were repulsed by surprisingly effective resistance. On Port Royal Island, Yankees captured Confederates. Then an attempted rebel landing at Brickyard Point on Ladies Island was aborted under heavy fire. Toward the end of October, on the north side of St. Helena Island near Eddings Point, freedmen guards opened fire on three boats of attackers, sending them rowing quickly back to deep water. Accurate rifle fire from night-pickets was probably the last thing expected from former slaves. But the army had trained them well to defend their home ground.

When Lincoln's government allowed General Hunter to call his First South Carolina Volunteers back into service, the men of Oakheart were ready along with hundreds more across the islands. They had issues to settle beyond the banks of the waterways surrounding their home plantations, where they had kept skills sharp warding off attackers. Now there was freedom to be won. President Lincoln had freed them to serve, and to a man, though without their leader BB, they responded as a unit.

★   ★   ★

After spending months on a ship supporting the blockade, Will was reassigned as the junior supply officer responsible for procurement of local food for the troops. To do his job successfully, he wanted to include Lucas and promptly arranged a visit to Oakheart.

Upon arrival, Will secured his boat to the dock, listened, and looked around. The grounds were strangely quiet and no one was visible from the front yard to the barn to the cookhouse. Laborers in the fields worked with little zest or rhythm in their chants. Callie spotted him first from the big house porch and ran to him. Catching herself slightly, she came to a stop a foot short of Will, who stood watching her approach.

"I heard, Callie. I know what happened here. I hate it more than I can ever say." Will did not mention BB at first, for he did not want to touch such sensitive wounds directly. Yet he had to offer his sympathies. "I didn't know BB very well, though he always impressed me. He was such a good man."

Callie was not able to speak. Instead, she stepped to Will and put her arms around him. With only support and kindness intended, Will was surprised to feel Callie clutching, holding her head to his neck, and then he felt her quiet sobs. For whatever reason, safely in Will's embrace, she finally allowed herself to cry openly about her dead brother. The night of his death, her tears were about the shock and immediacy of seeing BB fall to the barn floor. Now Callie's denied emotions, ones that Lucas had been living out daily, spilled onto Will's shoulder. Their embrace lasted until Callie's trembling stopped, her breathing settled, and her tears were absorbed into Will's jacket.

That night, after the quick dinner Callie made especially for him, Will sat with her and Lucas, sharing his knowledge of the world beyond the South Carolina sea islands. Though the war had been going poorly for the North generally, it seemed a large battle in Maryland—Antietam, they called it—gave Union forces renewed enthusiasm. Right after it, President Lincoln made public his plans for the Emancipation Proclamation. Will was impressed that Callie had already learned this big news from Washington. "Well then, smart one, let me tell you some things you don't know."

"Don be too sho. I heah ting you know. I taak to people." Callie may have been in mourning, but her quick mind still moved in ways that impressed Will. She gestured for him to proceed.

"The Union navy has been catching a lot of boats trying to run the blockade these days—three this month up around Charleston. I think we are really making it hard for them to ship their cotton out and to get their food and weapons in. They can't even get real coffee for Southerners anymore. So, if this blockade works, the Confederate states are gonna lose this war. And if the Union prevails, all the slaves will be freed."

"Glory hallelujah!" Lucas sang out just before Callie whispered, "Praise Gawd."

Callie and Lucas were indeed impressed and willing to believe what Will told them. Hoping it could be true, they spread the word over the next few days. Could slavery everywhere soon end? Callie and Lucas both felt a thrill at the prospect as Will described it, but when their conversation was done, they realized that they still could not share the joy with BB.

As they left each other that night, Will stopped to offer Callie one more embrace in recognition of the heartache and pain she had been through. To Will's great surprise, Eva arrived on the porch after an all-day outing. Her face registered the pleasure of seeing Will again, and then confusion from seeing how familiar Callie and Will seemed to be. Eva quickly shook her head, indicating either her disapproval or her involuntary reaction to such a sight.

Will stopped short. "Though I owe you no explanation, I can tell you that what you see is nothing more than comfort for Callie over BB."

Will thought that should suffice, but Eva said, "It certainly did look comfortable."

Will redirected Eva's thinking, as he had before. "Do you not think that there are more fruitful topics for us to discuss? For instance, what brought you back to Oakheart?"

"I heard that my father died here," Eva started to explain.

"Of course, I am sorry for questioning." Will wondered all the more how Callie and Eva were able to spend time together, but he hesitated to ask.

"And I'm back here on the islands where I grew up—where I saw slave children grow up beside me. Now I want to help the children get through this war, and, if I can, I want to help them get over slavery."

Will was favorably impressed as Eva sounded resolute in her commitment. They had indeed changed the discussion to a more purposeful subject. Will said, "Any time we focus on the needs of the children, we do the right thing." Will gave Eva a quick good-bye hug and some encouragement. "Keep up your spirits and the great work you are doing."

Will then returned to Callie for a slightly longer embrace.

Callie also praised Eva's work the next time she was in conversation with Miss Laura, letting her know that this caring white woman was very familiar with St. Helena Island, especially the north side, and wanted to help teach some of the young children there. Within another week, Callie was pleased to hear that Eva took the assignment offered by Miss Laura and began living at a plantation not too far from her family's land. Callie was pleased to help Eva right wrongs, nearer to her home.

Before Will's visit could end, of course, he and Lucas had to go fishing. Will sensed his friend's exhaustion after weeks of nightly patrols on the river. He learned that Lucas was deeply hurt and distrustful of the Union military and not able to understand how his God allowed BB to be taken. When Lucas said he didn't know God like he used to, Will was quick to urge him not to lose his faith. "BB would not want his death to cause you to lose something so important. He would tell you that God did this to move you on to a higher place." Will wondered where exactly he was going with this but knew he wanted his friend to continue to have faith. "Maybe in some way, you can help more people. You know, do something worthy of BB's sacrifice."

Lucas knew Will wanted to help, but just then, weeks after BB died, Will's best-intentioned words had trouble permeating the thickening crust around Lucas's soul. Will tried a familiar angle. "Think about it, man. You know there's something good around the next bend in the river."

That phrase moved Lucas to speak sharply. "I tell you bout da. Wha I talk bout now be de real bend in dishyuh riba. You wuk on de big wada, but deh be real wuk right yuh. We try fuh keep buckra way from yuh en da git BB kill. Ain gah fuh go roun no bend fuh fine trouble."

Will acknowledged Lucas's perspective on the war, which had been all too real for Oakheart's finest, BB. "Seems crazy that men are dying, more each day, since there's not much change down here now. Rebs have their mainland, and the Union controls the sea islands and all these creeks with your help. It ain't right that BB got killed over that."

"You mean BB die fuh nuttin, Will? Da wha you say?"

"You know I don't believe that, Lucas. BB fought this war as a US Army man; he fought for freedom, and he also fought his own war against Captain Bowen." And then the young sailor said, "But he also fought for me." That made Lucas look up, engaging Will's gaze directly for the first time in the conversation.

Will went on. "That's right, BB fought my wars, taking on my stepfather while saving Callie's life, and finally he got killed breaking the neck of a low-life slaver. Yeah, BB died for me."

They pulled castnets full of shrimp and mullet without talking for a long while. Then Lucas said, "Guess you know BB unit been call back. Ummm-hmmm. De First South Carolina Volunteers. Dem men been ready fuh go, da fuh sho."

Will understood Lucas as he transitioned from the painful discussion of life without BB. "Sounds like you are a little more enthusiastic about these war matters than you are letting on."

"Jes cause I don weah no unifoam, da don mean I don wan beat de man wid him boot on my neck."

"Whoa, Lucas! Whatever happened to forgiveness?"

"Time for da maybe some time, but da ain now. Eye-fuh-eye right now. BB tell me fo he dead he grow up haad. Maybe how BB git kill da wha mek me grow up."

They clasped right hands and drew each other close, rocking the boat in calm water. Lucas forgave Will for not being able to feel the depth of his pain.

Chapter 22

After Lucas sent Will back to his ship with fresh seafood any crew would envy, he considered Will's advice carefully. He decided to increase his ferry and patrol services as the flow of visitors to St. Helena Island had grown during 1862. Most came to observe and report on the success of the Port Royal Experiment, the new name of the effort to lift former bondsmen from the lingering constraints of slavery. Some were assigned specific tasks, like the US tax commissioners.

In late October, Miss Towne told Callie that the federal government had sent the tax commissioners to Beaufort because there were taxes to be paid for wartime costs. If taxes were not paid on land the planters owned, she said there might be an opportunity for freedmen to buy the land they had been working. All that was too much for Callie, and she showed her doubts with a head shake. "Pardon, Miss Laura, but I have to see da fuh real, to believe e."

After discussing the land issue, Miss Towne surprised Callie with her next idea. "Please, Callie, could you come to dinner at the Oaks this Saturday? Some special people are coming, and one is a new teacher for Penn School named Charlotte Forten."

"Sure, mahm, I'll be there, just tell me what time you want me to get cookin and servin, and I'll fix things to yo likin." Callie was enthused to be entrusted with the responsibility for such a fine dinner.

"No, Callie, please understand. I would like you to be our guest at dinner, along with others whom I'm sure you will enjoy."

"Can't quite imagine dinner guests be actin for my enjoyment." Callie hesitated. "Don't tink I should be no enjoyment neither." She looked at her new friend to discern intent.

Laura Towne was smiling. "Please let us share dinner together Saturday. We will all enjoy each other's company, I'm certain."

Through her shock, Callie managed a small grin and said, "Yes, Miss Laura. If you sho thas what you want."

"It is, dear, it is."

★   ★   ★

For Callie, the occasion of a meal being served to her rather than by her was not a cause for celebration. For sure, she was glad not to be serving, but she feared sitting down to dinner with persons who had more understanding of the world than she, or so she thought.

But it truly was a dinner to celebrate the arrival of Charlotte Forten. Callie was shocked to see that Miss Forten was a black woman like herself—well, not really like her at all. Miss Forten was highly educated and raised in the finest cultural mix Boston could offer. She spoke of famous poets, such as John Greenleaf Whittier, as family friends. While she did not put on airs, her refinement was evident. Callie was at once impressed and thrilled to see how well Miss Forten carried herself, noticing that, somehow after traveling for days and barely settling into her new surroundings, Miss Forten managed to look fresh in a plain but beautiful dress and well-coiffed hair. While admiring Miss Forten greatly, Callie checked to make certain that her hair remained brushed into a simple bun. Despite wearing an attractive navy-blue dress from Missus Bowen's closet, Callie began to feel inferior.

The dinner guests gathered at the table: Laura Towne and her best friend, Ellen Murray, who helped manage the work at Penn School; Miss Forten; two army officers who had arrived at the Oaks that afternoon; and Callie, who was not at all comfortable with the situation. In her anxiety, she stumbled slightly over the chair that the major had pulled out for her. "Thank you," she murmured quietly. "I'm used to servin dinner more than sittin for it." Around the table there was laughter at the clever truism, a measure of the ongoing change.

Callie was fairly sure that the laughter was not at her, but she had some doubts. As the dinner wore on, she mostly just listened—her habit as a lifelong server.

The gracious hosts described their new school now meeting at the Brick Church. They said there were so many children, sometimes as many as four classes were held in the open sanctuary, which made it awfully hard to teach. And yet they were thrilled that most of the youngsters and some of their parents worked so hard to learn their letters and other basics.

The youngest of the two officers asked if slavery was as cruel as some people said. Callie started to answer but waited when she saw Miss Forten lift her hand. In a shaky voice, Miss Forten said she was horrified that day to hear from a former slave whose master had not believed the slaves when they said they were sick, and withheld food from them until they returned to work. She told the story of another woman too fevered to move, let alone work. Her master held her under water to break the fever, but the lady drowned.

Callie decided not to tell any of the stories she had lived.

Miss Towne quickly intervened to suggest that there might be items more favorable for digestion than the awful ways of slavery. She was especially pleased with the progress she had seen in her first half year on the islands. The freedmen, she said, had moved from being fearful and distrustful to cautiously accepting of the US government's help. She said that the island people demonstrated their gratitude for the education, clothing, and freedom to associate with their loved ones by bringing food and other gifts. She turned to Callie to suggest that "all may not yet be perfect, but we are working on it, aren't we, Callie?"

Callie took the cue to describe the great help that Miss Laura and Mister Pierce had been to all the freedmen, and then she particularly praised their good judgment in allowing Oakheart work to proceed without supervision. "It give us a chance to prove what we kin do. We too proud and pleased to be workin in a freedom way now."

"What we are seeing, gentlemen," Ms. Towne explained, "is that the experiment the US government has undertaken here on these sea islands is working. Contrary to what many believe, these people from Africa, kept in cruel bondage, are more than able to function as free beings, and to fight in their own defense."

"Indeed," Charlotte Forten said, "there was a great debate running between one of Boston's finest theologians and one of the leading ministers from right here in Beaufort. This local minister defended the nobility of Southern slavery as consistent with Christian purpose, to the point that he questioned whether slaves could function well at all if they should become free." Miss Forten concluded rather strongly: "It seems this work in his own backyard has proved him to be frightfully wrong in his assumptions." That said, she rose, saying that the subject moved her to play the piano. She immediately pounded out an impassioned version of "The Battle Hymn of the Republic."

With that testimony and performance, and the custard dessert finished, the party moved onto the porch for conversation. It gave Callie an opportunity to thank her friend for caring enough to invite her to dinner. Before Callie rushed away to row home in the twilight, she pulled Miss Laura aside and expressed her doubts about ever being comfortable in such a social setting.

Her host responded, "My dear, you just did fit in, beautifully."

"I ain neba gon have all the high-minded ways and things to say, like I seen tonight, Miss. Thas not the way I ack mos times, and I sho don be standin roun talkin like a missus and her frens."

"You may not believe it, Callie, but you speak very well when you want to. I was very pleased to have you at my dinner table, seated, and in conversation with my friends."

Callie said, "Seein Miss Forten just remind me more of what I not, not what I am."

Miss Towne was saddened, and she proceeded to tell Callie what she needed to hear. "You must know that you have the same innate worth and potential as any other person. The only difference between you and our lovely friend Charlotte is that she has had twenty years of education that you have not. Do not compare yourself in that way. You are strong and very smart and should be proud, no matter anyone else. Look what you can do, look what you know, look how you care, look who you are!"

★ ★ ★

The week after the dinner party, the First South Carolina Volunteers were officially mustered in. The men, who had gone back to their island homes in August disappointed and without pay, returned in November wearing the uniforms they had kept. Their unit, reactivated with the approval of President Lincoln and with a promise that they would be paid, became the first regiment in the US Army made up entirely of freed slaves. It was November 7, 1862, one year after Union occupation brought freedom to the enslaved people of the sea islands. Two companies of the First South Carolina, one in which BB would have served, began immediate preparations for an expedition down the coast to Florida.

The will of the US government was imposed up and down the Atlantic coast as the blockade tightened. Fewer ships left Charleston with cotton and fewer returned to bring Southern citizens much needed supplies like clothing, leather, shoes, and coffee. Despite Union control of most coastal areas, the Confederacy mounted isolated attacks near mainland strategic locations to keep the Yankees off-balance. They surprised the Union command at Fort Pulaski, near Savannah, with all-day shelling on November 22, 1862. Civilian and military casualties were brought by boat to hospitals in the old homes and churches of Beaufort.

Laura Towne was summoned by authorities to help and asked her oarsmen to row to Oakheart on the way to town. Callie had just left the dock hauling a full basket of oysters to the cookhouse. Her enthusiastic greeting of Miss Laura simmered to uncertainty at the prospect of caring for the injured soldiers again. Callie knew she could handle the work, but it was so soon after watching the life ebb from BB. She hoped her memory of that terrible day would not diminish her ability to serve.

Miss Laura helped Callie into her light jacket for the boat trip to Beaufort, and they were on the way. The injured were waiting. As before, Callie treated each new patient as if he was her first. She sought to comfort, cleanse, and lift the spirits of those who had cause to be down. Though she recognized her limited experience, she reached out with gentle intent and was well received.

One of the military physicians asked Callie to attend more soldiers in the downstairs area of an old house by the water. Upon descending the narrow stairs to the ground floor, she saw men, but she saw no beds, cots, or pallets, or any semblance of such. There were ten men on the dirt, partially covered with blankets, and no one was tending to them. The dim light made it hard to discern at first, but then she saw that all the patients were black men.

After several hours down there with the men, Callie retuned to the upper floors of the home where Miss Towne was working. She saw that Callie was not herself, seemingly bereft of the spirit that defined her. Miss Towne learned that she had been down to the dank, fly-infested ground floor treating injuries, and she thought she understood what was bothering Callie. "I am told, Callie, that they want to improve the conditions for injured Negro soldiers. I assure you, I will speak to General Saxton about this."

Callie was barely responsive, though she said, "Thank you, Miss Laura." By Callie's passionless demeanor, Laura Towne knew she had to ask. "Callie, what is wrong? Are you ill?"

"No, mahm. See, oh missus, I can't believe it."

"What, Callie, what?"

"I found my Sunny's father down there. Firs time I see him since Massa lash him almos dead and send him off, away from me."

Laura Towne looked on with questioning compassion in her face.

"I knew he got move to Edisto back then. I heard someone saw him when slaves—scuse me, missus—freedmen, got move off Edisto to St. Helena by the Yankees. Today, all he say is he cain't catch any air in his chest after bein in a big explosion down at Pulaski."

Of course, Miss Laura's questioning did not end there, and Callie wanted to talk. Callie told her that this was the only man she felt special in here, as she pointed to her heart. "When I got ready to have my baby, Massa so mad, he lash my man bad. I didn't really know I done wrong. I jes know Massa sent him away more than six years ago." Callie waited, lost in thought. "I tell him bout his daughter and how she fine. He different man now—no warm smile I used to see anywhere on his face. Not man I used to know."

"That could be his injury, Callie."

"No, mahm. True he hurt, but Ben I know back then find way to smile when he hear bout Sunny. He show nothin when I tell him. I most sho that bein slave done kill his spirit, and dis explosion workin for Yankees takin his body. If he live, maybe the freedom fight will bring e back."

"I hope so for your sake and Sunny's, and for Ben's too."

"Well, mahm, I'm not expectin nothin for me. Fuh true, he been special fuh me. E felt good, mahm. But now e feels gone." Her friend looked doubtful, and Callie noticed. "No, Miss Laura, fuh real, I got no feelins for him. 'Sides, he has his people from Edisto now."

"Family?"

"No, miss, people took him in though. You know, we islanders heah in groups is all not family, if you mean blood family. No, miss, we been broken up and sold away too much to only look out for blood family. Peoples take in other peoples, to give them help, or home, or hope. We be generous people in tha way."

"I didn't realize how much so, Callie. Your community is better for it. Thank you for helping me see you more clearly."

"Not even my brothers, Lucas and BB, are my blood brothers, Miss Laura. Peoples always tell me Mama Ruth took me in as baby, and when she did, she tell her boys, Lucas and BB, dey my brothers. We not blood famly, miss, but in every other way under this hot sun, we famly."

As Christmas neared, Ben healed enough to travel out where his people stayed on the northern end of St. Helena, across from Edisto.

Callie remained at her home on Oakheart Plantation with her daughter, brother, and extended family.

* * *

In celebration of the season, Callie accepted Miss Laura's invitation to help teachers decorate the Brick Church for a Christmas Day gathering. The pulpit was draped in Spanish moss, and green ribbon had been hung between the church pillars, tied with sprays of red berries and magnolia leaves. Callie and Sunny loved their job, collecting pine cuttings and binding them together for wreaths to decorate the church. The scent overpowered them both as they worked to rub the sticky sap from Sunny's fingers. Many of her fellow students and their parents joined the celebration. When the teachers proudly announced that more than twelve hundred children were taking lessons on the islands, Sunny couldn't clap without her hands sticking together.

Again there were speeches and singing, and the children performed songs and poems they had memorized. One highlight was a new song, written for the occasion by John Greenleaf Whittier, Miss Forten's friend. Callie could not believe how well Sunny and the other children pronounced the words. She even memorized the last lines with Sunny.

> "Oh none in all the world before
> Were ever glad as we.
> We're free on Carolina's shore;
> We're all at home and free!"

As much as she loved the words, before she knew it, Callie had started thinking about them too much. Next thing she knew, she had walked up to a group of teachers and said in her most firmly polite voice, "Miss Laura, may I speak with you please? I just love the pretty words at the end of that poem by John Greenleaf."

"Whittier," added Miss Laura.

"Don't you love it? 'Oh none in all the world before were ever glad as we. We free on Ca'lina's sho, we all at home and free.' Ummm-ummm-ummm!"

After Callie allowed the wonderful sentiments to linger in the air, she asked, "What does bein free mean exactly, the way President Lincoln talk in his proclamation? I'm askin cause a man at Oakhaat ask me, and I respek this man."

"Go on, Callie." Miss Laura shook her head. "As if I could stop you from asking your questions."

"He say: 'Why bein free madda if man won't let you get up? Say they give you money but e don't come?' I couldn't argue with him, Miss Laura—when was the last time we got paid? September, Miss Laura? Then he say, 'In slave days buckra planter never promise nuttin, so he didn't break his word. Northern people promise lots but don't always come true.' Then he say, sounding kinda smart, 'Union got to be different from de buckra planta—if makin promises to we people, need to keep em.'"

Miss Towne looked perplexed that Callie would have such things on her mind on Christmas Day. She asked her to consider the season and let some of these business concerns pass for a few days.

To which Callie responded without missing a beat, "Seem to me, people's problems and questions don't go away for a day, even on Christmas Day. My belief in God don't let me take a day off. But I'll come back with it another day." And before her white mentor began to speak, Callie continued from her heart. "It's just that the smartest people at Oakheart been askin about this Mancipation and all. They say, 'I know slavery times be much worse and I sho don't want dem times back. But we din put ourselves in dis situation, in no way aks fer it. Now we free, let us up so we can be we. We jes want see all the fancy words come to life.' That's what they say, Miss Laura."

"Is that what 'they' say, Callie, or did I hear a little Callie in those words?"

"Maybe just a little bit of me, Miss Laura. But I been hearin questions. Just passin on what I hear. When I can answer em, maybe I be more joyful even den I am now."

"Those are all good questions, Callie. I didn't know there were so many doubts left among the freedmen. Maybe we'll learn more of the answers together in the new year."

"Got one more question, miss. Isn't part of bein free that you can have questions, and then aks the people in charge about em?"

"That is absolutely correct, Callie. You can ask them."

"Well, then, I just askin." Callie sighed through a small, twisted smile. "But I can wait til next year for the answers."

That new year arrived as promised by the calendar, one week after Christmas. There was excitement on this first day of 1863. The Emancipation Proclamation from President Lincoln was to be read for all the freedmen to hear.

As Callie told friends at Oakheart, "Mancipation is Yankee fancy word for bein free."

Camp Saxton, two miles south of town on the Beaufort River was the site chosen for the reading, in a grand ceremony to which all were invited. A huge crowd turned out on the beautiful day, in part because many freedmen believed that, in order to actually be free, it was necessary to be present to hear the document read. Many arrived over land, but hundreds came by water in all manner of floating stock, including a few steamships provided by General Saxton. Those approaching from areas south of Camp Saxton were helped by the surge of the incoming tide from the Atlantic, and they arrived in a timely fashion. They were, therefore, more likely to be up near the stage where important things were to be said, or first in line near the fire pit where five big oxen had been cooking all night. The aroma of smoked oxen meat drifted upstream to visitors still coming against the tide from Beaufort. Though they might be a little late, with perseverance they could still hear President Lincoln's "fancy freedom words."

The people gathered in all manner of finery fit for a Sunday occasion on a Thursday, under a canopy provided by giant live oak trees. The festivities were enhanced by the women's colorful clothing and headscarves. Companies of the First South Carolina Volunteers were at ease in files near the stage, brilliant as flowers in their red pants and blue coats. Dignitaries filled the platform as Callie watched, not surprised to see Miss Laura among them. Bright sunlight caused the Spanish moss to appear illuminated while wafting in the breeze off the river. With great anticipation, freedmen filled in all the gaps between groups of white civilians and military officers.

The man chosen to read President Lincoln's proclamation was Dr. W. H. Brisbane, a South Carolinian who had freed his slaves as a matter of principle before the war began. When he finished, and as Colonel Higginson received a gift of the US flag and prepared to speak, one of the elder freedmen began singing, his strong voice lifting above the crowd.

"My coun-try 'tis of thee." More voices joined in. "Sweet land of liberty, of Thee I sing."

Amidst flowing tears, the voices swelled during the rendition until all sang the last line as one, "Le-et free-dom ring!"

PART V

January to July, 1863

Chapter 23

For the former slaves, hearing the Emancipation Proclamation was a profound experience on that first day of 1863. They joined their liberators to celebrate with song, ceremony, food, and fellowship. As grand as the occasion was, however, the former slaves knew that freedom meant continuing to go along with US government work requirements.

The very questions Callie put to Miss Laura on Christmas Day were given voice by the newly proclaimed free people of Oakheart during Callie's first meeting with them in January 1863. Callie stood on the front porch steps before more than fifty workers who had gathered under the massive live oak branches. Her peers were wary, having been free of enslavement for only fourteen months, yet seeing that each day could change the shape of their freedom. They had come to expect that living their own "free" lives would require more pain and sacrifice, a situation not changed by a proclamation.

The worries of the people came to her rapid-fire. "Tell your Yankee friends we ain gah pay fuh fo months." "Dey gon leh rich folk buy dis lan, chase we people off? Da fuh real?" "Why we soljuh join army and still ain git no pay?" "Mancipation mean we no more wuk cotton?" "Why Yankee soljuh tek we pig en wegetable anytime dey want?" "Yankee man ebba gon leh we be free on we ownt faam?"

Callie heard more stories of field workers choosing to take jobs with military and civilian organizations. She learned that many men had begun working as laborers in Union warehouses and on the docks; as craftsmen with products to sell; as "independent" farmers marketing their produce; or like Lucas, earning their living from the sea. Women had been hired as cooks and laundresses in support of the army and navy personnel based around Port Royal Sound.

If Callie had not committed herself to making Oakheart work, her skills would have been valued by any officer trying to run a tight outfit. The streets of Beaufort were lined with headquarters for the operations of the Union army and a bevy of new businesses designed to meet the needs of the military, for a fine fee. Old homes on Bay Street that overlooked miles of the Beaufort River were commandeered by Union generals, the quartermaster, and the signal corps, while others were converted into hospitals and centers for relief organizations.

Callie had no time for such outside interests. Her hands and heart were busy raising her daughter while managing Oakheart. When her mind was free of immediate worries, Callie thought about questions she should ask the Yankees—what could be coming around the bend in the river that she could not yet see?

In spite of the uncertainties and lack of compensation, the Oakheart freedmen continued to labor in the fields, train to be soldiers, serve the needs of the Union forces and organizations, and feed the extra mouths. For that loyalty, Callie felt that her kinfolk were right—the Yankees needed to fulfill the promise of freedom in some real way.

★   ★   ★

Over the next month, Callie listened to discussions between Miss Towne and visitors at the Oaks Plantation, learning that the land sale just might come to pass. She also heard that the Congress told the president that his tax commissioners should make sure that taxes were paid in every Confederate state that seceded and where the Union had gained control. Miss Towne convinced Callie and other freedmen that they would have a chance to buy plantation land, if their former masters were not able or willing to pay the taxes to the federal government.

There were problems, however, and Miss Towne worked hard to get the Union generals to agree with her solutions. She feared that the parcels of land would be too large, or the cost of the land too high, to allow any freedman to bid successfully for the property. Miss Towne was fighting for some land to be set aside specifically for freedmen to purchase. General Saxton agreed with her because the US military shared the freedmen's interest in maintaining the current arrangement without the encumbrances that new land owners might impose.

One afternoon, Callie happened to overhear a discussion between Miss Towne and General Saxton, confirming her excitement about the possible land sale. So she decided to interrupt and press her luck with the agreeable general, instead of attending a lesson on lettering.

"Excuse please, suh."

"Yes, young woman, what would be your name?"

"My name would be and is Callie, suh."

Saxton was intrigued, saying, "Please go on then."

"It's just that, suh, I hear that you are a fair man, and we mos proud of what our men been doin in the First South Carolina. They been workin up and down the coast over las three months. Fuh true? Ummm ... Is tha true, suh?" Callie looked General Saxton straight in the eye when she rephrased her question, talking as she imagined he would say it.

"Fuh true," General Saxton said with a smile. "That is in fact quite true, and we are grateful for their service."

"Well, suh, when I ... was ... helpin Miss Towne in the hospital houses heah in Beaufort, I went down to the ground floor to find the Negro men deh ... there." Callie worked hard to speak with care so that the general could understand her fully. "Suh, I know you know how haad it be ... is ... to git soljuhs well when they sick an hurt. Think how haad must be for our people, our soljuhs to get well, kept on wet ground down there. You see, General, I'm a person re-spon-sible for helpin them get well. Make my job ... haader, suh. Take longer to get them back to fight fuh you."

"You have painted a fairly full picture for me, haven't you, Miss Callie? I'll talk with the people of the US Sanitary Commission next week. They will make the situation right. Thank you for your willingness to tell me this, Miss Callie."

"Scuse please, but suh, what is the US San ... San-i-tare Commission?" Callie really didn't begin to understand.

"Of course, how could you know that? It is a group composed mostly of women who have volunteered wherever our troops are, to work very hard to keep them healthy, by providing clean places for the injured or ill to recover."

"Oh, you mean the hospitals we have all around Beaufort?"

"Indeed, Miss Callie. They help there as well. Again, it was a pleasure." As General Saxton tipped his hat to Callie, she could feel a flush rising to her face. She was overwhelmed by his kind reception and his response to her question made her believe he would act. So stunned was Callie that all she could say was, "So nice to talk to you, suh."

The general walked on, and Miss Towne approached Callie from the side, placing an arm around her shoulder. "You should never doubt what you can do, the impact you can have on people. I have seen you in action, 'Miss Callie.'"

⋆   ⋆   ⋆

General Saxton acted according to his word. Shortly after he met Miss Towne and Callie, he persuaded General Hunter that delaying the proposed land sale would facilitate military objectives. The generals were concerned that they would lose full control of the islands if they were purchased by private citizens, and that they would not have enough places to put all the former slaves seeking refuge. Besides, they believed that the current satisfactory status of freedmen on the islands would be disrupted.

While the matter festered in Washington, Miss Towne and most plantation superintendents focused on helping the former slaves to manage their new freedoms independently. Miss Towne saw the land sale as a measure of that freedom, when those who had worked the land as slaves could buy some of it.

As freedmen waited to become land owners, Union forces left Port Royal Sound, moving south to probe and raid the Georgia and Florida coasts. BB's fellow soldiers in the First South Carolina Volunteers not only fought well but also were effective in gathering supplies, wrecking salt works, stealing machinery and products from lumber yards, and generally weakening the Confederacy's supporting network.

By land and by water the freedmen were finding work and reasons to travel beyond the boundaries they had known as slaves. Through their vast network of communication, of which Callie was a proud part, communities of freedmen learned the news rapidly. For those watching closely, the ebb and flow of the war was understood by the freedmen to a degree that continued to surprise their white Northern brethren. In this regard, Callie, while remarkable, was not unique. From the many disrupted lives that were the products of slavery, surprising capability and unbreakable determination arose.

Callie remembered overhearing a conversation between Miss Towne and Colonel Higginson, after he had commanded the First South Carolina Volunteers for several months. She was pleased to hear such admiration in his voice as he spoke of the island people. After Miss Towne complemented his firm but kind approach to his troops, the colonel described his men as keen observers of people—first their former masters, and now their current Yankee allies. "Though they despised the state of being owned as slaves, they discerned the good from the bad among their white masters. They knew who treated them with any degree of kindness." *** Then he paused: "They see us equally clearly."

Callie thought to herself that being able to read white people was, to her, no trickier than Lucas reading the river currents. Watching how the wind changed the top of the water could fool you, so you had best know the current beneath the surface. Sometimes you could not even see swift currents that could control your direction and your ability to reach your destination. In the same way, Callie had learned from watching and listening to the white people she had known. She heard their words, watched their faces, studied their bodies in motion, and then most times could accurately predict their actions and describe their reasons for them.

"Comes from watching the tides flow, don't you know?" Callie muttered to herself, as Lucas guided their small boat toward Beaufort on a chilly February morning. Then louder, she said, "If you gon mek yo way in dishyuh day en time, den you bes know how fuh read de face uh folk same way you read spot on a riba fuh fish. Da way you know mo bout wha odda folk gon do, en how you kin git wha you wan. Jes gah fuh know wha oona wan (*Just got to know what you want*)."

Lucas had been lured to the bait by his sister. "Supm tell me you talk bout mo den how fuh fish, sistasweet."

"You know da fa sho. I watch en listen to deese Yankee fren real close, en see one ting bout dem jes like buckra—like Bowen." Callie talked past Lucas's questioning look. "Dirt!"

Lucas's surprised brows furrowed. "Callie, wha you talk bout?"

"I say don madda wha white people say, dirt be wha dey afta—deese yuh islan, brudda. Maybe I kin tell a lot uh ting like Colonel Higginson say, but one ting be true, we bes value land we stan on same way white folk do."

"I still say we gah fuh buy mo boat now fuh tek people wey dey wan go. We gah too much lan roun yuh." Lucas knew firmly where he stood, or floated.

"We gah lan? Wha lan we gah? Wey I been when we git lan?" Callie knew the limit of jabbing at her brother, stopping just as he smiled slightly.

"All I mean is we wuk lan all we life—who gon mek we move?"

"Lee brudda, how kin you aks da? I know BB been see why we gah fuh git lan fuh we sef. Oona say ting lika da, mek me see maybe we ain smaat like Colonel Higginson tink." Callie snapped her fingers as she jumped off the boat onto the newly built Beaufort dock. Rope in hand, she quickly tied to the piling set deep into the pluff mud. The new dock Lucas used was a block closer to the little town than where they tied up before freedom time. It was bigger, safer, more convenient, and available for everyone to use—military and civilian, freedmen and whites.

Callie's tense words with Lucas reflected her own uncertainty. When she mentioned BB to her little brother to persuade him about the land, she masked her sadness, just as Lucas could not hide his.

Such was the nature of their debate as they walked up Bay Street to their first destination. Though Callie needed more spices to season her cooking and cloth to make Sunny's new school outfit, both she and Lucas wanted to go to the bakery shop in town that had been opened by Harriet Tubman. Callie had told Lucas the stories she knew about "Moses," and they both wanted to see her in person. If she did all those great things, leading slaves to freedom up north, why was she down in South Carolina?

Callie was especially excited to meet this woman. "I be too pleased fuh fine Miss Moses. She gah fuh be real smaat to keep buckra off her trail. Negro ooman da smaat. She fine huh way tru swamp en crik en woods fuh lead people to freedom. She know all bout herbs and how to fine em and use em too, jes like I do. No tellin what we may learn from dis ooman." Lucas was still interested in the visit, but Callie's mention of BB had set him back a bit.

As they entered the shop, the smell of fresh-baked piecrust was overwhelming. Lucas went directly to the three pies displayed near the door, while Callie made her way to the back of the store. A small woman with flour-caked hands and arms was just opening the oven when Callie approached, asking, "Pardon, missus, can you tell me where I can find Harriet Tubman? I unnerstand she run this pie shop."

"Yes, ma'am."

"Yes, mahm, you can tell me, or yes, she run dis pie shop?"

"Yes, ma'am, you found the person you seek," said the woman as she closed the oven door. "I see you come in here, young lady, with that lovely strong jaw firmly set, like you aim to get something done. What would that be?"

"Don't know—try fuh do right ting in dis war—try fuh hep we people git by on de Oakhaat Plantation."

Harriet Tubman watched Callie intensely and then responded. "Even in the dark I done look in the face of many a man, woman, and chile when we set out tru de swamp to git to freedom. I seen worry, I seen fear, and I seen troubled heart. I seen the joy when we reach a safehouse of stranger that welcome us to rest along the way. You and me we done what we had to do, but there always something deep, deep in our heart we wear on our face. Your face, young lady, wear more than worry bout crop and the people you been trying to help."

Callie's eyes widened and then cast down to the floor. "Try fuh git pass wha happen tuh my brother—he died savin me. He de fus ting on my mind each monin."

"Well, girl, you know like I know, mens and womens been dyin long time before now. Not in war—just men bein evil."

Callie quickly said, "Thas right."

Harriet Tubman concluded. "So I do what I have to. Just like you say your brother did. He fought his war, fought for family, earned their freedom—and his own."

Lucas sat at one of the two tables near the entrance, allowing Callie's conversation at the counter to continue without him. Harriet Tubman asked, "He your brother, too?"

"Yes, mahm."

"He look lost," said the woman whose reputation was to help people find their way.

"Yes, mahm, been that way since our brother passed. We don't mean to be a burden to you. Just wanted to take one of your best sweet potato pies with us, and, pardon me, mahm, to see if you are as real as the stories some tell."

"Don't rightly know what stories been told, but I've had some fun helpin folks run away from slavery, if we talkin bout the same thing."

Callie nodded and looked on in admiration.

"Your pie be ready directly." "Moses" moved down her counter to serve another customer.

As Callie joined Lucas at the table and chairs in the front corner, he quietly kept his head down. Callie studied Harriet Tubman as she greeted her next customer, asking the young black man about the pending government decision on land sales. The man expressed hope that the federal government would allow the people to live on their own land and care for themselves. Callie began to watch the man as he sighed deeply, looking out the window over Beaufort Bay to the east where islands stretched between the town and ocean.

Catching himself from being too serious, he laughed aloud and compared one who would lead people through dangerous nights to their freedom to one who would bake breads and pies for the army. Obviously, he knew her reputation too.

Callie grew more excited as Harriet Tubman demurred, speaking of the great work being done right here in South Carolina by all the freed people, especially the First South Carolina Volunteers. Miss Tubman was very pleased that the men were getting to show their bravery in the uniform of the US Army. Then she stopped abruptly, saying to her customer, "But then you know the courage it takes to risk your life for freedom, don't you, Mister Smalls?"

At that, Lucas lifted his head from the table and joined Callie in rapt attention. Robert Smalls appeared embarrassed by Harriet Tubman's recognition of him. He thanked her for her kindness and simply said he did what anyone would do with the knowledge and resources to do it. He said that, just like Miss Tubman, he worked with others determined to gain their freedom, and that together, they made a plan and carried it out.

"Ah, but you were the leader," Miss Tubman insisted. And with that, he agreed that they both cared enough to make a difference, and that they each had more work to do.

Robert Smalls then asked her, "Is it true that you have been given the authority to act independently in the name of the Union generals?"

She pulled a slip of paper from a satchel behind the counter and showed it to her customer. He seemed to fumble for his glasses and, when he did not find them, Callie rose to the counter to assist. "May I read it for you, sir?"

"Why, yes, young lady, of course. Can you? Please do." Smalls was enthused at her ability and her willingness to assert it. She focused on the awkwardly formed letters. Hiding her newness to public reading, Callie proceeded haltingly:

Pass the bearer to Beaufort and back to this place, and wherever she wishes to go, and give her free passage at all times on all government transports. Harriet ... is a valuable woman. She has permission as a servant of the Government to purchase such provisions from the Commissary as she may need.

D. Hunter
Maj. Gen. Com'g.
HQ Dept. of the South ****

Robert Smalls thanked Callie, before smiling at the small, brave woman behind the counter. He reached out to shake Harriet Tubman's hand, saying that he was honored to have her in Beaufort and asking if he could please take her out on the river sometime. With that, he eagerly took his box of pies and said he started smelling her bakery while crossing on the ferry from St. Helena Island, where a day with the students of Penn School had made him quite hungry. He then excused himself with a nod to the proprietor of the shop and its two customers sitting at the corner table, saying he wanted to hurry home to his family to share the wonderful pies.

Lucas seemed to gain energy from his brush with two such powerful people. After he and Callie thanked Miss Tubman for the pie and headed out the door, he paused briefly and turned. "Paadon, Miss Tubman?" She looked up from rolling dough. "I know ebby nook en cranny in dis riba, ifn some day you wan see some secret spot, I kin show you."

She nodded yes and invited him back the next week to make plans. In that instant, Lucas lifted from his melancholy and walked away with renewed purpose. On their return trip to Oakheart, all he could talk about was helping Miss Tubman tour the waterways and learn about the currents. "I kin take Miss Moses ebby place she wan fuh see."

Callie saw Lucas as a new man, suddenly strong again, like his old self—and like BB used to be. But she could not join in his enthusiasm if it meant he might be heading into danger. "Plenny soljuh en navy man round yuh kin tek Harriet Tubman on de riba. Da don be yo job. Done los BB awready, don wan you fuh git kill."

Lucas decided not to respond or in any way encourage Callie to give the matter further thought. They did not need to debate the reasons why such an action would be poorly advised, in her opinion. Lucas knew what he was going to do.

As he thought about touring Miss Tubman, Lucas heard Callie say, "Now wha bout de money we git? Wha betta you tink—buy boat or some lan fuh tie boat tuh?"

Lucas was not going to take that bait again. Callie continued her side of the debate. "Don need fuh fight no mo Lucas, like BB say. We git dis lan fuh BB. Sence we earn dis cotton money togedda, we gon buy dis lan togedda."

Lucas concurred with Callie for the most part. He did not want her worrying about him anymore. Callie was right about the land, of course, and he was grateful that she would handle it. For now, he was too busy thinking of his own plans which he hoped to share soon with a baker, the conductor of the Underground Railroad.

★ ★ ★

As February wore on, Callie talked with Laura Towne almost every day when she brought Sunny to Penn School. She would look expectantly to her for news about the land sale, especially when Miss Towne was hosting visitors from out of the region. Callie imagined that they were the ones bringing word from Washington that the land sale could proceed in a way Laura Towne thought was fair to the freedmen.

Finally, her hopeful look was met with unbridled joy from Miss Towne. With wide smile and dancing eyes, her friend informed Callie that Congress had passed a law allowing small portions of available plantations to be kept for charitable purposes. President Lincoln had ordered the tax commissioners to set aside these parcels for purchase by freedmen.

Before Callie knew it, Miss Laura had grabbed her by the elbows and they both were dancing in a circle, laughing wildly. When they slowed to catch their breaths, Callie looked across the salt marsh, winter brown and windblown, but with moss green sprouts growing. With tears forming in her eyes, she said, "When we bring dis land tuh we famly, BB soul res bedda." Miss Laura's laughter calmed as she appreciated the meaning of this moment to Callie.

The US Tax Commission operated out of the Rhett house in the middle of Beaufort, the very house in which, a few years before, firebrand secessionists wrote documents leading South Carolina to secede from the United States. The newly authorized commissioners' duty had been amply described in law and they set about it in earnest. Some sixty thousand acres were made available because land owners could not or would not pay taxes to the federal government in Washington. Of that amount, more than fifteen thousand acres were set aside for purchase by freedmen. Notices were posted and properties listed in a publication by the commissioners.

As March arrived, Callie called the Oakheart freedmen together. From the notice she read, they learned that their home land had been partitioned into five- and ten-acre parcels for sale, like so many other plantations on the islands.

Callie, BB, and Lucas had been completely fair and honest when distributing the cotton money. Divided among the fifty adults at Oakheart, the $3,000 did not stretch very far. For those who saved the money, their $60 allotment might be enough to buy a parcel or combine with someone else to make a purchase. Callie urged the people to meet and discuss the different possibilities.

After Lucas agreed that Callie could purchase land as she saw fit and that she should use his money along with BB's share, she grew more excited as sale day arrived. She began considering her options, since her savings and shares combined with her brothers' money totaled almost $200.

With nearly one hundred acres of Oakheart Plantation available, Callie realized that she could buy a large portion of it, a thought both thrilling and impossible to believe. To own land so soon after being a slave was beyond her imagination. She proudly joined the lines of persons waiting to pay the tax commissioners and watched acquaintances from other plantations and friends from Oakheart walk away with deeds to the land they wanted.

Callie chose not to combine her family funds with others to make a purchase. The portion she wanted was quite large and varied slightly from the maps the commissioners had before them. They asked Callie to search for any Bowen records that could confirm property lines before they could complete the sale.

To Callie's great surprise and relief, just as she turned from the commissioner's desk in disappointment, there was Will. He had known of the land sale and worked his supply run schedule to be in Beaufort that day. When Callie explained the status of her land purchase, Will at first suspected foul play of some kind. But after talking with a commissioner, he was reassured that the men in charge were being fair, but quite meticulous. Will advised Callie to search Bowen's documents well—he offered to help, but she declined. He was sure that the land sale would go through with or without additional Bowen records.

After examining the maps of Constant Island, Will realized how much land was still available and made an impetuous decision. He had been given a sum of money by Uncle Harris as a "graduation" gift, with a note that said, "You will know the appropriate time to use the money for yourself or someone you love." Will offered some of this inheritance to Callie so that she could purchase more of Oakheart.

Again, she refused gently, reminding him that he had done too much for them already, and that maybe he should think of his own best interests. In fact, Callie suggested that Will buy some acreage of his stepfather's plantation. He could then argue that at least he had tried to keep the land in the family.

Will smirked to himself at the perfect irony—the land purchase would be his way of repaying some of his debt to his stepfather. Though Will never intended to pay Bowen's taxes or otherwise secure the land for his use, he entered the land sale office with great enthusiasm and the promise to return the next day with $100 to cover his purchase. He was relieved that several choice parcels were still available, but he wanted to check with Callie before buying land that Oakheart freedmen wanted.

The gathering outside the Rhett house was a celebration that could not have been envisioned two years earlier by its owner, the advocate of secession. Newly freed slaves exited the house, many with deeds to properties all over the islands. As they talked excitedly and sang, they praised their God as ever watchful and pledged their lives in service to him!

Callie joined many others as they walked the short block down to the bay, where their boats waited to take them on a joyful journey down the river—former plantation slaves now turned into landowners. They rowed swiftly on rolling swells, as northerly breezes at their back joined the strong outbound tidal flow. A lowering sun reflected off countless waves as if millions of silvery fish skimmed the surface of the water simultaneously and repeatedly. Moving with the currents, the freedmen basked in the colors of the setting sun, brightened by the river's mirrored brilliance and … the reality of owning dirt.

***   Adapted from *Army Life in a Black Regiment*, Thomas Wentworth Higginson, W. W. Norton & Company, Inc., (New York: 1869), 236.

****   Conrad, Earl, ed. "The Charles P. Wood Manuscripts of Harriet Tubman," *The Negro History Bulletin* 13, no. 4 (January 1950), accessed December 29, 2013, http://www.harriettubman.com/cwood.html.

Chapter 24

Callie satisfied the paperwork requirements of the US Tax Commission with documents discovered in the same box that contained Bowen's slave records. She asked Lucas to row into Beaufort on the morning tide to deliver them so she could continue to delve through boxes of Bowen secrets.

In her search, Callie found an envelope that had decayed around the edges and appeared to be years—even decades—old. Scratched through the upper corner she could see "Fel" and though other letters had faded, somehow Callie knew it referenced Feller. Inside was one page with a paragraph documenting the sale of a slave woman named Selena for $1,250 in 1838. Both Bowen and Feller had signed.

Callie shivered upon seeing their names, but then she turned full thought on Selena. Now she had confirmation that a slave woman named Selena was sold in the year she was born, and a note made in the margin seemed to read, "as soon as baby comes."

This discovery set Callie off anew, and she began questioning some of the elders at Oakheart. She asked about the name of a woman sold away around the time when she was born, whose name began with S. Then she said the name out loud: "Selena." Two of the women apologized and then turned and moved away from her. Then Callie came to Bella's cabin asking her the same question.

After a considered pause, Bella glanced at the door of her cabin and spoke softly. "Callie, Massa mek all slave too scaid fuh say huh name—nobody talk bout huh on Oakhaat."

"Huh? How Massa tie ebbybody tongue so?"

Bella held her hand to Callie's lips, and then one finger to her own mouth. Whispering to Callie, "Chile, Massa so mad when oona bone (*born*). Jehori mek joke bout who be yo daddy—Massa tek him tuh de shed en lash him close tuh dead."

Callie was so startled to hear confirmation of her birth that she ignored the next story of Bowen's cruelty and started to interrupt. Bella shuddered and slowly went on. "Den Massa grab Jehori ... en pull back him head, say 'Stick out your tongue! You want de lash some mo? Stick out your tongue!' Massa be too mean sometime, you know."

Bella took a deep breath. "Den he say, 'Jehori, you wan me cut off supm else, stick out yo tongue!' When he say da, Jehori give up, en Massa grab him tongue and wid one skroke cut em off. Jehori mos bleed out fo I stitch de cut shut. Massa shout all roun da no one bes neba speak de name of dis chile mama agin! He look at ebbybody deh, knife drip wid blood, dey mout hold tight shut—and da slave ooman name ain neba been say on dishyuh plantation til you say so jes now."

Callie shivered at the horrifying description. She was confused about why Massa Bowen reacted so strongly when Selena gave birth to her. "Bella, you know who my daddy be?"

"No, chile, no. Da supm nobody know en nobody wan talk bout sence da day."

"Wha mo kin you tell me? Please, dis supm I gah fuh know."

Bella shook her head in pained silence.

Unaware how either of her parents looked, Callie could not know whom she resembled, or from whom she got her own brown complexion. "Bella, kin you ansa me one mo question?" Bella nodded. "My mama, she be light like me o she be daak?"

Callie looked into Bella's face as if her gaze could extract the answer. "She ain been light like oona, chile. She been mos daak, mos daak." And with that Bella turned away, knowing she had just given Callie a mind full of more questions. But Bella had told all she knew, or felt comfortable sharing. The fear of Massa's hard heart had walled Callie off from her ancestry.

*   *   *

Lucas was pleased that Callie made the purchase for their family, and that there was land for his kin and offspring. But he was not content to be a landowner, always more at home on the water. Lucas sought a destiny that would be worthy of BB's sacrifice, and his too if necessary, far beyond the bend in the river where they now owned family dirt.

Though he had been lifted from his sadness by the inspiration of Smalls and Tubman, he still carried his brother's memory like a torch lighting his way. And although some light was shed upon the current that carried Lucas forward, his nearness to the intense torchlight obscured his vision. He moved on the energy of passion more than plan.

Lucas sought the opportunity to serve and to emulate the bravery Robert Smalls needed to steal a boat and escape enslavement. He was sure that he could help Harriet Tubman learn how best to use the local waterways.

After delivering Callie's documents to the tax commissioners, Lucas went to the bakery to share his ideas with the proprietor. He saw her immediately begin to consider the possibilities and to decide what direction she would take. She asked him to come back the next week after she had time to consult with the generals in command.

*   *   *

Contrary to the approach Lucas had adopted, going out and looking for action, Callie hoped that the freedmen of Oakheart would simply settle in to work their newly acquired land. She also hoped that somehow the hardships of the war would diminish, at least for them.

But soon more men were called to serve in the army, again creating great concern among the families on the plantations. Although Union raiding parties continued their success down the Georgia and

Florida coasts, the biggest focus was the impending Yankee attack on Charleston. After the two Confederate iron steamers blasted their way out of Charleston harbor months before, Union navy commanders resolved to bring their own ironclads into the action with a determined assault on Charleston in April 1863.

They failed to dislodge the Confederate defenses, and casualties from the Charleston attacks streamed into Beaufort once again. Despite her best intentions only to manage Oakheart, educate her daughter, and tend to the needs of the people of the island, Callie felt compelled by the rightness and the firmness of Miss Towne's request to care for the wounded at the Beaufort hospitals.

As before, Callie worked energetically. Her talents in mending minor injuries and changing wound dressings were exceeded only by her demeanor—how she gave her care and lifted soldiers' spirits. Callie treated each of the injured as if he was one of her brothers. Miss Towne was asked about Callie by other staff members, now including the US Sanitary Commission volunteers. They appreciated her work and the many extra hours she devoted to the men without taking long breaks.

At the end of two full days, with only short periods of rest, Callie and Miss Towne boarded a military launch to take them down river to Oakheart and the Oaks. Though exhausted, Laura Towne praised Callie to the fullest and mentioned that others had noticed her competence, asking whether Callie would be able to assist more often. They even suggested that Callie might want to get some training to advance her nursing skills. Callie was too tired to think of such things, her sole desire being to return to the relative calm of her home. Her answer showed on her face. Miss Laura had come to know Callie well by then and responded to her silent message. "Callie, my dear, you could do so much more good for so many; you could learn fast from these Sanitary Commission volunteers. It would help you get what you want in the future."

Callie deflected the suggestion. "What I laan from you now is so helpful to me—it tell me all I need tuh know tuh help people betta all over deese islan."

Miss Laura continued to encourage her. "Wouldn't you like to see more and learn more beyond what you can do on these islands?"

"Yes, Miss Laura. So much more. I got all kinda questions bout this world. But I got questions bout my life right heah too. Like, why is my baby girl growing up so fast? And why was the planter people so cruel to we people? And what new day will freedom bring for we people who been through so much? Don't you wan tuh laan things like that, Miss Laura?"

Callie received and returned a quizzical look. "Miss Laura, I kin be happy, free, workin heah, laanin from you, raisin up Sunny. You don't tink da be nuff?"

"Yes, it's just that I see all that you can be. There were times when I was a young woman that there was too much talk about right ideas and not enough right action. I was too content with my life as it was and not concerned enough with what it could be."

"Yes'm. Funny you say that. I been tellin Lucas look roun the next bend in the river, so he kin help hissef get there." Callie smiled at their common understanding and looked up to see Miss Laura looking at her, eyebrows raised, head cocked, as if to say, "And so?"

Again, Callie hesitated. "Thank you, Miss Laura, but I know for now, unless some tings change, here with my daughter is where I need to be."

After being subjected to questioning about her wishes and dreams, Callie sensed that there were currents within her wanting to surge beyond her perceived limits. At the same time there were low-tide pools and swirling eddies in which she found familiarity and comfort. Callie would nestle into those comfortable waters until high tides flooded her out into the mainstream. Just as she fended off opportunities presented by her mentor and friend, she realized that perhaps Lucas should receive less nagging about what he should do with his life.

★   ★   ★

Lucas returned from Beaufort one afternoon in mid-April to report that a blockading ship, *The Kingfisher*, had captured some Confederate spies on Edisto Island, just north of St. Helena. While Callie praised the news, she did not understand why Lucas would have such an excited look on his face, unless there was more to tell. After he had been rejuvenated by his brief association with Robert Smalls and Harriet Tubman, Callie had seen Lucas steady his emotions and conduct his business in a solemn but purposeful manner. "Wha? Why you gah da foolish look on yo face? You gah supm fuh tell me?"

"Yeah, sista. Capn Bowen been captcha (*captured*). Yankee pick em up when e try fuh come back tawd Beaufut las mont, preten fuh be cotton agent."

Callie could feel layers of tension fall away; her face muscles eased, her shoulders slumped, and she sank to the ground, offering prayer. Lucas interrupted. "Fo you say da prayer, sista, deh be somebody you bes talk tuh fus."

"Wha, Lucas? Don tease me bout Capn Bowen."

"I come by dis wud bout Massa—from Missus. She down on we dock now. She wan come up tuh de house."

"Lucas, why did you bring huh yuh? Julia Bowen? You bes tell me she by huhsef!"

"Yeah, I brung huh down by huhsef. She ain be no problem. Say she wan see Will and aks you bout huh clothes fo she head nawt (*north*). Seem like she ain wan wait fuh Massa Bowen git free. Seem right fuh we tell huh bout Will. She ain de one wha wrong we Callie, oona know da."

"Bring huh on up den, I spose. I wait fuh huh up yuh. Stay close by, brudda."

When Julia arrived on the porch, she stopped briefly to greet Callie with a sincere but distant, "Hello, young lady," and went into the house. Her tour allowed her to see how the rooms were being used now. Callie and Sunny shared the master bedroom, and Lucas slept in the small bedroom upstairs where he and BB had kept pallets. Lately, some of the cookhouse workers had been sleeping in the drawing room downstairs, so they could get to the outside kitchen quickly to prepare food as needed for the Oakheart community's varied work schedules. This was another of Callie's new ideas.

Julia returned to the porch and sat beside Callie. After an awkward silence, she asked, "Callie, have you seen my dresses? I hoped to take them with me back north."

"Yes, mahm. I seen six or eight of em just today, on the women and young ladies of Oakhaat." Julia frowned, and Callie continued. "I want you to know how grateful some of them be to you, Missus. I give bout twenty of your dress to ladies who had only one or two dress all they life. I tell them you asked me to share yo things when you went away."

"Why ever would you do that, Callie?"

Callie's look of satisfaction turned very serious. "I figyuh you be glad they see you as betta person than yo husband. They call you Sista Bowen since you been heah. That man they call Massa Bowen was meana than a hungry coon meetin a snake at night."

Julia Bowen seemed to receive these messages on the many levels Callie intended. She decided to assert herself, however meekly, in the face of these strong words. "Well, you certainly have made out well here, haven't you, Callie? Got the run of the place, for now. No longer a slave. Why, you aren't even talking like a slave anymore."

They exchanged a chilled stare for several seconds before Callie spoke. "Missus, we don't make out well here at all. Struggle every day. Glad I'm not yo slave no more, that's fuh damn true! Doin real well? Guess time will tell that." Callie stood and turned away from Julia to enter the house. "Well, I bes be takin care uh my chile. Is that why you are here, to see about yo chile? Cause Will not here—you may know he workin on one of the Yankee ships out in the ocean."

Julia acted as if she knew that. "Well, I didn't expect to see him, but ... you know, the captain has been captured by the Yankees and I'm leaving to go back to Annapolis. I was going to leave him even before he got taken away."

Callie looked at her former Missus without empathy. "Really, Missus, I sorry you can't see Will, but I have no more time to talk about the captain, or yo married life. I hope yo boat arrives safely in the North, and though I do not do it for you, I will help look after Will while he's around these parts." And she climbed the stairs quickly.

Julia called up behind her. "I apologize for the wrongs of the past. And I want you to know that I forgive you for pleasuring my husband—he needed more than I could give."

Callie came down the stairway far enough to look at her former master's wife. "I assure you, Missus, it weren't no pleasure for me to ever be touch by your husband. What I did I did because he made me do it, and I did it fo my famly. And I'm still workin on forgivin you for what you did."

"Whatever do you think I did?"

"All due respect, Missus, you stood by and let that man do whatever evil he wanted to do. And by your words I'm hearin that you knew what he was doin. Much as I be thankful that you taught me to read, en much as I care fuh yo son, ain got no place in my heart for you, Missus, hearin you speak so."

"Well, just let me stay the night and—"

"I can't do that, Missus. Not in this house. The people on this island suffered too much and feel too free of you and yours. So tomorrow dayclean can't find yo face around this place. Meaning no disrespect." Callie leaned out over the railing. "Lucas, Missus Julia has to go!"

When Lucas came through the front door, Callie went on. "I know you want to see that Missus is cared for, for Will's sake, and I do, too. Please tell her all about Will, but she can't stay in this house or anywhere somebody at Oakhaat can see her. I know Will would understand that. Good-bye, Missus."

★　★　★

Lucas honored his sister's strong urge to move Julia Bowen from the house, but he also had to honor his relationship with Will. After brief instructions to Julia to stay put in the boathouse, Lucas left the plantation around nightfall to cross the sound to Hilton Head, hoping to bring Will to see his mother.

The dedicated friendship Lucas displayed was rewarded. Against the odds, he located Will's ship, and Will was able to gain approval for a quick "supply run" to St. Helena. An hour later as Lucas handled the boat, Will jumped onto the Oakheart dock to embrace his mother for the first time in sixteen months.

Once in the privacy of the boathouse, Will told her of his exploits, first on ships hunting Confederate blockade runners and now as junior supply officer. He shared his excitement about using his local knowledge and contacts to gather provisions for the troops. They even had a small smile together when Julia noted that the last time she saw him, he was in the supply business for the Confederates. Julia seemed hesitant but asked her son about the boat gift, the *Southern Will*, and what happened that morning. After Will's description, her brow furrowed.

"That's not quite what the captain told me." With prodding from Will, she continued. "He said you never made it to the fort."

"That's true."

"That you turned the boat and fled back down the river before your boat was sunk."

"That is not true. Mother, when I arrived at Bay Point, the Yankees fired at me, and sank the *Southern Will*. Don't you see? The captain lied to you again."

While convinced that her son's account was true, Julia said that her husband had felt betrayed.

"By whom?" Will was incredulous.

"His slaves, Lucas and BB, when he returned from the battle."

"He cannot be serious."

"His stepson to whom he gave an education and a sailing vessel."

"Please, Mother—in which he sent his beloved stepson off to war."

"His wife whom he—"

At this Will could hear no more. "Small wonder he was betrayed if that's what he calls it. To a person, yourself included, all of us had reasons to do what we did. You know better than any."

Will's disgust was evident, but he wished to be more positive with his mother and remembered to tell her of the land purchase. "For my part, I've done something kind in spite of the captain's ill-tempered ways. I have used funds given me by Uncle Harris to buy back a part of Oakheart that the captain lost when he failed to pay taxes." Will went on, a bit cynically, bragging that he kept his pledge to his stepfather—to always supply and support the defenders of these islands.

Julia smiled slightly at the irony and, with no spirit of reprimand, remembered Harris's words to Will. "Your internal compass is too resolute to go awry."

"Remember, Mother, my compass comes from my feelings, and my heart, and they come from you. They are telling me that these people here at Oakheart are my family, too!"

Julia looked on without understanding.

"Mother, what we had here was wrong. What we had here is gone!"

"Well, son, I am gone too. I am leaving Daniel Bowen, and Oakheart, and I do not plan to ever return to the South."

"I am surprised, but I am not sorry, Mother. I look forward to seeing you back in Annapolis in a matter of months, after we end this war. When you go back, I hope you rediscover your life there. It is too late here." Their connection reestablished, Will left his mother again, this time in service to the Union.

Lucas kept Will in his captain's good graces with a quick trip back to his ship and a couple buckets of crab. The Missus slept in the boathouse for a few hours until the first sign of morning light. Then Lucas took her from Oakheart to Beaufort on the rising inbound tide.

* * *

Lucas planned to visit Harriet Tubman that day, hoping she was ready to tour some plantations upriver. He was convinced that the war was taking too long to free other slaves, and that someone should do something about it. His determination was strengthened, if possible, when he learned that the Confederate president had issued an order to shoot black Union soldiers upon capture. If the hope was to discourage black men from the fight for their freedom, Jefferson

Davis was woefully misinformed about the character of enslaved men newly freed.

As Lucas entered Harriet Tubman's bakery, he was prepared to be disappointed by the slow decision-making process in the Union chain of command. Lucas's eyes grew wide as she told him that the generals had given her the authority, under Colonel Montgomery's command, to guide a military action to help others to freedom. She told him that the generals were willing to send large numbers of troops to raid the rice plantations north of Beaufort, up where the tidal flow met the Combahee and Ashepoo Rivers. But first, to learn all she could, Moses needed help from someone who knew the rivers.

Over the next several weeks, Lucas took the diminutive woman on night reconnaissance trips, piloting the narrow, sleek boat he had used on his own lonely patrols. Several times each night, Moses left Lucas on the boat at the riverside. He waited for her call or song when she returned from exploring the terrain and meeting with some of the people. Eventually, she was satisfied that conditions were right for the operation, having found sites where those still enslaved could meet the Union transports and escape south to the secured freedom zone around Beaufort.

The days Lucas spent waiting for the raid were very busy, as he traveled between Oakheart and Camp Saxton where Harriet met with the Union command. Though he missed his comfortable fishing routine and had to share some of the ferrying with other Oakheart boatment, he was excited about the task ahead.

Then, too, he also was enthused after several visits to Camp Saxton where he had conversed with a young, free, black woman whose job was to teach the troops to read. One evening, and only briefly, she and Lucas managed to share a moment near the dock—Lucas knew that he would seek other such moments with her. Despite these most welcome distractions, Lucas remained intensely focused on the impending mission.

Finally, the word came from Moses that it was time. On the first day of June, two gunboat steamers were loaded with 150 Union soldiers, black troops from South Carolina and white from Rhode Island. Once it was dark, Moses guided them upriver on the incoming tide, Lucas at her shoulder on the bow.

Through the night, limited rebel resistance from the riverbanks scattered as troops landed on the mainland to raid one plantation after another. All the while, streams of black men, women, and children filled the designated riverbanks where Lucas and others maneuvered small launches on a full flood tide to ferry the bondsmen to their freedom aboard the steamers. So many came that Lucas sought to reassure them that there would be room for all, though he knew no such thing. He heard Moses singing to her people to ease them through their fright and uncertainty.

In all, more than thirty mansions were burned as the Union expedition liberated livestock, cotton, and rice, along with nearly eight hundred people, formerly "property," who never expected such a day to come. The packed gunboats followed the winding river southward toward Beaufort, as a full moon raced toward the western horizon before the sun greeted the new day.

Back on board with the refugees, Lucas relaxed on deck near the bow and watched a woman trying to calm her pig. Next to her, a younger woman nestled into her man's arm, while he held their child in his other arm. Lucas felt his eyes water in the first light from the east, as he understood the significance of the freedom brought to these people more than he had been able to appreciate his own at first.

Tears cascaded down his cheeks as he shouted out to those who now shared his liberation. "Yeddy (*Hear*) me, good people, oona gah fuh know deh be whole lotta folk ris (*risk*) dey life en done gib dey life fuh mek oona free dishyuh night!" He stopped after gaining their attention, his voice catching in his throat. "My brudda git kill when he fight fuh my sista freedom, fuh my freedom, en fuh yown." He had to stop again, shoulders shaking against the tide of his emotions. "Dishyuh night I mek him proud. He done show me how fuh live, en I know in him eye, I wort supm (*worth something*)."

Lucas saw mostly puzzlement and weary looks in the eyes of his listeners. "Wha I try fuh say," and he elevated his voice to be heard, "dis be a great day fuh oona, but dis bout mo dan be free. Wha oona gon do wid freedom? Da wha count mos." With that he stopped, leaned back against the rail, brought his hands to his face, and whispered, "I jes pray to Gawd oona unnerstan."

Soon a crying woman touched his arm and held on to it for a few seconds of mutual assurance. A child grabbed Lucas at the knee, causing him to boot the pig gently. It went squealing along the deck, dodging around tired bodies, and setting off a nearby hound dog. All those around had reason for laughter. They began to ease—they were free.

★   ★   ★

Word passed quickly to Laura Towne at the Oaks Plantation that hundreds of newly freed slaves from the mainland had been brought into Beaufort. She was thrilled at the wonderful news and overwhelmed by the enormity of the task. Of course, she stopped by Oakheart to give Callie this great opportunity to serve.

Callie could not and would not say no. But she wished it weren't so, for once again she had set aside time to go exploring the attic secrets of Daniel Bowen. In just a few minutes that morning, she had uncovered but not opened two promising envelopes when she heard Miss Towne calling her name on her walk up from the dock.

Minutes later, with Bella again willing to take Sunny on short notice for an undermined length of time, Callie was on her way to Beaufort in a rowboat crewed by four young navy men who happened to be white. Callie was not so upset with the change in her plans that she had lost her wry wit. "Miss Laura, you know times changin when the Negro lady get rowed upriver by white men." And she laughed the kind of laugh that should be reserved for others' jokes.

Just after disembarking on the Beaufort dock, Callie spotted Lucas on the wharf in an embrace with a young lady. For an instant, Callie considered giving him space and being low-key about it and then stepped off quickly in his direction while uttering, "Nah!"

"My brudda, whey you been dish yuh day? Oh, scuse me. I ain mean fuh butt in." And then she just stood looking on. Having no choice in the matter, Lucas made the introduction. "Miss Lilly Bradley, dis my dear sista, Callie."

Callie couldn't go on with the ruse of giving Lucas such a hard time, especially since she recognized Lilly, having seen her conduct a reading class at Fort Saxton, where the First South Carolina Volunteers were camped. They had talked briefly then about doing such good and important work with the soldiers.

Lilly said, "Truly pleased to meet you, Callie." A little shorter than Callie with more meat on her bones, Lilly carried the same confident air that buoyed Callie. Her animated facial features lit up as she greeted Lucas's sister.

"Good to meet you, Miss Lilly. I saw you teachin, rememba? Very impressed by you then." Callie turned to her brother. "So, Lucas. What am I lookin at heah?"

"Well, don hole back yo questions, sista. May seem skrange to you, but dis special lady tink I do awright like I be. I know dis, she be de smaates ooman (*smartest woman*) I know."

Callie did not take it as personally as Lucas may have gently intended. Instead she turned toward Lilly, who explained, "Lucas says he likes that I read and teach. He even said I put him in mind of his sister." Lucas grimaced.

Callie decided to wait to use that information against Lucas. "Well, I'm sure he thinks you are a sight for his sore eyes. I'll tell you true, he's a worthy work for some talented soul."

Lucas was so relieved. "Well, tank you, sista, I tink."

"So, fuh real." Callie asked, "Wha you been doin?"

"I proud uh mysef fuh two tings, sistasweet. I keep dis secret bout Lilly from you, das de fus ting. En de nex ting, I jes git back yuh wid Miss Harriet Tubman, en we jes bring whole bunch uh people off dey plantation—steal em from up de riba."

Callie was awestruck at both accomplishments but still had trouble believing him. "You speck me fuh tink you do all da?"

"Well, we git some hep from lotta Union soljuh."

Just then, Harriet Tubman approached the group, stopping to acknowledge Lucas. She said, "This young man is pretty smart—tell me all I need to know about the water to make free people by the hundreds." Then she laughed, recognized Callie as his big sister, and leaned toward her. "And I tell you one more thing—these heah young'uns, they met in my pie shop few weeks ago, and I gave em a pie. Saw em next day down near Camp Saxton ..." She waited, perhaps for timing. "I'm pretty sure they been nibblin on sumpin other than pie."

At the height of Lucas's embarrassment, and Miss Tubman's amusement, she went on. "Got to be serious to say how good dis young man is. Could not a planned it or done it without him. His brother would be proud, and I am too."

Callie was speechless, almost. "His sista be mighty proud too!"

At that, they went their respective ways: Miss Tubman to report to Union command, then to serve again, whether it be pies or freedom; Callie to tend those who had been enslaved just hours before; Lucas to rest, and then rest some more, and then probably fish; and Lilly to give lessons to Union troops, after making sure Lucas would rest.

Chapter 25

Every day presented change and challenge for freedmen who found themselves at the vortex of forces warring for superiority. Although the freedom zone provided by Union occupation stabilized, the influx of hundreds more fleeing from slavery presented logistical nightmares for the Union quartermaster staff. Wherever troops camped or refugees settled, greater demand for all goods followed.

The island soil continued to grow crops just as the sea produced its bounty. Lucas and Will were actively involved in "the procurement" of both. Lucas was delighted that he could keep filling Will's orders, and he arranged with friends at nearby plantations to have their seafood and produce ready for Will on a regular schedule. Will built relationships with the people of the area to become a supurb junior supply officer.

On finishing his sweep at half a dozen docks on the southern tip of St. Helena, Will headed toward Chowan Creek. While passing the large Union military dock that had been built at Lands End, he noticed that a whole regiment of black army troops in blue uniforms had just landed. He continued on to Oakheart to gather Lucas's catch and to share the news that the First South Carolina Volunteers were not the only black men serving in the United States Army.

Callie had already heard from Miss Towne of their impending arrival in the area and even teased Will with the question, "How was the Massachusetts Fifty-Fourth like the First South Carolina?" When Will answered the obvious—that both were filled with black soldiers, Callie laughed triumphantly. "Will, anybody kin see that. But you ne-va know that both colonels in charge of the regiments be white men from Massa…chu…setts?"

Will was further stumped when Callie asked him the next question. "What be different bout them two regiments?" He yielded to the prospect that any answer he would give would only allow Callie to gloat more. "I tell you. The boys from up nawt been free men. Mos ne-va been slave befo they join the army. First South Ca'lina boys all been slave." Callie found herself wondering briefly how free black men from the North would differ from the men she had known her entire life. But she had no more time for such considerations.

Will pushed off from the Oakheart dock, needing to get on with his assignments, since Callie clearly was well informed. "All right, smart woman. Be about your business."

"I am busy today, Will, got places to go." Her already full day was compounded by the fact that the US Freedmen's Inquiry Commission, formed in Washington several months before, had arrived in Beaufort to investigate the condition of former slaves. Callie planned to attend the hearings so she could tell her stories. Though she did not testify, other leading members of the freed community from around the islands were there to make certain that the realities so many had endured would be recorded.

Callie left Beaufort satisfied that truths were being told, and she reported as much to Laura Towne. She also was able to tell her friend that there was a new hospital in Beaufort, which, at first, Miss Laura did not think remarkable since she knew of more than ten already established. But she watched Callie's face for clues and knew that it was something important to her. Callie couldn't wait to report that, in a big old house downtown on New Street, she found a hospital dedicated to treating black soldiers. "When I been outside theah, I see a group uh people listen to a lady name Clara Barton of the US Sanitary Commission. She say she happy that this place be the first US Army hospital for black soljuhs." Callie beamed.

Now Miss Laura understood why Callie was so excited. "Well, General Saxton told you he would make it happen, didn't he?"

"Yes, mahm, but not everything promise happens, you know. So, I am too please to see this be done for the hard-fightin men down here. Too please."

Callie also was quite happy that the Massachusetts Fifty-Fourth had set up its camp at Lands End, not too far around the bend in the creek from Constant Island. She had heard that they were well-drilled troops and that they were strong just like the men of the sea islands, but that they were very reserved and quiet in their interactions with the islanders.

So it was good for Callie's curiosity when Miss Laura informed her that the officers and some of the men would be attending the July Fourth celebration at Brick Church where they held Penn School. Of course, Callie agreed to help prepare the grounds and cook up her famous fish stew with ingredients supplied by Lucas.

For the first time, former slaves had cause to celebrate the birthday of the nation with their white brethren. After being officially proclaimed free by President Lincoln seven months before, island freedmen turned out in large numbers, validating the organizers who ordered extra provisions.

Among the expected visitors, as promised, was a contingent of the Massachusetts Fifty-Fourth. Callie had started moving toward them to find a place to watch the program when she was tapped on the shoulder. To her great astonishment, Eva was there too.

"I just want to thank you, Callie, for helping me get started teaching near Tidal Flats. It was good to get back near home and to work with the children in that area."

Callie nodded with pleasure at Eva's sincerity. She had heard the school was thriving.

"You know what else? I even went back to my home plantation and, at first, some of the adults were scared. But I talked to 'em and they understood that I was just there to help. I'm teaching some of their young'uns now, too."

Callie caught herself before speaking, as her voice would have cracked had she started. She hugged Eva briefly and whispered, "You

make me feel like we people can all work it out together, peaceful-like."
As she pulled away, she and Eva exchanged glances, caution in their
eyes but smiles on their lips.

Just then the program began with everyone singing "The Star
Spangled Banner." There were readings and speeches, even a brief
one by Edward Pierce, who was there to salute the deployment of the
Massachusetts unit. The children sang beautifully as they had learned
to do at these public events.

When the program ended, and the eating began, Callie was drawn
to the gathering of uniformed Union officers who began an animated
conversation. The fixings were not nearly so fancy as on New Year's
Day, when thousands gathered for the reading of the Emancipation
Proclamation. None of this mattered to the group of officers, though;
they were too engrossed in their debate to move toward the food. So
was Callie.

Callie overheard a major exclaiming how impressed he had been
by the light in the children's eyes. "I say, these young learners inspire
me. We have seen surprising leadership rising in the ranks of our black
regiments, and when I see these wonderful youngsters, it seems to me
that we may have their next great leader with us today. What say you,
Colonel Shaw?"

No wonder Callie was enthralled. Here was the commander of
the Massachusetts Fifty-Fourth and his officers. He hardly seemed an
authority figure, but for his uniform. Though small in size and gentle in
demeanor, he presented an air of kind confidence. And then he spoke.
"Maybe the next great leader for us all. What would you say, boys?"

Their muted responses led him to conclude, in a mock scolding
tone, that they should not doubt what might be possible. "After all,
we are witnessing miracles down here. Who could have imagined
just two short years ago that secession speeches would be replaced by
the sweet sound of abolitionists working with freed Africans to build
their future?"

His officers listened intently, as did Callie. "Now these island people
are going to school, adults and children, they own land, and they work

for wages. Two years' change only, mind you. Imagine how well-off they may be in ten or twenty years after we win this war."

So involved with the line of discussion was Callie that she did not see the large blue uniform loom behind her. A Union sergeant stood tall, a strong, black face with smile lines that showed as he spoke: "You sure are doing some hard listening, young lady."

Turning abruptly, Callie whispered, "Well, I guess I was. They talkin bout beautiful ting. I jes couldn't stop listenin."

The sergeant tried to stifle his smile but was cut off as he started to speak.

"That's how I learn what I need to know, you know. Pickin somethin up here and somethin else up there."

"What would you like to pick up from me?" The sergeant enjoyed his question far more than Callie's response.

"Why, not a thing, suh. Why ever do you think I would?"

"Say, you are different from anybody I've seen here, or anywhere else. You don't seem like some of these other folks roun here."

"I don't?" Callie protested. "But I am of these folks, you can know that."

Callie had not thought much about how or who she appeared to be. Knowing all her life who her people were, the fact that there were differences of color or facial features never made her doubt her place in her community.

"Easy, girl. I just was wonderin where you came from, is all."

"Well," Callie said, "I wonder that too sometime."

"You mean you don't know your mama and daddy?"

"Nah, never knew. Got by jes the same, though."

"Did you now? How do you know you got by just the same?"

"I just say I done real well for myself and those I kyah fuh."

"How do you do that, miss? I'm sorry, I don't know your name."

"Sergeant, you ask so many questions, I hope you carry good intentions. Now, my name is Callie, and you have one less reason to be sorry." She passed a look with her last sentence that softened the blow and walked off to find Sunny.

The sergeant called after her, "I thank you for your time, Miss Callie."

* ★ ★

But the sergeant's questions hung in Callie's mind that night, long after the celebrations were over. The next morning she went back in the attic to the letters she had found tucked in a pocket of the slave record book. Still unopened, she studied an envelope with marks resembling clothesline poles. *HH* was written in the upper corner. She quickly opened it, nervous that she seemed to actually have time to press her search for answers. It read:

> I regret our disagreeable departure when last I was in SC.
>
> I assure you I have no interest in your slaves, or who they look like. Our idle conversation about your slave girls need not spoil our lucrative arrangement, through which your fine vessels are sold to my customers around the Chesapeake.
>
> Do not hold my personal peccadilloes against me, Daniel, as I assure you it was only horizontal refreshment, long ago. You may know what I mean, old man.
>
> Looking forward to renewed good will and partnership.
>
> HH — 1852

Callie frowned. "Da maak again—wha da stan fuh? H? Two H? Who Bowen know name staat wid H? H ... H ... Hew-itt. Hewitt! Da ain Will fuh sho. Ain Missus. Wha Will uncle name?" She thought hard enough to bring rain. "Why dis person pologize tuh Massa Bowen—jes fuh bein interested in his slave?"

Just then a small piece of paper dropped out of the envelope, with a barely legible, scribbled note. Callie saw that it was in a different handwriting from the first note, and she struggled to read it.

"Tell him it's simple. If he comes back, the gal gets sent away, or worse. If he stays away, she gets raised right here at Oakheart, safe under my supervision and attention, with Julia's assistance, of course."

Then down at the bottom, in yet another handwriting: "Yeah, that should do it."

Callie searched for meaning. "Who's 'him'? 'If he stays away' … Who's 'the gal'? Selena? No. Check the date—1852." She slept fitfully that night, knowing that she must put these matters from her mind to make room for the full life she must lead. After awaking early, she was sitting on the porch admiring the sunlit sway of Spanish moss in the morning breeze when she heard the sound of a large boat banging into the Oakheart dock, and then voices.

Will came bounding up the path from the water. "Callie, dear Callie, I'm here with a patrol crew and have very little time, but I have something to give you."

Obviously pleased at his presence, the thought of a gift delighted Callie more. "It so nice to have you back again, Will."

"Well, I need to tell you something, and I have just enough time to do it." Will had seldom been so abrupt and determined.

Callie could not wait to tell Will of her discovery that a woman named Selena might be her mother, and the other pieces of information that gave her some understanding of her parentage. "Will, I've got things to tell you, too. Almos too good fuh be true. Something I pray for, but … then I have some questions for you about your uncle."

"I have news about my uncle, too. I'm afraid mine may not be nearly so positive as yours."

"Maybe you should go first then." Callie wanted to share her joy after dealing with any other worries.

So Will proceeded. "Two things really—I have received an envelope from my uncle Harris." He paused.

Callie whispered, "Harris, of course: *HH*." Callie focused intently on Will and his next words.

"It seems hard to believe, Callie, but my uncle has found your mother—living near Washington."

Callie's heart raced. She had never really allowed herself to think that she might one day see, touch, or hold her real mother. Her already profoundly wide eyes grew larger in wonder at her mother's existence, and her face asked all the next questions.

"I know no more, Callie, and my uncle told me no more than this. He just instructed either my mother or me to make certain you received this envelope."

As she waited to tell her story, she saw him hesitate. "But I'm afraid I have more news—this also involves my uncle Harris, directly. You should read the note from him before I tell you any more."

She took the envelope, starting to speak. Will gently cut her off, saying, "Open it, Callie, learn of your mother. I think you should read first."

Reluctantly, she did so, opening the carefully sealed envelope to find five one hundred dollar bills, wrapped in paper, and then another envelope within. In it, there was a note in what was a precise, but basic, writing style.

> Callie, I intend to tell you one day much more of your father. He is filled with regret that he has never known a day in your presence. I too am so sad to have not seen you again after you were born. We are thrilled to hear reports from young Will that you are strong and successful despite your bondage. Your father and I have wished for your freedom every day of your life. He loves you deeply, though from afar, as have I, always.
> Your mother, Selena

Callie looked up at Will, uncertain though grateful. "She pass all this money to me and speak of my father." Her eyes welled with tears.

Will corrected her. "I think the money was added by my uncle. See, it wasn't in the other envelope, just wrapped in the paper."

Callie heard but was on to other concerns. "She speaks of my father like it is not him."

"Who, Callie?" Will earnestly asked, still without a notion.

"Will, I think your uncle and my mama know each otha a long time."

This caught Will completely by surprise. "Callie, whatever are you saying? Can you share the note with me?"

He read it and looked up at her, still confused, to find her eyes cast aside. "Does this prove something about my uncle to you?"

"Will, I must tell you what I find." He started to speak, but she leaned forward, insistently placing her fingers on his lips. "I find papers in the big house attic that Daniel Bowen came back to get, along with some money. I pack it all away and can give it to you. Massa hated your uncle and keep him away from Oakhaat startin around 1852. There's a letter from your uncle apologizin to Massa for supm bout what your uncle said bout slave women roun heah."

Callie hesitated, just a moment. "One ting more I laan. I know my mama name is Selena, before I read huh note. Massa so mad right afta I was born that he sent my mama away." She pointed to Selena's name at the bottom of the letter. "I didn't understand why Massa so awful in the story Bella told me, but now I do. Now afta I read my mama's words, packed in with your uncle's money." Callie's report finally slowed to conclusion as she reached both hands to hold Will's face. "I know fa sho that your uncle Harris ... is my daddy."

"Callie!" Will leaned back in surprise and then opened his mouth without words. His training had not prepared him for this—but from his loving spirit guided by his internal compass, he could only say with a laugh, "Then that makes us cousins."

At this, they fell into a natural embrace, devoid of any sexual tension, and full of need for family support. "So good to learn these things in the arms of family," whispered Will, as Callie cried and held on to him. He went on, "All this time ..."

"Our fathers were brothers." Callie marveled at the fact.

"And we never knew." Will moved back to see Callie's face and held her at arm's length. "No wonder we had such a strong set of feelings between us—we have the same deep currents running through."

"Fast, strong currents—we both do." Callie nestled to his shoulder again, shaking her head. "Can't ever be one current, is all."

"We're cousins!" Will protested. "We are one family, we just haven't been able to live it yet."

"From today on, Will?"

"Ever more so, Callie, because of the news I must share." Will pulled back from their shared joyfulness, his troubled face now out of sync with Callie, whose smile faded.

"What could be so bad, now on top of this good feelin?" Her expression pleaded for no bad surprises.

"You see, I received my uncle's envelope a few weeks ago—when I went to visit his home in Maryland. Obviously, he wanted very badly for you to receive this information and money, or he wouldn't have—"

Callie looked on with great excitement, as she heard her father spoken of for the first time. "He wouldn't have what?"

"He wouldn't have left it to you in a bank box for safekeeping." Will looked up to see Callie's confusion. "It seems my uncle Harris had a habit of conducting secret business for the US government that was frought with peril, and ..." Will stopped. "Oh, Callie, I can't. This is too cruel." He broke down briefly before composing himself. "Callie, dear cousin, I came into possession of his letter for you ... I know of my uncle Harris finding your mother, only because ... he has been lost at sea."

Her comprehension stopped. To find out consecutively that she has a mother and knows where she lives, and then to realize that she has a father, but he might be—lost! Callie sank to the earth, folding herself over the large root of an old live oak tree.

She quietly prayed to find the comfort and guidance that lay nowhere else. When she was finished and looked up, Will was still there, waiting for her process to include him.

Will wanted to be hopeful. "They still believe he could have survived where his ship sank in the Chesapeake Bay, near the Virginia shore. My uncle Harris, your father, is tough, and too good a man to go down easy. But for the last two months, there has been no word."

Will wished to comfort her and explain more, but he had no time or additional information. "You know I can't stay, but I will be back soon. Do you have any idea what you might do about all this?"

As she shook her head, they embraced again. With an apology for the necessity of his departure, Will was gone.

Callie had no easy answers to the questions presented by Will's revelations, so wonderful and so tragic. Even if she knew what action to take to find her parents, what could she really do? Over the next few days, she considered her options while handling the myriad responsibilities she had taken on. She kept the story of her mother and father quiet, not wanting to tell Sunny or Lucas before she understood it herself. Callie was so immersed in her deliberations and tasks that she did not notice the signs all around her—the Union army and navy were preparing for a major advance on Charleston.

One evening after fishing near the ocean, Lucas reported that all the ships with fighting men on them had headed out of Port Royal Sound and straight up the coast toward Charleston. Quiet had descended on the plantation grounds as Callie and Lucas began a walk without destination.

When they arrived at the far side of the fields, Callie said, "Les sit yuh by our family tree and tink on some ting." They settled, watching the tidal creek moving with its outbound flow toward the sea. "Brudda, some beautiful days come our way, days full of amazin grace. We been able fuh do ting we ain neba tink we could. Who say you ain be man fuh army? Da be me. I proud uh wha you do wid Miss Tubman, mos proud."

"I kin look roun de bend in de riba pretty good, huh?" Lucas leaned back, hands behind his head, enjoying his phrasing as much as his success.

"En now dis fine gal wan be round you—Miss Lilly. You tink she so smaat ifn she wan talk tuh you so much?"

Knowing his sister was mostly teasing and that he already had her full approval, Lucas shrugged his shoulders. "Gawd work in mos mysterous way, sista. Jes may be I spose fuh do good in dishyuh worl, wid Lilly by my side."

"Ting turn out good eben in dis awful waw. We praise Gawd—en we see tru all dis da we kin do wha we gah fuh do (*and we see through all this that we can do what we've got to do*)."

Lucas agreed, but grew somber. "Da go fuh BB, too. We been tru sad en moanful time, sista. We kin see da when we see back roun some dem bend in de riba. I aks why we go tru da? How long fo we git from unda dis hebby feelin? Callie, BB need fuh be yuh!" Lucas stood up, tears on both cheeks as he quickly wiped his forearm across his face. "Why good man like da be dead when he do wha right?"

Then Lucas asked Callie if he could say one more thing. "Ga fuh say sorry, sista. Lilly hep me unnerstan bout de way ting be on mos plantation—bout you en Massa. I ain know fuh real wha happen …" He began to sob gently. "I know e ain right ifn you gah fuh lay wid da man. I so sorry, Callie!"

"Lucas da don be yo worry now. Ain eben my worry no mo."

"Da worriation might stay wid me no madda wha I wan. My sista suffa wid da ole buckra? I neba tink nobody suffa mo dan me when BB git kill. Lilly hep me see deese ting."

Callie had let him stand alone in his misery too long and moved quickly up under his arm, grabbing him by the waist and moving over to a nearby bench. They held each other until both could breathe in regular cadence again. Callie kissed her brother softly on his cheek and gently insisted that they move on from that sadness. They stood and started walking again.

Then she told him of her discoveries—Selena and Harris. She described where they were now and where they weren't, suggesting that Will may have lost his uncle at sea, as she may have lost her father.

Lucas, absorbing her joy and sorrow, insisted that all could be well. "Will tell me his uncle be good boatman. Da man be safe. Now he yo daddy—ain time fuh him jes disapeah."

Then Callie said to Lucas what she had not admitted to herself. "Idea run in my head bout go up nawt—gah fuh see bout ting wid dem da might be famly."

Returning the respect Callie had given him, Lucas said, "You gon do wha be right. Ifn you go, me en Lilly en Bella gon tek kyah uh Sunny. I don wan yo haat fuh ache in time come (*don't want your heart to ache in the future*) cause you ain do wha you gah fuh do now. When you tink back on deese yuh time, leh joy be in yo haat fuh wha you do." Lucas reached for her hands with a smile. "You kyan see round de bend in dis riba—kyan see till you git round de bend. Jes gah fuh go wey da riba flow fuh fine out bout yo Mama en Daddy."

Callie felt the love in Lucas's care and counsel. The sweet and good man that Callie knew him to be was emerging for all to see.

★   ★   ★

The next morning Callie awoke to the muffled roar of faraway cannon. It continued for most of two days, after which she was summoned once again by Laura Towne to nursing duties in Beaufort. Apparently, Harriet Tubman and Clara Barton had gone up near Charleston to witness the Union attack on Fort Wagner, led by the Massachusetts Fifty-Fourth. Having seen the carnage, they rushed back to Beaufort to ready the hospitals and summoned Miss Towne and others to come quickly.

On the boat to town Callie told her friend, Miss Laura, all she had learned about her life in the weeks since the Independence Day celebrations. She said she was trying to decide whether to take advantage of the offer to train as a nurse in the North, if being up there would help her locate her parents. Laura Towne was both empathetic and supportive but encouraged Callie to put it from her mind over the next few days, if she could, while treating the soldiers.

When they arrived at the headquarters of the US Sanitary Commission, also in one of the grand old homes overlooking the river, Laura Towne recognized Clara Barton standing in front of the building near the water. "I say, Miss Barton, I would like to introduce you to an impressive young woman, Callie this is—"

Callie spoke right up. "Oh yes, missus, I know your name. You are Miss Barton who started hospitals for all de soljuhs. En you fix up a fine hospital in a house right over heah for our African soljuhs. We are too please! Thank you, missus."

Miss Laura finished her introduction, which was intended to praise Callie. "Miss Barton, this young woman is one of the most amazing people I have met on the islands. A natural healer is our Callie."

Callie was honored and embarrassed, so she quietly deflected the attention by pointing to all the houses where there were injured men needing help, wondering where she should go. Like Miss Laura said, with hundreds of soldiers needing help, there was no time for personal concerns. As before, Callie responded quickly and calmly to each urgent condition with her healing hands and innate ability to concentrate on the here and now.

In the course of nursing the soldiers, to her great sadness, she found the sergeant she had met at the July Fourth celebration lying on a gurney barely conscious, and without one of his legs. The minute she started speaking to him, he became more aware and soon tried to sit up. Callie urged him to rest on the gurney.

After the third day of work in Beaufort, Callie prepared to leave, telling Miss Laura, "I'm goin home to think about my choices."

"Don't tarry long in your thinking—there will be hospital ships heading north next week. Miss Barton and I had a splendid conversation. She has already signed papers approving your transit, so that you can begin your training and work in the Sanitary Commission's main facility in Washington."

It was almost too much for Callie to contemplate. But she still could not commit to a decision to go, to leave her daughter and the people and the work at Oakheart. "I come back soon to this whaaf to work with these men, or catch that northbound boat. But I got to tell you, Miss Laura, if I live to be sixty years old, I know my people will never forget you."

"Oh, Callie, you exaggerate—I only did what any well-intentioned person would do."

"Well, missus, then I not see a lot of sech well-intention people in my life! No matter, I just can't say thank you enough times for all you did." With that, her eyes filled, and she pulled Laura Towne to her. Exhausted, Callie turned to board the boat back to St. Helena Island.

On the way downriver in the longboat that ferried islanders closer to their homes, she shared the ride with one of the First South Carolina Volunteers, who was returning home, where his mama's cooking and love would help him heal from a battlefield injury. Callie was tired and preoccupied as they crossed the waters between islands, but she began listening to the soldier.

"We been ready fuh fight fuh we freedom. When dey tell bout dis waw en de black man in it, dey say we stan skrong gainst treble fiah (*terrible fire*) from rebel soljuh. We show we been brave den, en we show da ebby day on dishyuh soil befo de waw (*and we showed that every day on this here soil before the war*)!" He grew louder with each phrase. "I know I mo den eaan (*more than earned*) my freedom—en I be ready fuh fight agin, if we git call fuh keep we freedom and save dis Union."

Then an older man who had been listening spoke up. "I don tink you gah fuh fight much mo, son. Leh yo spirit tek some peace."

"Why da be?" The young soldier asked with respect.

"When de Nawt en Sout git back togedda, deese yuh Suddon (*Southern*) folk gon be awright. Dey know we bedda dan Nawden folk know we (*They know us better than Northern folk know us*). Suddon folk unnerstan why we fight fuh freedom—dey know wha we been tru bedda dan anybody cep we. Dey gon unnerstan we do wha we gah fuh do. Dey be awright by en by."

"How long oona tink da gon tek?"

"Oh, maybe five yeah, ten yeah, twenty. Might tek a whole generation befo ting be bedda. Meantime, we tek kyah we sef. We need fuh laan fuh read en git train in all kine uh wuk da show wha we kin do. We gon be awright en dey gon cept we fine."

The young man shared the hope but kept his doubt. "I yedde (*hear*) in de hospital de buckra bes git ready fuh cept dis (*to accept this*), cause Nawt done beat em bad in a lee town in Pennsivania call Geddys-burg. Say da be de bes win yet gainst ole General Lee. Abe Linkum done bring de Negro intuh de fight—Suddon boys give up fo long."

Callie did not hear the last few sentences. She had slipped from war talk to much-needed rest, barely waking when the longboat hit the dock.

★   ★   ★

Callie quietly went out before first light the next morning. Only the tops of the marsh grass, undulating with currents and gentle waves, were showing above the full-moon flood tide. The sweet silence of a soft breeze combined with the slightly cool air of a July morning. As Callie arrived at her "flectin" spot between the marsh and the river, the silent silhouette of a great blue heron passed by, unnoticed.

She was back where she had always found peace, if not answers to every question. Quiet reflections in still waters always let her see clearly so that she could face her biggest problems. The first time somebody called her pretty around twelve years ago, she had to see for herself and the "flectin" spot let her see it was true. In times of sadness she came back for the solace of her special place in the world—loss of her childhood to the probing hands of Massa, then loss of the only man she ever loved when he was lashed and sent away. At times of doubt when she was a new mother to Sunny, Callie found herself in her "flectin" spot. Even when the wind blew the water surface so as not to allow a clear image, Callie had found her balance here.

Now, Callie wondered aloud. "What kin you tell me bout when to leave my chile behind? If I go, she be safer here—I know that she be better here. And I have to go, don't I? Jes didn't know I would ache so …."

As in the past and again this time, Callie's favorite place of solitude elicited her prayerful spirit. In the presence of the sea, breathing salt air on a growing breeze, she called out, "Dear Gawd, what You gonna say if I don try to find out bout my family? My baby girl in Your hands, I know. But I thank You jes same for bringin sweet little Lilly's hands to help Lucas and Bella care for my precious girl." She paused to look up. "But now I know who my mama and daddy be ... kyan say they in good hands ... don't even know fa true how they be at all ..." The wind picked up, ruffling the waters and whispering in the trees. Callie's voice joined in. "I jes gah fuh fine out bout my mama and daddy!"

Callie saw only shimmering images on the surface, but she knew how the current ran beneath. She lifted her head, finding comfort in her decision and strength in her resolve. Her future could only be revealed by searching for her past.

As day broke, Callie told Lucas of her decision. "See, Lucas, I kin leave Sunny wid you cause I trus you like I trus my sef. Bella en me glad da Lilly gon stay yuh on Oakhaat some. Da be de wuk uh Gawd. I ain scaid no mo fuh leave Sunny heah like I be befo. I know she be in good, lovin hand and all de time in de sight uh Gawd."

Callie asked Lucas to bring Lilly from Camp Saxton to meet her at the Beaufort dock the next morning. There was a departing hospital ship that she expected to be on. She then visited with Bella for more than an hour, describing her plans and asking from her heart for Bella's love to enfold Sunny once again. Of course, it was granted immediately; such was Bella's nature.

The rest of the day was spent with Sunny. Mother-daughter time always took multiple forms. From schooling, to wading, to catching shrimp, to watching sailing clouds move across the blue sky. It was at that time, when they were flat on their backs, that Callie explained what she had learned about her parents, and that they might be living up north. She also explained her need to find them and talk to them and hug them.

Sunny's response, a tribute to the community that had raised her, was to hug her mother's neck tightly. Then she whispered, "Mama, don worry bout we, we be fine. We gon worry bout you."

Callie pulled back from the hug to see who she was looking at. "How old you be?"

"Seven, tank you."

Thank you indeed, said Callie to herself as her daughter had eased her greatest fears. Callie rested better than she thought possible, arms around her daughter all night.

Lucas had done Callie's bidding once again by getting out to Camp Saxton early to pick up Lilly. Callie and Sunny had boarded a boat with four Oakheart oarsmen when Will, always with amazing timing, arrived in the creek. On escort duty, Will had gone to the Oaks, where Laura Towne told him to come to Oakheart swiftly, as Callie's decision might take her north soon.

After Will informed his crew that they were transporting a nurse to the hospital ship, they arrived at Oakheart dock to find that the nurse's young daughter needed transport as well. Sunny proudly wore a new vest, fashioned from excess material when Callie converted one of Julia Bowen's fine linen dresses into a new travel suit. The steam-powered boat gave the well-dressed mother and daughter a ride against the tidal currents like they had never experienced.

When they arrived on Beaufort's wharf, just as the last patients were boarding the hospital ship *Cosmopolitan*, they waved to Lucas and Lilly, who were walking toward the ship. Then Callie recognized the sergeant from the Massachusetts Fifty-Fourth as he sat up on the gurney to look her way while being carried up the boat ramp. She realized that she should have boarded already and that there were only a few minutes before the ship would depart.

Having said her good-byes several times over by then, Callie moved toward the ramp but then heard Sunny's footsteps and turned back to her family just in time to catch a jumping hug. Callie released her clasp around her daughter's little body as she handed her over to Lilly, who received Sunny and retreated a few steps. After Lucas moved forward for a final embrace, the only reason he let go of Callie at all was that he knew he must.

Will took Callie's arm and escorted her to the ramp. "As soon as I can, I'll be by your side to help steer your search for your parents, if you wish. Until then, here is a list of my friends in Annapolis. I guarantee they can be trusted to help my cousin."

"Yes, Will. Thank you for all you do. This day and every day."

"Hey, we're family, aren't we?" After one last hug between cousins, Callie boarded the ship. Just like Lucas, Will wished both to hold her close and to send her on her way. "I know you will do well. I have no doubt that wherever you go, soon after you arrive, folks will know the name Callie Bowen."

Callie leaned over the railing, speaking distinctly. "No, they not ever gonna know Callie Bowen." Since he knew she had great expectations for herself, he studied her for clues. Callie was pleased she had confused him. "Where I go, I will be known as Callie Hewitt!" The sad lines on her face disappeared. Callie's radiant smile beamed back at him.

On board, as the ship moved away from the dock into the swift currents of the incoming tide, Callie waved good-bye to her daughter, brother, cousin, and perhaps a new sister. Then she rushed to the bow of the steamer so that Sunny could not see her cry. From there, she craned her neck to see what she could not see beyond the bend in the river. The corners of her smile caught the teardrops trickling down her cheeks. "Jes another dayclean, Callie Hewitt. Jes another dayclean from Gawd."

Gullah Glossary

Chapter 1

wuk – work
haad – hard
mek – make
dey – their
bret – breath
fuh – for/to
yosef – yourself
jine – join
tarectly – directly
kyah – care
oona – you
leh – let
gi – give
wey – where
gon – going
dishyuh – this here
laan – learn
yuh – here
neba – never
fuhgit – forget
speck – expect
smaats – smarts
needuh – neither
roun – around

da – that
afta – after
regla – regular
tass – task
tawd – toward
gah fuh – got to
tuh – to
swimp – shrimp

Chapter 3

memba – remember

Chapter 4

das – that's

Chapter 5

aks – ask
cah em – carry them
e – it
figyuh – figure
kyan – can't
guh – am going
riba – river

wada – water
skrong – strong
scape – escape
supm – something
maash – marsh
nuf – enough
pass – died
holla – holler
yeah – year

Chapter 7

ebba – ever
huh – her
ooman – woman
hahm – harm
buckra – white person(s)
skrent – strength
hep – help

Chapter 11

big wada – Atlantic Ocean
jes – just
ebon - even
fus – first
anodda - another
foat – fort
creachah – creatures
smaat – smart
bedda – better
wen – when
cuz – because
deh – there

lee- –little
fine – find
tawd – toward

Chapter 13

sho nuf – sure enough
scaid – scared
slabe – slave
yeddy – hear
monin – morning
haat – hearts
madda – matter
shree – three
shawt – short
huhsef – herself
daak – dark
shaya – share
soljuhs – soldiers
haad – hard

Chapter 14

stan – stand
sto – store
wedda – whether
aw – or
faah – far
fayah – fair
trut – truth
blieb – believe
leh em – let them
faah – far
fait – faith

Chapter 15

feebah – fever
haid – head
tawd – toward
injuh – injured
follah – follow
lessn – unless
haffuh – have to
planta – planter
whey – where

Chapter 16

tief – thieve
gi – give
yer – year
eyeschuh – oyster
swimp – shrimp
tas – tasks
splain – explain
holla – holler
chirrun – children
anodda – another
oudda – out of
heaby – heavy
ack – act
shree – three
togedda – together
ebbybody – everybody
dut – dirt
waw – war
mine – mind
sence – since

kine – kind
sef – self

Chapter 18

wort – worth
layda – later
tawd – toward
spose – supposed
kyetch – catch
ebbyday – everyday
injud – injured
gwine – going
tuhday – today

Chapter 19

whaaf – wharf
hih – his
bol – bold
ris – risk
speck – expect
han – hands
crack my teet – smile
sutla – sutler
malasse – molasses
quaat – quart
ovah – over

Chapter 20

lef – leave
stubbin – stubborn
hongry hongry – very hungry

bidness – business
ancha – anchor
kine – kind
eben – even

Chapter 21

ansa – answer
huht – hurt

Chapter 23

odda – other
tru – through
ebby – every

Chapter 24

skroke – stroke
captcha – captured
wud – word
skrange – strange
smaates – smartest

Chapter 25

maak – mark
moanful – mournful
suffa – suffer
buhn – burn
disapeah – disappear
time come – future
whaaf – wharf
sech – such
treble fiah – terrible fire
Suddon – Southern
Nawden – Northern

Bibliography

Branch, Muriel Miller. *The Water Brought Us: The Story of the Gullah-Speaking People.* Orangeburg, SC: Sandlapper Publishing Co, 1995.

Billington, Ray Allen. *The Journal of Charlotte L. Forten: A Young Black Woman's Reactions to the White World of the Civil War Era.* New York: W. W. Norton, 1903.

Brooks, Geraldine. *March.* New York: Penguin Books, 2005.

Clinton, Catherine. *Harriet Tubman: The Road to Freedom.* New York: Little, Brown, 2004.

Conrad, Earl, ed. "The Charles P. Wood Manuscripts of Harriet Tubman," *The Negro History Bulletin* 13, no. 4 (January 1950), accessed December 29, 2013, http://www.harriettubman.com/cwood.html.

Conner, T.D. *Homemade Thunder: War on the South Coast, 1861–1865.* Savannah, GA: Writeplace Press, 2004.

Eighth Grade Humanities Class. *Nov. 7, 1861: Crossroads in Beaufort History.* Beaufort, SC: Beaufort Middle School, 2004.

Elliott, William. *Carolina Sports by Land and Water.* Charleston, SC: Burges and James, 1846. Reprint, Columbia, SC: University of South Carolina Press, 1994.

Faust, Drew Gilpin. *Mothers of Invention: Women of the Slaveholding South in the American Civil War.* New York: Vintage Books, 1996.

Ferguson, Ernest B. *Freedom Rising: Washington in the Civil War.* New York: Vintage Books, 2005.

Garrison, Webb. *The Encyclopedia of Civil War Usage: An Illustrated Compendium of the Everyday Language of Soldiers and Civilians.* Nashville, TN: Cumberland House Publishing, 2001.

Goodwine, Marquetta L. *Gawd Dun Smile Pun We: Beaufort Isles.* Brooklyn, NY: Kinship Publications, 1997.

Graydon, Nell S. *Tales of Beaufort.* Beaufort, SC: Beaufort Book Shop, 1963.

Helsley, Alexia Jones. *Beaufort, South Carolina: A History.* Charleston, SC: The History Press, 2005.

Higginson, Thomas Wentworth. *Army Life in a Black Regiment.* New York: W. W. Norton, 1969.

Holland, Rupert Sargent, ed. *Letters and Diary of Laura M. Towne.* 1912. Reprint, Salem, MA: Higginson Book Company, 2007.

Hurmence, Belinda. *Before Freedom, When I Just Can Remember.* Winston-Salem, NC: John F. Blair, 1989.

Jones, Norrece T., Jr. *Born a Child of Freedom Yet a Slave: Mechanisms of Control and Strategies of Resistance in Antebellum South Carolina,* Hanover, NH: The University Press of New England, 1990.

Kozak, Ginnie. *Eve of Emancipation: The Union Occupation of Beaufort and the Sea Islands.* Beaufort, SC: Portsmouth House Press, 1995.

McFeely, William S. *Yankee Stepfather: General O. O. Howard and the Freedmen.* New York: W. W. Norton, 1968.

McPherson, James M. *The Negro's Civil War: How American Negroes Felt and Acted During the War for the Union.* New York: Vintage Books, 1965.

Mitchell, Patricia B. *Plantation Row Slave Cabin Cooking: The Roots of Soul Food.* Chatham, VA: Patricia B. Mitchell, 1998.

Romero, Patricia, ed. *A Black Woman's Civil War Memoirs.* New York: Markus Wiener Publishing, 1988. First publication, 1902.

Taylor, Susie King. *Reminiscences of My Life in Camp with the 33rd US Colored Troops, Late 1st South Carolina Volunteers.* Boston, MA: Susie King Taylor.

Rose, Willie Lee. *Rehearsal for Reconstruction: The Port Royal Experiment.* Athens, GA: University of Georgia Press, 1964.

Rosengarten, Theodore. *Tombee: Portrait of a Cotton Planter: With the Journal of Thomas B. Chaplin.* New York: William Morrow, 1986.

Rhyne, Nancy. *Before and After Freedom: Lowcountry Folklore and Narratives*. Charleston, SC: The History Press, 2005.

Stevenson, Peter and Evelene Stevenson. *The Spirit of Old Beaufort*. DVD. Directed by Peter Stevenson. Beaufort, SC: Sandbar Productions, 1995.

Taylor, Michael C. *Historic Beaufort County: An Illustrated History*. San Antonio, TX: Historical Publishing Network, 2005.

Wise, Stephen R. *Lifeline of the Confederacy: Blockade Running During the Civil War*. Columbia, SC: University of South Carolina Press, 1988.

Whyte, Mary. *Alfreda's World*. Charleston, SC: Wyrick & Company, 2003.

Chronology of Actual Events Depicted or Referenced in *Swift Currents*

This chronology is composed of two types of items: listing of dates and actual events; and excerpts (in italics), by date, from the *Letters and Diary of Laura M. Towne*. As a Unitarian abolitionist volunteer from Philadelphia, Laura Towne's position of importance evolved during the Civil War as the Oaks Plantation was central to civilian relief operations and a frequent stop for Union military personnel. Her contemporaneous notes from 1862–63 describe significant events that impacted the lives of freedmen and the Union war effort. The diary entries cited here describe the real events encountered by the fictional characters of Oakheart Plantation.

In the summer of 1861, the lighthouse on Hunting Island was blown up by Confederate forces. This event occurred several months earlier than depicted in *Swift Currents*. Because it dramatically foreshadowed the Union naval attack, please allow the author creative license to change the date of the action to late October. As such, it is the exception, as the timing of all other actual events included is accurately represented.

1861   November 1–2   Atlantic Ocean storm

   November 7   The Union navy is successful in a five-hour attack on Forts Walker and Beauregard at the mouth of Port Royal Sound.

	December 5	Union troops take possession of Beaufort, SC.
	December 20	Colonel William Reynolds arrives in Beaufort as US agent to collect contraband cotton.
1862	January 15	Edward Pierce arrives representing the Lincoln administration to assess the situation and make recommendations.
	February 3	Pierce reports to Treasury Secretary Chase regarding the need to have educators and missionaries assist newly freed slaves, and to have freedmen work cotton for wages.
	March	Missionaries and educators arrive to become on-site plantation superintendents.
	April 18	*"There has been a little rebellion upon Mr. Philbrick's plantation (the old Coffin plantation). Two men, one upon each estate, refuse to work the four hours a day they are required to give to the cotton, but insist upon cultivating their own corn patch only." (Letters and Diary of Laura M. Towne, p. 9)*
	April 24	*"The cotton agents promised last year and now are just paying for the cotton picked on their promise, one dollar in four—the rest in orders on their stores, where they sell molasses at fifteen cents a pint ...." (Laura Towne, p.16)*
	April 24	*"We go again tomorrow upon a visit of cheering to the poor anxious people who have lived on promises and are starving for clothes and food while patiently working for Gov'ment. ... They say, 'Gov'ment is fighting for us and we will work for Gov'ment.' " (Laura Towne, p. 16)*

April 28	"'Why for we burn de cotton? Where we get money then or buy clo' and shoe and salt?' So instead of burning it, they guarded it every night, the women keeping watch and the men ready to defend it when the watchers gave the alarm. Some of the masters came back to persuade their negroes to go with them and when they would not, they were shot down. One man told me he had known of thirty being shot." (Laura Towne, p. 27)
May 9	First South Carolina Volunteers is formed, consisting of freedmen.
May 12	"... General Hunter [commanded] Mr. Pierce to send every able-bodied negro man down to Hilton Head today. ... About four hundred men ...were taken to Beaufort tonight and are to go to Hilton Head tomorrow." (pp 41,46)
May 12	Robert Smalls, et al., take the Confederate ship Planter from Charleston docks, give it to the Union navy, and then bring it to Beaufort and on to Hilton Head for service in the Union navy.
May 19	"Mr. Whiting has not been a Government agent for two months, and yet he lives in Government property, making the negroes work without pay for him and living upon 'the fat of the lamb,' — selling too, the sugar, etc., at rates most wicked ... It is too bad. The cotton agents, many of them, are doing this." (Laura Towne, p. 57)
May 19	"Last Saturday the provisions from Philadelphia were distributed, and I heard our folks singing until late, just as they did after their first payment of wages when only then they sang till morning." (Laura Towne, p. 55)

May 23	*"The first rations of pork—'splendid bacon,' everybody says, was dealt out the other day and there has been great joy ever since, or great content." (Laura Towne, p. 61)*
May	Harriet Tubman arrives in Beaufort, stays for fourteen months.
June 3	*"Mr. Pierce is going home—perhaps not to return, and who can take his place here with the negroes?... Some began to bless and pray for him aloud, to say they 'thanked massa for his goodness to we.' " (Laura Towne, pp. 61-2)*
July 14	*"Edisto is evacuated!—and all the negroes brought to these islands." (Laura Towne, p. 73)*
July 17	The Militia Act passed by the United States Congress "provided that Negroes who rendered military service were free and that the mothers, wives and children of soldiers were also thereafter free." (Willie Lee Rose, *Rehearsal for Reconstruction: The Port Royal Experiment*, p. 187)
July 22	*"Our guns have come. Captain Thorndike brought over twenty and gave Nelly instructions." (Laura Towne, p. 80)*
July 31	*"Pay day for the negroes.... at the rate of $2 per acre." (Laura Towne, p. 83)*
August 6	*"Hunter's negro regiment disbanded." (Laura Towne, p. 83)*
August 16	*"Heavy firing heard before sunrise. Two gunboats stationed at the mouth of our creek. Am preparing my Philadelphia money for safety and I shall have the guns loaded." (Laura Towne, p. 84)*

September 1	*"The rebels are getting bold. They landed at Brickyard on Friday. This is the third attempt lately." (Laura Towne, p. 90)*
October 24	*"Three boats full of rebels attempted to land on these islands last night, two at the village and one at Eddings Point. The negroes with their guns were on picket; they gave the alarm, fired and drove the rebels off." (Laura Towne, p. 93)*
Late October	United States tax commissioners arrive in Beaufort to conduct land sales.
November 22	*"We have been wrapped all day in the smoke of battle and the people hear the roll of cannon. They say it is an attack on Fort Pulaski." (Laura Towne, p. 96)*
1863 January 1	The Emancipation Proclamation is read to all assembled for the celebration at Camp Saxton, Beaufort.
February 3	*"[Freedmen] had not been paid since September, and they begin to believe that Government never means to pay any more." (Laura Towne, p. 102)*
February 24	*"Hurrah! Jubilee! Lands are to be set apart for the people so that they cannot be oppressed, or driven to work for speculators, or ejected from their homesteads." (Laura Towne, p. 103)*
March 9	The land sale occurs.
April 7	The Union ironclad fleet attacks Charleston unsuccessfully.
May 1	A decree is issued by CSA President Jefferson Davis that captured black Union soldiers should be shot.

June 1	Led by Harriet Tubman, Union forces raid plantations along the Combahee River, freeing nearly eight hundred slaves.
June 3	The Fifty-Fourth Regiment Massachusetts Voluntary Infantry, composed of African American men, arrives in Beaufort and camps at Lands End on St. Helena Island.
July 4	*"Then we marched out and stood under the flag and sang 'The Star Spangled Banner' ... There were many officers of the Fifty-Fourth Massachusetts, Colonel Shaw, Major Ned Hallowell, and the surgeon, Captain Hooper..." (Laura Towne, p. 114)*
July 16	Union forces attack Fort Wagner near Charleston, SC.
July 20	*"I came home yesterday and today I am summoned by Mr. Pierce to Beaufort to help nurse the wounded soldiers who have come down from Morris Island. They are coming in by hundreds. We hear the guns all day and night. The Fifty-fourth Massachusetts behaved splendidly at Fort Wagner." (Laura Towne, p. 114)*
July 27	The steamer *Cosmopolitan* leaves Beaufort with wounded soldiers.

Note from the Author

My commitment to civil rights and the experiences of my diverse family inspired me to write *Swift Currents,* a historical novel about how slaves became freedmen beginning in 1861. In it, I combine my longstanding interest in the Civil War with my deep respect for African American tenacity in times of despair, to tell about the end of slavery.

My grandchildren, identified as 'minorities,' are growing up in a world still troubled by cross-cultural divisions. Through *Swift Currents,* a historically accurate story, I hope to engage readers so that young people and their parents will come to a greater understanding of our shared racial history and abandon the inherited prejudice of generations.

I live in the South Carolina sea islands where actual events in *Swift Currents* took place. If you wish to contact me about *Swift Currents, please do* so at swiftcurrents1861@gmail.com.